CURSE & FATE

Book 1 of **Memoirs**

By

Eric Lindquist

Contents

For Karine

PROLOGUE

Sunlight fell softly between the birch trees, outlining the leaves clinging to the white branches and casting their shadows over the barren ground. The season had come early, but the trees still held most of their red and yellow leaves; those that had fallen blanketed the forest floor in dull gold, a colorful playground for two children, a brother and sister. The pair tried to best each other with games that had no specific set of rules, mixing fun with torment as they tested each other's patience and will.

While the forest was dense, most of the trees were tall and slender, with only occasional thick black oak trunks and alders towering above like dark guardians overlooking their young. It was the only supervision the children had, as their parents' warnings to avoid the temptation of the forest had gone unheeded.

The woods were old, and with them came old tales told by elders that were filled with mystery and excitement around some moral lesson that was simply another reminder for the children not to go wandering off too far from home. Silver Wood wasn't all that far away, mere moments from the Rhyol lumber sheds, and even Alvyn Poldr's farmstead bordered a good section of it on the southern side of the valley; his sheep were occasionally lost in the birch trees. Still, the forest was vast, and grew denser the farther north one went, until it reached the craggy coastline several miles away. There, the trunks grew right up to the edge and overhung the cold waters of the North

Sea below like long fingers reaching to touch the waves. There were no sheep or lumber sheds that far into the wood . . . or children, for that matter; silent forests have their way of deterring children's interest much more ominously than any elder tales could.

Not so far away from Alvyn Poldr's farm, on the eastern edge of Silver Wood, was another village where the sunlight did not reflect so brightly through the trees. This was more directly the reason for parents' warnings. It was this village that became visible to one of the children, the boy, no more than thirteen years old. He climbed a tree whose branches were low enough for him to reach, to study the empty houses in the distance.

"Seth," his sister called as she emerged from behind a fallen tree and noticed that her brother was yet again distracted. "Don't even think about it," she warned.

"I'm just looking." Seth cast a quick scowl over his shoulder at Millie before returning his attention to the houses. Mischievous curiosity gleamed in his eyes. He lifted a dirty hand to brush dark curls from his face before bracing his other against the tree to jump back onto the old wagon path they had been following for the last hour. Landing softly as a fox, he adjusted his calf-high boots, taking the opportunity to scoop up several broken twigs and forest refuse, which he tossed at Millie as she approached.

With a hiss of disapproval, she stepped back quickly, yanking her green dress out of the way of the flung dirt. He chortled, and she scowled back. Being a hand taller than Seth and a couple of years older, there were several more violent responses she could have used to teach the little monster a lesson, but her mother had made her responsible for her brother this afternoon while their parents tended to business in town. Her dress and shoes were not what she would normally wear for this activity; she hadn't expected their walk to take them into the forest, let alone away from home at all. Her dress was almost too elegant to play in in the woods.

"What are you scared of, Millie, ghosts? Or the mine monsters?" Seth's lips twitched with suppressed humor as he looked at her.

She wasn't going to admit it, but Seth was close to the truth; she was too affected by the stories they'd been told.

"They have fangs . . . and fire that drips from their eyes and mouths." He advanced slowly and methodically, imitating those unseen horrors as theatrically as he could, his hands clawing through the air, his mouth snarling. Millie held her ground. "They have teeth so sharp, they can snap your bones in half!" Seth stomped heavily on a dead branch underfoot, snapping it with a loud crack that made Millie shriek and jump.

Millie realized that she had lost whatever authority she might have held as her brother clapped his hands and hooted with laughter. "That's not funny," she scolded, her voice quivering in both dismay and anger. "There are no such things as ghosts—or mine monsters; the Council says so." She strove to sound confident, but she glanced nervously around, expecting some response to emerge from the trees to refute her assertion. Realizing that her fear was showing, she immediately felt foolish and said in a common-sense tone, "It's simply too old and dangerous here—from the drift clouds. Uncle said that's why he got that cough. I don't want to cough all the time, do you?"

Millie referred to her Uncle Travor's description of the days when the mines were in operation, hoping she'd remembered correctly. It seemed to have the desired effect on Seth, who sniffed and looked back toward the abandoned village. More confident now, she waited, twirling the end of one of the little blue bows securing her braid before tossing it back over her shoulder and lifting her chin.

Looking more irritated than discouraged, Seth began to pluck leaves that had somehow become woven into the fabric of his clothing, along with twigs. "We're not even near the mines," he retorted, but with a wolfish grin, he bounded off down the path toward the abandoned village before Millie had even taken breath to reply.

"Stop!" she yelled, but instinctively followed him, carefully holding up her dress. She knew where he was heading. "Seth! Stop, you're too fast!" She hated when he did this. He was her responsibility, and mother trusted her to take care of him . . . *Why does he never listen to me?* The breeze picked up and she slipped on the fallen leaves that had gathered in ruts in the path as she ran. Realizing that she had lost sight of her brother, she panicked, dropped the hem of her dress, and pushed herself faster down the path. Low-hanging branches brushed against her and she cringed away from their sharp points. *He is going to make me rip my dress,* she thought with an unladylike curse that the leaves crunching under her sandaled feet drowned out. She continued to call out to him as she half sprinted, half stumbled through the fallen leaves.

When the pathway turned into a road of small black

and gray pebbles, she stopped. The wind dropped off, as if she had entered a sheltered cave rather than an open-air village. The silence made her shiver as she remembered the stories that she'd have preferred to forget. A sharper kind of panic slid up her neck as her eyes took in her surroundings.

It was not the first time that she, Seth, or many of the town children had been in Mir Town. Yet this was the first time that she had been nearly alone, and she whispered to herself about the nonsense of those stories, rebuilding her courage by remembering exactly which direction her home in Rhyol was from here. She pulled her vest more tightly around her, against the chill.

Where was the fire billowing out of cracks in the ground, made by evil, ugly creatures clawing up to the surface after escaping their underworld cages? She moved along down the road, but couldn't keep her eyes from straying to the ground, searching for the monsters.

Where were the yellow clouds of rot and decay that floated behind the houses, breathed in by unsuspecting travellers to dissolve them from within? She saw only dead rose bushes and moldering crates.

Where were the sinister, marching trees, misshapen and bent with hatred as they roamed the streets, ready to capture would-be intruders to this forgotten place, and make them suffer horribly for their trespassing? Holding her breath, she waited for them to appear. They did not. Astonishingly, the wind returned, pulling at her dress and bringing with it the sounds of life that had seemed suspended in those moments.

Her paranoia became curiosity. She remembered the

other times she had been on this same road without her parents' knowledge. This was just a village, like hers . . . almost. But it had emptied long ago, for reasons that her father had explained away with "You're too young to be troubled by politics." She hesitated a moment longer, just to make sure that she did not miss anything horrible and beastly, then, satisfied that she was overreacting, she took a deep breath and continued into the place she knew she shouldn't be.

She examined the small wood and stone houses a short distance from the road, looking for swaying doors or open windows that her stupid brother might have gone through. On most, the wood had rotted away on the sides, leaving ragged holes that revealed the framing underneath, and most of the shake roof shingles were loose or had blown off; many stone foundations bore gaping cracks or had crumbled. Some houses had even fallen in on themselves, and she wondered what nice things may have been buried under all the rubble after the community had left as suddenly as Father said they had.

Gardens lay untended, forgotten by those who cared for them and by nature in general, as not a hint of overgrowth lay within the patches; it was as if the soil had been ruined by salt wash. In fact, the only things telling Millie they were gardens were the dust-covered hoes and shovels propped near the abandoned plots. She passed larger buildings—stables and barns. Once they may have been noisy with bleating sheep, whinnying horses, or grunting pigs, but now they stood silent with vacant, shadowed stalls.

Lettering etched on the rusted entrance doors of one

large building declared it to be the Mir Town meeting hall; it stood half erect, its rear and part of the roof victim of some violent storm that had passed directly across it, leaving it open to the sky. A school was next to that, much to Millie's delight as she recognized the large bronze bell on the roof; the school was patterned much like the Rhyol School, where she heard that bell ring every morning to start the sessions for the bright-eyed children skipping into the classroom. This bell was not ringing now, and dense cobwebs had imprisoned the clapper.

The solitude of the place sank into her, and the farther along the road she travelled the sadder she became by the lack of life; this was worse than the horror stories the elders told of Mir Town. She drove thoughts of what had been away, and focused on why she was there.

She came to an intersection where the road forked and realized that she had reached the center of town. One fork continued through Mir while the other seemed to turn into the forest, just past several larger homes. A well near the edge of the road across the way caught her eye, its peaked red roof pocked with holes and a bent and rusty windlass dangling from a coil of rope beside it. She thought she saw the bucket sway and nearly forgot about her brother in her sudden desire to run back down the road down which she'd come. Breathing heavily, her heart thumping, she stared at the well for several moments, frozen by panic like a rabbit trapped by a hound. The bucket didn't seem to be moving at all now. Still . . . she'd heard too many uncomfortable stories about what lurks inside unattended dark wells, and decided that this would be the extent of her investigation of the bucket; she continued on down the Mir Town road.

The wind carried with it a faint voice, and she looked frantically around, trying to identify its source. Nothing. Then she heard it again—a shout, then laughter, coming from behind one of the larger houses on her left, where the forked path returned to the woods. She recognized that laugh, and both her terror at the well and her curiosity about the town disappeared in a flash of anger. Visions of her mother, red-faced with rage at Millie for losing her brother, filled her mind. How long had she been wandering around this whole time while something terrible could have happened to him? She frowned in frustration, disappointed that she had been so easily distracted. Now all she could think of was throttling her brother.

But upon turning the bend in what might have been a track on someone's property and not a road, what she saw was completely unexpected, and pulled her mind away once more.

The path didn't return to the forest, as the birch trees cutting off a view of the path had led Millie to assume; instead it crested a steep bluff and dropped down the other side into another part of Mir; it seemed almost as if the town was separated into levels. From her vantage point, this area looked smaller than Mir proper, with the houses replaced by tall, skinny chimneys all surrounding one large domed building in the center. Railway tracks still bearing small carts connected all the structures together, then ran out toward a partly hidden mountain of rock a short distance away.

Millie immediately pictured Rhyol's wagonmaker, Master Lairn, and how his workplace back home was larger than any of the other buildings in Rhyol—not including the town hall, of course. His home was kind of rounded like this one was. Yet this place was larger still, larger even than the town hall; it was probably the largest building she had ever seen.

She focused on the dome only briefly, because the most astonishing sight drew her eye to what lay behind all of this: the cold waters of the North Sea, shimmering deep blue with the reflected brilliance of the afternoon. It lapped up against a beach just steps away from the farthest cart. She had forgotten just how close Mir Town was to the sea, and its enormity nearly overwhelmed her.

The waves rippled to the horizon, where the sky and water merged, deep blue and gray blue, in the distance. White gulls called coarsely to each other as they glided above the waves, occasionally dipping low to capture an unsuspecting fish. The smell of salt hung in the breeze that now blew past Millie, a smell she'd not sensed in Mir Town behind her. The surprise of it, and the deep blue beauty of the ocean, warmed her inside, making her grin in wonder. She never would have imagined something so wonderful was hidden just past the desolate and frightening town.

The large mountain of rock partially hidden by the dome behind her was one of many, Millie realized as she saw several dozen more jutting from the ocean, zigging and zagging from the black shoreline out into the waters like a broken peninsula of miniature mountains, until they grew small against the horizon. They broke the flow of the tide, and Millie watched with fascination as the white-tipped waves crashed against the oversized boulders, repetitive violence in an otherwise peaceful afternoon setting.

The shoreline was shallow, running nearly horizontal up from the water in this part of the mining town; elsewhere the bluffs rose tall and sharp from the rough sea washing around their base, sometimes through them where, over many lifetimes, the constant probing of the waves had carved caves and passages in the rock. Precious stones and minerals had been discovered in them years before. The protected alcove where Millie stood might just as easily be filled like a well bucket if the tides grew high. It had not happened in anyone's lifetime that Millie knew of, but it was one reason that Mir Town had been abandoned.

A blast of white water smashed upward against one of the nearer boulders in the water, the crash distracting Millie from her thoughts

"That's why nobody can bring a boat here."

The voice behind her made Millie jump and whirl around, the quick turn nearly costing her balance. She caught herself and glared at her missing brother, who sat cross-legged on a stone as if he had been there with her the entire time. He smiled at her stumble, but the humor in his eyes faded to shame as she felt her face grow hot with anger.

"I saw you looking at the sea," he mumbled as he shifted uncomfortably on the rock, eyeing Millie's clenched fists. "The water's too dangerous to bring boats, even ones small enough to fit between the boulders." He was trying to change the subject, or at least start one to distract her, but Millie wasn't having any of it.

"What's wrong with you?" she screamed, ignoring

what he had just said. "When Mother is not around, you listen to *me!* Do you understand? She doesn't like it when you run away, and I don't like it either! We are not allowed in Mir Town and we're especially not allowed here in the camp. Do you know what she will do to us if she finds out? *Do you?*" She stopped to catch her breath, shaking visibly. She didn't like to yell; she would rather have beaten Seth, but if she tore her dress in the scuffle, Mother for sure would know they had been up to trouble. She drew in a slow, deep breath to calm herself, but her sudden anger was slow to recede.

Seth said nothing, but his guilty eyes were clearly avoiding hers; he scratched and picked at his boots.

"Now let's get out of here before Mother worries," Millie announced, calmer.

"No! Not yet, please! Just a little longer?" Seth pleaded. Millie knew this ploy well, and glared. "I won't run away again, I promise . . . You can come with me! Aren't you even wondering what's in those carts?"

Millie crossed her arms, one hand toying with one of the blue ribbons on her braids, as she often did when she was troubled or uncertain.

"Come on, Millie! We'll just take a quick look, and come back—that's all." Seth grabbed at the hem of her dress, trying to pull her forward toward the rocky path. She was still angry, but the discovery of this place and the sea itself were enough to deter any retreat. Her sandaled feet actually seemed to move of their own accord toward the work camp.

"Alright." She spoke firmly, making sure he understood that it was her decision in the end. "But stay by

17

me, and do what I tell you." Seth's face lit up with a smile. He hadn't listened to the last part, and she knew it, but she returned his smile anyway as he took her by the hand and led her carefully down the path that snaked around boulders and outcroppings.

"Do you know what they dug here?" Seth asked, glancing out at the big rocks in the water.

Millie nodded, remembering more about the sad history of Mir Town from her classes. "Metals," she replied. "For the war."

* * *

"Wow! Millie, look at this!" Seth called.

His sister came out of the small, ramshackle shed attached to one of the skinny chimney things in answer to his call. In her hand she held a large hard hat made from double-layered leather. It was heavy and awkward, a protective cap worn by men that worked deep in the mine to keep rocks from crushing their heads, but it also had two hollows in the front for securing candles for light. She was studying it when Seth had called for her.

He waved to her from atop the chimney he had somehow managed to climb. "I think it's an oven." Seth sat dangling his feet within the opening where a closed top might have once been. "It looks cooked inside, and I can see burn marks."

"Maybe they used to cook little brothers who don't listen to their sisters." Millie snickered as Seth pulled his legs over and slid back down the outside of the chimney, landing roughly beside her.

"No, it's probably something to do with melting the stones," he replied, as if he hadn't heard or really expected

18

an answer to what he'd surmised. He pointed to the series
of small carts leading from the large oval building behind
them. "Let's see what's inside those, before it starts to get
dark."

Caught up in the newfound curiosities, she followed
the tracks to the closest cart. They looked eagerly inside,
only to be disappointed by the absence of jewels and
baubles. It contained only more rocks, dusty clothing, and
other useless junk. Seth picked up a torn shirt, wrinkling his
nose before dropping it back down onto the dusty pile.
They moved on to the next cart, hoping for treasures or
something of interest, and the next again, finding only
stones, a glove or two, chunks of wood, more candle-hats,
and a lot of bird droppings. Stroking her braid nervously,
Millie watched the seagulls gliding across the sky as Seth
scratched his head.

"I don't get it," he muttered. "What's the big deal?
Why did no one come and get their stuff? Why don't they
work here anymore? There are no monsters!" His tone
suggested that he was more upset that the last statement
might be true.

"Don't you remember what I said about Uncle?"
Millie answered. "The mine got too soft . . . with too much
dirt and water getting into everybody when they breathed.
They thought that fixing it wouldn't make any difference,
since the mine is so close to the sea—the same thing would
keep happening."

"What about the ghosts?" Seth argued, "You heard
them talking about things down there that would cause men
to scream and run. Like Jerrod's pa—he has that weird look
in his eyes when he talks to you about it, like he's still

scared of something. He used to work in the mines."

Millie shuddered as she recalled those other stories, the ones that effectively kept the children away and at the same time hungrily curious to visit. She turned the hard hat nervously in her hands, trying to come up with a response that would sound reasonable and adult. This was not the time to be acting like a frightened child; she didn't want to accept those tales of monsters and ghosts. She had seen nothing in the village above and nothing here . . . so far.

Seth reached impatiently for the hat. The act brought back her maturity. "Don't just take things! Ask first!" Her brother frowned while retracting his hand, probably fearing she might slap it . . . or his head.

"That's pretty neat! Did you find that in the house?" he asked more politely. He didn't wait for an answer. "I have my kit with me; do you want to see if it works?"

"Of course it works!" she said confidently, as if she herself had constructed the device, "I don't think anybody used it before, and I don't want to use it now anyway; we can still see fine."

"Not out here, stupid." Her brother turned and pointed to the rock face where the tracks went, no longer partially obscured from view.

When Millie saw the entrance to the mine, her uneasiness returned like a sudden breeze. Her first thought was how dark the small square entrance to the mine was. It seemed out of place against the rock face shining bright in the sun, like a square that had been cut out of the world, leaving a black nothingness.

How men could dig into something so big and thick . . . She looked around the entrance at the massive rock wall, sensing the enormity and the strength of it even from a distance away. It was much larger than it had seemed from above, even larger than the large oval building nearby. The angles of the jagged stones above made it look like a stone rooftop to some underground creature's home. The rocky bluff went from the land into the water, disappearing a hundred or so feet out in the North Sea where whitecaps slapped. The whole lay of the rocky terrain made the square-cut mine entrance look like the entrance to a tunnel leading under the sea.

Seth waited only an instant, watching her sister stare in awe of the mine, before he snatched the hard hat out of her hand and bolted for the entrance, ignoring her screams of protest. Millie set out in hot pursuit.

The chase did not last long. Millie crashed into Seth when he stopped abruptly at the opening, causing him to drop the handful of little lighting sticks he had begun pulling out of the brown bag tied at his belt. "Be careful! I don't want to lose any of these!" he snapped, ignoring the fact that it was he who had initiated the chase. She slapped him across the side of his face, hard enough to knock him back a step.

"Ow!" he moaned, rubbing his reddened face while trying to gather his fire sticks. "I just want to see if it works!" he shouted, trying to turn away from her reaching hands.

Millie finally stopped when she realized that her beating him wasn't going to change anything, and in her moment of anger she'd forgotten about keeping her dress from damage. She pouted. "I hope you fall and break your neck," she hissed through her teeth. "And if not, I'll be here to finish the job!"

"I'll give it back," he replied, his tone placating. To his surprised relief, she dropped her arms and her lip stopped quivering. He watched her carefully. Satisfied she would be still, he began searching for the fire sticks he had dropped. Finding them, he nodded in approval and returned to attaching candle stub to the hard hat.

Knowing that he would always find some way to torment her, and that there was little point in scolding him constantly, Millie walked over to the mine entrance and looked inside. It was still frightening, but there was something else in the blackness, something peaceful and relaxing, as if she were at the entrance to a quiet study or a place of solitude, a place where she actually thought it might be nice to wander around—if anything, to calm her mind after her brother's infuriating behavior. She took another step toward the black entrance.

The sensation of peace and seclusion vanished as her eyes fell upon a family of large spiders draping their webs across the arched passageway inside. She let out a shriek, and her voice shrieked back at her from someplace within the depths of the mine.

"Knock it off!" Seth reprimanded like a parent tired of his children's noise, angry while not in the least concerned about why she had shouted. "You're going to let all the ghosts know we're coming," he finished.

Millie grimaced as she pulled her dress more tightly around her so the fuzzy black creatures wouldn't jump on her. She was still a little frightened, mostly from the surprise of seeing the spiders . . . hairy, disgusting things. But she felt different about the mine itself, confident that it wasn't as scary as it had seemed. It was as if being so close to it took away all the fear and left only the mystery. *Like when I first got over my fear of going into the sea,* she thought, remembering swimming around in the dark waters not knowing what else might be out there, but not allowing it to bother her after a while, until it became something exciting, exhilarating.

She looked over to Seth as he was awkwardly tried to strike his flint with his hands already full. She reached for the hard hat when he released a discouraged sigh, and Seth stiffened up immediately. "You can't hold it and light your sticks at the same time, stupid," she said with a touch of superiority as his eyes furrowed in mistrust.

Seth glanced over the flint, the lighting sticks, and the hard hat in his hands and finally handed the hard hat back with a sigh.

Sparks flew from the flint, igniting one of the sticks with a crackling sound. The candle was old and dusty, but lit quickly enough before his stick burned through. He dripped wax into the hollow in the leather, pressed the end of the candle into it, and the two exchanged smiles as the yellow flame danced pale in the afternoon light. Seth placed the luminous hard hat on Millie's head.

Laughing, they vanished into the mine.

CHAPTER 1

It's always the same . . .

Soft light penetrating the darkness, changing the shadows against the walls of the . . . cave? No . . . a tunnel . . . a series of tunnels. I am moving through a series of tunnels, brushing past the rough gray rock wall, knocking away small particles of dust and dirt as the walls crumble. The tunnel takes me down, as always . . . takes me down farther.

I know what waits for me at the end of the tunnel. It calls me.

The tunnel vanishes and it appears from the darkness: the basin. The bowl of rock that keeps it safe from them . . . spirit—it is filled with his spirit. No . . . not spirit, but something heavier, something more real . . . thicker and richer.

I gaze into the metallic sheen. It is metal liquefied . . . hot, burning metal. No . . . not quite . . . It is something else, something different, something greater.

It's always the same.

Something is wrong.

There is movement! Something swirls and churns in the blackness of the tunnels. And then it is with me—a girl. Such calm . . . such peacefulness . . . such wisdom.

She speaks. "It is time, Kav. Wake up!"

The young man's eyes opened, and he sat bolt upright on his bed. Slowly, the images of his dream dissipated from his mind.

24

"Basin . . . tunnels . . . girl." He swept his eyes around the room, seeking a pen and paper to write the fragments down. "Blood . . . girl . . ." He saw them on his wooden writing table and leapt, but his legs tangled in his blanket and he stumbled. "Whoa!" Freeing his legs, his toe stubbed on one of the many books on the floor and he slipped more than sat in his chair, just narrowly missing the table edge. Several books that had been crookedly stacked on the table tumbled to the floor.

He rested only long enough for a curse before pulling a scrap of parchment toward himself and dipping his pen into his inkwell. He began to write down what he remembered of his dream, but it was too late—all memories of it fled in his dance with the furniture. Glancing at the illegible sentence he had scribbled, he muttered in disgust and crumbled the parchment into a ball, which he tossed toward the collection already accumulating in the corner. Returning his pen to the well, he bent and snatched up the culprit text from the floor.

The Balance—Articles and Theories by Haved Gar. He had been studying its pages in his free time from chores, reading about the history behind the Rav'agas political and theological ideology, and its obvious conflict with Quetalian fundamentals. Smiling ruefully at the ironic title, Kavriel rubbed his sore toe and tossed the book onto his rumpled bed. He wasn't too discouraged about the elusive dream; he would dream again of . . . whatever they were about, in coming nights.

He leaned over to his washbasin and splashed cool water on his face, sweeping his wet hands up through his straw-colored hair to smooth it. Straightening, he contemplated the two days' growth of red beard on his dimpled cheeks in the clouded glass of the mirror, decided against shaving it off quite yet and, scratching absently at it, reached instead for his clothes, draped over the foot of his bed.

He pulled a shirt over his head while walking to the window, where he threw the shutters aside, letting in the morning brightness and his thirst for knowledge of the new day. There were so many questions and answers waiting to be discovered, fresher in the morning, it seemed, and more so this last month as his dreams held a new mystery. If he could only remember them . . .

A door opened in the next room, followed by muffled voices engaged in a serious discussion. Men's voices, and the rhythmic *knock-knock* of wood on wood identified his father, who walked with a cane, as one of them. Wondering what all the commotion was about, Kavriel quickly opened his door and stepped out into the hall.

"Are you sure it's him?" Kavriel recognized the gruff voice of Cyr Soelle, his father.

"Of course it's him," the second voice replied quickly, but without any agitation. "I came with his group from Teltraum directly."

The two moved to the dining area, and into Kavriel's view as he walked down the hallway.

Cyr propped his thick cane against a table and awkwardly up-ended a bucket of water he had been holding in his other hand into another. He was tall—or he would have been tall, if not for his handicap. He was still taller than his younger son, who stopped to watch from the doorway. He swayed under the weight of the bucket, having to compensate for his gimped left leg, but Kavriel could see the muscles in his left arm tighten like pulled cords underneath his skin as he accommodated for his uneven balance. The chore complete, Cyr set down the bucket, wiping his forehead with his hand and then pushing his fingers through his short, salt-and-pepper hair. Noticing Kavriel watching him, he stood up straighter. He was a proud man, and certainly healthy despite his handicap, but not one to hide his difficulties from others just to satisfy his pride. He knew who he was and what had happened to him, and that didn't lessen his authority in his home or anywhere else in Rhyol.

The other man was not as proudly relaxed, but moved about as if he were a cat in a room full of hounds. Heavyset and with a disheveled look about him, he didn't seem quite sure where to go, if he should sit down or help Cyr with the water. He was obviously distracted, rubbing his hips under his dirty riding coat, suggesting to Kavriel that he had just arrived from a long journey.

Kavriel knew Aurel Femaor well, and respected him for his quick mind and tongue. He had a habit of rubbing his hands together when he was nervous, and would often need to push his spectacles up from the end of his nose, but despite his quirks, there was a deep and knowledgeable look in his eyes, much like Cyr's.

Femaor was reaching into his coat pocket for a book of notes when he noticed the fair-haired young man in the doorway, and his eyes lit up. "Kavriel, is that you? Why, it has been a long time," he shouted warmly from across the room. Forgetting his notes, he moved spryly across the room despite his girth.

"Hello Master Femaor . . . It is good to see you, too," Kavriel wheezed as his breath was squeezed out by the older man's bear hug.

Femaor released him with a grunt and stood back with a chuckle, giving Kavriel a good once-over. Femaor shook his head and tsked. "It's only been—what? Six months? A year? And look how much of a man you've become." He leaned back and turned his big head to look at Cyr, now searching for something in the pantry. "It looks as if you did a good job raising him, Overseer. And he's fortunate that he doesn't look at all like you!" He roared heartily at his own joke, causing his spectacles to slide to the end of his nose. Kavriel smiled.

"He takes after his mother," Cyr replied, still occupied with searching the pantry. With a whispered exclamation of satisfaction, he pulled a small bag from one of the shelves.

"I don't know, Cyr; Lyssa didn't have that color hair . . . the eyes, maybe. Not too common, west of the Oenes Mountains." He waved a fleshy hand as if dismissing what he had just said. "I apologize, Kavriel. I ramble, and I am sure you have heard comments from others besides me about your uniqueness. All this riding has displaced my manners. It is good to see you!"

"No need to apologize, Master Femaor," Kavriel replied with a nod of understanding. He knew all too well the villagers' opinions about his fair hair. "Father told me that my mother's mother was from Loellen, which would probably explain it. You have just returned from there too, have you not?"

Kavriel had loaded his question, wanting to take every opportunity to hear about Femaor's adventures. His father tended to leave out detailed explanations whenever he pestered him about Master Femaor's business on the mainland. Cyr was more distant about political news to Kavriel, but Femaor knew what kind of person Kavriel was. He nodded back and his eyes became more focused.

"Yes, my lad, I have. Well, more recently, Teltraum City, of course." He tapped a sausage-like finger against his lips, as if thinking of something forgotten. Then he shook his head and moved over to the center of the room, where chairs and a table had been placed in front of an unlit fireplace. He sat down, removing from his pocket the notebook he had been searching for earlier while motioning for Kavriel to join him.

"Have you seen the Council? Did they decide about the scrolls?" Kavriel asked, moving immediately to sit down, hoping that this wouldn't be a pick and taste method of getting information from the man. He was much too hungry for that.

"Yes, but the Nine are at a standstill with other concerns," Femaor replied. "They have not decided on the scrolls—or at least, they hadn't when I left. I doubt very much things have changed since." He grunted, as if reflecting Kavriel's disappointment. "The Loellen representatives have taken residence in the upper city, awaiting any decision. They are not a . . . *patient* Council, but who can blame them? It's been months since they arrived, and the Council Nine can't seem to decide which day it is, let alone determine the fate of the scrolls. It is a tiring affair and the Loellen nobles are not used to such tedium." He pushed up his glasses and leaned forward, warming to his subject.

"It is the south that concerns them, and I'm afraid we are in for a difficult conflict. Negotiations with the Patriarch's envoys are riddled with complexity, I have heard from my contact in the Council. The issue with the scrolls is only going to make it worse. You're lucky that your father has been able to keep you and your brother from the fighting. It is a terrible ordeal and too many lives are being lost." He lowered his head in sorrow, as if remembering a personal horror.

Kavriel looked to his father, who had since finished fussing in the pantry and was listening to their conversation. It was impossible to read in his eyes how long he had been listening. Femaor's visit was more for him than for Kavriel, he knew, and Kavriel should be grateful that his father hadn't chased him out of there by now. Cyr had a discouraged look on his rugged face.

"They are needed here. The life of a soldier is not for him, nor his brother," Cyr said firmly in reply to Kavriel's expression. He took a sip from a mug that emitted a pungent odor—the result of the small bag he had searched for earlier. Kavriel knew that his father's leg must be afflicting him greatly today, if he was drinking tykat leaves. It dulled pain, as long as you could stomach the taste.

Femaor raised his head again to smile at Cyr. "You are right of course, Overseer. I wish I had had your resolve in that matter with my own son." His expression suddenly sharpened to something more confined and deep as his gaze shifted toward the empty area of the room. But only for a moment. He returned his eyes to Kavriel with a jovial smile, his deeper thoughts blown away like a passing breeze. "And you! Your father has told me of your advances here, the water piping, the irrigation, and the housing. Yes, you will do well here as the village overseer, just like your father has done all these years. It's too bad, though; they could use your quick mind in the city!"

Femaor's praise served to change the subject, although Kavriel's achievements with the village in truth had been executed by his older brother, Vaemalin. Kavriel had merely crunched numbers for him so that material could be cut correctly and water kept at clean levels. Femaor's comment burrowed into a long-held dream of his, though.

Teltraum, the largest city in the mainland, located nearly in the center of Quetal, was not only the seat of all political power in the country, but it was the repository of all the records and histories of every town, village, and tribe, everything stored away in the city's magnificent libraries. It was where the greatest scholars spent years unraveling the mysteries of the past while creating new ideas of the future; where people and culture blended together to create a haven of intellectual ingenuity; where all roads led—to the center of Quetal and to the center of civilization. The desire to experience that wealth of knowledge and culture was like a thirst he was unable to quench. Teltraum City . . . *one day.*

Cyr placed his empty mug heavily on the table, jolting Kavriel back to the present. He cast his father a cold look. Noticing this, and knowing something of Kavriel's dream to leave this small island village, Femaor frowned and began to rub his hands together.

"There are other matters that are more important to discuss now, if you'll remember," Cyr Soelle stated. "You and Kav can discuss the needs of the city another time."

"Yes, yes, of course!" Femaor nodded quickly and flipped several pages in the notebook that he again produced. Finding what he needed, he stood with a grunt and walked over to hold the book out to Cyr, a thick finger marking a place on the page. He waited patiently while Cyr scanned the page.

"These are all of them, I imagine?" Cyr asked gravely.

Femaor nodded. "Yes, they're the main points of discussion that took place between the Council and . . . and *him*. Well, what I could get from the committee hall, of course. It is quite large in there, you know, and it makes it difficult to hear everything when they are all talking at once."

Cyr stared ahead with troubled eyes. "Yes, I know. How was he able to get an audience with the Council so suddenly?" he asked, lifting his cane and moving toward the table where Kavriel sat.

"You know the general's reputation . . . he has more leeway with the Council Nine than most overseers," Femaor replied, taking the notebook back, since Cyr seemed to have forgotten about it already.

"But why did he come here? This is not a military affair. Something doesn't feel right."

"The general?" Kav asked aloud, wanting very much to become involved in the conversation from which the two older men had excluded him. "Who are you talking about?"

His father and Femaor gave him a look that didn't favor interruptions. "Saire, Kavriel," his father replied coldly after a pause. "The mighty General Saire has decided to grace our village with a visit." His eyes drifted toward the floor before he turned quickly to the front door. He pulled it open letting the cool autumn wind blow in, reminding Kavriel that he stood in only his undershirt and pants.

His father snatched a heavy coat from a peg beside the door. "A meeting has been called, and I must prepare for it," Cyr stated as he pulled on the coat. "When you hear the bell toll, Kav, make for the town hall. Do not dawdle, as you have had a tendency to do these last few mornings—this is an important matter and must be taken seriously. And get your brother; he should be there as well."

The door slammed shut behind Cyr, and Kavriel was left staring dumbstruck at it. Femaor only nodded and prepared to leave.

Kavriel stepped over to him quickly, before he could escape. "Wait, Master Femaor . . . what is this all about?" He reached out as if pleading; this sudden news was more than intriguing.

Femaor waved his hand away with a smile while keeping his distance. "I am truly sorry, Kavriel, but I cannot take the time to explain this to you now." He did look genuinely abashed as Kavriel lowered his arm slowly. "Your father has much to do before the other elders arrive, and I must assist him."

Kavriel was used to his father's sudden departures to deal with the affairs of the village—he was, after all, the overseer, and the other elders or head tradesmen certainly had the right to know more about what was happening than he did. It didn't make him feel any better, though, and he wished he could pull at least Femaor away for a time, to understand what was happening. Unfortunately it didn't seem that Femaor knew much, either—otherwise he would have said *something* more instead of being so quick to leave. Kavriel would have to keep his questions to himself. He nodded to Femaor, who responded the same way before disappearing out the door.

General Saire . . . is it possible? Kavriel thought, standing alone in his home. He repeated the name in his head.

In his readings of Quetalian political history, certain names were often mentioned as a focal point of change. They were the authors, teachers, leaders, or champions who stood out above the rest, whose thoughts and actions had changed the world, either benefitting civilization, or spiraling it in another direction; people whom future scholars considered worthy of study. Calvyn Terout, the stonemason from Loellen; the refugee doctor Fiola Garet of Bairn; Chairman Dar of the first Teltraum Council—these were just a few names that came to Kavriel's mind when he thought of great Quetalians, most long dead but some still alive to add pages to the history books. But *Saire!* He was legendary! An orphaned child, raised in the deserts of Rav'agas by nomads, had risen to become the most brilliant war tactician in recent history.

It was General Saire who led the Quetalian troops, outnumbered four to one by the superior Ay'vol forces, from the city of Taivr to push back the Southlanders across the fast waters of the Viliros, where the Rav'agas still hadn't been able to regain the border town that the Patriarch of Ay'vol City seemed so desperate to claim. General Saire also succeeded in cutting off their supply route to the port town of Viskye at the river's delta with a swift naval battle, leaving minimal Quetalian casualties and eliminating any direct access to the north from the defeated southern forces.

It was General Saire who personally discovered the scrolls east of Loellen, within the Oenes Mountains, and brought them to the Council of Teltraum, where their fate and legitimacy was still being debated. The scrolls were the only intact records possibly dating before F.T.—the Fall of the Temple. Their script, written in a dead language identified only as Temscript, supposedly held prophetic explanations of the current and future struggles against the Patriarch's Ay'vol forces, and the reasons why northern (and other lost) civilizations had drifted away from the faith nearly two thousand years ago. *Supposedly*, since scholars hadn't been able to find any correlating active language to translate much, if any, of it. Similarities were only speculation and from what Kavriel gathered from his brief conversation with Femaor, negotiations with the Patriarch might become worse *because* of the discovery of the scrolls. He wished that he had time to learn more, since he and Femaor shared similar theories about the scrolls and how understanding might be found in the south and not in the east.

At any rate, General Saire was not only known for his strategy and prowess, but also his political acumen. Many times he had fought with the Council on decisions that could have turned out for the worst, if not for his advice. Although asked, he never accepted a seat on the Council, instead accusing them of corruption and idealistic inbreeding, just for starters, which would have put any other man in the stockade. Yet his status, not to mention his admirers both high civilian and military, made him practically untouchable. The Council of Teltraum and the country of Quetal owed much to the man during the past few years, when the struggle against the Patriarch's Ay'vol forces seemed to reach a new ferocity.

Kavriel had never met the man, but General Saire's accomplishments were the stuff of wonder. He had an intelligence and skill far above most in Quetal, and his self-confidence seemed unbreakable.

What is he doing here? Kavriel wondered, repeating what his father had said earlier. It did seem a little odd. The legends of General Saire on the borderlands put him in a far more effective place than this northern isle, especially with Ay'vol's push; that was where he was needed most, defend that region. Even his influence with the district overseers on the mainland would prove far more effective for any political wrestling than up here on this sleepy island that was half forgotten by the Council Nine. It was a little shameful to think that way, due to his father's position as one of those overseers, but his old man would agree, having mentioned it often enough himself after being called to the city for some bureaucratic assembly. So whatever had drawn General Saire away from the fighting, both military and diplomatic, must be very important indeed. Kavriel began to understand why his father was in such a hurry.

Realizing that he had been standing alone in the empty house, muttering to himself, Kavriel hastened to his chambers to finish dressing before the town hall bell tolled; he doubted General Saire would allow extra time for this fool to get his boots on.

CHAPTER 2

Rhyol, the largest town in the Highlands, second only to Port Dior on the southern tip of the island, was lively with activity this morning. It was market day, and the villagers bustled like worker bees, browsing the market stalls, stockpiling the fruits and vegetables of the recent harvest for the coming winter. Merchants set up their wares along road intersections; lumbermen and woodworkers guided horses dragging heavy logs from nearby Silver Wood between barrels of peppers and salted fish; farmers paced amidst their flocks of sheep and goats, guiding them through the center of town with touches from their heavy crooks. It was a beautiful spectacle of chaos.

Stepping out of his doorway, Kavriel was nearly run over by a ram that had separated from its flock in the excitement. He patted the creature's rump and turned it back toward the apologetic shepherd's son who seemed a bit flustered by the number of people in town. Market day, held once every couple of weeks, always swelled Rhyol's normal population, but the end of season bounty tripled it, drawing people from all the nearby villages to the larger center to buy and trade. Realizing that the traffic might make it difficult to get to his brother in time, Kavriel leapt over the rail fence behind his father's house to navigate along the narrower streets and alleys. These were still filled with people, but less crowded than the main thoroughfare, where most of the large carts and wagons travelled.

Most were heading south toward the public square, where there was more space for the vendors to set up stalls and tables. The town hall was also in the square, and

Kavriel wondered how much time he would need to fetch his brother and make it back to the hall in time if the bell tolled with this mass of people everywhere. He moved east, away from the market district bordering his father's house, and quickly reached the outskirts of town, where coastal bluffs cut a steep recess into a valley where the storage sheds and silos were housed. The morning sun gleamed off the distant ocean and made the little facets in the pink rock walls on homes he passed sparkle.

Historically, the town was named after those rocks, which contained valuable minerals that gave them their dark pink, red, orange, or yellow color. The variety of unique minerals concentrated in this location in the Nostrac Highlands, the only place west of the Oenes Mountains where mining was possible, made it a haven for earth scientists and ore hunters. Rhyol, along with nearby Mir Town, Jovan, and Wood Side, had all been simple fishing and farming communities before the trade for metals brought prosperity and recognition to the Highlands. That was, of course, until the mines were closed down by the Council.

The official documents, which Overseer Cyr Soelle had been reluctant to sign, declared it to be a matter of health and safety; the proximity of the mines to the ocean, the properties of the minerals, and the underground heating wells combined to produce poisonous vapors that had afflicted numerous miners with a sickness known to the locals as red-eye, named for the discoloration of victims' eyes that accompanied a mental disorder and seizures. Kavriel had understood the concerns of the Council, reading the reports later on (he was only a baby when the mines had shut down), but he also understood his father's reluctance.

The sickness was real, but not as treacherous as the Council had publicized. The sick comprised a small percentage of the miners, and of those sick, only a few became as ill as the Council said—suffering uncontrollable fits and violence that could and had led to death. Most were no sicker than those with a common winter fever, which would generally burn itself out in weeks, leaving the person as healthy as he was before.

Unfortunately the dire description of the illness quickly fired public imagination on the mainland, their concerns prompting local overseers and the Council Nine to intervene in the livelihood of this distant district. The Highland clans were infuriated, calling the declaration unjust and a political maneuver pushed by the Oenes masons in Loellen, long wealthy from their trade and most likely feeling threatened by the prosperity of Nostrac. Plus having a Council Nine Chairman of noble Loellen blood only helped the conspiracy. Kavriel believed his father thought much the same as the clans, but he was still a representative of the Council and had needed to calm public concern before any talks of referendums began. Not that that was possible.

Though the mines and the riches of Nostrac had always benefited Quetal, it would continue to thrive, with or without the metals. The north and Rhyol had survived, the number of vendors and buyers on market day was proof of that. As for the mines, they remained full of minerals and ores that the funded scientists of Teltraum and the curious affluent tourists of the mainland came to see. Still, with less tangible work for the young, other places like Jovin and Mir Town were deserted. Their location against the ocean and the Silver Woods didn't offer much work, now that the mines were gone, and the clans of those communities dispersed to the rest of the island, their departure observed with a sadness that Overseer Cyr Soelle had found hard to stomach.

Kavriel frowned, thinking of the delicate position that had placed his father in, as the pinkish building stones twinkled against the black slate roofs and dark green landscape that gave way to the deep blue sea beyond. He wondered how such a beautiful place could be damaged by politics.

Yet today was market day, and for a time the villagers traded more goods than old stories. This was always an exciting day for Kavriel, who normally would be talking with the peddlers, who brought news from the mainland capital about a culture that he knew little about.

Teltraum was known for its artistry almost as much as its politics. New plays, concerts, and books popped up all the time in the large city, teeming with a creativity that caught Kavriel's interest even more than its political system. Femaor was generally a reliable source, but his responsibility was in the Council Halls with the other politicians. It gave him little free time to indulge in other interests, let alone speak much of them.

Unfortunately Kavriel had no time for the peddlers today. The curious arrival of General Saire was first in his thoughts. He did notice, from glances along alleys that led back to the main road, that this market day seemed more exotic than usual; the arrival of Saire seemed to bring an entourage of unlikely visitors from the mainland. His curiosity got the better of him and he turned back to the main road for a moment to watch the flood of people pass by with a grin on his face.

He recognized several of the Nostrac clan crests sewn onto coats and dresses, and the shell bracelets and armbands on the people of Port Dior, as well as the thick leather straps worn by the Sai Mariners, but for the rest, he was baffled. There were men and women wearing long, brilliantly colored robes with tall matching hats, and tattoo-faced men who looked more animal than human in their furry shoulder pads and not much else below, and even a group with skin so dark he wondered if he might be seeing Goern Islanders, that race of people who lived on an archipelago southwest of Viliros Bay.

Kavriel shook his head in awe, bidding a good day to the men and women passing by, who looked at him strangely and made him wonder if they understood his tongue. He loved seeing such cultural variety in his town. It gave him a chance to experience the outside world, if for only a short time. Being somewhat trapped here, this was all he could do, until the time came when he was able to leave for the mainland himself, and truly live the experience. That was if his father the overseer allowed for that in his plans. Kavriel tried not to let the thought discourage him today. His wishing for greater things was a battle that he had been fighting with his father for quite a while.

With a slight frown, Kavriel returned to the alleys to cover the final distance to the bluffs, which were now visible between the homes. A few moments later he was out of Rhyol and making his way down the wagon trail under the morning sun.

A tingle crawled up his spine, and he stopped. He didn't quite understand why, but he felt something *unusual* pass through him, like a dizzy spell. Standing in the middle of the trail that meandered lazily around the jutting rocks and stones, he blinked at the bright sun, wondering if he just needed to catch his breath. Then something just on the edge of his field of vision caught his eye, and he turned to look north, scanning the gray bluffs that climbed upward from the coast, looking for what had caught his attention. Atop the bluffs, some five to six hundred paces from where he stood and about the same height from the ocean below, several large cylindrical white rocks gleamed in the sunlight, completely out of place from the rest of the landscape—Moonstone Shrine. It wasn't truly a shrine, or any place of worship, for that matter. In truth, nobody actually knew what it was.

Within their shadow he saw the silhouette of a man.

Kavriel watched the man move cautiously around the circle of rocks—six columns circling a seventh, twelve to fifteen feet high and as thick as two men standing together. There was nothing else like them in all of Nostrac and history put them as old as the island itself, when nomadic clans began to congregate to form towns. Some believed the circle a magical place built by the gods, for the stones were unbreakable, and chipping even the slightest fragment off for study was impossible. Scholars from the mainland wishing to study the stones needed to bring samples with them from elsewhere for comparison; Kavriel had heard from Femaor that even Teltraum University took interest in the stones.

Science explained them as a result of massive pressure buildup, likely from a once-active heat source below the earth, that forced the glossy stones up to the surface. They said the pressure continued below, but at such a slow rate that the columns continued to rise from the depths only inches every thousand or so years. Of course there was no solid proof of this, but the theories seemed solid enough, and fishermen had discovered hollowed-out caverns under the ocean's surface where trapped air and salt mingled together to form crystalline formations. The person now surveying the stones was likely some scientist, or one of the many drawn to Rhyol out of geological curiosity.

Yet rather than dismissing the man, Kavriel continued to watch him as if drawn to him.

A voice near the storehouses in the valley below startled Kavriel, who turned his head toward the sound. A girlish laugh followed, and he had an idea of what was going on inside one of the buildings. His brother Vaemalin often spent time with his lady friend in the valley on chilly mornings; perhaps "dawdling" a bit longer, as his father had called it, wouldn't be such a bad idea. Not wanting to disrupt their intimacy, he turned back toward Moonstone Shrine.

The person there seemed to have noticed him, and after a few moments of trading stares, Kavriel decided that maybe he should introduce himself. In truth, he felt that he needed to. The tingling sensation seemed almost to draw him forward. He clambered up the steep path toward the circle of stones. The man's features became clearer as he neared.

The lone man was a bit shorter than Kavriel, but heavier set in the shoulders. He was wearing a dark blue, double-breasted vest embroidered with an intricate golden filigree over brown leather riding pants that were tucked into bulky looking black boots. A heavy cape, the same color as his vest, fell from his collar to just above his thighs, and was patterned with the same golden filigree. A skullcap covered his short-cropped hair. It was all quite different from anything on Nostrac.

Kavriel's eyes fell to the scabbard of a long broadsword hanging at the man's side, concealed from his view by the cape until Kavriel reached the perimeter of the stone circle. He slowed his pace, not used to seeing armed men in his village—other than the Quetalian guardsmen stationed in Rhyol, who generally wore their blades across their backs; this man clearly was not one of them. Suddenly nervous, Kavriel shifted his gaze from the sword back to the man's face, etched by a life lived at least twenty years longer than Kavriel's, and he realized that the stranger's eyes were even lighter than his own. They were a strikingly brilliant blue, almost translucently clear, and they regarded Kavriel with an uncomfortable curiosity. It sparked an interest in the man's origins.

"Greetings to Rhyol, stranger," Kavriel said after what seemed like an eternity under that gaze. "I hope our village finds you well, and that you are comfortable and content during your stay." He placed an open palm upon his breast before holding it passively toward the newcomer in the common Highland introduction.

The stranger remained silent, raising a gloved hand

to his face to casually to stroke his chin with two fingers. He cocked his head to the side slightly and his eyes narrowed; Kavriel's own eyes flickered back to the sheathed weapon. He immediately hoped his nervous reflex went unnoticed.

It hadn't. The man's hand fell from his chin and he tucked his thumb casually into his belt near the sword hilt. Kavriel swallowed with difficulty, telling himself the movement seemed more habitual than calculated. "You must excuse my manners, stranger," he said. "Visitors to Rhyol rarely carry weapons on their person."

The stranger finally spoke. "Are you a lawman?" His deep, grandfatherly voice was soothing to Kavriel's ears, but unusual, coming from a man who didn't seem to fit the role.

Kavriel stumbled over his reply. "Um . . . no. I meant—no, I . . . I just haven't seen it here before. Pardon my offense." He blinked rapidly, as if something had fallen in his eyes, and shifted, suddenly weak-kneed. He wasn't frightened as much as nervous, and he noticed that the tingling sensation he had felt earlier seemed to have wrapped around his head, causing his ears to hum slightly. It lasted only a moment; as the stranger suddenly opened his mouth in a white, toothy grin, the sensation dissipated as if lifted away by a slight breeze.

"There is no pardon required, young man," the stranger said. "You were only concerned for your well-being." His light blue eyes moved down to the protruding cross hilt of the blade, and he tapped its black leather pommel. "I have been on my own for some time now. The blade is a part of me, and I forget sometimes that I carry it at all . . . and how it might look to others."

He offered one of his gloved hands. "My name is Xavr."

Kavriel hesitated before reaching to shake the other man's hand, but as their hands touched, he felt calmness settle in him, as if he were greeting a long forgotten friend. "My name is Kavriel," he breathed. "Kavriel Soelle."

The man named Xavr withdrew his hand and clasped it with his other hand behind his back. He moved away from Kavriel slowly, walking back among the white columns, following their height with his eyes like a man casually taking a stroll through secluded woods. Kavriel watched him curiously. "I was admiring the stonework." Xavr spoke to the columns more than to Kavriel. "The smoothness is magnificent. Pureon is not an easy rock to manipulate."

It took a moment for Kavriel to understand what the man had just said. "I'm sorry. I am not familiar with that name." Kavriel's mind burned through memories of his past studies about Moonstone Shrine. He was quite certain he had never heard it called . . . that . . . before. "What is it that you said it was?" he asked.

"Pureon," Xavr repeated, his voice sure as he glanced back at Kavriel with a grin. "It is rare this far south, but not impossible."

Kavriel blinked again, more from confusion than unease. Who was this man? "This far south?" he repeated, mentally picturing maps of the vast expanse of North Sea past Nostrac. "I'm sorry, but there is nothing farther north than us. Did you mean the Oenes Mountains to the east, maybe? I have heard that similar rocks have been found there."

Xavr turned with an irritated glint in his light eyes that startled Kavriel. He swallowed nervously again, hoping that he hadn't angered the man. It was strange; normally he was quick and able to speak with strangers, but this Xavr fellow had him balancing on his tongue.

"Similar, yes . . . but not the same." Xavr spoke so low that Kavriel thought he had heard a growling undercurrent.

"Forgive me," he said humbly, "but you have me at a disadvantage. I have never heard of these things about the shrine before . . . and I thought I had heard them all!" Kavriel tried to throw out a quick chuckle, but it refused to come out. "Anyway . . . it sounds very interesting and I would like to hear more about it. The Rhyol Overseer would also be interested to hear what you know about the rocks. I would be happy to introduce you to him, if you'd like."

Xavr watched Kavriel, his face a mask. "He is your father, is he not?" he asked calmly.

Kavriel opened his eyes wide with interest. "Yes. How did you know?" His unease returned.

Xavr simply shrugged. "I have a good sense of people," he replied with a smirk. "For the moment, I believe your father might be more interested in another visitor, and I believe he is preparing to meet with him in your town meeting hall."

"Yes, he—" Initially awed by the stranger's knowledge, Kavriel started to suspect who this Xavr might be. "Wait . . . you are speaking about General Saire. Did you accompany him here?"

"I followed him," Xavr replied matter-of-factly, which seemed more than necessary for the simple reply. "But I am here on other matters." He turned back to the white columns behind him, placing his gloved hand almost tenderly on the smooth surface of one. "I have an interest in this . . . what did you say it was? A shrine?" He sounded amused.

Kavriel's smile was defensive. He shook his head. "It's not, really. But we call it Moonstone Shrine for the color and for its similarities to the fallen ruins of the Temple of Ciele. Well, so they say, since I have never seen those before." Kavriel tried to chuckle again, forcing it out in an effort to ease his tension. It helped, for Xavr's amusement suddenly turned into a sad frown as he looked solemnly back at the columns. Kavriel almost felt that he needed to apologize again for what he had said, but Xavr spoke before he could.

"Interesting." Xavr's voice was low, almost a whisper. "I have never thought of it like that."

There was a brief and uncomfortable pause. Xavr quickly stepped back from the column as if it had just burned him and turned toward Kavriel. He adjusted his cape, then moved past Kavriel, striding down another path that led directly to Rhyol, moving rapidly, as if Kavriel wasn't there. But he called back, "It was a pleasure to meet you, Kavriel Soelle." He waved a hand in the air without looking back. "I am afraid, however, that our conversation about your shrine will have to wait. Your father is planning to speak with the general very soon, and I hope to be in the audience. I bid you farewell."

Kavriel stood alone within the white columns,

49

baffled by such a strange parting after an even stranger conversation. He thought about calling after Xavr, hoping to prolong their chat, and wondering if he might have insulted the man by mentioning the temple. Rhyol was not a community of believers, but the stories of the fallen gods were still told in certain towns, and villages north of Rav'agas continued to worship the old ways. The Fall of the Temple was a immense part of that faith, and cause for great sadness to those that still believed. Was it possible that this Xavr fellow was a follower, and Kavriel had unknowingly reminded him of that story?

It was too late to say anything now; Xavr was just disappearing into Rhyol. A chill breeze from the bluffs woke him from his thoughts and he remembered his own obligations. He turned back toward the path into the valley and ran down it.

Moments later Kavriel entered a cluster of low wooden sheds that extended from the trail. A mischievous grin split his face and he picked up his pace, sprinting toward the large oak doors of a two-storey grain silo. Leaping forward, he drove a kick against the double doors, driving them open to crash back against the walls within. Luckily the hinges held. Kavriel landed awkwardly in the arched entry and shouted in the most authoritative voice he could muster, *"Vaemalin Soelle! What are you doing with my daughter?"*

A girl's shriek came from the loft as a man, covered in nothing but bits of straw, tripped and fell over the railing with a startled curse. He fell about six feet to crash onto a pile of barrels on the floor, the impact bursting several open to ooze grain and seed over the wooden floor.

A cloud of dust exploded above the whole mess.

Kavriel jumped back, his humor swinging quickly to fear for the fallen man's safety, but the groan that came out of the dust cloud was one of embarrassment rather than pain, and he couldn't help but snicker.

The man, dirty but otherwise unharmed, pulled himself free of the broken staves and lurched to his feet. "Damn you, Kav," he shouted, fist raised toward Kavriel, "Father's going to hang you when he finds out what you did! This is six months' worth of grain that you just spilled!"

"Me?" Kavriel replied, still overcome with laughter. "And what are you going to tell him, Vaem? That you and Tess were fooling around in the silo when I scared you out of your roost like a startled hen? Master Taloe would be interested to hear that as well, I think."

Vaemalin couldn't argue that. His lips curled downward, then pulled up in a menacing grin as his hand reached for one of the barrel staves. "No, but I could tell him that you had an accident, and that you are going to have to drink you meals through next winter." He charged, wielding the stave like a sword.

Kavriel cursed and scrambled back, trying to escape his brother's wrath, but his feet slid on the grain underfoot and he slipped to the floor. Vaemalin was on him instantly. He threw his arms up, trying to protect his face as his brother slapped him several times across the shoulders with the stave. Vaemalin didn't hit him hard, just enough to make him wince and gasp between gusts of laughter. He barely heard Vaemalin's lecture about never doing what he had just done ever again.

"Alright, alright!" Kavriel pleaded, palms up in surrender. "I submit!"

Vaemalin ceased his pummeling and straightened, standing, chest heaving, over Kavriel. With a satisfied smile he tossed his makeshift weapon across the room and grabbed his brother's arm to yank him to his feet.

Kavriel made a show of flinching at his brother's nakedness. "For the love of the Creator, would you put something on?"

Vaemalin smirked and gave his brother one final shove before he turned to search for his shirt and pants in the mess of broken barrels. Pulling them from a mound of seeds, he brushed them off while muttering curses interspersed with his brother's name.

Vaemalin was two years older than Kavriel. They shared the same mother and father, but that was the only thing they had in common. Kavriel was considered a man of average height by village standards, while Vaemalin was easily a hand taller, with shoulders like a bull. The muscles in his arms and legs were nearly double the size of Kavriel's own, his chest chiselled from long hours of working in the fields and forests. Though he was the overseer's firstborn son, it was his physique and virile, handsome face that made him popular with the ladies. He was also smart, friendly, kind, and overly protective of his villagers, which made him popular with everyone.

Compared to his brother, Kavriel was simply another villager in Rhyol, despite his unique appearance, which occasionally caught the eye of curious girls from the Highlands. His handsomeness was a flicker of light compared to his brother's radiance. Vaemalin's dark eyes were deeply compassionate. His loyalty to his neighbors and friends was more than commendable—he would give everything he had for the benefit of Rhyol, let alone Quetal. A woman who won his heart would be the luckiest person in all of Nostrac.

That woman called down to Kavriel from the loft where she had been hiding. "Hi, Kav!" Tess waved, and immediately Kavriel blushed. She was sitting in a pile of mixed thatch and hay without a stitch of clothing on above the waist! Whirling, he rushed to pull the open double doors shut against the eyes of any passing villagers.

"Tess, are you mad!" he scolded to the oak doors, refusing to turn around to face her. "If anyone should see you . . . " He was unable to finish, knowing Tess had a wealth of self-confidence and anything he said would make little difference in how she behaved. It wasn't the first time Kavriel had seen Tess in nothing but her skin, but still it surprised him each time.

"Relax, my wholesome little brother," Vaemalin said. "Remember what day it is? All the Highlands are in Rhyol today to trade, everyone except you." Now dressed, Vaemalin was arranging the barrels that had not been destroyed in a reasonable pile in the corner. Noticing a broom propped against the wall behind Kavriel, he nodded toward it and waved for Kavriel to bring it to him. Meanwhile, Tess had clothed herself, to Kavriel's relief, and was now climbing down the ladder from the loft above.

"What do you want, anyway?" Vaemalin asked as Kavriel tossed the straw broom to him.

"Pa's holding a meeting at the hall and he needs us to be there," he said.

Vaemalin frowned. "Today? It must be important, if he needs to speak with the tradesmen. Pulling them out of the market could hurt their business, and they need the push before winter."

Always the people's champion. Vaemalin would be the next overseer of Rhyol when Father stepped down, regardless of what Femaor had said earlier in his father's house. Not only did Vaemalin have the support and faith of the town, he was a man constantly involved with it. When there was a problem that Cyr Soelle needed solved, Vaemalin was there. When there was a new idea or development in the works for Rhyol, Vaemalin was there. He was right for the town, and the people knew it. Kavriel was also there, of course, as another son to the overseer with responsibilities of his own to uphold. Yet unlike Vaemalin, his heart and passion went beyond this place. His desires were much greater than anything the Highlands could offer him. As soon as his brother took the reins of Rhyol, he would no longer be needed here and he would pursue his dreams on the mainland.

Tess had reached the bottom of the ladder while Kavriel was thinking of the future. She walked over to them, twisting her long dark hair into a loose bun. Tess was noticeably shorter than either of them, more so next to Vaemalin, and she smiled up at Kavriel with a glint in her dark eyes. "You know, Kav, Vaem is going to start getting jealous if you keep trying to peek in on me," she joked. Several dark ringlets escaped the knot in her hair and bounced on her lithe shoulders. "What is the meeting about, anyway?" she asked.

"Not about the tradesmen, as far as I know,"

Kavriel replied as his mind returned to the errand his father had sent him on. "General Saire is here, but neither Pa nor Master Femaor seem to understand why. They both are confused, and Pa seems on edge about it." He shrugged, but he felt a twinge of excitement as he said the general's name. "Either way, we need to get going before the bell sounds."

Vaemalin must have had the same reaction as Kavriel had when he learned Saire was in town, for his face lit up with a generous smile. By contrast, Tess paled, eyes wide and her lips compressed.

"Saire . . . I don't believe it! This is a great day for Rhyol, if he's come." Vaemalin spoke proudly, glancing over to Tess, who barely nodded back. "And old Fem is back! Wonderful. I wonder if he came across any Pasavian ale." Vaemalin eagerly collected his and Tess's belongings and opening the silo door, the embarrassment of Kavriel's intrusion and the spilled grain forgotten.

Vaemalin's almost childish excitement distracted Kavriel; he barely felt Tess's hand until she closed it tightly over his arm. Looking at her, he saw her ghostly expression and it worried him. "Do you think the general is here to declare his right to conscription?" she asked softly, with a fearful glance toward Vaemalin. It was rare for Kavriel to see her bothered and he did not like it one bit.

"Don't worry," Kavriel replied quickly, placing his hand over hers to calm her distress. "We are . . ." he glanced at his brother who, oblivious to the conversation, was already waiting out on the wagon trail, "ineligible." He smiled at Tess and tried to sound reassuring. "Having an overseer as a father has its benefits."

55

It seemed to work. Tess smiled back with less tension in her expression, and released her grip. "Of course." She sighed. "I forgot, is all . . . thank you, Kav."

Vaemalin shouted back to them, "Let's get going, you two!"

CHAPTER 3

Tess Taloe was always around the Soelles, even as a child. Master Kair Taloe, her father and also one of the village elders, often joked that occasionally he forgot if Tess was his daughter or Cyr Soelle's, as she had practically grown up in the overseer's house, playing with the brothers. The heads of the two respected families were both colleagues and friends; they had known each other a long time, and had been present at the birthing of their respective children, so it was understandable that their offspring had grown up like siblings.

Tess's older and only brother, Grieg, was in the company of the Soelles nearly as often as his sister. He was the same age as Vaemalin and so in the same grade in school; sharing plots with Vaemalin to terrorize their younger kin created a strong bond between the two boys.

Kavriel, in turn, was forced closer to Tess, simply to have safety in numbers whenever Vaem and Grieg tormented them. Their similar personalities drew them even closer with age, until they were like twin siblings, finishing each other's sentences and sharing opinions on subjects of interest they studied, while the two older boys preferred the more concrete bonding of sport or roughhousing.

They both were social enough, but Tess was Kavriel's only true friend. Kavriel had been shy when it came to playing with other children, who teased and ridiculed him for his hay-colored hair and blue eyes, unique among all the dark-haired children of the Highlands. All children tended to set apart the unfamiliar, he understood as he grew older, but Tess never did. She was protective of her substitute brother, a victim of the abuse often doled out by her brother, who tended to be on the supply end of name-calling. Maybe it was a maternal instinct, one passed on by her own possessive mother that she reflected onto Kavriel, who'd never known his own. In fact she found his unique features fascinating, and they created "Kavriel's origin" theories that grew from their shared interest in far-away, exotic cultures.

It was obvious that she preferred his company over that of the girls her age, who prattled empty nonsense. Tess and Kavriel spent many days sitting in the fields east of the village, talking about Highland politics or simply walking along the beach to the west, searching for shells. As they became older Tess remained Kavriel's confidante and surrogate sister, but it was Vaemalin who began to notice her beauty as she approached womanhood.

When the Quetalian military passed through Rhyol over a year ago, drafting recruits, Tess's true brother had been fascinated. Kair Taloe was an official elder of Rhyol, but that did not give his family immunity from enlistment, as it did Overseer Soelle's family; while neither Kavriel nor his brother had any desire to fight against the Patriarch in the borderlands, the draft had not been necessary for Grieg, brought up on the historical glory of war. After one night in a tavern with several of the battle-hungry Quetalian cadets, he decided that his place in life was going to be on the front lines, where the action still was. He signed up as a soldier the very next morning and was on the boat to the mainland within days.

Kair Taloe, the old soldier and veteran along with Cyr Soelle and General Saire of the forty-year "border's battle" when the Patriarch had first made his push into the southeast, was tremendously proud of his boy when he learned of his son's decision, and eager that he share the experiences of military life that he had once lived.

The fighting was constant, though minimal now, with the war that once had Quetal youths fighting to keep the southern tyrant from claiming their homes now eroded into a lethargic annoyance more than true conflict. The initial three years had been violent, but Quetal had pushed back the gold- and black-armored Ay'vol Force of the Patriarch, creating a stir in Rav'agas that had the provincial leaders reassessing their allegiance to Ay'vol City.

Unlike her father, Tess was devastated by her brother's enlistment. That left Vaemalin, kind and sensitive Vaemalin, to take the place of Grieg, becoming the emotional rock that she needed, involving himself more and more with her and Kavriel's group of friends . . . and then just with her. Vulnerable in her brother's absence, she found Vaemalin, Grieg's best friend, naturally filled an emotional need. Recognizing his obvious attraction, her love for Vaemalin blossomed from affection for a childhood companion into a mature, adult relationship. If Kavriel had any pangs of jealousy he did not show it, instead supporting her decision to be with his brother as a true friend and confidante would. She was like a sister to him, more so now than ever. He couldn't be happier for their joining.

Rhyol was the largest town in the Highlands, but the Taloe and Soelle families were known in every community within and around, watched like characters in a long, ongoing novel. Two things were certain: Vaemalin would become overseer when Master Cyr Soelle stepped down, and Tess would be his wife. Together, the two would govern with kindness, intelligence, and understanding. It had been all but decided by the people of Rhyol, Overseer Cyr Soelle, Kavriel, and especially between Vaemalin and Tess.

Yet Kair Taloe would not allow a marriage to take place until the entire family was present, which meant when his son Grieg had finished his tour of duty and returned to declare with his father the merging of the families. It was an age-old Highland tradition that could not go unrecognized, even though the people of Rhyol and *especially* Master Taloe were not foolish; they knew that young men and women would always be able to find a moment or two away from prying eyes to enjoy each other's company. Vaemalin and Tess, out of respect for the community and more importantly their conservative fathers, kept their trysts from general knowledge as best they could—to Kavriel's amusement.

"Do you think your father will mention the missing girl?" They had climbed the wagon trail back onto the Rhyol's main road when Tess broke the silence with her question.

Vaemalin replied by frowning uncertainly. "No," he said. "What happened is Kessor's concern for the moment. The Guard will get involved only after a certain time has passed . . . normally after a full day. Until then, the family will do what they can on their own."

"What are you talking about?" Kavriel asked, trailing behind them as they entered the mass of people that he had been able to avoid earlier.

Tess glanced back at him with a look of astonishment while slipping between slower pedestrians en route to the main square. "You can't be serious!" she exclaimed. "Half the village woke during the night, and the Kessor place is just across from you."

Vaemalin snorted. "You don't live with him," he said. "Lately he's been sleeping like a corpse. I don't think even a pack of howling wolves outside his window could wake him."

He followed his comment with an elbow jab that Kavriel was barely able to avoid. "You should stop reading at night," Vaemalin said. "Filling your head before you sleep is a bad idea."

Kavriel responded with a snort of his own. "Filling one's head is never a bad idea, my simple brother. Reading a book or two might even do *you* some good." He tried landing a punch on Vaemalin's shoulder but with an agility belying his size, his brother dodged it easily with a taunting smile.

Kavriel turned his attention back to Tess. "What happened . . . really?" he asked.

Tess seemed to fall into her thoughts for a moment, staring down the road before she answered. "Lady Kessor's children went into Silver Wood yesterday afternoon." Her face clouded, and she frowned. "They didn't tell her where they were going, and when they weren't home at sundown, she came to the town hall all in a panic. Father and I were there discussing market day with Master Kessor and several other tradesmen. We all searched the town most of the night, causing quite a ruckus, but we couldn't find them." Tess paused to adjust her dark hair, which had begun to slip

61

out of the bun she'd wound it into.

"How did they know the children had gone into Silver Wood?" Kavriel asked, frowning himself. Silver Wood was a dangerous place for children. It went on for miles, and if the trails weren't followed, anyone could easily become lost.

"Finally, near dawn, Farmer Poldr came up the road fast, with Seth Kessor, the girl's brother, in his wagon. He said he found him in a clearing near his ranch when he went out to check on what was spooking his flock. The boy was unconscious and chilled to the bone when they brought him into the Kessors' house, and I thought he was dead." She shivered.

"I was sent home then to get some sleep—as if I would be able to sleep! Apparently the boy woke a few hours later. My father had stayed with the family, and when he came home he told me. Father thinks he's in shock, but he seemed unharmed. They don't know what to make of it . . . the things that the boy said when he woke up."

They had stopped walking now, all disturbed by this news. The brothers were staring intently as Tess finished the story. "What did he say?" Kavriel asked.

Tess shook her head. "Father wasn't sure. Seth was in and out of his head when he began talking, but he mentioned fog, darkness, and blood."

Vaemalin's face paled, and Kavriel could feel the blood draining from his own. "You didn't tell me that part," Vaemalin said softly.

She gave him a tight smile and put her hand on his cheek. "I'm sorry, but it has all happened so fast. The other child, Millie . . . she's still missing."

"Do you think this mention of blood . . . ?"
Vaemalin began, but Tess was quick to interrupt him.

"I don't know, my love. It is still too soon to
understand what happened. The men were organizing a
search party this morning when I left to meet you. The boy
was found . . . and they will find her, too."

Vaemalin pressed his lips together and nodded
once. There was no point in continuing this subject without
more news about the missing girl. Kavriel tried to picture
the Kessor children, Seth and Millie, but he couldn't bring
details of their faces to mind. He never paid much attention
to the children in the town, aside from the occasional name
and whose boy or girl belonged to whom; certainly not
enough knowledge to be effective in helping if something
happened to them. He suddenly felt quite shamed at that
fact—as the son of the town overseer, he should be more
accountable to Rhyol's citizens.

He frowned, trying to recollect images. He knew
what Edan Kessor, the children's father, looked like; there
would be similarities to his young. The boy Seth might
have been that short, curly haired boy who was always
running through his father's yard, which would make sense,
since they lived close by. Yet when he tried to envision the
sister, he suddenly felt an odd and almost guilty memory of
something that he couldn't quite place. It was as if she had
been an important part of his life, but he was without any
direct memory of her—she'd simply always been there and
then one day she wasn't. It was a strange sensation, and
Kavriel didn't think there could be any possible proof to
that idea if he couldn't even bring her face to mind. He
shrugged, dismissing it.

The loud clang of a bell cut through the monotonous chatter of the passing villagers, signalling that the meeting was about to begin. The noise woke Kavriel, Tess, and Vaemalin from their thoughts and they shouted to one another to hurry as they ducked and dodged their way to the town hall.

The road widened as they entered the center of town, joining several other streets and alleyways in merging into Rhyol's Market Square. The larger space meant the crowd grew less dense, and Kavriel and the others were able to quicken their pace, crossing to the large rectangular building on the southern edge of the square. Rhyol was the capital of the Highlands, and the town hall was the largest building in town. Members of clans and those from all nearby towns and villages came here to discuss trade, the harvest, the weather, the economy, and myriad other subjects within the wooden walls patterned after the Council Hall in Teltraum, the governing seat of Quetal.

Overseer Cyr Soelle spent much of his time in the town hall, as his duties did not differ much from those of the Quetalian Chairman of the Council Nine, delegating and officiating and sending reports to the mainland as Head Representative to the Council. Each district overseer had the same responsibility, and Kavriel imagined a Cyr Soelle in every corner of Quetal, doing exactly what his father did, and what his brother would do, in time. Holding a position of constant public audience did not appeal in the least to Kavriel, and he was glad that the people of Rhyol favored Vaemalin as future overseer. *If* other names appeared during the next inevitable election, Kavriel doubted that his name would be one of them.

They arrived at the entrance to the town hall as the two tall arched oak doors swung open to admit the crowd of people gathered in front of the hall. Nervous-looking guardsmen, unused to the large turnout, waved people into a single file past a large table next to the entrance bearing a sign instructing those in attendance to leave weapons outside.

"What is this about?" Vaemalin said immediately after reading the sign. Kavriel shrugged. The sons of the overseer knew that it was Quetalian law for attendees of large public meetings not to carry arms, but this was the first time a *notice* had been posted to remind people of that law.

"It must have to do with the general," Tess said as she stood up on her toes to get a better look over the crowd near the table. "With all the people in town, every clan in Quetal must be here today . . . maybe from even farther away. The general's reputation draws followers."

Kavriel nodded for her reasoning was sound, but she didn't seem to approve of her own words. It might have been because there was a surprising amount of steel atop the table, all shapes and sizes of weaponry, as varied as the array of people who had come to market day this autumn afternoon.

Kavriel's memory went back to the man he had met on the ridge, Xavr, and the broadsword he wore, so unlike anything he had ever seen. Leaning closer to the table, Kavriel scanned the pile for the broadsword.

Tess's shriek of joy distracted as much as startled him. Before he was able to react, she was running toward a small group standing near the entrance. Kavriel recognized one of the men in the group as Master Taloe who, grinning, stood facing the arms table. His white hair, hanging in ringlets around his shoulders, drew the eye. The two others he was speaking to had their backs to Kavriel.

Tess broke through the line of people like a sickle through a corn field, and leapt onto the back of one of them, nearly knocking him into Master Kair.

Kavriel's first reaction was to wonder what sort of lunacy had overcome his friend, that thought quickly followed by a mental image of steam shooting out of a red-faced Master Kair's ears because his little girl had so rudely interrupted his conversation. Instead the white-haired elder, retaining his smile, stepped back to avoid getting hit. Tess was laughing like a madwoman, still hanging onto the stranger's neck. This all happened in an eye blink. The victim of Tess's assault, quite a bit larger than she, reacted immediately, reaching around his neck to yank the girl off of him and pull her around to the front, as if she was no heavier than a bug. The motion brought his face to view, and Kavriel and Vaemalin exchanged a smile. Now grinning with Tess, the man pulled her into a powerful hug. The brothers laughed openly, and quickly hurried over to the group.

"Oh, Grieg! It's so wonderful to have you back!" Tess exclaimed, her eyes glittering with tears.

"I missed you too, Tess." Grieg released his sister but still held her arms, keeping her close. "I hope you received my letters?"

She nodded, too overcome with joy to reply, and brushed the tears from her eyes with a choked laugh. When

Kavriel and Vaemalin arrived, Grieg released his sister, throwing his arms wide with a roar of happiness to embrace them both.

Grieg Taloe was the spitting image of Tess, though five years older. He had the same dark eyes that lit up when he smiled, the same dark, curly hair that bobbed when he laughed, and the same smile that could warm any heart. He was a little taller and more rounded in the middle than Vaemalin, making him a giant compared to Kavriel and Tess, but his fighting in the borderlands had clearly tightened his bulging muscles. Kavriel realized this as the bigger man squeezed him against his mail armor, pushing the air out of his lungs. Only when he started to turn red did Grieg realize it too, releasing him to find the ground with his feet again.

Tess beamed at the three of them, her clasped hands pressed to her mouth in joy. Master Kair continued to smile at his prodigal son, nodding happily to Tess and her friends. He was the image of a dignified father, proud of his son's choice but also relieved for his safe return. Excusing himself, he entered the town hall as Kavriel and his brother began bombarding Grieg with questions about the borderlands. Grieg was happy to reply, describing his adventures on the battlefields with an excitement that seemed to waft from him like perfume.

It had been almost a year since they had seen Grieg. His letters, shared among the three of them, didn't come close to the awe conveyed in his vivid descriptions of abandoned villages, night storms in the desert, and the camaraderie he shared with his fellows. Several of the townspeople entering the hall stopped to listen to the large man as, waving his hands dramatically, dressed in his uniform and armor, he spoke of the Patriarch's Ay'vol Force.

At last his rapid retelling of his past year on the mainland fluttered out as the last of the townspeople entered the town hall. He clearly had more to talk about, but he seemed equally eager to hear about the life he had left behind. "So, Rhyol hasn't run the Soelles out of town yet? I'm surprised you're still here, Kav."

Kavriel was still lost in what he had listened to, and only responded with a smile and a nod.

Grieg was on a roll; he turned to Vaemalin. "And Vaem, have you been taking care of my little sister for me . . . treating her right?" Grieg pushed out his barrel chest and lifted his chin to look down at Kavriel's brother. He adjusted his steel-reinforced gauntlets menacingly while Vaemalin replied with an unnerved laugh.

"What's it to you, Ox?" Vaemalin jeered. "Surely a big, handsome man like you had better things to do than worry about your little sister."

The two men stared each other down like a couple of puffed-up roosters for a moment before they both hooted with laughter and slapped each other's shoulder. Kavriel shook his head while Tess mumbled several unkind words while still keeping her smile.

"Speaking of better things, my friends, I have someone you should meet!" The second soldier with Grieg had been forgotten in Grieg's arrival—yet in hindsight Kavriel wondered how he'd possibly noticed anything *but* the second soldier.

The soldier was a *she* . . . and *she* was stunning.

Clearly a warrior like Grieg, she was dressed in the blue
and silver uniform and armor of a Quetalian soldier, but it
was tailored to a feminine body that only heightened his
awareness of her. Her boots were those of a soldier, thick
leathered and steel-toed, but with low heels to add to a
woman's smaller stature—something she clearly did not
require. Her greaves of black leather went up only just
above her knees, where the rest of her long legs and
shapely thighs were only lightly protected by a split mail
skirt that hung loosely from under a mail shirt. Her bare
arms were wrapped with numerous bands and bracelets that
were of a deep green and violet color—quite different from
Quetalian standard, but beautiful against the polished silver
of the scale armor on her shoulders and her incredible dark
bronze skin. A collar guard made of tiny ringed mail
protected her neck, and a sculpted breastplate protected
exactly what it suggested it did.

Swallowing uneasily, Kavriel pulled his eyes away
from her body, lifting them to her gold-beaded and braided
black hair and finally to her face. Again he was instantly
transfixed by her almond-shaped eyes that were almost the
color of sand.

He must have been looking at those eyes longer
than was proper, for she tilted her head back slightly and
drew her brows together in a frown. Her hands went to her
hips.

It couldn't be helped. She was the most exotic
creature he had ever seen, but she was also armed with two
slim, nasty looking curved blades in shoulder scabbards
that crossed like a gold hourglass on her back. Kavriel had
only read about sicca blades in books, as they were not

popular to the northern armies but remained a standard weapon of the south, their origins in Rav'agas. She also carried a black whip coiled neatly at her belt that, combined with her exotic appearance, only fed his fascination.

Tess cleared her throat with a loud "ahem" that woke him from his stare. As he turned away in embarrassment he saw that Vaemalin had been hypnotized by this strange woman's appearance as well, and Tess's irritation was meant for him. Being the master of charm, Vaemalin recovered quickly and first smiled innocently at Tess before welcoming the new woman with an open-palm greeting.

"Welcome to Rhyol, my lady," he began. "I apologize for not greeting you sooner. Our friend has been gone for a while and we were only eager to speak with him. Yet now that I see you in his company, I think it would have been more proper to address you first. Female soldiers are rare in Quetal, and you deserve the greatest respect we can offer."

Very smooth, Kavriel thought as he glanced over to see Tess's reaction. The fire seemed to have left her eyes but she kept her lips pressed together, watching Vaemalin. Grieg remained silent, a knowing smile on his lips. The woman didn't say anything in response, but instead suddenly looked expectantly over to Kavriel.

"We . . . um . . ." Kavriel stumbled for a moment, wondering what he should say. A passage from a novel that he had recently read suddenly sprang to mind. "We hope that you find our people hospitable and that the beauty and grace of our home may be matched only by your own." The immediate silence was enough to stop his heart, but the amused grunt from Vaemalin quickly brought the heartbeat back. He shot a discouraging glare over to his brother as the strange woman finally reacted by raising a dark eyebrow.

"Well," she drawled, "if I knew there were such captivating men on Nostrac, I would have visited earlier." Her voice bore a heavy accent that Kavriel hadn't heard before, making her i's sound more like ah's. He blushed; Vaemalin seemed unaffected.

Tess finally decided to say something to the woman. "Your visit would have been disappointing, my lady." Her voice held an edge. "*Captivating* men are rare in Nostrac, and I, unfortunately, have claimed them already." She had to look up to meet the soldier woman's eyes as she approached, and a smile was growing on her lips. She startled Kavriel by grabbing both his and Vaemalin's arms. "Still, it is market day here in Rhyol ,and I would hate to disrupt the tradition. Perhaps we can talk trade?"

"Tess?" Vaemalin said uncertainly as he and Kavriel looked at the petite woman holding them at her sides. Grieg bellowed laughter; the new woman smiled.

"You must be Tess, Grieg's little sister. Grieg has told me much about you." The woman spoke with a look in her eye that reminded Kavriel of a cat toying with a mouse. "Your people are blessed to have the strength of a true woman in their town. If your love for them is only a fraction of your love for your brother, then this place is greater than it can imagine." Now she gave the open-palm greeting, but it was followed by another that involved a turn of her wrist and a bow.

Tess released her smile to its fullest. "And you must be A'zia. I am honored to finally meet the woman who has

71

captured my brother's heart."

Hearing the name, Kavriel's thoughts suddenly pulled together. The initial shock of her beauty dissipated gradually, but he remembered the woman's name from the letters that Grieg had sent home throughout the year. There hadn't been much detail about her besides what one would expect from a man bragging about his new lady . . . there was certainly no exaggeration. Yet there was something else that Grieg had quickly mentioned in an afterthought about her home, and the sicca blades across her back jolted Kavriel's memory. "A'zia," he repeated, drawing her attention back to him. "You are the one from Rav'agas?" The suspicious look that garnered reminded Kavriel once more of his inadequacies at small talk.

She replied firmly, with words he would have expected. "The *one* from Rav'agas?" She said, shifting her large eyes for a moment back to Grieg. "Are you implying that there are others I should be aware of?"

Again Kavriel stumbled over what he should say. Luckily, Vaemalin was there to quickly take the lead as he too glanced at Grieg with a devious glint in his eye. "Well, my lady, I cannot speak for my friend here, but he does have a reputation."

Grieg lunged at Vaemalin, and the two grappled a moment amidst bouts of laughter and curses. A'zia regarded Tess with a confused expression; Tess only shrugged with palms up, as if to say, *Don't worry about this.* Kavriel wondered if the new woman truly understood what she had gotten herself into by becoming Grieg's companion.

When the scuffle began to peter out, Kavriel noticed

that A'zia was now closer to him, and the suspicious look in her eyes had returned. "You seem to have an interest in Rav'agas, my blue-eyed one. You know my name, as well. I am afraid you have me at a disadvantage."

The scent of her perfume made Kavriel perspire, but he had unwittingly caught her attention and now he must deal with it. He cleared his throat before speaking, hoping not to sound too foolish. "My apologies if I was out of line," he said. "My name is Kavriel. I haven't met many people from the south." He decided to throw in a bit of his knowledge of Rav'agas to see if she might stop looking at him like a wolf might look at a small rabbit. "Are you by chance from West Point?"

The smile that she responded with only heightened her beauty. "I am, and there is no apology needed. I was born in Kairn. My people do not support the Patriarch's interests in conquest—our history can tell you that. Our army has recently joined with your Quetalian defenders. You look like a smart boy; I am sure that you know this already?"

Kavriel wasn't sure if she was trying to be sarcastic, but her smile didn't change and her eyes held his. The other three were now listening to their conversation with interest. "Yes," he replied shyly. "I have read of the provincial powers in Rav'agas, and we are honored to have your support."

Rav'agas politics were almost as complicated as those in Quetal. Like the north, the country was separated into districts, but called provinces, each with its own overseer that they called a bishop. Unlike Quetal, whose district authority still needed to pass through the Council of

Teltraum, the provinces retained governing rights separate from the Rav'agas capitol of Ay'vol, the greatest and wealthiest province, ruled harshly by the Patriarch. At one time Ay'vol had absolute power over all of Rav'agas, like Teltraum over Quetal.

Governance was deeply rooted in a common religious ideal that the ten provinces adhered to; since the system was faith-based rather than politically tangible, the provinces began to separate from the Patriarch, reinterpreting their own version of *The Way*, and in turn their own version of rule. They still retained the old titles, but the once united nation had fractured into smaller, independent pieces.

A great river, the Viliros, formed the border between Quetal and Rav'agas. Historically the devout south and the "heathen" north exercised only conventional distrust between one another, but occasionally real physical disputes erupted along the borders. Closer to the Oenes Mountain Range in the east, whose enormity actually touched the two nations, the island of Ciele remained independent from either nation, at one time a great seat of power for a religious order that was said to be even greater than the order ruling Ay'vol. The religion had been considered banal and primitive, even barbaric, and the two nations had exiled that nation to its own ways, before the religion of Ciele had either died out or moved away from the island. The current Patriarch of Ay'vol had recently begun a campaign to assimilate the island, now a nation within the nation of Rav'agas, winning the support of several of the provinces near Ciele that led to the amassment of troops known as the Ay'vol Force.

Disagreeing with the Patriarch's notion of assimilation that was simply a softer word for genocide, the Council of Teltraum brought Quetal into the affair. The Quetalians were used to the Rav'agas rattling their swords from across the river, but the massacre that this current Patriarch was proposing went beyond politics. Only passive farmers and nomads now occupied the island. And the island of Ciele was near the southern Quetalian city of Taivr, whose populace had grown nervous about the Patriarch's intentions.

The Patriarch's new Ay'vol Force was quite different from the past Rav'agas army, its members rumored to have been chosen by the Patriarch himself for their skill, their violence, and of course, their loyalty. Bloody skirmishes between the Taivr Guard and the Ay'vol Force were inevitable, but the Patriarch refused to acknowledge any blame, simply calling it *divine intervention*.

Immediately the Council of Teltraum sent soldiers from the north, initiating the struggle that Quetal and Rav'agas had been embroiled in for forty years. The eradication of Ciele never came to pass, but the two nations remained enemies. The battle front stretched past Taivr to encompass the entire length of the Viliros to the West Sea.

The loss of what the Patriarch had promised to be a "swift end to the northern plague" caused a stir in the provinces that had backed the Patriarch's crusade and most pulled out, leaving only his loyal Ay'vol Force. Strangely the Patriarch did not enact vengeance against those who withdrew support, still focused on Ciele, though no Quetalian scout or messenger had been able to enter Ciele to verify that. The Patriarch had withdrawn from the public eye, and interprovincial trade dwindled to a minimum as the provinces farthest from the fertile lands of Ay'vol began to feel the squeeze of the conflict. As a gesture of good will (but more likely good politics), the Council in Teltraum had initiated negotiations to assist the people of Rav'agas who had fallen out of the Patriarch's protection, and three of the ten provinces, including the northwest peninsula of West Point, allied with Quetal.

Naturally, the Patriarch ended all relations with the provinces now taking up arms with the Quetalian Guard against his Ay'vol Force on the borderlands. Three years ago, in his last known announcement, the Patriarch had officially declared that this desertion from the nation and from *The Way* was an act of heresy. Since then, the Ay'vol Force remained just outside of Ciele, a stone's throw from the Quetalian border, and Quetal took the opportunity to strengthen their relationship with the new provincial friends from the south.

Kavriel was not presuming the general mindset of his people when he mentioned his honor to A'zia.

"Thank you, Kavriel," A'zia replied, her pronunciation of his name making his heart jump. "Do you know much about West Point?" she continued moving closer.

Kavriel wished he could find a way out of this conversation. His unease must have been obvious, because Grieg and Vaemalin began whispering to one another with smug grins on their faces. "Not much." He glanced over to them, and they instantly fell quiet, as if trying to hide their behavior from him. Or waiting to hear what he had to say.

"It's . . . uh . . . a peninsula . . . A sea-based economy mostly, not much agriculture." Kavriel grimaced inwardly, wishing he sounded more intelligent than a student answering a teacher's question, but Grieg and Vaemalin were irritating him while A'zia's nearness was simply intimidating.

"And the women?" A'zia asked, choosing a loaded subject. "What do you know about the women of West Point?" She drew close enough that Kavriel could feel her breath on his face.

A muffled grunt of laughter came from his brother's location, but he dared not look away from A'zia. Her gaze was mesmerizing. Somewhere in the back of his mind he knew that this wasn't right, that the Rav'agas woman was testing him to see how he would answer her question. He knew this, but she was so stunningly beautiful that he had a hard time putting up any kind of defense. Her question had been intentionally awkward, since there were *many* rumors about the women of West Point, and their dominant matriarchal society. For one thing, if women were rare in the Quetalian Guard, as Vaemalin had said to her earlier, the opposite was true in West Point, where women held the majority of power. Even the bishop of West Point was apparently a woman—which was one of the many ancient reasons for West Point's independence from Ay'vol. The local traditions were nearly unbelievable to northerners—the right of a woman of high status to have multiple husbands being one of them. He wondered if this woman staring at him had that right.

"Um . . . well," Kavriel squeaked out as A'zia's almond-shaped eyes seemed to grow larger, and Kavriel nearly lost himself in the desert-color of them.

She interrupted him. "So you haven't heard that when one of the women decides to take a man—or many men—to her breast, it's traditional for the man to accept that decision or face the penalty of death?" Her eyes fell across his body, hungrily, as if he were a ripe piece of fruit just waiting to be plucked. He felt as if he would faint as her long fingers came up to touch the growth of beard on his face, her light caress tickling cruelly. He knew it—that she'd bring up that particular part of her culture! It confirmed his assumption that she was only toying with him. Now his damn brother wouldn't keep his amusement to himself.

Her touch was ever so pleasant, but her teasing cleared his head of her entrancement. He smiled roguishly back to her, deciding to try taking the upper hand in the conversation with a bit of charm straight out of Vaemalin's repertoire. "I have, as a matter of fact," he said with confidence, however dry it might sound. "But a man would have to already be dead, to deny such an honor from those women." He heard a hum of approval from those behind him, but he couldn't tell if it had come from Grieg or Vaemalin.

A'zia held him in her gaze for only a moment before her seductive gaze softened and she smiled as if agreeing. "Well said, my blue-eyed one," she responded. "We will not have any problems at all." She actually tapped his face, a light blow that didn't hurt so much as knock him from his hastily constructed tower of bravado. Her words implied she didn't agree with him completely, and he wondered what she meant by "not having any problems."

Behind him, Vaemalin and Grieg roared with laughter. Only Tess, frowning and shaking her head, didn't find A'zia's words amusing—though Kavriel thought he saw the trace of a smile tugging at her mouth. He felt overwhelmed.

Grieg slapped him on his shoulder with a force that nearly took him off his weak knees. "Don't let A'zia scare you, Kav." A'zia softened her expression to a devious smile while moving over to her man. Grieg put a thick arm over her shoulder plates. "I will try to give you warning when my lady decides to have her way with you." He roared out a laugh again that was echoed by Vaemalin, naturally.

Tess, desperately trying to conceal a grin, finally spoke. "Alright, alright, that's enough." Kavriel gave her a frown for the failed effort.

"What?" Vaemalin replied, lifting his arms in an innocent shrug. "You were the one who offered us up!" Tess nodded in acknowledgment as Grieg and A'zia chuckled in reply. Kavriel's embarrassment began to ease.

"Do not worry, my dear," A'zia said, speaking to Tess now. "I wouldn't dream of stealing your men from you. Your brother is more than enough to satisfy my needs." She pulled out that hungry gaze again, but it was directed toward Grieg, who leaned over to give her a peck on her luscious lips in response.

Just then Master Kair Taloe returned from the front doors of the town hall. Kavriel noticed the procession of people entering the Hall had trickled down to a few stragglers. "My family," Master Kair said. "I am pleased to see you all together again, but we will need to reminisce at a later time. The meeting is about to begin, and you must all hasten inside." He motioned to the entrance.

Vaemalin took Tess's hand, while A'zia held onto Grieg's arm. Kavriel trailed them, and Master Kair put his arm around him with a smile, unaware of what had just transpired as he guided him under the arched entry. The guards outside closed the doors behind them.

CHAPTER 4

A fire cracked and sparked within the great fireplace of stone, as tall as a man and twice as wide, at the far end of the town hall. Large slices of oak logs burned away from the inside, filling the enormous reception room with a comforting warmth. It was a new addition to the town hall—"new" meaning within the last hundred years, since the former temple had been renovated to accommodate the modern, more practical beliefs of Quetal.

The Way, still practiced in Rav'agas and occasionally found in southern communities of Quetal, had once been the faith followed by all the people in all parts of the known world. Domed temples patterned after tented origins, with large oval windows to allow in the most possible light, once inhabited every town, village, and city, and no expense had been withheld to make sure it was the largest and most luxurious structure there.

The town hall in Rhyol retained much of its temple architecture, with only slight and obvious changes to make sure it did not cause too much discomfort to those with more liberal contemporary views. The stained glass windows depicting the story of The Becoming had been removed and replaced with standard cloud glass. The altar had been redesigned as a podium when the fireplace was constructed (and where the deacon's throne had been) and the religious paraphernalia of shepherd's crooks, golden masks, and blade insignia had been placed in storage bins for safekeeping, hidden away in the tiny cellar underneath the reception room. The citizens of Rhyol who had once congregated in this place to rejoice in the priests' sermons of their god's gift to humankind now instead came to speak with the town elders about droughts, the economy, and the current trade rates to the mainland.

From the history books he loved to read, Kavriel learned that the reception hall, once the nave, was built to accommodate not only Rhyol but all the other local communities nearby that did not have a big enough population to pay for a flashy temple. Mir Town had one, but not nearly as large or pretty, so Rhyol would find itself with a sudden rush of souls several times during each season for worship, similar to the rush market day now drew. To accommodate this wealth of believers, aisle benches had been built across the room, enough to seat about five hundred people on any given prayer day. Later generations never had any reason to remove the benches, as they were still practical and would only need to be replaced by something else to sit on. But they never saw the capacity drawn by the temple worship ever again. It was another reason to build the great fireplace—to keep the huge hall warm when only a dozen or so tradesmen met with the elders.

Walking into the town hall, Kavriel wondered exactly when the hall had last been filled to the brim, since he would have never imagined the attendance today in all of his dreams. Everyone had come to the town hall, to be packed in like straw in a bale. The bench seats were full, and those unfortunate enough not to have a place to sit lined the walls, eyes scanning the benches before them for a bit of space anywhere they could find it. The cacophony of voices was deafening. Within moments of entering,

Kavriel began to sweat, the heat given off by those gathered nearly as great as if he were standing next to the massive fireplace on the other side of the hall.

Frowning at the unnecessary flames, Kavriel glanced back to the closed double doors, wondering if he should open them a crack. Master Kair, who had been standing behind him, was gone. He noticed him desperately trying to push through the crowd to the podium at the front of the hall. Vaemalin and the others seemed to have melted into this cauldron of humanity. Forcing patience with a deep breath as he felt the sweat on the back of his neck, Kavriel tried to remove his coat, bumping elbows and arms with those around him, apologizing while trying to move to a more practical place to stand other than directly in front of the entrance.

He looked toward the podium again, where his father sat at his assigned place in the high-backed chair adjacent to it, with Femaor next to him. His father seemed preoccupied in his thoughts while his heavy associate was peering over the crowd, most likely seeking Kavriel or his brother, since they should be there standing behind the overseer. Kavriel muttered a curse.

A familiar hand suddenly took him by the arm and pulled him toward one side of the hall. "Over here, Kav," Tess said, speaking loudly to be heard over the crowd. She pushed through the crush of taller people, guiding him to a corner bench where Grieg had successfully found a few empty places. He was talking intently to A'zia when Tess and Kavriel sat down next to them.

"Vaemalin wanted to try to speak with your father before the meeting begins." Tess leaned close to his ear so that he might hear her as she pointed to his brother, squeezing his way to the front of the hall, and chuckled. "I don't think he'll make it."

Kavriel smiled in response, watching his large brother stumble over feet and sidle past shoulders. Even if there were fewer people in the hall, his popular brother still would have a difficult time moving without saying at least a few words to the townsfolk who smiled when they recognized him.

Kavriel leaned over Tess to look at Grieg and A'zia. They had fallen quiet, regarding the front of the hall with grim expressions. He followed their eyes to a lone figure near the stone hearth that he hadn't seen from his earlier place. He glanced back to Grieg and A'zia, seeing the unease in their eyes before squinting at the person by the fireplace. Whoever seemed to distress his friends had his back turned to them, so all he was able to determine was that the person was very tall, had long silver hair, and wore a long, dark red riding jacket whose hem brushed the backs of his black boots.

Grieg and A'zia's conversation resumed, and Kavriel listened closely to the words A'zia spoke. "No, he is not the same one, but he is from the same tribe. I am sure of it."

Grieg's expression went cold as he continued to stare at the person.

Kavriel's curiosity got the better of him and he leaned over. "Who are you talking about, the man at the fireplace?" Tess frowned at him, since he was practically in her lap.

"No. We know who he is," Grieg replied after a

short pause. Kavriel saw his gaze shift to the man at the fireplace before returning to the person he *had* been watching. The icy glare returned. "It's *that* one . . . to the left."

Kavriel leaned back, looking to the man at the fireplace again before sliding his gaze toward a small recess shadowed from the orange flames of the fire. As if materializing out of the eastern wall, a man was suddenly there, leaning against the wall as casually as if he had always been there. "What the—where did he come from?" Kavriel blurted, convinced that he should have seen the man earlier.

Grieg chuckled softly. "Don't be surprised, Kav; I bet half the people in this room haven't noticed him. You see his outfit? How it blends with the moving light?" Grieg outlined the silhouette of the other man with a wave of his finger. "His people are known for being invisible when they want to be."

"And deadly," A'zia added, and Kavriel saw that her desert eyes were staring intensely at the man leaning against the eastern wall, as if she would lose him if she blinked.

Kavriel focused more on the person, somewhat easier to define, now that he knew he was there. The man was about his height and build, dressed in a robe of sorts that looked like leather strips and plant leaves. The blend of brown, green, black, and every other somber shade he could think of hung about the man like an actual forest shadow. Long sleeves covered his arms, which were crossed over his body, and he had a foot up against the wall while his cloaked head tipped forward as if contemplating

85

the floor—or taking a nap.

"Who is he?" Kavriel asked.

"A Wylyn," A'zia growled.

Grieg quickly explained with a bit less bite in his tone, "A'zia has had some . . . *trouble* with their kind in the past."

As if he had heard Grieg from across the room, the Wylyn lifted his head and turned calmly toward the crowd. His hood fell back. Despite the darkness of the recess, Kavriel could easily see the man's auburn hair, worn in an odd spiky style. Silvery shards, arranged about his face like jewelry, shimmered with reflected firelight and gave the man a fearful, formidable look.

Kavriel started to remember more about these other people of Rav'agas: Like West Point, Wylyn was another of the three provinces that had separated from the Patriarchs flock. Yet unlike West Point's mostly barren, windswept landscape, Wylyn's was deeply wooded. Its northern society remained extremely isolated from the rest of the nation, even when they were supposedly allied with Ay'vol. Supposedly, for it was difficult to know what kind of system operated underneath the thick canopy of trees that hid the province from even the Patriarch's eyes. The community lived apart from the rest of Rav'agas, remaining self-sufficient and only agreeing to join Quetal as long as it stayed out of their internal affairs. The Patriarch's interests in the nation of Ciele were of no concern to Wylyn, but the Patriarch's interest in uniting Rav'agas under his control was. Quetal, interested in acquiring a new ally against the Patriarch, had agreed to the terms.

Kavriel had heard from Femaor during the negotiations that the Bishop of Wylyn, which was no longer the title he went by, was an eccentric man who dressed more like a wild animal than any kind of religious figure, and the guttural Wylyn dialect made him and his representatives difficult to understand, when they spoke at all. There wasn't much else known, and since their way of life was so secretive, nobody really knew the actual number of Wylyn in the province, or what they did in their forests. Kavriel might not have understood A'zia's animosity toward the strange man who dressed like a game hunter, but he had heard enough invented stories about the "wildmen" of northern Rav'agas to wonder if A'zia might be able to shed some truth on the stories. West Point was a neighboring province, after all. Her expression when she looked at the Wylyn was hardly encouraging, but not enough to stop Kavriel from asking his questions.

"I thought they remained in seclusion, rarely leaving their homeland?" Kavriel said softly, as if the man might overhear him.

It was Grieg who replied. "They do. Occasionally the tribes have been known to hunt around the Viliros. Some of my squadron said they had even seen a few close to the lines. But in general, they keep themselves hidden in the trees. It's extremely rare to find them on the mainland, which is why we're wondering why he is so far from his home."

"Maybe he's following you, A'zia." Kavriel smiled coyly at the woman, hoping that his small joke might get her to talk more about the Wylyn.

Her mouth widened in that wolfish grin. "I certainly

hope so."

A wooden gavel struck the podium three times, and the hall fell immediately silent. Kavriel chafed at the interruption, hoping to speak more with A'zia about the Wylyn, but he understood the regulations of the hall, and as a son of the overseer it was also his duty to respect them. He leaned back in his seat and waited for the man at the podium to acknowledge the crowd. He'd keep his remaining questions for A'zia for later.

Overseer Cyr Soelle set the gavel down as he calmly regarded the people within the town hall. His was an expression that might be seen on the face of the tired, but still respected head of a family, which was an accurate analogy to how his father addressed the townspeople. The overseer waited a few moments more; as the last sounds died down, leaving only the crackling fire, he spoke.

"Thank you all for coming. Many of you I know already, and I welcome also our newly arrived guests who have journeyed far from their duty and homes to gather with us today." His eyes slowly took in the crowd. "I am also pleased to see that many of our young soldiers have returned from the borderlands. The struggle against the Patriarch's Ay'vol Force, unfortunately, continues still. We can only be grateful that our friends and family are back with us . . . if only until their time of duty calls them again."

Kavriel saw several heads in the audience turn toward young men in blue and silver uniforms. Tess also glanced over to her brother with a loving smile.

The overseer continued. "We also must think of our friends and family who remain far from their homes, dedicating their strength and loyalty to protecting our nation . . . and remember those who have paid the ultimate price with their efforts."

The mood of the audience changed, becoming more somber and humble. Kavriel heard several muffled sobs within the crowd from those who were part of that unfortunate percentage of soldier families. Leaning away from the podium to give the people a moment of silence, the overseer rested a hand on Femaor's shoulder. Femaor managed a smile and a quick nod to Cyr, struggling to control his emotion.

The overseer shifted as he turned back to the podium, and Kavriel recognized the discomfort his gimp leg was causing him. He was used to standing for long periods of time, however, and would accommodate. He cleared his throat to capture the attention of the audience. "I will not keep you for very long. Market day is today and with the turn of the season, I understand the importance of your businesses. It is a happy coincidence that our many new visitors have arrived on the same day, so they may truly get a sense of a Highland fair—whether for good or ill, depending on your bartering skill," he quipped, to elevate the previous mood. His words sent a soft rumble of chuckles across the hall. "But to be honest, these new arrivals and the return of our soldiers from the battlefield are not without reason, as you may have already heard. It has been many years since Rhyol has been honored to receive a renowned guest from the mainland. Now one such person has come. I have asked him to take a moment to speak to you before he returns to his duties as our champion of Quetal, so we can welcome him together into our town."

Stepping aside, Cyr Soelle looked behind him to the tall man in the red jacket. "General Saire, would you be so kind?"

Suddenly animated, the crowd stood and applauded when the man smiled modestly and walked to the podium. Awestruck by the energy of the crowd, Kavriel rose, feeling awkward and ignorant; he should have somehow recognized the famous general earlier. There was no way he could have, of course, as he had never seen him, but the man's presence suggested greatness. Wanting to share his amazement, he turned quickly to his friends and saw that A'zia and Grieg had reacted similarly. But Tess had remained seated, her hands in her lap, a bleak expression on her face as she stared straight ahead. He was about to ask her what was wrong when the noise of the crowd began to die down, and Kavriel turned quickly to see the overseer shaking General Saire's hand before taking a seat. The audience also sat.

Kavriel stared intently at the general. When he'd been standing by the fireplace, Kavriel had initially thought the man was tall, but he had no idea *how* tall until the man stood next to his father. He was large, but not in a weighty sense like Master Femaor; he was simply massive. He was a head taller than the overseer (which would make him two heads over Kavriel), and younger. Kavriel had heard that the general had been involved in the early battles, but with the stories that followed him, Kavriel expected to see a man at least the same age as his father. The difference couldn't be more than ten or fifteen years, but it did strike Kavriel as strange.

Underneath his jacket the general wore a formal, black-plated armored suit that was streaked with branches of scarlet red. It was not standard field issue, nor the uniform colors one would expect on a general, but instead the Council colors of Teltraum. Kavriel found that a bit odd. The lines of red reminded him of burning embers tracing through the last log in a fire pit. Kavriel also wondered about the general's long hair, not silver as he had originally thought, but instead such a pale gold that it seemed to be white. The most notable feature was General Saire's fierce eyes. They were such a piercing blue that they shone across the hall like full moons during the blackest night of winter. Kavriel's thoughts went back to Xavr, the man he had met at Moonstone Shrine. General Saire reminded Kavriel of him, especially in the eyes.

Standing against the dancing shadows of the flames in the fireplace, the general hadn't given the impression of greatness, but now, in front of the audience, he drew every eye. It was as if he could control their attention. Kavriel could understand how General Saire had grown into such a popular figure, even without his military record; his presence was like the sun itself.

"Greetings, everyone," the legendary general said in a rich tone that carried warmth across the hall; it touched every soul, enveloping the audience as if his voice were a soft blanket. "It has been many years since I've seen Rhyol; my duties have not allowed me to visit much of Quetal north of Teltraum, but I remember the Highlands fondly from my past and am pleased to find her residents still warm and welcoming to strangers."

The locals in the audience smiled in harmony,

wooed by his simple compliment. Tess grunted quietly. Kavriel shot her a hard glance to keep quiet. She ignored it.

"Your overseer is too kind, calling a gathering of his people simply to welcome me into your town. Yet he is mistaken, for it is not you, but I who am honored by this act. Many of you know my name, but I unfortunately do not know yours; I can only thank you all for your kindness during my stay.

"I am not here on behalf of the Council, as you may suspect. Yet my status and the many years I have put into the service of our great nation has allowed me certain freedoms from my responsibilities. You might simply call this a temporary retreat." He paused with a humble smile on his lips, allowing the audience time to respond in amusement. "Yet be that as it may, I always have several agendas that I must review whenever time allows. One of those has brought me here, in fact, and try as I may, I do not think I will ever truly be able to escape the needs of the Council, no matter where I find myself. Their concerns always seem to coincide with mine. We share similar causes for our nation, and if my theory is correct, this retreat might be considered an important cause indeed. I will explain."

Kavriel thought he saw a small smile on his father's lips when the general spoke of his feelings about the Council. Saire was not *directly* insulting the Nine, for even a man of his elite status must respect the rules of leadership, but his eyes seemed to reflect irritation. It was a good way to captivate the Rhyolian crowd, but Kavriel wondered what the mainland visitors might think.

"The Quetalian struggle against Ay'vol is not

recent. If it's not this particular Patriarch dictating and attempting the rule of the world, then it has been another before him, another before that one, and so on. Ay'vol has never been in need of ambitious men with ideals of grandeur. Yet what has happened in our most recent struggle, which involves the nation Ciele, is something that goes beyond the time-honored Rav'agas tradition of enlightenment in The Way. This is clear in the minds of not only Quetalians in the north, but many Rav'agas in the south, whose decisions to leave the Patriarch's flock have been welcomed here by the people of Quetal. A hostile move into a defenseless nation simply to expand one's range of power is not an honorable one." The general paused, reflecting on some personal thought. Kavriel wondered about the past battles that this man had seen with his own eyes, in exotic places that Kavriel could only dream about.

"The brave men and women of Quetal, encompassing all communities including your Highland capital, joined together to halt this madness, pitting themselves against the formidable Ay'vol Force, which remains like stubborn coals, refusing to burn out long after the fire has been extinguished. This is not news to you. The return of your youth from the front line is proof that the heat of the Patriarch's will is close to fading. Yet there is some flame left in him, and I believe that I am partially responsible for that."

A murmur of curious whispering rose from the audience. From his quick talk with Femaor that morning, Kavriel had an idea what Saire meant. He leaned forward and rested his elbows on his knees, supporting his chin with his fists, anticipating the general's next words.

"In the eastern district of Quetal, notably in the region of Greater Loellen, there have been many new developments. Historians working with archaeologists have made discoveries in the Oenes Caverns, and successfully acquired additional grants and funding from the Council to continue their research and the building of their camp. After the realization that bringing the teams back to either Loellen or Teltraum during the winter has been more costly than simply leaving the station operational with provisions year round. Implemental in that Council decision was the discovery of the Temscript Scrolls. They have decided that this year, the scientists will move farther into the mountains to accelerate the project."

Kavriel couldn't help but smile at the general's modesty. The Temscript Scrolls, or Loellen Scrolls, as the eastern districts liked to call them due to the location of their discovery and out of notorious Loellen pride, was what had caught Kavriel's interest in the legend of General Saire in the first place. He knew Saire's beginnings were in Rav'agas, in the Seccacian Desert, a remote and arid part of the country northeast of Ay'vol City. The desert was so large that it was actually in two provinces, but the only inhabitants were nomadic tribes that rarely traded with the western towns and villages. They were similar to the Wylyn people in that respect, but living in more remote areas and with fewer loyalties.

With origins in such a remote and dangerous place, where not even their customs or mores were known, it was always difficult for historians to confirm the legitimacy of Saire's past. The general insisted that he had spent his adolescence on the wind, living, sleeping, and eating on horseback. As a child he had visited the western towns with his tribe on trading missions, and by some event or another he had ended up in Taivr—he'd either been sold or kidnapped; he couldn't recall which, as he had been too young to remember. He was raised by farmers who were killed during the first attack by the Ay'vol Force in their invasion of nearby Ciele, and eventually he found himself in the Quetalian Guard, fighting against the Patriarch. His skill with the sword and bow were flawless, and his intellect was keen, with his gift for military strategy earning him many battle victories and the eventual promotion to general over the southeast borderland companies. He was a great figurehead in Quetal. The story of his past was incomplete but still rich with delicious tidbits.

Saire's modesty in speaking of the scrolls might have been intentional, but Kavriel knew, along with everyone else in the town hall, that it was Saire himself who had discovered them.

The project in the Oenes, hundreds of leagues north of Loellen, had been one of many initiated by Teltraum's intellectual upper class over the last several years. Since the Patriarch's unsuccessful attempts at conquest, along with the alliance of the provinces to Quetal, the struggle had died down enough for theoretical politics to rekindle in the Council. Some of those involved a group who had discovered a series of caverns in the mountains while mining for ores and metals, about three summers ago. The reports were filled with eerie details of a once-inhabited system of interconnecting caves, with discoveries of beds, furniture, cookware, and even paintings and sculptures being pulled out of the caverns by curious hands. Immediately, the scientists and theorists petitioned the Council, asking for involvement.

The Council was reluctant at first, still thinking of the borderland and the financial burden of the Quetalian Guard. Spending needed funds on projects in the endless Oenes Mountains was simply unreasonable. That was, until General Saire became involved. It was strange to see the military man take on politics head on, but he had a knack for it and his presence drew attention.

Both Kavriel's father and Femaor had met the man for the first time during one of the overseer's obligatory visits to the capitol, and they had been there during the general's request that the Council follow the case of the Oenes Caverns. After hearing the general's speech, Kavriel's father told him and his brother of Saire's theory of a lost people deeper into the Oenes Mountains, a civilization that he had heard about when he was a child travelling among the nomads. It apparently had come from several sources, and may or may not have been a key in understanding the Ciele people, whose nation was surrounded by the Oenes on three sides. The coincidence of the Patriarch's interest in the nation was something to consider.

The Council and everybody in attendance were hooked by the general's enthusiastic speech. They agreed to Saire's request for a small expedition, handpicked by him, with only a week's worth of provisions. This had been accepted with surprise, as the Council had expected and were ready to give more. Saire said he was content with the minimum, as if he knew where he would be going once he got to the Oenes Caverns.

Either through amazing talent or simple luck, he discovered exactly what he had theorized all along—proof of his theories in the form of three ancient scrolls. The only problem was, the scrolls he had found had been written in a dead language that was indecipherable to anyone in Quetal.

This did not discourage the general, who safeguarded the scrolls on his own person. He studied them, with the occasional assistance of Teltraum scholars, for weeks that became months and then a year. He had become a man obsessed. His duties along the borderlands were on hiatus, much to the disapproval of the Council, while he spoke about a nomadic group that might be of help, located in north Seccacian, near the southern rim of Ciele. By now the Council had begun to lose interest, already unhappy about the general's dereliction of duty, especially since the Patriarch seemed to have caught his second wind and was recruiting soldiers to his Ay'vol Force. They needed the general on the front lines.

The Loellen nobles also had become active upon the discovery of the scrolls, striking at the Council from another angle as they screamed about their claim. The eastern aristocracy and the Council Nine were like cocks stuffed in the same pen, ruffling their feathers at each other over their hens. Plus, to make matters worse, rumors of the scrolls had crossed the border into Rav'agas, awakening the Patriarch's curiosity, like a sleeping lion lured by the scent of fresh blood. It had become a political mess.

To save face with the Loellen, as they didn't need an internal dispute on their shoulders, the Council Chairman accepted the request by the nobles to bring in their specialists and scholars to study the scrolls while the general was ordered back to the border. Yet to soften Saire's mood, not wanting to upset one of the nation's greatest battle commanders, the scrolls were to remain in the capitol city of Teltraum for study. The nobles argued, and the general wasn't all that pleased, either, but the Council had spoken, and their rules must be followed. The nobles went to the capitol, Saire went to the border, and the Temscript Scrolls went to Teltraum, where they remained to this day, safeguarded by a platoon of researchers in the Council's Great Library with no further advances in their discovery.

This resumption of exploration in the Oenes Caverns was news to Kavriel. He knew that the settlement, a mixture of scientists and miners, remained in the mountains, but he'd assumed that the Council had decided to completely end the project. Saire must have continued his attempts to persuade the Council otherwise. Believing there must have been an important reason for that decision, Kavriel listened intently as the general spoke.

"This could not come at a better time, for all of us," Saire said, "for the Patriarch seems to have eyes and ears located all across the country, and the translations have come to his attention."

Astounded, Kavriel wondered if he'd heard correctly. He noticed that his father, sitting next to the podium, had given Femaor a sour look, as if he had swallowed something that didn't agree with him. The heavy man only nodded in reply, though his face paled.

Whispers also rose from the audience, until the general held up his hands and said quickly, to suppress the sudden anxiety, "This news is not meant to startle you, kind people. The Patriarch does not need much motivation to continue with his corrupt cause. This is only another hunger, driven by his madness, that our strong men and women of Quetal and our southern allies will suppress. Do not be troubled."

The words seemed to calm the audience. Kavriel was still hanging onto the part about the scrolls being *translated*, which, if it were true, went beyond any threats the Patriarch made, in his mind.

Saire continued. "The reports from the borderlands have remained uneventful. However, the Patriarch does seem to know more about what has transpired in the Council Halls than would seem possible. It has also come to my attention that the Patriarch has learned of *my* involvement in this, and as Ay'vol and I are not on the best of terms . . . " He threw out a haughty grin that built the crowd's confidence, knowing quite well Saire's meaning. "Well, let's just say that any attempts on my life or to capture me will come at a high price." The audience chuckled arrogantly as he sneered his disdain. "Still, to get back to the reasons why I am here, it has much to do with what the translations of the scrolls have revealed."

Kavriel didn't think he could listen any harder, and he sat precariously on the edge of his seat as he fixed his gaze on the man at the podium.

"They are not yet fully understood, mind you, but they're viable. What has been decreed official by the Council is that within one of the scrolls, the only one that we have been able to translate to date, there are references to other records still to be found in the Oenes Caverns, as well as in other places around the world. Teams have begun excavating in the Oenes already, but there is also a reference to an isle off on the northern horizon, mountainous, with precious metals that were once traded with the Oenes Cavern people. The Council is unsure, but I believe personally that the scroll is referring to Nostrac and more specifically, the mountains here in the Highlands."

If Kavriel thought he was astounded before, he had been mistaken. The general had just confirmed countless ideas that he and other curious laypersons had about their homeland. The uniqueness of the rock of the Nostrac Highlands and that of the Oenes Mountains confirmed it. Moonstone Shrine was the most obvious abnormality; the strange, poison-producing minerals trapped under the old Mir Town mining camp had never been heard of anywhere else on the mainland north of Rav'agas, either. Specific reference to Nostrac in the Temscript Scrolls—older than the records of any other known civilization—was something that would keep him awake for nights.

"So that, my friends, is why I am here in your homeland today," the general said. "The scrolls are a personal obsession of mine, and I would be betraying my better nature not to further explore your island in hopes that I might uncover more of their secrets. Not only would it be a tremendous historical discovery, but it could be an advantage that the nation of Quetal would have over the Patriarch and his minions of Ay'vol." With a nod, he stepped back from the podium.

After a short pause, the volume of voices discussing what General Saire had said rose. Saire nodded to the overseer, a silent indication that he was finished speaking and Kavriel's father rose slowly to take the general's place at the podium. He calmly lifted the wooden gavel and struck it twice against the podium. The audience fell quiet.

Kavriel sensed a troubled aura radiating from his father as the overseer regarded his community with a furrowed brow, despite the general's inspirational words. His tone when he did finally speak was further confirmation that his father was worried.

"We have heard the words of General Saire, of his intentions and of his cause," Cyr Soelle said slowly, as if distracted by other thoughts. "I can assume from your reactions that you feel that this is a most peculiar development. Our interest and how we feel about it seem to be unanimous. Yet we also must realize the dangers that General Saire's proposal entails, and I am not referring to the Patriarch's unknown intentions for Quetal, the Cielean nation, or even the general himself, but of a danger that is closest to all of our hearts. To put it simply, the general's project involves exploration of the source of our once rich heritage, the mines. As we all know and remember, the people of Rhyol and her neighboring communities have spent many hours within the mountains, prospering from the mining of ores and metals. For years we travelled under the earth, excavating our underworld. Nothing we encountered has ever confirmed the existence of what the general believes he can prove. Still, the caverns are numerous and deep, with many secrets still undiscovered."

The overseer paused to sip from a mug of water resting atop the podium. It had been untouched until now. "Yet before any of those mysteries can be further explored, there are real dangers within the mines that must be taken seriously." Kavriel noticed that some of the locals had shifted into defiant postures, arms crossed, backs straight. The overseer continued. "Accidents have occurred, as one would expect in such a hazardous trade. The walls are not structurally safe, the ground is unstable and soft, and the *sickness* is an issue that cannot be ignored. One could argue that the mine is cursed, and those who have lost loved ones can certainly understand why."

The overseer paused longer than Kavriel thought necessary. He shifted position, and Kavriel wondered if his father's leg was beginning to give him problems. Whenever his father spoke of the mine, the pain of his leg seemed to reflect the trouble in his heart.

"The general's proposal is intriguing, and worth further investigation if his theories are sound. But it has been many years since the mines were operational and we cannot know how safe they are for exploration. This is quite a sudden request, and if I had been given earlier notice of what General Saire intended, perhaps I could have prepared. Personally, I disapprove of this. It is too dangerous to enter the mines until their stability has been secured. However, I understand the importance of this possible find in our homeland; if General Saire believes that time is of the essence, then I can only take his word on that. He is a respected man of Quetal and a representative of the Council, and that is something of great worth."

He paused a moment, glancing aside, collecting his thoughts. When he spoke again, Kavriel noticed that his words were directed at individuals in the audience. "It was never my intention to close the mines, but at the declaration of the Council there was no choice. I know there are those among us who do not agree, believing that the loss of my wife to the poisons of the mines was my motivation to follow the Council's order. I understand economics well enough to know that our community struggled after all operations ceased."

Those in the audience who were the overseer's obvious opposition were the same clansmen who had been sitting with arms crossed and backs ramrod straight. Kavriel didn't like them, and felt that his father was still being judged unfairly for what he had done all those years ago. He glared at the dozen or so clan leaders who had argued against the overseer, too loyal to their trade to understand that they were still ruled by a government. The death of his mother from the red-eye sickness was not something that made Kavriel feel forgiving toward their heartless disputes. Kavriel had never met his mother, who had died during his birth, but that didn't make her any less important to him and certainly not something to be used as a political piece played by the clans. Kavriel understood the shadow over his father's face now, and listened supportively.

"Still, I will grant General Saire's proposal to re-enter the mines. He has my word that the Highland clans will give any assistance he needs." The overseer looked hard at the audience before he turned toward the general. "But only if I can guarantee that *you* will use your influence in the Council to re-evaluate the need of our island to return to our most important resource."

Kavriel nodded at his father's words, noticing also the clan leaders glancing at one another, their angry expressions shifting to something more amenable.

The general smiled coyly before nodding. He couldn't truly make decisions outside of the Council, but his reputation was solid. The people of Quetal liked him—and the people of Quetal elected the Council Chairs, who in turn elected the Council Nine, who then chose their chairman. Democracy was like a waterfall, Kavriel thought.

As the audience rumbled, Kavriel smiled at his father, who seemed to relax at the agreement. It wasn't a promise for change, but having the general recruited to their cause was a powerful step in the right direction to restore Nostrac, and more importantly, bring back a sense of solidarity in the Highlands. The clans would never truly be a threat to the overseer's rule, custom was much too established for that, but the issue was an old stain on the overseer's reputation that he hoped to one day remove. The general had been right in saying his visit couldn't have come at a better time—just not for the reasons he had said.

His mood seeming lighter, Cyr Soelle extended an open palm to the people. "As always, I would like to open the floor for any opinions from the audience about the matter discussed today."

Master Kair reappeared, moving quickly from the front row of seats to take the overseer's place at the podium to direct the community discussion. Kavriel watched his father walk over to the general. The two huddled together in conversation that Kavriel was much too far away to hear before he was distracted by the questions from the community.

They were standard questions—how the mine would be stabilized, if Mir Town or Jovan would be rebuilt, where the funding would come from, but most importantly who would be in charge of the expedition. The mines had been out of service for twenty years, and the clans were a proud people not about to allow a mainlander to run the show, even if it was General Saire.

Kavriel listened, amused, to Master Kair's reply, assuring the people that until a more productive and secure method of exploration could be established *by* the clans, the general would for the moment only be studying the main cavern passages to determine where to begin.

The questions continued, but Kavriel noticed his father turn in their direction, looking straight at them as if he had known all along where they sat. Lifting a hand, he gestured for them to follow as Femaor appeared at his side to escort General Saire to a chamber adjacent to the main hall. Kavriel responded with a nod and a surreptitious wave, nudging Tess with his elbow. She stood with Grieg and A'zia and the four of them moved out of the aisle. As the meeting was adjourned, attendees started shuffling out the exit, leaving only several smaller groups of farmers and tradesmen waiting to speak with Master Kair concerning other matters. Kavriel led the others along the side wall toward the front of the hall, avoiding the river of people heading the other way. They crossed the podium platform and passed through the door his father had used, entering the vestry, remodeled as the overseer's office. The small room, furnished with its own compact fireplace, table, and chairs, had only one north-facing square window to provide natural light, and as he closed the door after they'd all entered, it felt crowded after the large audience hall. He squeezed past Grieg and A'zia to stop in front of the table.

Vaemalin had arrived earlier. He was sitting at the

table going over maps and reports with Cyr Soelle behind him, nodding at things Vaemalin identified with his forefinger. The general conversed quietly with Femaor near the window, looking even taller beside short, heavyset Femaor. The woodland-garbed Wylyn leaned up against the eastern wall near the door, looking as contemptuous as he had in the audience hall. Kavriel felt uncomfortable being is such a closed place with the oddly dressed man. The man's earthy odor reminded him of a wet rock covered in moss. Kavriel looked away from the distrustful green that met his, wondering how the Wylyn had traversed the podium platform before them without his noticing.

The overseer looked up from the table. "Good. You are all here." His voice was soft; his eyes looked heavy.

Seeing the new arrivals, General Saire pulled back from Femaor and smiled. Grieg and A'zia immediately straightened and together saluted their high-ranking officer. Kavriel hesitated. He had never met a general before and certainly not a man like Saire. Panicking, he clumsily mimicked the two soldiers. If the general took offense he did not show it, simply saluting back as his blue eyes regarded Tess with what Kavriel imagined as amusement. He glanced over at her. She stood stiff as a board with her arms folded across her chest and her eyes staring blankly at the tall man.

"It is my pleasure to meet all of you," the general said in a low, authoritative voice, passing his gaze over the rest of the group without any obvious mood change. He nodded casually toward the Wylyn. "This is my associate, E'mon."

The man he introduced lifted his chin slightly. He

nodded to the group slowly, his eyes sliding away as if he didn't care. Kavriel did notice that his eyes paused on A'zia for a moment longer than the rest of them, and his green gaze flickered with interest. The woman from West Point simply looked back, ignoring his peculiar interest.

The general continued, looking over to the table. "I am pleased by the hospitality of your townspeople, and their overseer. He has offered his son as an escort for me and my associates to Mir Town, which I understand is a perfect place to begin my expedition."

For a moment Kavriel felt a surge of pride, thinking he was the son General Saire spoke of. Then, as Vaemalin looked up from the papers on the table with a smile, he realized that Vaemalin was the son the overseer meant. Tess grunted her disapproval, and Kavriel saw his brother's eyes widen, but Vaemalin gave no other response.

The overseer said quickly, his eyes on Saire, "This is not an expedition, General, as I have already stated." He spoke firmly, making sure the general understood he was still the governing voice in Rhyol. "You will keep to the caverns indicated on these maps, and no more, until I am convinced of the security of the mines." The general's eyes seemed to flare up, but his face remained impassive. Cyr Soelle continued less vehemently, noticing the general's reaction. "It has been many years since these routes were taken." He pointed to the maps that lay in front of a wide-eyed Vaemalin. "I cannot guarantee your safety, and I do not wish to be responsible for any harm that might befall one of Quetal's most respected citizens. I owe that much to our people and to the Council."

The tension left Saire's face and the tall general

responded with a respectful bow. "I appreciate your concern, Overseer . . . and your integrity. I will respect your wishes."

"Overseer." All eyes turned toward the Rav'agas woman. "I offer my services to General Saire's mission. I am only to return to Taivr when he has returned to Teltraum. I wish to use my time for his assistance." The room was quiet for a moment as the overseer regarded the woman as if seeing her for the first time. She added quickly in the silence, "I am A'zia Rhe'to'am, Kairn blade-sister and company liaison to Quetal third battalion." Kavriel thought she would salute again, but instead she gave his father the same hand-wave she'd given Tess outside of town hall, modifying the ending by crossing her arms against her breastplate and dropping to one knee. She rose just as quickly, waiting for the overseer's response as he glanced over to the general. The tall man nodded to him.

"A blade-sister?" Cyr Soelle asked, and the woman nodded sharply. Kavriel didn't quite understand what her title meant, but it must have been some kind of warrior order in her culture. His father seemed to know; he looked impressed as he nodded. "Very well, *Gar'i'or-Fe'oam*." He spoke a Rav'agas dialect that Kavriel, with his basic understanding of the southlander language, still couldn't understand.

A'zia went through her greeting motions again, a small smile cracking her face as she finished. His father's knowledge had obviously impressed her. Grieg smiled at her as the overseer turned to him with a nod. "It is good to see you again, young Grieg."

Grieg responded with a bow. "And you, Overseer

Soelle."

"I apologize that I was unable to speak with you more today, son. You will go with Vaemalin. You boys have spent enough time in that village and the mine to know just about all that the general needs to get started."

"I am not sure what . . . ." Grieg began, his denial fading under the gaze of the overseer. Kavriel almost laughed, seeing Vaemalin stiffen in his chair as their father gave him a sidelong, knowing look. Vaemalin looked over to Grieg, who quickly straightened and barked, "Understood, sir."

Kavriel shook his head in amusement, until he noticed that the general was now looking directly at him. He quickly tensed. If it had been disconcerting to see the general's strange crystal-blue eyes regarding the audience in the town hall, having those moonlit eyes watching only him was enough to steal his breath. The gaze was so cold and unforgiving that Kavriel wondered if he had unwittingly insulted the man.

The others must have noted a change in the general's mood, for the overseer quickly spoke up— quietly, as if calming a skittish horse. "This is Kavriel, General Saire. He is my younger son." Kavriel's father turned and gave him an apprehensive look, as if there were some secret he did not know. Kavriel looked wide-eyed at the both of them, not quite sure what he should say. The general responded in his place.

"Your son," he echoed, as if it had been a question, and not an introduction. A strange sensation, as if he were tethered to the general from across the room, seemed to come over him, and Kavriel physically felt that he needed to lean back against the pull of the tall man's gaze. Saire crossed the room in two large steps, stopping just in front of Kavriel to look at him curiously.

This close, the general's outfit was clean and proper for a man who had just arrived from a long voyage, but he had an antique scent that reminded Kavriel of the dusty, leather-bound books in his father's study. The tall man's analytical gaze raked over him. Kavriel felt like one of the unique shells that he and Tess collected on the coast and turned slowly over and over to understand every last detail.

"Is there something wrong, General?" Overseer Soelle asked, his voice sharp with concern as he regarded the tall man with a defensive frown. The others stood motionless until the scene played itself out. It didn't last long. When the general finally released Kavriel from his gaze, he felt as if the invisible rope that had leashed him had been severed. He blinked rapidly, as if waking from a daydream, realizing that he had been staring back into Saire's eyes almost hypnotically. It had been a strange introduction.

"I apologize for my manner." The general offered a humble smile as the gleam in his eyes seemed to dim. He tilted his head toward the overseer, addressing him but keeping Kavriel in his view. "Your son has the look of someone I once knew, very long ago. I was simply caught by a memory. " The calm words sounded genuine, but his expression remained hard and uncertain.

"I hope a *good* memory," Kavriel joked, trying to lighten the ominous atmosphere.

The general didn't respond, only smiled secretively back to Kavriel as his eyes seemed to flare up again.

Turning quickly, the general stepped back over to the front of the table, regarding the papers with interest and seeming to forget that Kavriel was ever there. "I am honored to have you all with me in this pursuit of mine," he said, his uncaring tone belying his words. "I have my personal guard with me, but having two local experts will only hasten this project."

"I will be coming along as well."

Kavriel gaped at Tess. Her interruption was inexcusable, and her demand baseless. Her attitude toward the general was disrespectful, which had not gone unnoticed by the overseer. He straightened and replied quickly, "Tess Taloe, you are *not* to be making demands. You are the daughter of a village elder, but that does not give you any rights here. You will apologize now and leave this room!"

The overseer's words struck hard, and Tess's wide-eyed expression indicated she had been chastened. Normally Vaemalin would have spoken in her defense, but he remained silent, as did her brother.

"I . . . " she began timidly, thrown off guard by the overseer's quick retaliation. Kavriel could see the confidence returning in her posture, however. It would take more than words from his father to tame the young woman. The general had taken an interest now, watching her, waiting. "I apologize for my impetuousness, Overseer, and to you, General Saire." She was trying hard to keep her tone polite. Her eyes had darkened, and her face paled— signs Kavriel had seen just before she exploded over something that displeased her. Vaemalin must have noticed as well, for he watched his ladyfriend, though his eyes

111

didn't touch hers. "I spoke in haste. But there is another concern that we have not discussed, and it is of grave importance."

The frowning overseer was about to say something when the general suddenly raised his hand. "Peace, a moment. I do not wish to intrude on your wishes, Overseer, but this young woman is obviously troubled by something. Perhaps we should give her leave to speak." His voice was calm, but powerful.

Tess swallowed, clearly not expecting this. The overseer continued to scowl, though it was softening. Kavriel wondered if the general's years of field command had given him this gift for relieving tension. Even the Wylyn man had departed from his otherworldly attitude to take an interest in this argument. Kavriel noticed that the man continued to watch A'zia. The West Point woman wore a small smile of approval as she watched Tess. Grieg seemed to have turned into a statue.

"Very well, Tess," the overseer said, capitulating to the general's request. "You may speak your mind, but this is not the first time we have had this problem, young lady, and you will learn to guard your tongue in my chambers." He spoke firmly, but his voice had softened to a more fatherly tone.

Tess nodded respectfully, her posture relaxing. "I understand, sir. Overseer Soelle, last night a child from the town went missing. Her brother was found and returned but there is no news about the girl yet."

The overseer's expression softened and he nodded. "Millie Kessor, yes, of course."

Tess continued. "I was with Edan Kessor and his

wife late last night, taking care of their young son Seth after he had been found. We believe that the children were in Silver Wood yesterday afternoon. They might have entered Mir Town and possibly the camp."

"What do you propose, Tess?" the overseer asked when Tess paused.

"It is possible that they entered the mine," she said. "While the general and the others will be focused on this other project, someone should be there to focus on finding the girl, if she was trapped in the caverns."

"It's too risky, Tess." The words came from her brother, who had been silent until now. Vaemalin murmured agreement. "The mines are not safe. The overseer said—"

Tess silenced him with a glare, shifting it to Vaemalin, as well. "I know what the overseer said. All the more reason that I should be there to look for her." She swung her gaze over the others in the room. "None of you here, besides the overseer and myself, know who this girl is. I won't be in any less danger than the rest of you—or her."

Her words were enough for Grieg and Vaemalin to lose their patience. They both began voicing their disapproval. She retaliated heatedly, and the room suddenly seemed even smaller to Kavriel as the noise level rose. The overseer merely sighed uncertainly, while A'zia continued smiling at her proudly. The general looked interested.

"She's right." Kavriel had to nearly shout to be heard, and since he had been relatively quiet until now, his voice caused those in the room to fall silent. They turned to him. "She's right," he repeated, feeling a bit uneasy about getting involved, but Tess was watching him intently. "If there is any chance that she is lost in the mines, then she will most likely frightened, more so if there are strange men rumbling through the tunnels. We have a duty to the Kessors."

It was rare that Kavriel was able to sway the opinion of his brother or his father, but he sometimes needed to remind them that their role in the Highlands didn't always involve politics. Femaor had taught him that, and remembering the man was still with them, Kavriel glanced his way to see him nodding in approval from his place near the window. Tess beamed up at him. The overseer and Vaemalin exchanged a glance, then nodded at Kavriel.

The general spoke first. "Well said, young Kavriel. Your dedication to your townspeople is commendable. Your father has done well in raising you." He looked over to Tess. "I admire your directness, young lady. You have a fire within that surprises me. But I am curious to know why you think the children entered the mine. As I understood it, the place was off limits." He looked at the overseer.

Cyr Soelle sighed and placed his hands on his hips. "Children will be children, General. Even the Council would agree with me on that."

Saire chuckled in understanding as he turned his attention back to Tess. The gleam had returned to his eyes. This issue with the missing girl seemed to intrigue him. "You mentioned a boy. Can you elaborate on his condition when he was found?" The question was strange, coming from a man whom Kavriel figured would be more interested in politics and military strategy than the health of missing children.

Tess didn't seem to find his question odd at all, and replied quickly with what she had told Kavriel and Vaemalin earlier. The general showed concern as Tess described how the boy was and the words he had mumbled in his delirious state, but there was something else in the tall man's expression that Kavriel couldn't quite place. As Saire glanced over to his Wylyn associate, a sense of danger made Kavriel twitch, as if he had just been spooked by a moving shadow in the middle of the night. Something stirred in his memory with the mention of *girl* and *mines* together; it didn't sit right with him, but before he could explore the feeling, his father spoke.

"Then it's decided." He indicated to Vaemalin the maps and reports on the table, then looked to Saire as his eldest son began organizing those. "I must attend to my other responsibilities today, General. If there is anything else . . . ?"

The tall man smiled and shook his head quickly. "You have provided all that I need to begin, Overseer. I thank you, and I will give you any reports you require when we return." General Saire looked at the others. "We will leave immediately. My company is waiting at your town stable, and I wish to take advantage of the day."

Vaemalin had rolled the maps and tucked them along with the reports into a leather satchel, which he handed to the general. Accepting them, Saire nodded briefly to Kavriel and Femaor as he moved quickly to the door, which the Wylyn opened for him. The others followed Saire.

A silence followed as Kavriel and Femaor waited

patiently for the overseer to say something. Kavriel wasn't entirely sure what that might be, but he hoped to have the time to continue his conversation with Femaor that they'd started that morning. He turned to the large man who smiled, waiting. "Is it true that the scrolls have been translated?" he asked, moving closer.

Femaor nodded, though hesitantly. "I believe so, yes. However, despite the general's words, I cannot say for certain if this has been confirmed by the Council. According to my contact in the Trade and Commerce Committee, this knowledge is as new to them as it is to us. He heard the same speech I did, after all, and it is even more disturbing if the Patriarch has caught wind of this also."

"So he says," the overseer interjected as he walked slowly to join them at the window. He had the same notebook in his hand that Femaor had shown him earlier and was skimming over certain sections. Kavriel looked to Femaor, feeling a little lost; the big man shrugged, pushing up the glasses that had slipped down his nose. The overseer looked from the book to Femaor. "Do you trust him, Aurel?" Kavriel wasn't sure if his father was referring to the general, or Femaor's contact.

Femaor looked hard at the overseer. "I don't know, Cyr," Femaor replied, almost in a whisper, which Kavriel thought strange. "His popularity is high, his reputation inspirational to a lot of Quetalians. The Council takes that very seriously." He paused. When the overseer didn't react, Femaor continued. "But I have been friends with Councilman Richart a long time, and *he* thinks there is something we're missing."

The overseer nodded, finally, glancing at the book once more before closing it. "So do I."

Kavriel suddenly felt like a ghost in the room. "I'm sorry," he said, "but . . . what's going on?"

The two men looked blankly at Kavriel for a moment, as if remembering he was still there. "Kavriel, I would like you to go with the group," his father said.

"With the group? Why?" Kavriel asked, both curious and confused. He looked at Femaor, who was watching him without expression.

"You must listen very carefully, son," the overseer said, "and continue to listen with both your ears and your judgement." He rested a hand on Kavriel's shoulder. "I don't believe the general revealed everything to us. This interest in our land is poorly timed for his responsibilities to the nation. This rumor that the Patriarch has knowledge of the scrolls does not seem likely, even if the security of the Council had been compromised."

"You mean like, by an Ay'vol spy in the Council?" Kavriel interrupted, looking quickly to Femaor, who frowned.

The overseer shook his head. "No, nothing like that. Pay attention please, Kavriel." Pausing, he breathed deeply, thinking on his next words. Kavriel's mind spun with curiosity conjured by his father's behavior. "The Temscript Scrolls are old news to the Council, and Saire's interests in them are not recent, as you already know. *If* he has been able to translate them, then this is important for the Council. Yet only Saire has guaranteed this, with his own handpicked men from both Teltraum *and* Loellen, as I have just recently found out." The overseer glanced at Femaor, who nodded. "This coincidence of the Patriarch's push on Ciele at the same time Saire has brought us this needful cause seems overly fabricated. The Patriarch could not know what the general has been doing, let alone be disturbed at Saire's involvement, as he said in the hall. That is, unless . . ."

"Unless this project had been known earlier, maybe from the beginning," Kavriel said. His father did not seem to mind this interruption; in fact, satisfaction flashed across his face. "That would mean that someone in Saire's circle could have been contacting someone in Ay'vol this whole time," Kavriel finished, and the overseer nodded knowingly.

"I was thinking about someone with more influence."

Kavriel was stunned, hearing what he thought he heard his father say. He glanced quickly back and forth between him and the expressionless Femaor before he replied.

"Do you think that General Saire is . . ."

"I am not sure, Kavriel," his father replied, his face now gloomy. "I need you to be my eyes and ears. I wanted to inform your brother about this, but I didn't have time. Vaemalin has been given a task to help the general navigate the mines and he must focus on that. Grieg and his friend are in the same position. And Tess . . . " He smiled slightly, as one might smile mentioning to neighbors about an unruly child under his charge. "Well . . . Tess's feelings about the general are obvious, which puts you in a neutral position." He released his grip on Kavriel's shoulder, but held his eyes. "I am depending on you, son. Can you do this for me?"

Kavriel nodded quickly, feeling his face flush. The overseer nodded. "Good. Now move quickly, before they leave. If the general asks, just say that you're there to help Tess with the missing Kessor child."

"Do you think that he will believe that?" Kavriel asked, feeling to the weight of responsibility settling on his shoulders. He remembered how intently the general had looked at him, and wondered if his excuse would be credible.

Cyr frowned, seeming to understand without Kavriel needing to elaborate. "Probably not, but he'll have no reason to argue your coming along. Now get moving."

Too overwhelmed to ask anything more, Kavriel nodded to Femaor, who smiled confidently, and exited his father's office. Moving along the side of the audience hall so he wouldn't disturb the meeting still in session between the tradesmen and Master Kair, he left the building and jogged past the fruit and vegetable stalls in Market Square, his thoughts still on his father's plan.

As he headed toward the north road where the stables were located, a solitary figure clad in a gold-embroidered blue vest watched Kavriel intently until he passed out of view. Several moments later, he followed.

CHAPTER 5

Kavriel wrapped his horse's reins around a rusted iron spike that time had buried in the earth. He was just outside the dome-shaped forge, twice the size of Rhyol's town hall, located in Mir Town's mining camp, having caught up with the group accompanying General Saire. Noticing the dark clouds thickening on the northern horizon, out over the ocean, he mentioned that it might be better to keep the animals inside the forge, all but empty for the past twenty years, save for a few storage bins and smaller blast furnaces.

Unfortunately, the group was preoccupied with jotting down information about the primary mine entrance in relation to the bluff caverns. They were not concerned with the horses, as General Saire had mentioned in passing that his men would "deal with any emergency, if required." Kavriel wasn't quite sure what that meant. Saire hadn't even looked toward the sky, let alone the horses after dismounting. Kavriel tucked the general's reaction into his memory as something of possible importance to tell his father later.

Besides the group from Rhyol, Saire had with him some half-dozen soldiers hovering around him like a cloud, visors lowered to cover their faces and red-painted splint-mail over their chests. They spoke very little if at all, creating an aura of tension. Two Loellen stone-scholars, as Kavriel liked to call them, had also accompanied the general all the way from Teltraum. A far cry from the soldiers, these were old, fidgety men in long, pale blue robes who skittered around the broken slate and iron tracks, scratching down information about the camp. Kavriel tried to stay out of everyone's way.

During the ride from Rhyol that had begun immediately upon departing the hall, Tess and Vaemalin had taken the lead, heading toward Alvyn Poldr's farm at the eastern edge of Silver Wood. They could have gone directly north on the lumber trails and then cut across to Mir Town, saving some time on the ride, but Tess had insisted on speaking with the farmer again about the boy he had found. He was willing to help, but looked nervously at the armored group travelling with Tess, and so she thought it best to speak to him alone. While they waited, with the horses snorting at each other impatiently, Kavriel had eased his steed over to the Loellens for conversation. To his chagrin, he discovered that the stone-scholars were even less charming than the soldiers Saire had brought with him. They were seedy little men with heads too big for their necks and arrogant personalities to match. Kavriel had wanted to hear their thoughts on Saire's project, and ask about their trade. The old men, assuming that a simple island villager couldn't possibly understand the intricacies of their career choice or the general's research, had brushed Kavriel aside as one would an annoying pup sniffing around their robes.

Tess had returned to the group with no more information than she had already, and an hour of gentle riding took them from Poldr's farm to the abandoned mining camp.

It wasn't so much a coast as a small bay, Kavriel thought, observing the mining camp, hollowed out of the frighteningly tall black and gray banks as if a large shovel had come and scooped out a section of the island. What remained was cluttered with makeshift hovels, sheds, and chimney-like kilns. The ore carts remained where they had been left twenty years ago, with some actually half swallowed, along with the tracks they sat on, by the creeping ocean. Atop the banks to the west, silver birch overlooked the camp like wiry sentinels, thick and plentiful despite the constant salt breeze from the ocean. That stand of wood, he knew, continued several miles deep and farther west. Mir Town was behind him to the south, atop another bank that wasn't nearly as vertical.

North and east was where things got interesting. Mountainous boulders jutted from the ocean surface like enormous fish heads, some even possessed of menacingly jagged sides that Kavriel thought resembled teeth in open-mouthed monsters rising from the depths. Kavriel and his friends had counted twenty-three mountains in the water on their numerous illicit trips to the camp. They ran out toward the horizon like a half-submerged peninsula. One enormous triangular behemoth that blocked the camp completely from the setting sun to the east was where the primary adit into the mines was located, half in the water and half against the banks.

As a child, Kavriel played in the forge, the sheds, and the carts and to some extent the chimneys, though care had to be taken there, not to fall in. His father and the other village elders had forbidden any kind of recklessness in the camp, obviously not wanting anyone to get hurt, but also to keep the place unspoiled, a monument of sorts to this aspect of Highland life before the declaration of the Council. The clans had taken care of the place for a few years afterward, but eventually it just seemed pointless and the camp was left to its own demise. It was a sad memory for the adults, but a paradise of exploration for the children, who continued to think that their parents didn't know they played there.

The elders had sealed the mine entrances for additional safety, and removed the more dangerous tools that had been left behind. They were not foolish, and knew that when their children disappeared for several hours they were exploring the camp; they simply tried to make it *less* interesting for them. The idea backfired; the elders' attention to securing the town and camp had only inspired young minds to create stories about the elders' real motives—was it to keep them out of the caverns . . . *or was it to keep other things in?* The red-eye sickness that from a child's viewpoint could be a frightening illness both mentally and physically was the catalyst for stories of ghosts and curses. All of which made the camp that much more interesting!

Kavriel and his friends, suppressing any fear of monsters, occasionally crept behind the rotten wooden barricade at the mine entrance—but only so far. Their courage had limits, once inside the darkness of the caverns. As far as Kavriel knew, no Rhyol youngster had ever ventured past the first corridor. Vaemalin and Grieg had tried, looking for forgotten treasure, but it was nightmarishly dark, and the wind's constant battering at the rocks outside sounded like screams echoing from the depths of the earth.

Kavriel had not passed the first corridor for an entirely different reason. The place frightened him, to be sure, but he would always suffer stabbing headaches after crossing the threshold. It happened every time he tried, and his brother joked that invisible guardians that didn't like Kavriel's pale hair and eyes were bombarding him with hundreds of needle-sized arrows and lances. He knew it was the closed quarters that bothered him. He had read in the town records that not everyone could work in the tight confines of the mine, which made him feel less unusual. He had a hard enough time as it was with his unique appearance, and didn't need any more flame in that fire. So he would sit by the water's edge whenever Vaemalin and Grieg decided to do their treasure hunts, waiting with his thoughts on the water and the horizon until the others returned.

Now, Kavriel walked over to the water's edge, watching the cold black water lap against the gray rocks and glinting shells as his mind returned to those memories he had forgotten until arriving at the camp. What should he do? His father depended on him to keep an eye on Saire, but he didn't know about the effect the mine had on Kavriel. He assumed his two sons had visited the camp, but since they weren't *supposed* to be there, Kavriel had never revealed the pains he felt whenever he crept into what his father thought was the most dangerous place in the world for young children. It would have been like handing his father the rope to hang him with.

Kavriel looked uneasily at the group already at the mine entrance, kicking away the dilapidated wooden door. Others were lighting torches that they had brought. In only a few moments, Kavriel would be alone in the camp while the others explored the caverns. It was like being a child all over again, and the feeling of helplessness frustrated him. He had a duty to do!

"It's beautiful, isn't it?" Tess said, standing next to Kavriel. Her voice startled him; he hadn't heard her approach. He forced a smile, nodding in agreement, wondering what she was looking at.

"It's a shame the camp is like this, smelling like rotten fish and dust. It doesn't do justice to the skyline."

He realized she was looking over the water, where the black clouds were parting and moving away from the camp. It didn't look like it would rain after all. Rays of sunlight had broken through the cloud cover to dance across the surface of the water and highlight the white-capped waves as they crashed against the half-submerged rocks. She was right. It was beautiful.

It conjured other childhood memories of the camp, of looking out over the sea with his friend, and he realized that whenever Tess had come with them, she would always stay behind with Kavriel while their brothers explored. *Probably at this very same spot,* he thought, and smiled genuinely this time, savoring the memory as he looked at Tess, wondering if she remembered the same thing.

A shout from the mine interrupted the moment. "Hey!"

They turned to see Grieg waving furiously to get their attention. As they walked over to him, Kavriel stiffened, realizing that it was now or never; he had to decide if he was going into the mine. Could he mention his father's request to Grieg, and ask him to fulfill it? No; something as important as spying on General Saire was best kept to himself. Grieg wasn't paying attention to them anymore, anyway.

"Look at this," Grieg said to them when they arrived, dropping to kneel in the dirt just outside the mine. He stood up after a moment holding a wooden stick no longer than his finger, wound with a scrap of cloth and blackened at the tip. Kavriel caught the skunk-like smell as Tess took it from Grieg to give it closer inspection.

"Seth was carrying others like this in a bag when the farmer found him," she exclaimed, looking questioningly at her brother. "What is it?"

"A firewick." He took it back from her. "Did you find flint and iron with him?" She nodded. Grieg looked into the mine with concern in his eyes. "Then that means there's a good chance he was in here."

Tess hurried forward, ignoring the red-armored guard Saire had posted at the mine entrance. The darkness swallowed her up almost immediately. Casting a worried glance at Kavriel, Grieg dropped the firewick and followed his sister. That left Kavriel with only the guard, who ignored him now, just as he had earlier, his eyes shifting watchfully about the camp. Kavriel looked uneasily at the mine entrance, wondering if he should stay and try some light conversation to pass the time. But he knew he couldn't.

It had been years since he had entered the mine, but already Kavriel felt the tiny arrows of pain pricking at his temples. He knew once he passed the adit they would only get worse. But there was no other choice. Closing his eyes, Kavriel passed under the archway.

The red-plated guard merely glanced at him before

continuing to scan the area for any signs of trouble. He didn't cast his eyes up the southern path to Mir Town. If he had, he might have seen the lone figure standing in the shadows between the trees, watching intently.

CHAPTER 6

As Kavriel stepped beyond the archway, the sense of open freedom vanished along with the afternoon light. The torches held by those in front of him cast eerie shadows along the rough gray stone walls of the corridor. Kavriel frowned down at the rotted wooden planks of the sloping walkway beneath his feet; the stony floor would have been better than the damp-damaged planks that gave slightly under his feet with a disgusting squishing sound. He followed the others, treading carefully until the corridor opened up into a large, circular room. In its center stood a dust-caked table stacked with rows of unlit torches. The group stopped in a ring around it. Their features flickered eerily in the light from the torches they carried.

Pushing aside the stacked torches, Saire removed one of the maps from the leather satchel he carried before handing the bag back to Vaemalin, who hung it over his shoulder. The general unrolled the parchment over the tabletop, revealing a schematic diagram of the mine, yellowed by time and looking like a black-inked spider web. Everyone huddled closer for a better look. Kavriel recognized his father's handwriting in the notes alongside corridors that ended in dead ends and unfinished sections, and he wondered how long ago he had written them. It must have been before he was born, Kavriel realized, looking from the map to the walls of the room. He saw several marked passages leading off in different directions from the chamber, and these corresponded to several markings on the map.

His interest in the map had distracted Kavriel from

the growing pain in his head, but when he looked at one of the passages to his left, the invisible arrows began to strike in earnest. Closing his eyes, Kavriel rubbed at his temples, cursing under his breath, until a disagreement near the table brought his focus back to the room.

The stone-scholars and Vaemalin were engaged in an animated argument, their voices low to avoid the general's attention. Saire remained absorbed in the map, but Kavriel listened in. Vaemalin was patiently but firmly reminding the two Loellen men that he had spent his childhood exploring the caverns (a great exaggeration), giving him a better knowledge of the safest and surest routes. The scholars disagreed, citing their experience in "this sort of thing" as they explained that the integrity of the rock in the caverns and shafts so close to open water could, and often would change, causing unpredictable collapses. The fact that the mine had been unattended for all these years only strengthened their reasoning, and Kavriel had to agree with them. The rest of the group seemed to follow the scholars as well, eyeing the stone ceiling above for any "weakened integrity" in their general vicinity. Vaemalin finally yielded to the Loellens with a shrug.

The arrows began burrowing farther into Kavriel's skull, and he wiped beads of sweat from his brow with the back of his hand. He looked toward the table, and saw that he had captured the general's attention.

"You." Saire's voice carried in the chamber as it had in the town hall, but now it carried a dark undertone that seemed amplified in the confines of the mine. Kavriel blinked stupidly, just as he had before when the general had analyzed him with those crystalline eyes.

"Kavriel . . ." Saire drew out his name as if just remembering it. "I don't think it would be wise to separate from the group. It is rather dark in here . . . and you don't look very well." Saire's concern sounded more like sarcasm as the man's lips crept up in a smile.

Kavriel blinked again, wondering *why* and *how* he was at the center of everyone's attention. Instinct made him look behind him, thinking foolishly that there was something there. He saw nothing but one of the corridors marked on the map but his unease remained. One more step and he would have been inside. He didn't remember walking over to it.

"Are you feeling alright, Kav?" Vaemalin asked, leaning over the table to peer at him with concerned eyes.

Kavriel knew that his brother was wondering about his head. Tess and Grieg wore similar knowing looks. The rest of the group merely watched, confused. Knowing his secret was close to being revealed, he blurted, "Yes I'm fine," and concentrated on mentally plucking the arrows from his brain as rapidly as they came. "I just think . . . well . . . we need to start somewhere, and this—" he jerked a thumb at the passage behind him "—seems like the most stable passage."

The words had absolutely no credibility whatsoever but they did distract the group as the scholars quickly responded. "What do you proof do you have of this theory?" one of them asked arrogantly. Tess grimaced at the old scholar, who obviously couldn't care less about her opinion.

Kavriel cleared his throat, using the pause to think

of something that would sound rational to this scientist. The dark silence of the passage behind him beckoned, an ideal place to escape their scrutiny, but it also gave him an idea. "The winds." He nearly choked on the words as the Loellens looked at one another. He quickly continued. "I don't hear the sound of the wind coming from this passage as much. That means it goes deeper, right? It might be safer than the other routes, if they run close to the water. It would make them more . . . more susceptible for rupture." He smiled nervously.

The group regarded him wide-eyed, absorbing what he had said. Saire was expressionless, but his eyes seemed to spear Kavriel, as if they were searching his very soul. Before the stone-scholars had a chance to refute Kavriel's claim—he saw their lips tighten and the loose skin under their necks waggled with suppressed laughter—the general broke the silence as he took a torch from the hand of one of his guards.

"I agree," he said, walking past Kavriel into the passage. He was gone from their sight before the scholars could protest.

Picking up their robes, they hurried after the general like two yapping pups following their mother. Kavriel moved aside quickly to avoid both the scholars and the red-plated guard behind them. The Rhyol party hung back only a moment longer, trading looks of puzzlement.

Vaemalin rolled and returned the map to the satchel before approaching Kavriel. "You know . . . " His voice was calm and reassuring, and it reminded Kavriel of his father whenever he consoled his youngest son. "You can wait outside if you need to. No one will think differently of it." He didn't smile, but looked deeply into his brother's eyes.

Kavriel nodded appreciatively, but his duty came before his discomfort. "Thanks, Vaem, but I'll be fine. I promise."

Vaemalin nodded, though he frowned his concern. He had become more protective of Kavriel in the last year; Kavriel didn't understand why, but he figured Tess's influence must have been part of it. Either way, it was a sincere trait of his brother that he respected and so he pushed back the pain in his head and forced a smile.

The group disappeared one after the other into the passage, leaving Kavriel hanging back, muttering while rubbing at his temples. He thought no one was looking—but someone was looking. He saw the Wylyn man from the corner of his eye, not standing by the table as the others had, but in front of the corridor that led to the entrance of the mine. The wan daylight that made it this far along the passage outlined him ominously, and the dark collage of forest colors that he wore seemed to have changed to dull gray and black, as if mirroring the cavern. The stealth of the man both impressed and frightened Kavriel and after a quick nod he turned quickly to catch up to the others in the passage. Being alone with the Wylyn made him uncomfortable.

They walked steadily downward, following a narrow set of iron tracks, half-buried in the dust and fallen rubble of twenty years, the light from their torches dancing along the glossy black walls. Shape and form lost all rules under the earth, Kavriel thought as he watched objects of the mining trade materialize from shadows touched by the torchlight. Axes, lanterns, spent torches, and shovels were just a few of the treasures revealed, while beetles and spiders that had likely lived their entire lives in darkness skittered from the light.

A large box-shaped thing appeared directly in the center of the tunnel, and the torches illuminated one of the carts that had once moved up and down the tracks they followed. It was still filled with its last load, but the wheels looked all but shattered and the wooden sides had bowed with ruin. Any disturbance might see the cart crumble into pieces right in front of them, so the group moved around it slowly. Workers must have been extending this particular tunnel instead of mining, Kavriel thought, noticing more waste rock in the cart than any significant ore, and the tracks ended soon after in a buffer stop built against the rock wall before them.

Uncertain, the group circled up around the cart, waiting as the general stood at the wall, brushing dust and grime away with his gloved hand as if expecting some kind of solution to emerge from the stones. Kavriel noticed that the pain in his head had lessened slightly and he must have been showing it, because Tess moved close enough to place a hand on his shoulder and ask, "Feeling better, Kavriel?" He nodded with a smile.

The general turned from the wall and gave him a curious look, and Kavriel wondered if his foolish idea had simply delayed a tongue-lashing. The stone-scholars seemed overly pleased by this dead end, crossing their robed arms and regarding Kavriel with smirks like a couple of haughty buzzards. Vaemalin had moved to the cart, unrolling his father's map atop its load and tracing passages with a finger while Grieg held a torch high beside him. The integrity of the cart proved sound and the two mumbled together a moment before Vaemalin addressed the group.

"This probably isn't the best time to mention this, but I think I now understand some of these notes." He motioned for them to move closer. The general stepped up first and gazed down at the map as Vaemalin explained, "You see these?" Vaemalin's finger circled several sections of the map where dark loops had been drawn. "These are unfinished tunnels, like the one we are in now. The solid line shows the passage ending. And these—" he moved his hand to touch smaller Xes crossing the lines in no particular pattern, but lighter lines continued through them "—are where the tunnels have been closed off. It looks like there are only four or five main shafts open now." He frowned, and Kavriel knew his brother was disappointed by their limited areas for exploration. Vaemalin and Grieg standing together in the tunnel reminded Kavriel of the two as kids, trying to further understand the mines.

Silent, the general studied the map with narrowed eyes that drifted slightly, as if something else was on his mind. Still, he placed a gloved finger on a section of the map where the shafts were neither looped nor marked with an X, they simply stopped, as if the map's creator had suddenly run out of ink. "What is this place?" Saire asked.

Vaemalin quickly turned the map in his direction as he walked his fingers into the mines. "I think it's one of the ore deposits," he answered. "And it looks like that was the first section to be closed off. You see?" Vaemalin leaned back so the group could see his fingers move along the map, following the route back to the entrance chamber where the table was. "The closed sections seem to follow a sequence . . . indicated by these numbers here. This was the first, followed by the others. Kavriel! Come over here and look at this."

Kavriel hesitated, wondering if movement might trigger the arrows in his head. He took the chance and moved over to the map, concentrating on the passages until he understood his father's work, and nodded in agreement with his brother about the closed passages. He also recognized the classification symbols that those in the trade used to identify different ore accumulations, or *veins*. He pointed out a few of them. "Vaemalin is right about the deposit . . . this is iron." He touched an icon—two swords crossed at the blades. "And this is silver." Several coins stacked together. "And this one—"

"Is gold," one of the Loellens interrupted, creeping up behind the two brothers like a ghost. Kavriel took his finger off the flower-shaped character on the map to give the scholar a blank look. "We are all impressed at your knowledge, young man, but I don't see what the point of all this is."

"What is this symbol?" The general's finger delicately touched a circle outlined by jagged lines, like a child's picture of a sun. It connected to six other, smaller suns surrounding it. He wasn't looking at it directly, instead watching the others in the group for a reaction.

The older Loellen leaned in between Kavriel and Vaemalin for a closer look. His lips were already parted to respond, but then a look of utter bafflement crossed the old man's face. "I haven't seen that before," he stammered, standing upright. Kavriel smiled at him in the same manner as the man had to him, happy to know that the scholar was not as all-powerful as his attitude suggested. "It must be something else," he hurried to add. "It is not a metal identifier, but a drawing of something on his mind . . . only a doodle from a mapmaker, probably fighting off sleep while working late."

The Loellen turned to the second stone-scholar, who immediately nodded in agreement. Vaemalin whispered something nasty under his breath. Kavriel heard it, and choked back a laugh as his brother winked at him.

"And you, Kavriel?" The slow, steady voice of the general reminded the two brothers what they were there for. They turned together toward the man. Kavriel felt an itch around his neck and waist as Saire stared, as if the man were mentally *roping* him up, as he'd seemed to do at the town hall. "What do you think this means?" Saire asked.

Kavriel was confused, uncomfortable with the way the man would bring him into the conversation, but he swallowed his anxiety and peered down at the symbol. Immediately the arrows flew, landing by the dozens underneath Kavriel's forehead. The sudden pain startled him, and he stumbled as one of his hands went to his head. The image on the map blurred. He felt his brother's arm around his waist, supporting him as he backed away him from the cart. The episode lasted only a heartbeat, but it was enough to draw worried comments.

Kavriel waited for the worst to pass while he leaned up against the black wall of the tunnel feeling more embarrassed than exhausted. Vaemalin remained at his side, and Tess had managed to get around the cluster of people to join him. They both looked at Kavriel with

136

concern, but the general was looking at him with fascination.

"Are you alright, Kavriel?" Saire asked in a thoughtful tone.

Kavriel nodded quickly, as if he needed to defend himself for a crime he hadn't committed. "Only a spell . . . the light of the torch on the wall made me a bit dizzy."

His answer caused more conversation than he'd imagined, as the stone-scholars burst into discussion of certain minerals that, when compounded with the breath of a man, could form poisonous gasses. Grieg was speaking softly to A'zia as she nodded, eyes on Kavriel. Kavriel could only guess what he was telling her, but he imagined that there was one more in their party that knew about his issues with closed spaces.

Again it was the general who broke through the discussion, snatching up the map where Vaemalin had left it on the cart. "Then we must double back," he said, not necessarily to Kavriel but to the group in general. He trotted up the passageway, his decision coming too quickly for the others to grasp the reason. They followed, regardless.

"General?" Vaemalin called.

Sensing the question, Saire said over his shoulder, "Your father has given us leave to explore the passages, and that is what we shall do."

It was clear that he considered the conversation finished, and Vaemalin shrugged as he looked over to the others in the Rhyol group, who had begun trailing after the rest. Kavriel again hung back a moment to make sure that his legs were steady, and Tess waited with him. After a moment, he nodded and they went on their way.

Saire, who had taken charge of the map now, stopped in front of a large door that had been ignored the first time they passed. He glanced down at the map as if for confirmation, and Kavriel remembered that this was one of the first "closed off" sections of the mine. The general grabbed the black iron handle affixed to the thick oak door, and pulled it open with relative ease. He was clearly a strong man, but even his expression was one of surprise as the door opened so easily, it barely disturbed the dust.

"This door has been opened recently," he said, waving his torch into the black opening to illuminate a tunnel wall that wasn't much different from the one where they stood.

"There are footprints." A'zia spoke for the first time since they'd entered the mines. She knelt, waving her torch slowly back and forth above the gray floor. "Two sets . . . no more than a day old, and not made by heavy bodies." She looked up at Tess with concern in her eyes. "They may have been made by children."

Tess pushed past Kavriel and grabbed a torch from one of Saire's unsuspecting guards. He relinquished the light without argument. Tess knelt by the Rav'agas woman to examine the tracks herself. Without a word she stood and moved into the new tunnel, but as quick as a snake Saire caught her by the shoulder.

"I really should go first, my dear." He spoke coolly, eyes surveying the passage.

Tess was visibly upset but seemed more startled by the speed of his hand. She shook the hand off and backed away from the tunnel without argument. The general stepped into the tunnel and the rest of the group followed.

CHAPTER 7

Shorter work tunnels split off several times from the main tunnel, but the group continued to follow the general as he led them downward toward the ore deposit chamber indicated on the map. They came across other black doors like the first they had entered, but most had already been opened. Increasing dampness mingled with the dust on the floor of the tunnel and the tracks of the two children became more evident in the layer of mud. With that reminder the group moved silently, listening for any sounds of distress ahead.

The air thickened with moisture, the humidity creeping from cracks in the walls to play tricks with the torchlight, now flickering weakly through a mist. The tunnel narrowed, zigzagging lower and lower into the depths of the earth, and water appeared on the walls, dripping through small pores of rock and forming actual puddles in some places. The Loellen, who were clearly enjoying this descent, explained that the water came directly from the ocean and it was possible that they were now travelling directly under the waters. Eyes slid nervously to the walls, and Kavriel could almost hear the odds of escape being calculated, should the ocean decide to join them in the tunnel.

They seemed to walk for a long time, though the passage of time was impossible to verify so deep underground. Finally the tunnel walls opened up into an oval-shaped cavern. Long fingers of rock hung from the ceiling, and Kavriel saw that there were similar narrow spires rising up from the floor, as if trying to touch those hanging above. Everyone paused, awestruck by the beauty of this underground chamber. The far wall was striped with thin lines of minerals, white, pinks, and yellows, and again the miners had marked their presence with tools stacked against open barrels and crates filled with ore samples.

They had arrived at the deposit, the first cavern sealed off after the declaration by the Council and the last place the miners had excavated in the many years of working the mine. Kavriel knew enough about the earth to know that caves like this one were not man-made and that it only took a tunnel or two to discover them, like breaking down a wall in a room to get to the next. There was a good chance that there were many more caverns like this still undiscovered, and he suddenly became inspired by the general's interests in future explorations. Yet he also felt a touch of disappointment, since this was the most distant place indicated on the map and the farthest place they would be able to go until the overseer was notified. They hadn't found anything that might have been what the general was searching for, Kavriel thought, but they seemed to have moved fairly quickly to this location without spending too much time in the other areas. He began to wonder why.

Then he noticed a strange marking behind several of the icicle rocks and his head began to vibrate. It was the same symbol that he had seen on his father's map, only larger and more defined, etched into the wall as if it had been carved. He forced the pain in his head back and concentrated on not stumbling as he walked slowly forward. The image was at about eye level, and he stopped unsteadily before it, ignoring the dizziness as he focused on the symbol. For a brief moment his head cleared and he thought he recognized something in the etched shapes.

A shadow fell over him, drawing his attention, and he turned to see the general standing behind him, looking at the same image. A restrained passion seemed to shine in his eyes and he licked his lips as if the symbol were a mug of water and Saire a thirsty man. The others, who had been exploring on their own, began to gather around them, eyes wandering, wondering what they were looking at. One of the Loellen scholars was intent on scribbling notes in a book he held open. He spoke up first.

"Why, this is extraordinary! I have never seen anything like it before. It seems to have been burned directly onto the rock surface, perhaps by an ancient civilization . . . a cave-dwelling society living here before our modern towns and villages," the Loellen exclaimed, speaking quickly to his associate, who was nodding eagerly while staring at the symbol. The rest of the group exchanged impressed looks.

"So my father wasn't *doodling*," Vaemalin said smugly behind the stone-scholars. "He must have seen this thing when he was mapping the mine and transcribed it onto the map. I wonder what it means."

"It means Creation," said Saire in a somber tone that caught their attention. "It is Temscript."

Immediately, the scholars were on him. "Are you certain, General? Is this part of the translation?" The question wasn't meant to be sarcastic, as Kavriel would have expected from the two men, but actually expressing genuine interest. The general responded with a nod, focused intently on the symbol. The scholars turned to their books, copying the image and scribbling down notes next to their drawings.

"There is a hole here," said Tess. She had been the only one of them to merely glance at the symbol before focusing on the ground to look for more tracks made by the children. They all turned to her, including the general, who watched in awe as she began crawling on her hands and knees into a smaller tunnel near the image. Vaemalin quickly called after her and tried to follow, but the opening was much too small for him. He called again, more irritated than scared by her actions.

The tall general approached and stopped behind him. "Step back, child," he said in a distant voice that made him seem older than he truly was.

Vaemalin's eyes went wide and he quickly moved aside, then watched in horrified wonder as Saire moved back a moment before thrusting his giant form into the rock wall. Hearing a crack, Kavriel wondered if the impact had smashed the general's shoulder, but the tall man stood back from the wall. Kavriel looked in amazement from the crumbling wall to Saire, who seemed unharmed, still looking distant and unaffected.

The small tunnel Tess had entered was suddenly revealed to be another passage that had been sealed up in the past. Unlike the rest of the passages closed off with oak doors, this one had been closed with rocks and mortar. It seemed much older than anything they had yet seen. As the dust settled, he saw Tess looking back at this new entry in shock.

Before anyone could comment about the general knocking down a mortared rock wall with his body, he was moving quickly into the tunnel, his torch held high. He passed Tess, moving quickly and confidently into the darkness until his light became faint. The others had no choice but to chase after him.

There was nothing obviously special about the new passage, but the arrows in Kavriel's head were relentless, increasing in number with every step he took. The ground seemed to incline slightly, as if they were climbing up now and not descending. Grieg came up behind him and placed his large hand near the center of Kavriel's back to steady him. The passage was only large enough to travel single file, and Kavriel glanced back quickly in gratitude to his friend, who merely nodded in reply. The general was someplace up ahead, and time again seemed to lose meaning as they trotted along.

Though he knew that this was an important discovery, Kavriel also knew that his father had specifically ordered them not to deviate in their explorations into the mine, and Kavriel knew the danger was very real. Tess, who had seemed to provoke this decision, was on the general's heels now, still seeking any signs of the missing Kessor girl. Saire seemed to have forgotten all about her as he strode forward with grim determination. The rest of the group could only do their best not to fall behind, and Kavriel noticed that the guards who had accompanied the general had been continuously shedding pieces of their heavy armor in an effort to keep up. Now left only in their mail shirts and pants, they bore expressions of uncertainty, and they kept their weapons. Kavriel wondered about the general's armor, not to mention the rather oversized sword across his back. They were there to explore, not go into battle, after all.

As they continued, Kavriel noticed that there was more light in the passage, and not from the torches, but some daylight source. He wondered if they had somehow doubled back to the mine entrance, and his were not the only spirits to lift at this possibility, because everyone moved with more determination. The pain in his head did not lessen, on the contrary, it seemed to increase to a constant drone within his skull. He fought his way through it, pushing on, one step at a time, until he passed under a grand archway decorated with hundreds of unknown symbols, and the tunnel opened up into another chamber.

Fresh air hit his nostrils as Kavriel entered the cavern. He smelled the ocean, and heard the crash of water somewhere above. Immediately he thought of the numerous mountains that dotted the Black Ocean in a line from the main island and wondered if they might actually have entered one via an underwater tunnel. The cave was so large and wide compared to others they had seen that he wondered if they were in fact in a different system of tunnels. The walls surrounding them were smooth, worn almost to a glassy finish. They rose fifty feet to the cracked ceiling, the source of the daylight, and the sounds of the ocean. Thin white pillars similar to the columns at Moonstone Shrine sprouted in a dozen different places, many topped by the nests of seagulls, which made Kavriel think of a white forest hidden underground. They must have been constructed by man, he thought, as the columns were much too precise and smooth to be natural. They rose from ground to ceiling like load beams supporting the cavern roof. Within the bizarre forest was a shorter column, wide as a man but about as high as his waist, situated in the exact center of everything.

The place was exhilarating, drawing exclamations of wonder from the group—everyone except the general, who stood like a statue in the center of the room before the short cylinder of white rock. His back was turned, but as Kavriel moved around several of the tree-shaped pillars he noticed that the general was talking to himself, and accomplishment gleamed in his eyes.

Kavriel looked curiously at the column, feeling the thumping in his head but sensing that the pain wasn't coming from within him, but from the white column, and merely echoing back against his mind. He didn't understand what that could mean.

Vaemalin and Grieg approached it from the opposite side, his brother running his fingers along its rim while tilting his head thoughtfully. "I think this is a cover . . . This is a container of some sort." As he spoke, he tested the weight of the stone top but it refused to move. Grieg set down his torch and tried helping his friend move the cover, but even their combined strength failed to budge the stone.

The general stared at the object, indifferent to the others. His lips still moved as the man continued speaking to no one in particular.

A muffled gasp drew Kavriel's eye and he glimpsed one of Saire's bodyguards stumbling backward into a darkened corner. *Odd,* he thought, wondering if the man was alright, but then he saw Tess and A'zia moving near the far wall of the cave, eyes on the ground, Tess kicking at small rocks and pebbles—the Rav'agas woman had decided to assist Tess in searching for clues concerning the missing girl. *Perhaps he's helping them,* Kavriel thought of the guard, glancing back that way. He didn't see the man and his eyes drifted to A'zia, scanning the dust for any unnatural change. They moved slowly in a semicircular pattern around the white rock forest. Tess showed little interest in that. A'zia looked up now and then with more curiosity, but she too was focused on the missing girl.

* * *

They didn't see the Wylyn man until they had nearly stepped on him. Tess jumped back quickly when she finally did notice him sitting on a large boulder that had once been part of the ceiling. He didn't acknowledge them, but continued to watch the general, absently turning white pebbles over and over in his hand. After a quick look, Tess thought that they might be bird skulls, but she couldn't be sure and certainly wasn't interested in asking. She moved past the Wylyn cautiously.

A'zia paused to watch him for a moment—or more accurately, watch him watching Saire. She too looked into his hand and her eyes narrowed in recognition. Sensing her attention, the Wylyn finally looked at her, and they locked eyes a moment before the man returned his gaze to Saire as if waiting for something. The skulls continued to tumble in his hand.

A'zia moved around him and leaned close to Tess to whisper, "Stay by me, girl. Do not get close to that man again. I do not trust him."

Tess lost focus on her search and blinked up at the beautiful foreign woman, wondering what the problem was. She glanced over to the Wylyn, who hadn't moved from the rock. She hadn't thought of him beyond thinking him some odd-looking crony of Saire's, but A'zia's eyes were fierce as she waited for some kind of acknowledgment. Tess nodded in confusion before continuing her search for clues to the missing girl.

* * *

The Loellen stone-scholars had finished their information gathering and now, their notebooks filled with fresh details about the cave, they approached Vaemalin and Grieg, who were still trying to muscle open the stone container. The oldest scholar waved his hand irritably and scowled at them. "It is no use, you fools. That is three fingers' width of solid rock; it will take more than you two to open it."

The two men backed off momentarily from their efforts, Grieg eyeing the old man with contempt. "You could help," he said.

"Nonsense," the scholar replied. "Whatever it is has been there longer than anything else constructed in this room." His eyes surveyed the white pillar forest surrounding them. "I suggest we return to the surface and equip ourselves with the proper tools. We need more of our references anyway, so that we might figure out what kind of rock this is."

"It's pureon," Kavriel said meekly from his place leaning against one of the pillars. His head was clouded and he felt dizzy, the effect of the cave starting to mentally wear him down, but he tried to remember what the strange man at Moonstone Shrine had said about the columns near Rhyol. *Why did I suddenly just think of him?*

The Loellen repeated the word, his expression revealing his irritation at Kavriel's interruption, but his

148

eyebrows lifted in curiosity. The general stopped muttering and looked past the cylinder to the Wylyn, still sitting in the back. There was nothing said or signalled between them, but Kavriel could have sworn some kind of message had just passed between them. As if suddenly remembering where he was, the general looked intently back to the cylinder. Two long strides took him closer to it.

"Pure-*what?*" the Loellen scholar asked Kavriel, as his colleague scribbled in his book.

Before Kavriel could answer, the general spoke. "Pureon." He gripped both sides of the stone cover that Vaemalin and Grieg had been trying to maneuver, and his muscles flexed, the red jacket tightening across his back. With one mighty shove and only a slight grunt of effort, he slid the great stone plate off the top of the cylinder. The white stone hit the floor and cracked into three pieces in a cloud of dust. Vaemalin and Grieg gaped at Saire as if they'd never seen him before. Kavriel hadn't attempted to remove the stone cover, but the gasps of effort from his brother and Grieg had made it clear that it was something Saire shouldn't have been able to do on his own.

The thumping in Kavriel's skull became a discordant roar, as if the opened container had released a full volley of the arrows inside his head. His legs gave way and he dropped to one knee, gripping his forehead with one hand while bracing himself with the other so he wouldn't fall completely to the floor. Tess was beside him in a heartbeat, the missing girl forgotten.

Kavriel raised his head with great effort. The general, who must have had seen him fall, was looking back at him, but with little concern in his crystalline eyes.

His lips pulled into a tight smile as he watched Kavriel struggle to get back to his feet. The rest of the party simply stared, aghast.

"There is only one place left where pureon can still be found," Saire said with calm darkness in his voice, as a father might sound when explaining to his child that there *are* bad things in life. "And you speak much too quickly of things you are not meant to understand. It would be wise for you to remain silent."

Without further explanation, Saire turned back to the cylinder of rock. He reached inside with two gloved hands and delicately extracted a large gold urn, the width and length of a man's leg. He placed it gently on the floor in front of the stone container and reached in again to retrieve another urn, identical to the first. He held it just as carefully, placing it next to the other as if he were a midwife assisting in the birth of twins. Then he backed away slowly and cupped a gloved hand over his chin in contemplation. Kavriel was dizzy, but he was still able to recognize rage when he saw it . . . and he saw it on the face of the general as he stared at the twin urns.

The others gathered around the open stone well to see what the general had removed, but they kept their distance from Saire, still unsure about what they had just seen him do. The Loellen stone-scholars hovered like flies over filth, caressing each golden vessel with trembling fingers. The older man tapped lightly on the top of one of the urns, eliciting a dampened echo from within. He tilted it to one side, then back and forth again, and Kavriel heard a sluggish sloshing, as if the container contained something viscous. "I think it's liquid," the scholar announced.

150

He pulled a small, flat-headed hook from his robes and tried forcing it under the lid of one of the urns. Struggle as he might, he was unable to open the urn; it was as stubborn as the stone cylinder that had contained it. It was not rock, or any kind of stone for that matter, Kavriel realized; it looked as if it was made of solid gold. Whatever the urn contained must have been of great value, to be hidden and secured so thoroughly.

The general seemed to have momentarily forgotten all about them. He paced around the forest of pureon pillars with his hands pressed together over his lips.

The old Loellen cursed as the flat-headed hook jerked free from his fingers when his hand slipped. With a frown, Grieg moved in behind the man, removing a thick-bladed dagger from his belt. He grabbed the neck of the urn with his free hand, pushing the old scholar back out of harm's way using the flat of the blade. Then he cut across the top of the gold vessel hard and fast, drawing a strange ringing sound from the urn when the metal blade touched it. The general whirled back toward the group as he'd heard a battle alarm.

A blast of red shot up from the top of the urn like boiling water from a spout, and Grieg shouted in surprise and threw up his hands to protect his face, dropping the urn. Its contents, a thick liquid with a metallic sheen, splashed over Vaemalin, who had been the closest to him. Everyone leapt back instinctively, and watched thousands of sparkling motes, highlighted in the light coming through the cracked ceiling, filter slowly downward, vanishing before they touched the floor.

As the cloud that had erupted from the urn

dissipated in the air, the general moved in closer, his face a mask of astonishment. Grieg cursed as he rubbed at his eyes. His face and hands were covered in a thin sheen of metallic residue that sparkled red in the light, but he seemed otherwise unharmed and very embarrassed. Tess and A'zia moved toward him but he raised a hand for them to stop, nodding his head with a reassuring smile. Vaemalin too was unaffected by the liquid that covered his hand; he stared at the red metallic slime gently flowing down his forearm with wonder-filled eyes. The scholars, now past the initial fright of the explosion, quickly moved to the toppled urn, trying to contain the slime oozing out with flat rocks and even their notebooks.

The general stepped in front of Vaemalin, studying him with an analytical look in his eyes. He glanced over to the Wylyn and gave him a nod, and the man shifted his otherwise empty focus to Vaemalin—or, more specifically, to the ooze.

Something had happened to the consistency of the stuff, Kavriel noted, watching the thick liquid become thinner, the longer it was outside the urn, until it became as transparent as water and evaporated into a sparkling cloud of red motes that resembled its initial release from the urn. The scholars leaned back from the urn with awe on their faces as the stuff that had been on their books and the stones dispersed into the air. They looked to Grieg and Vaemalin, and Kavriel followed their gaze to see the liquid vanish from their bodies just as eerily.

They looked at one another with idiotic grins on their faces. For them the experience had been a harmless surprise, like a quick joke to relieve an otherwise uneasy task in the tunnels. But the general was staring in silence at Vaemalin.

As Vaemalin reached for the second container, the older Loellen scholar waved his hands at him as if shooing away a giant bug. The man then placed his hands protectively over the urn, shouting some lecture to him about dangerous, volatile rock acids in airtight containers or some such that Kavriel could barely understand through the thumping in his head. His brother raised his hands and stepped back, then looked at his arm and hand as if seeking any lingering trace of the stuff.

Grieg seemed to have fallen into a state of bliss; he smiled broadly at nothing in particular. "That was amazing!" he finally said. Vaemalin smiled back at him. "What was that?"

The older Loellen scholar was quickly shouting for his pen, which he had apparently dropped, as he opened up his book. His colleague immediately stepped forward with another pen and he started scribbling down notes about Grieg and Vaemalin's reaction to the substance in the urns. The others moved closer together as if unconsciously seeking protection.

Grieg passionately described every last detail of what it had felt like—"Sharp and hot as a burn before cooling down, then like ice over my skin and eyes." Vaemalin said much the same, but he was not as quick to come up with words to describe the sensation, though he agreed it was as amazing as Grieg said it was.

As before, only the general looked preoccupied, listening yet at the same time seeming to hear something else. Kavriel looked at the second container cautiously, as if might suddenly burst open like the other. He noticed his brother staring at it as well, but with an expression of need on his face instead of worry.

* * *

Another of Saire's bodyguards, ignoring the activity in the center of the room, had drifted around to the entrance of the cave, searching for his missing colleague. He felt an arm wrap tightly around his neck as he walked past the dark archway and before he could react he was pulled off of his feet, disappearing into the blackness.

From across the room the Wylyn saw the abduction. He had been the only one watching the entrance, as Saire had wordlessly commanded him to do. Closing his hand tightly over his bird skulls, he rapidly spoke several words in Rav'agas.

Having never heard the man speak until now, everyone in the party looked over to him, hearing his gruff voice but not knowing what he said. Only A'zia understood the warning. She looked towards the cave entrance, her hands reaching behind her back to return holding the two sicca blades crossed defensively in front of her. Seeing the woman draw her weapons, the remaining bodyguards drew their own as they backed away from the black entryway.

Grieg's moment of bliss had passed. Frowning, he pulled out his soldier's blade and moved toward his beloved. The rest of the party could only wonder what was happening.

Saire nodded at his Wylyn associate, then lifted his head with a smile. "Come and join us!" he shouted. "There is no longer reason to stay in the shadows; I know you are here." He spoke calmly, despite the rage blazing in his eyes.

Kavriel looked to the others as they exchanged nervous glances. He only just then realized that the pain and dizziness that had been wearing him down ever since setting foot in the mines was gone . . . the arrows, the drums—everything. He felt more focused than he had in what seemed like ages, and as he stood up straight, the general glanced at him with what seemed like a knowing grin. Kavriel must have started to look as normal as he felt. The change was as fresh as the ocean air still seeping in from the ceiling, but concern for this unknown danger was quick to return as he saw his friends at arms.

Saire waited patiently for a reply to his words as silence overtook the cave. A moment later, soft footsteps were heard approaching the entrance to the cave, and a man materialized out of the darkness. He walked calmly into the room, his hands hanging casually at his sides; he ignored the

remaining bodyguards who quickly surrounded him. Their eyes slid nervously past the newcomer, realizing just now that their team of six guards had suddenly become four.

The man stopped several steps inside the chamber, ignoring the guards, eyes only intent on the general. Saire stared back. The others shifted uncertainly.

Kavriel reacted with surprise as he recognized the man from Moonstone Shrine; the same man he had just been thinking about. *"Xavr,"* he whispered, remembering the name of the man on the ridge. He was there with them now, underneath the rocks as if he had been there the entire time, dressed in the same clothes and wearing the same expression on his face. He did not seem to hear Kavriel but Saire had; his eyes turned to Kavriel a moment, carrying with them the rage that he had directed at Xavr. Kavriel suddenly felt the need to run, but before he could even begin to work his legs into motion the general spoke again, not to him but to Xavr.

"I must be honest. I was hoping that you would be here . . . I actually expected it." Kavriel let out a sigh of relief as the general returned his attention to Xavr.

"Did you, now?" the other man responded with a trace of sarcasm.

"You are very good at following me. I actually thought I had lost you at Chaven Glen, but you are a persistent one. When did you return to the island?"

"Seven nights ago," Xavr answered as matter-of-factly as if they were having a civil conversation over a cup of tea. The rest of the party watched silently, with no idea what to do.

General Saire nodded in acceptance of Xavr's answer. "So you knew where I was going?"

Xavr nodded, crossing his arms comfortably. His relaxed posture and empty hands prompted the guards surrounding him to lower their blades. They kept him in their circle, but the man didn't seem to be of any immediate threat.

"Then I must thank you for such detailed directions . . . I never would have thought of this place, if not for them."

Saire's snide compliment chilled Xavr's expression. "They were never meant for you," he replied, maintaining the comfortable demeanor. The general shrugged. Whatever relationship these two men had, it was obviously an old one.

The older scholar finally spoke. "Excuse me, but . . . who is this man?"

The general ignored him as he walked slowly over to the urns. The Loellen backed away from the tall man's approach but Vaemalin remained in place, staring hard at the containers without even noticing Saire. Kavriel wondered if his brother noticed Xavr's arrival at all. His worry must have shown in his eyes, or Tess had picked up on it, because she moved quickly to be at her lover's side. He didn't show any interest in her arrival.

"Vaemalin . . . are you alright?" she asked.

"Hmm?" he replied as if just waking up. "What . . . ? Yes, I'm fine." He blinked around at the group, then registered the situation with no obvious concern before returning his gaze to the urn.

Tess flashed Kavriel a look of confusion. He responded with a shrug. She looked over to Grieg, who seemed more focused; he held his sword defensively in front of him while watching Xavr. A'zia was at his side, standing in much the same manner, only she seemed more curious about the man. Was that a look of recognition? She seemed quite observant, he thought; maybe she had seen him in the town hall, even if he had not.

Saire reached down and picked up the empty urn from the floor. He was careful to not to touch the second, unopened urn as he watched Vaemalin for any reaction to what he was doing. Vaemalin's eyes stared ahead blankly. The general grinned again, while Tess scowled.

Saire turned toward Xavr, who had been waiting patiently. No, Kavriel realized, Xavr had been watching *him* until now. Xavr quickly returned his attention to the general when the man addressed him.

"It is of no matter what was meant for me or not," Saire said, continuing the conversation as if it had never ended. He turned the empty urn over in his hands and smiled. "You have arrived too late. What is done is done."

Xavr was clearly discouraged; he regarded the empty urn in Saire's hands with disgust. His eyes slid to the second urn behind the tall man, then over to Kavriel. "This is madness," Xavr said, looking back to the general, who had noticed Xavr's passing glance at Kavriel. Again his eyes lit up in curiosity, but Kavriel was certain that whatever his involvement in this, it was as much an unknown to Saire as it was to him. *Why did he look at me?*

He nearly bumped into Tess, standing next to his brother, and realized that he had moved over to the two without realizing. More importantly, he was next to the second urn.

"You are too ambitious, as always, toying with ideas that were never for us in the first place. Whatever you are planning will fail," Xavr said.

"You will stop me?" the general asked, his tone mocking as he touched his chest.

"You will fail," Xavr repeated, not answering the question but with a certainty in his tone that Kavriel knew was affirmative.

Grieg and A'zia seemed to stiffen to the implied threat, as did the four guards, who moved in closer to Xavr and lifted their blades. Unconcerned, he kept his eyes on

Saire. "This must not continue," he said softly. "You have gone too far already. You will only end up destroying yourself." His voice was calm, but also somewhat troubled.

Kavriel wondered again what kind of relationship was between these men. He saw the similarities in the eyes and in the hair color . . . brothers, perhaps? He didn't recall anything he had read about Saire having family. As a matter of fact, the general had specifically stated at one time that he was an orphaned and only child. Still, there was an obvious kinship between the two, and Kavriel put this to mind knowing that his father would be quite interested to know this.

Unaffected by Xavr's warning, Saire roared laughter. "Indeed!" he shouted. "And I am sure you would be quite distraught about that!" He laughed again, but fell silent just as quickly, his eyes narrowing menacingly, as if a new problem had suddenly come to his attention. The glitter of rage returned, and Kavriel began to grow fearful in his suspicions about the general. A'zia shot a strange look back in his direction, and glancing at Tess next to him, Kavriel saw that she was gripping Vaemalin's arm tightly. Vaemalin was still watching the urn.

"Do not take this matter lightly. This has grown beyond even your control. You must see that now?" Xavr asked, clearly trying to prolong the conversation and possibly defuse a hostile situation. Kavriel could understand why. If he was surrounded by armed men he would most likely be doing the same thing. Strangely, he didn't see the large broadsword Xavr had been carrying when he'd met the man on the ridge, but his vest was closed tight around him and it was entirely possible that he was concealing it.

The Loellen scholars had moved as far away from the situation as possible, clutching their notebooks defensively against their chests, their eyes watchful. The Wylyn man remained seated where he was in the back of the chamber, his eyes displaying a rage toward Xavr much the same as Saire's. Kavriel wondered how far back the history between the two men went, and how it involved the Wylyn man. *What is really going on?* He suddenly felt as if he had just stepped into a play that was being enacted before him and his friends.

As if somehow reading Kavriel's thoughts, Xavr looked calmly over to him once again. "Kavriel," he said, speaking his name with an assurance that suggested they had been friends for years, and not only recently met. "Take your friends out of this place." He glanced at Tess and Vaemalin, Grieg and A'zia, and even the Loellen scholars hidden in the back before settling his eyes back on Saire, who was smiling deviously. "This room is not your concern. Go back quickly to the village and forget all that you have seen here, before it's too late." It was not a suggestion.

Kavriel suddenly felt an ominous presence in the room. He was sure it was coming from the general.

"But it is already too late," Saire said to Xavr, and an icy chill ran down Kavriel's spine.

"Don't do this," Xavr said, almost pleading.

Grieg and A'zia looked at one another uncertainly before Grieg cast a worried glance back at Tess, who was trying unsuccessfully to move Vaemalin away from the cylinder of stone. Kavriel began backing away.

The general laughed, a menacing sound. He tossed the empty gold container at Xavr as if it was as worthless as a ripped sack. The scholars groaned as the urn landed with a loud crack on the ground several feet in front of the guards circling Xavr.

"Enough." Saire waved his hand, turning toward Vaemalin, who had picked up the second urn. Tess backed up quickly as the general approached, leaving her lover standing with a lost look in his eyes. Saire regarded Vaemalin with amusement, as if he could read something on the man's face. He then did something very odd: he lifted his gloved hand to gently stroke the side of Vaemalin's face. Vaemalin didn't try to move away, he didn't try to do anything; he simply smiled up at the tall man like a loyal dog being rewarded by his master. Tess looked genuinely frightened, and Kavriel almost let out a gasp in disbelief. *What has happened?*

"This will never go beyond my control," Saire said to Xavr, still looking at Vaemalin. "*Never again . . .*" He glanced back to Xavr, whose expression was sorrowful and distant. Saire smiled. "Kill him," he commanded his guards. He looked over to Grieg and A'zia, who had been watching the general with new doubt in their eyes. Kavriel realized that this had gone too far. "Kill them all," the general ordered.

Kavriel heard Tess let out a painful cry as the shadow of a man passed over him. It was the Wylyn, separating Kavriel from Tess with a quick shove as the Wylyn used the stone cylinder in front of them as a stepping stone, launching himself completely *over* the general like a trained stallion leaping over a hurdle. He crashed into A'zia and Grieg on the other side feet first, knocking them to the ground. Taken completely off guard, they both sprawled backward, their weapons skittering from their grasp. The Wylyn landed on his feet, agile as a cat, now gripping a pair of single-handed axes. Lips split in a grin, he rushed at the fallen duo.

Grieg's head had hit one of the white pillars in the attack, and he was slow to recover. The Wylyn should have finished the job—Grieg's condition was temporary and he was a formidable fighter. But, satisfied that he'd incapacitated the large soldier, the Wylyn focused on the West Point Rav'agas woman as the more dangerous of the two.

A'zia swung one of her long legs, deflecting the Wylyn's downward swing of the axe before spinning away. She was already crouched, waiting, when the Wylyn came in for another attack. Her whip shot out from her hip like a black snake, ripping a line of flesh from his hand as one of the axes flew from his grip. His grin vanished and she used the pause to slip back to where her blades had fallen. She dropped the whip while retrieving the thin blades with a quick flick of her fingers, then turned toward the Wylyn with a smile that bordered on flirtatious. He waited quietly, opening and clenching his wounded hand to test its function as he pointed the axe he still held at her.

Grieg had since gotten back on his feet and he stood, his sword in his hand and anger glinting in his eyes. He slowly began to circle behind the Wylyn, who hadn't even bothered to look at him yet. Grieg wasn't his concern. As the large man rushed at the Wylyn with a war cry, A'zia shouted out a warning that fell on unhearing ears. Grieg was larger and stronger than the scraggly Wylyn, but he had never fought with or against a Wylyn in his short time as a Quetalian soldier. His bulk and his armor overburdened him, and the man easily avoided him as he swung, then quickly downed Grieg with a series of fluttery motions from his feet and elbows, the multicolored coat furling like a dust cloud.

Grieg again fell. His eyes opened wide in disbelief as the axe blade swept down toward his forehead, but again the Wylyn was denied blood as a sicca blade deflected the killing blow. Grieg rolled from danger and struggled to his feet, watching his lover spar with the Wylyn in what resembled a dance more than a battle. He leaned against a white pillar, struggling to catch his breath as he gauged his next move.

* * *

A'zia lost one of her blades immediately after engaging the Wylyn directly. She knew and understood his methods of attack, as her people had spent years studying the Wylyn art of combat, which incorporated their naturalistic way of life even in defense. Yet that had not given her a mastery over his ways.

A'zia was considered one of the best sister-warriors in her society, schooled in combat at a young age and learning the techniques from all the provinces of Rav'agas and even the Quetalian discipline, but the Wylyn remained largely a mystery. Before she'd enlisted in the Quetalian opposition to the Patriarch's Ay'vol Force, her final test as sister-warrior was to engage a master Wylyn fighter, who in their society was referred to as a *Jag-wa-ru*.

Several villages on the Rav'agas border had been

looted by Wylyn that had become too ambitious in their raids and A'zia, along with eleven other women, had entered the forests to end this problem. Even the Wylyn's governing order had declared this group renegades operating outside the beliefs of the people, and so they had no complaints with these sister-women testing their strength against them while keeping the general peace between the provinces. Yet what the sisterhood in Kairn didn't say was that one of these renegades was in fact a Jag-wa-ru.

The test ended horribly. All but A'zia had been killed in an ambush, and she was wounded both physically and mentally. Her sisterhood granted her warrior status regardless, respecting and honoring her effort despite losing eleven other potential fighters. A'zia left for the Quetalian front, ashamed and vengeful. She understood the ways of the sisterhood, and their traditions, but she wished to have another chance against a Jag-wa-ru, both for vengeance and pride.

When she'd first learned that a Wylyn was in General Saire's company, she didn't think much of it until she actually saw the man. When she saw the trophies and artifacts of faith worn by the Wylyn that were only awarded to a respected man, her suspicions grew. This wasn't the same Jag-wa-ru that had slaughtered her sisters as easily as a wolf slaughtered sheep, but he *was* a Wylyn master. As soon as she'd come in contact with the man, she knew that they would battle.

She summoned all her skill and talents, but despite her readiness, the Wylyn Jag-wa-ru was still more experienced, and as he struck her other blade from her hand with a bizarre backward kick followed by an elbow to her head, she dropped to the ground. Cursing in her native tongue she pushed herself back to her feet, certain that the Jag-wa-ru was about to finish her off. Yet to her surprise, he stood waiting for her to recover.

She spat out a gob of blood and walked up to him casually, without her blades. The Wylyn dropped his axe and motioned for A'zia to come forward with open hands. She smiled menacingly in acceptance, and the dance began anew.

* * *

Kavriel was still dumbstruck by this sudden new series of events, and as the fight between the Wylyn and A'zia began he realized that the best thing he could do was take Xavr's advice and try to get them all out of there. His brother was still an emotionless statue, hands outstretched to deposit the urn into the waiting hands of the general, who was more immediately interested in watching Vaemalin's movements than the object itself. He couldn't begin to understand what was going on, and only worried for his brother's safety, being so close to the suddenly mad general.

Cries of pain and surprise from the cave entrance called Kavriel's attention, and he saw that Xavr had done extremely well against his opponents. Xavr had indeed concealed his great sword within his vests, although he hadn't drawn it from its scabbard yet. He saw in Xavr's quick movements the same refinement and precision exhibited in the Wylyn's style of fighting. He brushed the four armed guards away as mindlessly as a man swatting away a swarm of mosquitoes. In the time it took the guards to rush Xavr, he had already dispatched them unconscious across the cave floor.

Tess called out weakly for Kavriel, and he turned back to his friend. She was leaning against one of the white pillars where the Wylyn had shoved her, clutching her side with a pained grimace on her face. Kavriel rushed to her, seeing in horror the small bloom of blood soaking her dress and the thin knife in Tess's hand, its blade red with her blood. The Wylyn must have stabbed her as he shoved her aside. He looked back up to her face, feeling as helpless as a child, fighting back the urge to cry out.

Surprisingly, Tess reassured him, her voice strained, but still clear and focused. "I'm alright, Kav." She smiled, then mouthed a curse as she looked over to the fighting Wylyn. "I . . . I am only scratched." She was more frightened by what was happening, he realized as she lifted her hand from her blouse and Kavriel saw that indeed, the wound was thin, short, and shallow. She dropped the knife from her hand, more disgusted by the thing than anything.

Confident that she was out of immediate danger, Kavriel tried pulling her toward the exit after the two Loellen scholars who were making their escape. Xavr had just finished with the last guard, flipping the man from behind before glancing at the Loellen running out of the cave.

Thinking only of protecting Tess, Kavriel had forgotten his brother, but Tess hadn't. He was still blankly looking into the general's eyes. She screamed to Vaemalin to get away, and Kavriel screamed with her, trying to get Vaemalin's attention. Grieg heard them. Pushing aside the pain of his cracked ribs, he rushed over to pull Vaemalin back from Saire before he could release the urn to him. His intrusion broke the strange, meditative scene going on between Vaemalin and the general, but he was rewarded with a backhand slap from Saire. The general's unnatural strength lifted Grieg off his feet and hurled him several feet back to land unconscious.

Tess's scream distracted A'zia from her fight with the Wylyn, whose own strength seemed to be equal to Saire's. He cracked her forearm with an elbow, then spun, looping his leg around her neck and forcing her to the ground. Blood oozed from her smashed forehead as, like Grieg, she breathed slowly in unconsciousness.

As the Wylyn smiled down at her, Tess went mad with rage, breaking free from Kavriel's grasp to attack the general. The Wylyn saw her coming and leapt back up onto the stone cylinder between Saire and her. The general watched with a look of amusement. Kavriel moved forward to stop her, but the Wylyn had released something from under his cloak that flashed silver as it rushed to meet Kavriel. He gasped as the blade imbedded itself deep in his stomach, and staggered back against one of the white pillars. Hearing his gasp, Tess froze in fear.

Kavriel slumped to the floor, unable to think of anything except the burning in his stomach and the dizziness as the miasma of the mines returned to overtake him. He watched helplessly as the general turned toward Tess, raising his hand to forestall the Wylyn, who was perched behind him on the cylinder rim like some bird of prey. Saire stepped toward her, smiling wolfishly as he reached for her.

The sound of crunching metal echoed in the cave,

167

and a golden blur the size of a man's leg flew into the group like a loosed arrow. Xavr had seen what was about to happen, and with unnatural speed rushed to give the empty urn that Saire had tossed at him a mighty kick. Sensing or seeing it coming at him, the general leapt back, narrowly avoiding being struck by the urn. He stumbled against the Wylyn's knees, still crouching atop the cylinder, and knocked him to the cave floor.

The urn smashed against the second urn that Vaemalin had been holding to his chest like a newborn child, and the impact shattered the golden vessel and sent Vaemalin flying back to the far end of the cave. The red metallic liquid exploded from the shattered urn, covering him, Tess, and the general in one enormous splash, and covering the once white stone cylinder in silver liquid, darkening it so it seemed more aged. A memory flashed into Kavriel's mind, of a gray basin that looked exactly like what was before him now, and with Tess standing near the basin, the dreams that he had been struggling to remember for the last few months poured into his conscious mind.

The pain in his stomach began to overtake all of his senses, and the dizziness in his head made the room to blur and shake. He felt the need to sleep, despite the danger. The burning in his stomach suddenly became cold, moving down his legs, which he couldn't seem to move properly, and he realized that his hands hung at his sides. He struggled to keep his head up, the need for sleep was so intense, and he stared at the bloodied white hilt of the knife that had been driven into his flesh.

The general's roar shook him awake. He looked dreamily at Saire, standing before the stone basin. It might have been due to his unsteady vision, but the general seemed o be shaking in rage as he stared across the cave at the man who had kicked the urn. *"You fool!"* he screamed at Xavr, who had finally unsheathed his great sword in a slow, mechanical movement.

The Wylyn was back on his feet, but he'd shifted focus from Tess to Xavr. He watched Xavr hungrily, slowly rounding the basin that he had fallen from but remaining behind the general, not about to get between Saire and Xavr. Not yet, anyway.

The air had already begun to thicken with the cloud of red mist evaporating from the spilled liquid. It disappeared from the basin but the new gray color remained, as if a reminding Kavriel what he had forgotten in dreams. He struggled to pay attention to what was happening.

He saw Tess, her arms outstretched before her, watching the sparkling substance vanish from her clothing. Saire must have noticed this; forgetting his rage, he watched with eyes narrowed in interest. Tess's eyes became as vacant as Vaemalin's had, and Kavriel knew that she had fallen under the trance of the substance. She was oblivious to what was happening around her, to her lover, who sprawled on broken boulders, groaning in pain while trying to regain his feet.

Kavriel could not let go; he used anger to force himself awake, pushing the control back into his limbs while focusing on his fallen brother. His feet shuffled, and he found his arms again, using them to help slide his back up the white pillar. The general gave him a passing glance, but whatever it was about Kavriel that had held his attention was long gone now, and Kavriel could see nothing but an old anger radiating from the man that went far beyond him. The general returned his gaze to Xavr.

"It is finished," Xavr stated, broadsword raised. "You have lost it. It's gone from you forever now." His tone was firm, but he seemed relieved. He removed his vest with his free hand, his eyes constantly on Saire.

The general, visibly back in control of his emotions, smiled confidently and looked behind him to Vaemalin, then over to Tess. "On the contrary, old man," he replied. "It has only just begun."

Kavriel stumbled over to Tess, who was still staring at her arms as if she had just received them and only noticed that Kavriel was there when he grabbed her for support so he would not fall. He must have squeezed her harder than he'd intended, because she turned. She gazed into his ashen face, his own blood on his clothes, and something inside her must have awakened. Her blank look vanished, and she quickly caught him as Kavriel began to fall.

"Oh no!" she exclaimed. "Kavriel! Kavriel, we have to get you out of here!" She looked around in confusion, as if seeing for the first time the cave and the destruction that Saire had caused.

Kavriel couldn't respond. He couldn't spare the breath. He nodded over to his brother, who had struggled to his knees. His head was sagging, and a dark patch of vomit stained the front of his shirt as his hands clutched at his chest. He raised his head for a moment, and in his pained face Kavriel finally recognized Vaemalin who, despite his shattered arm and chest, still bore a look of responsibility.

170

His eyes widened as they took in his surroundings. He must have recognized Kavriel and Tess, for he forced himself to his feet and wobbled dangerously close to the general and the Wylyn to get to them. He didn't even look in their direction, or at the shattered pieces of the golden urn under his feet.

Saire merely smiled at the group, watching Vaemalin walk by as dispassionately as a man would watch a crowded street from a lofty window. The Wylyn was looking toward the opposite side of the basin, where the Quetalian soldier had gotten himself to his feet and was moving slowly over to the woman still unconscious on the floor. Grieg knelt to scoop A'zia up in his arms with great effort; the bloodied woman rocked back and forth as Grieg staggered toward the cave entrance. The Jag-ru-wa's lips twitched in dismay, perhaps wishing for another outcome, if his master would grant it.

Xavr watched all of this quietly, his expression concerned. "What do you think you have done?" he asked softly as his eyes followed Grieg, slowly approaching him with A'zia cradled in his arms. His eyes were unfocused and he stumbled while he walked. He didn't seem to see the man if front of him at all.

"This will only destroy them," Xavr whispered.

Saire laughed in response. "Then you must destroy them first," he answered through his teeth.

Xavr actually changed his position to face the approaching soldier, who stopped when he saw Xavr shift. Disoriented, swaying with pain, he looked at Xavr with an expression of anguished confusion. A'zia began to twitch back to conscious in his arms. Xavr's stance was that of a warrior ready to attack, but in his eyes was hesitation. Saire saw this.

"It is you who has lost," the general said, his voice arrogant. "But if you still believe that my efforts have been in vain, let me show you proof of my will—before I destroy you, as I did our brothers." His words seemed to strike at Xavr physically. Saire looked over to the Wylyn.

Kavriel wondered if, by losing so much blood, he had lost his sense of comprehension, for he saw the impossible happen. The Wylyn, nodding with a smile of appreciation to the general's wordless instruction, moved from the basin like a gust of wind, knocking aside Grieg and the woman in his arms with the force of a gale. His image seemed to separate into many hazy copies, and the axes came out, striking at Xavr in a flash of fury. Kavriel expected Xavr to be shattered into pieces like the golden urn he had kicked into Vaemalin, but the man parried the Wylyn's blows with a speed and confidence that only dreams could harness. The fight lasted hours—or perhaps minutes. Dust kicked up from the stones around them spun as if a tornado had entered the cave. The walls began to shake, and Kavriel felt the wind from their movements.

The fight held Kavriel, Tess, and Vaemalin transfixed. Approaching them silently, Saire struck Kavriel first, slamming him away from his brother and Tess. His chest caved in, and he felt the floor lift away; his back seemed to snap in two as the far wall of the cave stopped his momentum. Several pieces of pure white stone dislodged and fell with him as he dropped to the floor, and before consciousness fled, he saw that one of the pillars had been shattered by his impact. His eyes closed as the general closed his hand over Vaemalin's throat, but oblivion did not come.

Kavriel didn't know how long he floated in that limbo just shy of unconsciousness, but when he finally was able to open his eyes he saw that he was still half-buried in white rock and the sound of metal striking metal echoed around him. He leaned forward, unsure how he was still alive. Blood filled his mouth, choking his breath—that had been the reason he'd awakened. He vomited on the stones, seeing a great amount of blood.

Someone called his name. He struggled to focus, and saw Xavr now battling with the general in a deadly dance that only nightmares could fabricate. Sparks flashed between them. Xavr looked exhausted, and Kavriel could hear his heavy breathing even from his location on the far side of the cave. The general still smiled confidently, parrying and dodging Xavr's every effort with the blade.

Kavriel looked toward the cave entrance, and saw large black shapes falling like rain. Tess was just beyond the opening, and several other figures were behind her, trying to pull her away. She was struggling against them, staring back at him with desperation in her eyes as she shouted. Several more shapes fell, blocking the entrance. Kavriel looked up and realized that the ceiling was starting to break apart. The cave was coming down around them. He heard Tess scream his name once more before someone pulled her completely into the darkness, and the ceiling came down, barricading any chance of his escape with a wall of stone.

The only thing he could hear now was the fight between Saire and Xavr. He tried to get to his feet, but his body was destroyed beyond measure. Both of his legs had broken when he had hit the wall and his chest was concave, his ribs puncturing at least one of his lungs. He continued to choke on his own blood. He could move only one of his arms; the other was buried underneath a pile of white rocks. He wasn't even sure he had that arm anymore, because he was unable to turn his head that way to see for sure. He felt as if a rope were around his neck and he knew that his back had shattered as well. He was only denying death. The lack of air to his head was beginning to take his consciousness once again as the only remaining men still fought in the white forest of stone.

A scream of anger that could only have come from Saire forced his eyes open one last time, and Kavriel saw what had enraged him.

Kavriel wasn't sure what had happened to the Wylyn, but if he had bested both Grieg and A'zia only to be taken out by Xavr, then the general was a man to be reckoned with . . . if in fact he was a man. He fought like a thunderstorm, appearing and disappearing with such speed to strike at Xavr, the man must have been blessed with luck to have deflected them. His effort was magnificent, but the general was beyond all of this; he seemed almost to be toying with Xavr until the time when he decided he would end it. Xavr must have known that he was no match against the general.

At least that was what Kavriel and obviously the general thought. For Xavr suddenly changed his method of attack. Instead of trying to defend himself against Saire's heavy blade, Xavr became more aggressive, like a dying man fighting for his last breath—to which Kavriel could relate, as he struggled to stay alive just to see this. Xavr spun out of Saire's reach like a shadow slipping away from the burning rays of the sun. He turned his blade toward the white forest encircling them, slicing through the pillars of pureon one after another, as if they were made of chalk.

Saire screamed at Xavr, trying to catch up to him, but Xavr was too far away. The earth shook more angrily this time, and as the pillars dropped to the floor in giant chunks, the general shifted his effort to protecting himself from the collapsing ceiling. Xavr didn't seem to care any longer whether he lived or died, and as the stone sky finally collapsed altogether in one giant sheet, his eyes caught Kavriel's for a moment—and then the blackness took them all.

CHAPTER 8

It was familiar, in the way that dreams always seem familiar when you are in them. Kavriel remembered.

He remembered walking through the tunnels, the dim light thickening and thinning against the texture of the stones, as if a light fog were constantly being swirled by an unnatural wind. It had to have been unnatural, since Kavriel couldn't feel any actual breeze, only see the effects of wind as he continued down the passage. Maybe he was the reason the light moved, opening the path so that he could walk through unobstructed. Either way, it was a dream. It must have been.

Casually strolling through the darkness, Kavriel didn't feel any of the discomfort he normally experienced in the mines. He knew he was in the mine. He remembered the attack, the general, the urns. Yet there was more. He didn't feel pain, though he knew that he had been hurt, badly. Maybe this was simply a memory of his life, now ended. He paused, pondering this, wondering if he was truly dead and this wasn't a dream at all but another stage of existence that could only be experienced at the end of life. Strangely, this didn't bother him; on the contrary, Kavriel felt relief, realizing that he was now free from his suffering. He remembered his family and his friends, but in an almost nostalgic way, recalling only the good times, as if nothing that had transpired in the mines would matter for either him or them.

The world changed shape before his eyes, expanding outward farther and farther until Kavriel was no longer walking through a gray tunnel but a large cavern far beneath the mine. He recognized it immediately.

The cave was almost the same in this dream world as it was in reality, but the tall pillars of pureon could not exist in this place. Only the chalice-shaped basin, gray and weathered, could exist in both worlds, sitting directly in the center of this room as it had in the other.

Kavriel approached it without fear or worry . . . without anything, really. Looking into its hollow center, Kavriel saw the red metallic ooze swirling and bubbling like a simmering stew. He frowned, wondering if he was remembering correctly; had the liquid been in the basin, or in the long golden urns that the general had withdrawn from it? His eyes drifted from it in thought, and that was when he saw a shape standing near the far wall of the cave, hiding in the shadows.

"Hello?" Kavriel called softly and without anxiety, only curiosity.

The shape resolved into a person who stepped out of the shadows toward him. She stopped before reaching the basin, and Kavriel looked at the girl of about fifteen who stood patiently watching him. He did not recognize her. Her dark eyes were cautious, what one would normally expect to see in a young girl alone in a strange place with a strange man.

Kavriel smiled kindly. "I'm Kavriel," he said without emotion, as if he were merely speaking to the wind and not another human being.

She did not respond, but glanced down into the basin, as he had done only moments before. She placed her dainty hands on the stone rim and leaned forward with the curiosity of a child, smiling into the red metallic ooze. "It's beautiful, isn't it?" she asked in a tiny voice.

Kavriel approached the basin, placing his hands on the stone opposite hers. She did not move away but instead smiled politely up at him. Kavriel nodded. "Yes," he said. "Who are you?" Memory stirred. There *was* something familiar about her.

She stared at her reflection in the ooze as if it would provide the answer she needed. "Millie," she said, looking deeply into the liquid before repeating her name again, either to make sure that he had heard, or that she had answered correctly.

Kavriel remembered her now—the girl who had been lost in the mines. The conversation that he and Vaemalin had had with Tess was faint in his memory, but enough.

"Millie," he replied with a smile that must have been one of concern, though he didn't realize it. "There are many people looking for you," he finished, simply reminding the girl of the situation she had been in. It didn't seem to matter any longer in this world.

Millie didn't respond to his statement directly, but returned her attention to the basin. "There have been many people looking for you too, Kavriel . . . for a long time." She looked up at him with a deep knowing in her dark eyes, her hands still gripping the stone. Within, the metallic stew bubbled a bit more.

A strange sensation swept over Kavriel, like a chill breeze had disturbed his warm comfort. He blinked several times as the dull light in the cave seemed to flash, day to the night to day. He ignored it. "I . . . " he began, stumbling over his words. "What do you mean?"

Again the basin churned and the cave flashed. He began to feel pain in his belly, and he put his hand over his mouth as a fit of coughing overtook him. When he removed it, he saw that it was covered in blood.

Millie watched all of this intently. "You have been given a responsibility, Kavriel," she said, speaking to him yet at the same time seeming to speak into the basin. "A great responsibility that was passed to you in a gift, a gift that cannot be denied. You must accept it." She was only a child, but Kavriel didn't see anything childlike in her eyes, but something older, ancient and deadly. Looking into this little girl's eyes was like looking at a crystal clear lake under the afternoon sun and seeing only reflections of black clouds across the water.

Kavriel felt uncomfortable and helpless in the presence of such a creature, whatever she was. Anxiety and fear, two emotions that he had forgotten all about until now, grew within him like the bubbles rising up from the red metallic ooze, the basin steaming like a cauldron as the cave fluttered in and out of existence.

"Responsibility?" he repeated. "What do you mean?" He had suddenly forgotten the girl's name, even forgetting if she had ever offered it. She continued to stare at him. He backed away, feeling trapped. The cave had become a jail and the girl had become his jailor.

She smiled innocently as her image began to fade and his surroundings blurred. She removed her hands from the lip of the stone basin, and leaned back from it. "*Yes . . .*" she hissed with a hint of suppressed rage in her tiny voice, but her smile never left her lips. "You will do just fine."

"It is time, Kav . . . wake up!"

CHAPTER 9

A draft tumbled a ball of dust across the floor of the broken cave. Kavriel blinked, his eyes watering, watching the gray ball move in and out of focus. He blinked several more times, clearing the image as a thin, translucent bubble dissipated from around him like a steam cloud blown apart by the breeze. Lifting his head, he felt a sharp pain course through his neck and back, like stiffness left by a long sleep in an awkward position, and he felt something hard underneath his knees. Why had he been kneeling? He strained to push himself to his feet, wanting to see where he was, but managed only a crouch.

At first, everything seemed unfamiliar. But much like awakening from a deep sleep, his memory of the place slowly returned, and his arms went up instinctively to protect his head from falling debris. Yet there was no more falling debris, only the moon and stars high in the night sky overhead, shining down through the enormous hole in the rock to illuminate his surroundings.

His moment of anxiety passed and he lowered his arms slowly and found the strength to push to his feet, shedding a blanket of white and gray dust from his body as he rose like a corpse from the grave. The thought gave him a sudden chill, and immediately he looked down, examining himself with his eyes and his hands for the damage he remembered suffering. Strangely, there was none. He brought his palms to his face to ensure he truly existed. He flexed his fingers, feeling the cold and the dust as naturally as he should have. Then he looked around.

Kavriel saw all that he remembered. The cave was dark, but brighter, now that the roof had collapsed. Giant sections of it were jumbled over the cave floor, including under his feet. He thought that a bit odd, remembering vividly the feeling of tons of stone crushing him into unconsciousness. There was no way he should have been alive, let alone standing under his own power. The thin pillars of pureon had all been destroyed, pieces strewn about the cave and the remaining bases like white tree stumps, victims of some rampaging logger.

He remembered the man Xavr moving from one to the other during his fight with the general, slicing them apart in order to cause the cave-in. Kavriel glanced up at the open sky where the rooftop had been, recalling that when he had first seen the white forest, he thought that perhaps the pillars had been created simply to hold the cavern together. He had been right, and Xavr must have been thinking the same thing. It was what had saved him.

But where is Xavr? More importantly, where is Saire? The last thought came like a bucket of ice water poured down the back of his neck. Kavriel slowly walked over to the stone cylinder. It was the only intact piece of the mysterious chamber, and it was the last place he had seen the men fighting. As he remembered, the once white stone basin had been darkened by whatever the urns had held, but now the only thing in the cavity were sections of stone ceiling and chunks of pureon.

He walked in a circle around the basin, slowly at first as he made sure he wasn't simply dreaming that his legs were healed. He grimaced, remembering what they had looked like after the general had struck him hard enough to shatter one of the white pillars on impact, and he reached around to the back of his neck, caressing the place where he knew it had snapped. He felt nothing out of the ordinary except some stiffness, but it was enough to make him stop moving. *This isn't right,* Kavriel thought in a panic, wondering if he was alive at all or if this was just some fabrication of his mind as he lay dead under the stones. He had heard stories of men and women who had been on the brink of death, wounded by accidents or gravely ill, who had described in eerie detail their surroundings even though they'd lain unconscious under the worried eyes of their loved ones. The Rav'agas called it a "final separation" from the corporeal body to the ethereal plane of the heavens, with those who returned to the land of the living considered errors of circumstance, having not yet served their allotted time on earth. His people considered the phenomenon survival impulse—during times of danger, the mind would draw images from both memory and thought to keep the body active and alive. Kavriel didn't exactly know what to believe anymore, but he looked over to where he had been kneeling on the ground, fearful that he might see himself lying dead under the rocks, his body broken and ruined. Kavriel inhaled deeply when he saw only stones, tasting the cold salt air of the ocean and the dust of the cavern. Calmer now, he knew his answer was simple: he was alive.

That didn't answer the question of why, however, or what had happened to the others.

Moving quickly around the perimeter of the cave, Kavriel called the names of his friends, his voice hoarse. The cave echoed his calls back to him; that and the sound of the waves against the rocks outside were the only response. Gold glinted here and there, shards from the shattered urns, but he saw no signs that his friends were buried underneath jumbled stones. The thought that they had escaped and were safe buoyed him. Now all that remained was for him to do the same.

After one last pass over the cavern floor to make sure he hadn't missed anything, he rushed over to the cave entrance. That was when his high spirits vanished. He'd been afraid of this, he admitted as he stared at the wall of debris left by the collapse of the ceiling. After a moment in which he considered his chances, Kavriel clambered onto the pile of stones, carefully avoiding jagged edges while listening and feeling for any telltale draft or whistle from dark crevices that he might try to widen into an escape route.

One by one the smaller rocks fell, some on their own, jarred loose by Kavriel's climb, some he had pulled away. Soon sweat soaked his clothes, and cuts from the jagged pieces of stone crisscrossed his hands and arms, blood up to his elbows making him look like he'd dipped his arms in dark red paint.

Finally, exhausted of both hope and energy, Kavriel slid back down to the cavern floor, suppressing the idea that this place might very well be his tomb. He walked back into the chamber with hands on hips, looking up into the night sky and wondering if he could attempt to scale the wall to reach the opening. But looking at the smooth walls, he knew his chance of success was about equal to his chance of sprouting wings and flying out.

He had to get out.

He returned to the blocked passage, moving the

stones and rocks at the bottom of the heap instead of the top. He knew that his chances of success were even slimmer in this direction, but he had to try. He rolled aside a great boulder with surprising ease, revealing a small cavity that had been created underneath the pile of stones that opened up deeper into the tunnel. He nearly cried out in joy.

Lying flat on his stomach, he slid into the opening, trying not to think about how unsafe this truly was as he squirmed completely through into the passage beyond. Pausing, he whistled in the dark, trying to get some sort of vocal perspective, and heard it echo back. Swallowing his claustrophobia as the roof of the tunnel brushed the top of his head, he moved along as rapidly as possible on his stomach. The darkness was complete, his eyes useless. The dirt between his fingers was ice cold, and the air in the cavity was thin and moist. He had no way of knowing how long he squirmed, or which direction he was heading. He concentrated on his basic instincts and let his thoughts drift to deter his fear of being buried alive.

He remembered a time when he and his brother had helped the villagers excavate a waste runoff channel underneath Rhyol. Along with the numerous caverns running under the Highlands, there were also fresh water pockets that the residents had accessed since the town was built, usually by way of wells. The subterranean water was never at risk of drying up, but keeping the waste runoff from the wells tended to be a problem. The village elders had learned of a Rav'agas method called water transfer that made use of segmented underground channels to control water flow. Large reservoirs called cisterns were built on high ground in central locations within a community, and metal tubing carried the water away to numerous smaller wells for public access. Other metal tubes used some of the water to move waste far away from the populated areas. The system was quite ingenious, and had been operating most everywhere in Rav'agas where fresh water was needed.

Ay'vol City had the most sophisticated water-transfer design, so it was said, whose system had bred an artisanal trade of scultpers and architects even, fashioning the city with fountains and bath houses.

With the approval of the overseer, the villagers had attempted the same system on a smaller scale. Kavriel and Vaemalin volunteered as part of the work crew that installed a dozen canals under the city, solving the problem of the waste runoff. The work was difficult, and Kavriel had often waited long hours in the darkness while the miners planned routes to accommodate the hard ground. It wasn't much different from the tunnel he was in now, if only slightly larger—and he'd at least had his brother to talk to while waiting.

A new sound came to Kavriel, drawing his thoughts to the present. He stopped moving and listened. Voices? Were rescuers from his home searching for him? His hopes rose, yet as the sound became more consistent and repetitive he understood exactly what it was—moving water. He froze in panic, trying to see something ahead of him in the impossible darkness. Reaching a tentative hand forward, he touched a soft wall no more than six inches from his face. The miracle tunnel had ended, and he had absolutely no idea how he would manage to worm his way back the way he came. Stifling a sense of hopelessness, he rapidly tried to form another plan.

He felt something sliding over his hand, and bringing it back to his face, he tasted cold sea water on his fingers. It only took a moment more to realize that his clothes were also wet, and that the sound of the water he had heard was that of the sea starting to fill the tunnel. He remembered the passages that the group had travelled to get to the large cave with the basin, and more importantly, he remembered the two Loellen stone-scholars explaining that it was entirely possible they were walking under the sea itself. Xavr's destruction of the white pillars that had led to the collapse of the cave roof must have had an effect on the tunnels leading to it. Kavriel's squirming also must have disturbed the stability of this tunnel.

Fearing imminent death, Kavriel instinctively pushed himself back. The ceiling rumbled as if something had just rolled over it, and ice cold water trickled over his forehead. Within moments, the trickle became a torrent and Kavriel was trapped in a tunnel of black mud. He could no longer move, and the water gushed in from both the end of the tunnel and overhead. Before he could even use his last breath to scream, the ocean destroyed the integrity of the tunnel, and Kavriel was submerged.

Again instinctively, Kavriel kicked his legs behind him and, loosed from the mud by the amount of water, his body moved forward. He was blind and unable to breathe but he flailed his arms nonetheless, swimming through the tunnel for what seemed like an eternity as his lungs burned for air.

The need was too much for him to control, and his

mind told his mouth to open, to suck in anything that might save him. The icy water only heightened the pain in Kavriel's chest, but he gained control of his legs and turned his body upward, then pushed through sheer force of will.

He broke the surface, and his body immediately ejected the sea water he had inhaled and swallowed. He stood up reflexively, but a fit of coughing and vomiting forced him down to his knees, nearly submerging him again. He gasped uncontrollably, but as the air replaced the water in his lungs, Kavriel's thoughts became his own once again, and he forced himself to calm down and regulate his breathing. The spasm passed, and Kavriel raised his head, water running from his open mouth, pain pounding at his brain.

He saw rock icicles hanging from the ceiling and rising up through the lake that had once been a floor. He was in the ore deposit chamber. This realization made him laugh in joy. He had made it one step closer to freedom.

Feeling the strength return to his legs despite the numbing cold of the water, Kavriel stood. He was waist-deep in sea water that was slowly trickling in from small fissures in the ceiling. He looked behind him, unable to see the tunnel that he had crawled through to get here; it was underwater. The breach that he had made now connected this cavern to the other, and he could feel the sea water began pushing past him. He imagined the basin chamber now filling and wondered how long that would take. He wasn't going to stick around to find out.

Sloshing through the water, Kavriel clambered over a rock that had fallen from the ceiling near the exit, using it as a ramp up to the drier tunnel. He remembered this one.

Even without any kind of light to assist him, Kavriel moved confidently along the passage, using his hands as guides. Encountering one of the oak doors that had sealed this passage earlier, he pulled the door open without wondering why it was closed and stepped out into a cross tunnel. The light was better here—or perhaps his eyes had simply adjusted—and he paused only a moment to remember which direction to go before stumbling down the left passage.

He encountered another oak door. Again he yanked it open and stepped into another split corridor. Unfortunately, this choice was not as fortuitous as his first one; the passage he took was blocked by another cave-in, and he turned in the unfamiliar direction with trepidation, unsure of where it would lead and struggling to remember his father's map of the mine. He could picture it in his mind, but when he had looked at it with the others he'd been hampered by headaches and dizziness and the memory was unfocused. He was grateful, though confused, that the headaches didn't affect him anymore, but that didn't help him now. He could only follow this path with hope that it would lead to the main room near the mine entrance. One thing he did recall was that all of the completed passages did just that, so eventually he would reach the entrance. *That is, if there aren't anymore cave-ins blocking the way.*

As if thinking this prompted its existence, Kavriel noticed the walls of the passage narrowing, and he already knew that this was another dead end before he got there. Yet when he rounded a gentle curve he saw that it wasn't completely closed off; a large crack creeping up the curved wall allowed in the fresh sea air and what must have been moonlight. Gripping the edges of the fissure with both hands, he pushed his head into the opening and, eyes closed, inhaled the fresh air of freedom. His hope returned, and Kavriel pulled himself up into the crack. It was just wide enough for him to pass through.

The cold wind touched his wet clothes as he shifted himself through the rock, but to him it felt wonderful. He had escaped. At least he thought so.

The wind seemed to have increased threefold, and it froze his wet hair instantly as he clutched the rock so he would not be blown over. Quickly surveying his surroundings, he saw that he was indeed out of the mines and now clinging to the side of one of the many jagged mountains of rock that dotted the North Sea. It was a clear night and, judging by the position of the gibbous moon, Kavriel guessed it was about three hours before dawn.

He had entered the mine in the morning, and after the events leading up to his unconsciousness, he figured he must have been missing eight to ten hours by now. If his friends had escaped, they would have had enough time to reach Rhyol for help . . . *If they escaped.* He remembered Tess screaming to him from the entrance to the roofless chamber. There was no way he could know if she'd escaped with the others, let alone escaped the general or Xavr, if either of those men tried to go after them.

He needed to be certain. The only thing he could be sure of was that he had survived, but looking at his situation, clinging to an outcropping of rock out in the ocean with no direct path back to the island, he wasn't sure how long that would last. Grateful for the clear night that allowed him to easily see the sheds, the chimneys, and the large domed forge of the Mir camp from his location, he was also frustrated by his inability to *get* there. Or for anyone to get to him. He had no boat, no raft, nothing that would keep him afloat in the thrashing, white-capped black waves. No vessel could maneuver along this part of the shoreline. The currents were much too strong, also meaning swimming was not an option.

He looked the other way, seeing that the next outcropping was ten or fifteen feet away from his. The rocks were jagged, but if he moved slowly Kavriel thought he might just be able to reach it after only being in the water for mere moments. He was certain he could swim the ten-odd feet, but he had no idea how cold the water was and how quickly his body might stiffen up once he was in it. What he'd felt while in the mine was certainly cold. Add to that the wind, colder than expected, certainly colder than it had been during the morning. He looked back to the shore, and without wanting to ponder too long on it, Kavriel thought he actually saw *snow* in the camp—but he knew that was impossible, even in the Highlands. It was too early by far. Even so, this would be no bathwater he'd be swimming in.

Waiting for a lull in the gusts of wind, Kavriel pressed his body against the rock face and began shuffling along the ledge he stood on, moving around the outcropping. He kept his cheek to the stone, hands outstretched, seeking handholds as he moved inch by inch to the side of the rock closest to the next. He couldn't know where or how far the next outcropping would be from that one, or the next after that, but he knew he would at least be closer to the shore. If it came down to it and he had to swim, he would have a slightly better chance nearer to land, where the water might not be so deep.

He made it to a spot close to the next outcropping, where the water churned less, and summoning all his courage, he pushed off, propelling himself as far out and thus as close as he could to the next mountain. He hit the water with a splash and the cold blackness wrapped around him like the cold embrace of winter itself. He kicked as hard as he could, surfacing and then swimming for the jagged rock about an arm's length away from his outstretched hand.

Unfortunately the sea had other plans for him. A powerful current between the two rocks pulled him away as if he were grabbed by muscular arms and dragged. He struggled against the inexorable flow, unable to match its power as it forced him away from the rock and out into the open sea. He became blinded by salt water, feeling only his body bobbing uncontrollably in the waves like a cork. It was all he could do to keep his head above the water, and the intense cold was numbing his limbs.

The current abruptly changed direction, pushed aside by some larger underwater flow, and Kavriel was thrust upward, almost entirely out of the water. But his freedom from the sea's grip lasted only as long as the next white-capped wave. *The sea is playing with me, spitting me out only to pull me back in!* Kavriel thought as it smashed him back underwater. He clawed sputtering back to the surface, trying to stay afloat long enough to get his bearings. *It's going to finish the job the mine was unable to do.* He would not be crushed and suffocated by dirt and stone. No, he would die cold and drowned at the bottom of the ocean, if it had a bottom at all.

As the sea used Kavriel's body as a plaything, it hurled him against something hard, solid—a different sensation from the knocking of the frothing black waves. He no longer could feel pain; the ice water had numbed him, and his left arm had become useless. It smashed him against the solid thing again, and Kavriel saw that it was another of the many mountainous boulders that marched from shore to sea. *It wants to break me before drowning me,* Kavriel thought.

The waves picked him up and tossed him again, and this time his head smashed against the rock. The world turned silent and black. He no longer saw the water, felt the waves or the frigid wind; he could feel and see nothing. Yet he could still hear, the sounds dull and echoing in a world submerged. The cruel tide was gentler under the surface of the water, and it no longer forced him where it wanted him to go but gently guided him. It was almost peaceful. It was musical, the waves heard underwater harmonizing, singing to each other, and effortlessly lulling Kavriel to sleep. He would go now, Kavriel decided. He was comfortable. He felt safe under the many layers of dark blue blankets. His lungs did not burn, his body did not feel, yet something kept him awake, kept him conscious even without sight, sensation, or breath. The music of the sea rose in volume. His bed rocked.

Kavriel's limbs began to twitch of their own accord, and his legs pushed his knees forward then his feet down to stand, while his arms swept out, forcing his head to rise. A sharp pain suddenly attacked his body, moving from his chest and back to flow down his arms and legs and then his hands and feet as if he were caught in a firestorm that came from within his own body. He gasped as his lungs awoke, aching to inhale. A current pushed his bed from behind, and the music of the sea became clearer. Another sound joined the melody.

It was the wind.

Kavriel cried out as soon as the air entered his empty lungs, like a newborn child's first cry. He opened his eyes, seeing nothing at first but a dull grayness, then the stars shone brightly down, helping him focus. Cold wind rushed over his body, freezing on his skin and stiffening his clothes. He pulled himself to his feet again and he stood waist-deep in the water just off the shore by the Mir camp. He was saved. With his ability to see and breathe came the ability to feel, and a pain like a thousand swords pierced every part of his body.

Clutching his left shoulder to support the arm hanging limply at his side, he splashed ashore, imagining the ocean waves screaming their frustration behind him as he set foot on dry land. He didn't look back. He didn't care. He was alive again.

But he shouldn't be. The thought haunted him.

He tried to rationalize this miracle as he stumbled into the camp, legs wobbling as they began to weaken. He approached the nearest block-shaped shed, his exhausted body nearly crumpling on the threshold. His hand found the latch and he pushed the door open, then tumbled into the black interior, escaping the cold wind. With what was left of his energy, Kavriel stripped off his wet clothes, which tore away like old rags. He kicked off what was left of his boots, and now clad only in his skin, he searched for anything dry to clothe himself. A great shaggy coat, dirty with age and smelling of dust, hung from a hook near the door; he quickly pulled it over his shoulders, wincing at the pain in his arm. He continued to move, knowing that if he stopped now, whatever miracle had saved him from the sea would prove fruitless.

He saw a fireplace on one wall, with dry tinder and logs beside the hearth. He fell to his knees, tossing logs and tinder into the fire pit, teeth clenched, forcing himself to stay awake. Nearby he found a flint and iron and with painful difficulty succeeded in sparking the tinder into flame. Desperate to drive the agony of deep cold from his body, Kavriel grabbed everything and anything that would burn—tinder, books, wooden plates from a side table, even an oil lamp that he smashed open went into the fireplace. The flame grew, and the logs caught and began to burn, throwing heat out into the room.

Kavriel knelt directly in front of the flames, still feeling the rhythmic prodding of the invisible swords, though they had become less painful. The throbbing in his head began to recede and his eyes sagged shut. Before the first log in the fire pit cracked, Kavriel had slumped forward from his knees and was fast asleep.

CHAPTER 10

There were no dreams this time, as far as Kavriel could recall. Only a darkness as silent and deep as the mine itself. It took his thoughts, and his memories were only shadows. It was the first time in a long time that Kavriel had slept so peacefully and so deeply. His mind was his own. He was sharing it with no one and the dark was for him alone. If he'd been aware of it he would have been relieved.

A gust from the shoreline pushed open the door that Kavriel hadn't bothered to latch. An icy salt breeze tousled Kavriel's hair and his eyes opened to stare into a mound of ash in a long-cold fire pit that reminded him of where he was. It was still dark in the shed, and looking over at the open door wagging in the breeze, he was surprised to see that it was still dark outside. He felt as if he had slept for eons. He stood slowly and walked over to the door, clutching the heavy coat tightly around him.

The sky was still clear, the stars shining however faintly against the solid glare of the moon. Yet Kavriel noticed that the moon was no longer hanging over the eastern horizon, but higher and a bit more centered in the sky. He had slept long, and judging by the moon the night had passed into day and into night again. Almost two days had passed since the doomed exploration had begun, and if there had been any rescue attempt, the men of Rhyol would be focusing on the mines and not the camp. Not finding anything in the tunnels except cave-ins and water, the men would return to the overseer in discouragement. They would have to tell the father that his boy was buried.

Kavriel knew that he needed to return home as quickly as possible, but that it might be more difficult than he wished. His ordeals had weakened him; without a horse, boots and especially clothes, Kavriel might make it through Mir, but not through Silver Wood. Not only that, the wind was damp and cold—*Colder than I remember it being,* he thought, looking down at his bare feet and then at the thin layer of snow on the ground. *That should be impossible, snow this early in the season.* Yet there it was, and with no footprints leading from the water to the shed that would have traced Kavriel's route, he realized that it must have snowed again sometime during the night . . . or day.

The rescuers wouldn't even have bothered to check the camp.

Moonlight reflected brightly off the white ground, giving Kavriel a much clearer view of his surroundings. He felt very alone in the silent night, even more so than when he had awakened in the basin chamber in the mine.

Kavriel moved back into the shed and knelt before the fireplace. Lifting a poker, he jabbed at the ash and blackened remains of the logs, hoping for some coal to spring back to life. Nothing. Not even a hint of warmth remained of the once roaring fire. He looked around, seeing the broken lamp and the mess he had created the night he arrived, and knew he had overstayed his welcome.

Tossing the poker aside, he rose, letting the heavy coat drop to the floor. He looked over his hands and arms, his feet and legs, his chest and stomach for any sign of the damage that had been done to him in the mine and when he was in the ocean. There was nothing—no breaks, no cuts, no bruises, no marks. Absolutely nothing.

Kavriel bent to retrieve the coat from the floor and his confusion was further heightened as he realized that he had reached for the coat with the once useless arm. He raised it in front of him, flexing his fingers and moving his arm in a circle to test the strength of his shoulder. There was nothing wrong with it, and Kavriel pulled the heavy coat over his shoulders, puzzled that he could remember the agony of his arm the night before but there was no actual proof of it now.

I am losing my mind.

Reminded by the chill wind that he was wearing little, he glanced around the shed. It was larger than he had thought, and he wondered what its purpose had been. Besides the fireplace and a long table with almost a dozen chairs that he had slammed aside when he came in, there was a wardrobe near a few cots along the opposite wall that he had not noticed. A rest area or infirmary? It was far enough away from the noises of the forge for the workers who had been hurt or tired, or a place away from the dust and smoke to have their lunch.

He walked over and opened the wardrobe door, seeing with relief several pairs of pants, shirts, and boots stored within. He found suitably sized clothes and quickly dressed, pulling the heavy coat back on for added warmth. Kavriel wondered again about the place, looking at the clothes and the boots of fine leather he wore. There was absolutely no way someone would leave all this stuff behind, and after twenty years, it wouldn't be in this condition. It was as if someone had recently stocked this building. Was someone living in the camp without anyone's knowledge? The thought startled him, but then he felt guilty for being in this place that wasn't his and taking clothes that didn't belong to him. *Time to leave.* He would worry about whoever lived here another time.

Cinching the coat around his waist with a belt he found hanging on the wardrobe door latch, Kavriel stepped out onto the snowy shore, thankful for the boots, even if they were stolen. He carefully closed the door behind him, resetting the latch so the wind wouldn't blow it open, then moved quickly through the camp. He ignored the other sheds and shelters, the dome forge where they had tethered the horses, the bellows and the carts.

Kavriel stopped when he saw the opening of the mine, black against the heavy mountain of rock touching the ocean. He walked slowly over to it, as if it were the mouth of some dangerous beast that would swallow him again if he got too close. Yet as he approached, Kavriel noticed in the moonlight that the shape of the adit was still as he remembered, but it was closed off by a heavy metal gate, recently installed, and with a large circular lock to keep it shut. Kavriel placed his hands on the cold bars, giving them good shake. They were real, not figments of his imagination as he had feared, but he still did not feel any better for the discovery.

He stepped back from the gate, and Kavriel looked around at the snow as he thought again about the length of time that he had been gone. Worry greater than when he had been trapped in the water-filled tunnel under the mines made his heart pound. The snow was something that could be explained. It was early, but not entirely impossible. Having snow three months before the midwinter festival would be rare, but possible. The locked iron gate was not so easy to explain. Even if the overseer had called off the search for his son and ordered a new barricade to the mines to prevent further mishaps it would have taken longer for this. It would take at least a day just for the blacksmith to form and weld the metal, let alone install it in the adit. Shivering with a chill that wasn't caused by the wind this time, Kavriel turned from the mine and hurried to the path that would take him to Mir Town, then Silver Wood, and then home.

When he reached the top of the ridge overlooking the camp from Mir Town, he froze. Light glowed in the windows and the streets were alive with noise and movement. Had he actually awakened at all?

Rousing himself from his shock, Kavriel cautiously moved toward the main street through town. Flames flickered under the glass shells of the streetlamps, casting pools of orange and yellow light over the snow. A few people, bundled against the winter and leaning close to one another for conversation, walked down the road, snow crunching underfoot. Kavriel slowly walked past them, feeling delusional and lost. The people were certainly real; they nodded politely to him while passing.

He continued walking for a few moments more before the strangeness of it all suddenly began to make him dizzy. The smell of fire and food caught his nose, and following his basic instincts to distract himself from the more baffling details, Kavriel stopped at the door to a large, brightly lit building standing at a crossroads. He glanced up at the plaque nailed over the door; it pictured a miner standing with his pickaxe embedded in the top of a wooden barrel, from which a frothy liquid poured. Underneath were the words *The Backfill*. It wasn't until Kavriel opened the door that he realized he had found a tavern.

The heat from a roaring fire instantly warmed Kavriel as soon as he stepped inside, and hearty conversation mixed with laughter almost deafened him after his last two days in near silence. He moved quickly out of the way as two large men holding each other up stumbled out the door, still clutching half-filled mugs in their meaty hands. Spying a small vacant table, he moved along the wall toward it, knowing an empty seat was a rare find on a cold night, and after what he had experienced in the last couple of days, he needed to sit down.

Rhyol's own tavern, The White Rock Hold, was operated by the heavyset and boisterous Lady Cavyl, a true legend for years for her cooking and her social skills. Originally from a small clan in Port Dior, Amila Cavyl had relocated with her family as a child to Rhyol when the mines first prospered, and had grown up to be the most respected woman in all of the Highlands. She knew just about everything and anything concerning Rhyol, Nostrac Isle, and even the politics of Teltraum. The elders and even Overseer Soelle could barely tolerate the woman, but they had a deep respect for her boldness. Kavriel, Vaemalin, and Grieg were scared to death of Amila Cavyl but Tess loved her.

Kavriel was hoping to see Lady Cavyl running this tavern, if anything to give him some piece of mind, knowing that he hadn't truly gone over the edge of sanity. Yet The Backfill was about as opposite to The White Rock Hold as light was to darkness, filled with the most decrepit assortment of drunks he had seen in his life. They guzzled ale out of mugs and pitchers with ferocious thirst, stumbling around the room and pinching the bottoms of any figure that resembled a woman while shouting conversations to everyone and no one at all. Kavriel wondered if the name The Backfill referred to the mine or to its patrons.

He pulled out a rickety wooden chair that looked as tottery as the drunk patrons and sat down quickly, hunching forward and cupping his hands together on the table. He didn't wish to be noticed, but within moments a thin woman wearing a dirty apron that must once have been white approached his table. She looked at Kavriel silently and raised an expectant eyebrow.

He recognized her as a server, and cleared his throat as he looked up nervously. "Um . . . I'll have whatever that delicious smell is, please." He forced a smile.

Her sour expression relaxed somewhat. "Lamb," she said abruptly. "Potatoes and spice." Her expression didn't change, and it took a moment for Kavriel to realize that she had just told him what it was he had ordered.

He nodded with a more genuine smile, associating the smell with food that he liked. "That sounds wonderful . . . thank you."

"Ale," she continued in the same emotionless tone. Kavriel nodded again. It hadn't been an actual question but his response seemed to be all the information she needed; the woman turned and disappeared into the crowd, stopping at a few other tables where bleary-eyed locals sat nodding to her words, probably the same ones she had said to him. She had approached them with the same rigid posture, and Kavriel wondered if this was a nightly routine. Looking around at the crowd, he could understand her gruffness.

Even though he refrained from keeping his eyes on any one person for long, Kavriel noticed that a group of five men at a table nearby were watching him intently. He smiled politely, giving them a quick survey to see if they were men that he recognized. Mir was not that far from Rhyol, and despite the incongruity of a ghost town suddenly becoming a lively community during the time that Kavriel was underground, he hoped to find some anchor to his life that he remembered. One of the men seemed vaguely familiar, but he couldn't tell for sure.

Yet as five pairs of eyes watched him with the intensity of a pack of dogs eyeing a stray cat, Kavriel decided against introductions, and turned his attention away from the men. The server returned sooner than he had expected, making it easier for him to ignore their scrutiny. She placed a large bowl in front of him that was full of meat chunks swimming in a thick brown sauce, with some stone-sized white potatoes alongside. Thunking a rather sizable mug of dark red ale that she had been holding in her other hand onto the table, she pulled a cold loaf of bread from under her arm, deposited it on the table as well, and quickly disappeared.

Kavriel must have been hungrier than he thought, emptying the bowl of lamb stew and wiping the remaining bits of sauce from the bottom with his bread before he even touched the ale. The stew was overly spiced for his taste, but it was hot and tasty enough to quell the hunger in his stomach. Reaching for the mug of red ale, he took a long pull. He emptied the mug almost as quickly as he had the bowl of stew. As he placed the empty mug on the table the server returned as if summoned by the sound of an empty mug hitting the tabletop.

With his caution dampened by the effects of the ale, Kavriel decided to get some answers. "Excuse me," he said as the server quickly stacked his plate onto others that she had been carrying. She didn't glance at him but made a humming sound that Kavriel assumed meant "continue." Startled that she was open to conversation, Kavriel suddenly wasn't sure what he should ask without sounding too crazy. He hesitated, and the moment was long enough for her to shift irritated dark eyes to his face. She was obviously busy, and knowing that he needed to speak fast, Kavriel blurted the first words that came to mind. "I'm looking for some friends of mine."

She blinked wordlessly, her expression bored, but she hung around, so Kavriel figured she was probably waiting for more information. "Yes . . . um, a group of men and a woman. My age . . . my friends and my brother, not from around here. Uh, they might have come from the mine camp." Kavriel was stammering, trying to make sense to someone else something that didn't even make sense to him.

She must have sensed it, as her eyebrow rose again. "The camp? Nobody's been in from the camp since last fall. If you or your friends were down there, then you shouldn't be saying that aloud in here. Camp's off limits in winter."

Her eyes were studying him. Kavriel had known it was possible that his question might cause something like this, but he had already found out more from her response than what he had known. His shock at realizing that his two days in the mines had suddenly turned out to be much longer must have shown on his face. Her expression became inquisitive.

"I was . . ." he began, wondering what he could possibly say. "I only meant that they might have been in that direction. I . . . we are not from around here. We just arrived from Rhyol." He hoped his response might ease her curiosity, but instead she seemed hostile. Her eyes narrowed and her face stiffened.

"Rhyol," she repeated with more heat in her voice than he'd expected—with more volume, too. She put the stack of dirty plates that she had been holding on the table so she could rest her hands on her hips. She leaned down close to Kavriel's face and hissed, "You pay for your meal, and you get out."

The noise level in the crowded room abruptly dropped, as patrons turned interested eyes toward Kavriel's corner. He ducked his head and reached into the pockets of his pants for some coins—and suddenly remembered that the clothes he wore were not his own. His fingers desperately probed the empty pockets. She immediately interpreted the embarrassment in his face, and leaned back from the table. A small red vein began to pulse in the center of her forehead. Her lips tightened into white lines on her reddening face, and she nodded as if expecting this. Kavriel smiled humbly as he mouthed an apology for his mistake. It was too late. The server's anger blew out.

"You rotten, no good Rhyol trash," she shouted at him. "You're all the same, the dirty lot of you!"

Kavriel was stunned. He had seen Lady Cavyl give a defaulting client a harsh word or two, but she would

never say something so venomous. The server continued
her diatribe, full of curses, while pointing an accusing
finger at him. The curls on her head bobbed violently after
each word. The other patrons were quickly aware of what
was going on; Kavriel heard muttered comments in the
crowd that echoed her own opinions of people from Rhyol.
His attempt at anonymity had failed horribly. Kavriel knew
that it was only a matter of time before he found himself
strapped to the sink or tossed out the window.

A man approached behind the animated woman.
Kavriel immediately recognized him as one of the men
sitting at the other table, watching him. He placed a hand
on the server's shoulder and she whirled, ready to give this
new arrival the same tongue-lashing she'd given Kavriel,
but when she saw who it was, she suddenly became more
subdued. It was almost as if she was ashamed that he had
come over, and fearful. Kavriel didn't know what to make
of it.

"Easy, Mesi," the man said, keeping his grip on her
shoulder. "I'll pay for the meal, plus a little extra for your
patience." His dark eyes looked deeply at the server, who
quickly shifted her gaze to the floor. He released her
shoulder, and she bowed more formally than Kavriel would
expect to see anyone sober do in a tavern. She collected her
dishes and moved away from the table without a second
look in their direction.

The man remained, but Kavriel didn't feel any more
relieved. He had not been raised to feel this way with the
generosity of a helping hand, but recent events in his life
had shaken him deeply. He was ashamed at his feelings,
and he was nervous and scared. There was nothing that

could change that now. Kavriel only hoped that he didn't look as uncomfortable as he felt.

He surreptitiously observed the stranger standing proudly over him. He was slightly older than him, perhaps the same age as Vaemalin. He was fair, clean-shaven, and his eyes, dark brown beneath equally dark, thick eyebrows, regarded Kavriel with a peculiar interest. He wore a heavy brown coat over his shoulders, cut in the Highland fashion, but with no clan stitching that Kavriel could see or recognize. It covered a black, soft leather vest that was inlaid with some kind of reddish-gold pattern Kavriel couldn't make out.

Kavriel had no idea who this man was, but he was fairly certain by the man's posture and dress that he must be a soldier. The man was waiting for him to say something, and Kavriel cleared his throat, wondering if he had just escaped one problem only to drop into another. At least the other patrons of the tavern had seemed to lose interest, Kavriel noticed, their eyes returned to their mugs of ale.

"Thank you," he said to the strange man. "I am in your debt." Feeling awkward, he wiped a sweaty hand on his shirt before offering it to the stranger, who took it casually then held it in a surprisingly firm grip. Kavriel actually had to struggle briefly to have it returned to him.

"You are quite welcome," the man answered before looking down at another of the rickety chairs tucked under the table. "May I join you?"

Kavriel immediately held his open hand toward the second chair, smiling politely. The stranger had spoken calmly but much too precisely to both him and the server,

Kavriel suddenly realized, and there was something too particular about how the man had accentuated his words, as if he were making sure that he pronounced them correctly. Kavriel knew he should have been able to place the slight accent, but maybe it would come to him later.

The stranger pulled his coat aside to sit down, but he moved too quickly for Kavriel to see the symbol on his vest. He sat in the chair regarding Kavriel with keen interest, keeping his arm across the tabletop as if intentionally preventing Kavriel from seeing it.

"I am a little embarrassed," Kavriel said, shifting his gaze back to the man's dark eyes. "Things have been a bit strange for me recently. I don't seem to have a clear head." He spoke the truth with a smile, hoping that if indeed this man was a soldier, or at least a guardsman, he stood a better chance of getting back home than on his own.

The man nodded, his face a mask, as if he didn't quite understand. "I overheard you speaking with Mesi. I understand you are from Rhyol?"

"Yes." Kavriel nodded.

"Have you recently arrived?" the man continued, and Kavriel nodded again, not wishing to split hairs on how long he might have actually been in Mir. Until he knew for himself, he wasn't about to mention lost time to a complete stranger, even if he was a guardsman. The calm nod the man responded with was actually comforting, and there was something in his eyes that seemed to lessen Kavriel's tension. "That would explain things, then." The stranger spoke with a certainty that Kavriel didn't understand, but he nodded with a smile, regardless.

"What business brings you to Mir Town?" the man

asked, following with choices before Kavriel had a chance to respond: "Trade? Work? Drink?" The last word was accompanied by a shrewd smile that Kavriel couldn't be entirely sure was one of jest or simple cunning.

Kavriel chuckled—perhaps too over the top a response, but he was still in this man's debt and he wanted to continue to remain on his good side. He noticed that the man's smile didn't reach his eyes, however, and he continued watching Kavriel with almost interrogative attention. "Are you a guardsman?" he asked in a friendly tone, already assuming the answer.

Interest flared in the stranger's eyes and his smile became toothy, wolfish. "That would depend on your answer, man from Rhyol," he replied.

Kavriel immediately realized that his attempt at simple social interaction had made him look even more suspicious. He had answered the man's question with a question; who wouldn't think that he was hiding something? Kavriel knew then that if he wanted this man's help, he would have to be as honest as possible—within limits, of course. The complete truth was much too bizarre. The general, the urns, and the fight in the mines would make him sound all kinds of crazy. They were things that Kavriel hadn't been able to wrap his head around, especially while he was sitting in room full of folks in a tavern that shouldn't even exist. Still, he needed to find help from anyone who would offer it, if he was to understand what had happened.

"I'm sorry, as I said before, this isn't a good day for me," Kavriel said, trying not to sound too desperate. An idea came to him suddenly; it might sound convincing and gain the guardsman's confidence. "My friends and I we were looking for a girl from my town who was lost. It's possible she came here. She's young, no more than fourteen or fifteen years. Her family misses her. Have you seen anyone in town that might be her?"

Yet as he mentioned the missing Kessor child to the guardsman, something nagged in the back of his mind, a thought or a faded memory of something that he was certain involved the girl. He couldn't remember what.

The stranger seemed taken in by his concern; he pursed his lips together, nodding slowly. "Perhaps I would. A lost girl from Rhyol would be hard not to notice." There was no compassion in his voice. He wasn't sure if the man believed him or not, but Kavriel felt slightly reassured.

"The others in your party that you mentioned, your friends. Tell me about them," the man urged.

The question seemed odd to Kavriel, but without hesitation he described his brother, Tess, Grieg, and A'zia—anything to help him find an ally. He didn't mention the stone-scholars, Xavr, Saire's Wylyn bodyguard, or especially Saire himself. Kavriel wanted to be certain that he could trust the man before revealing anything more. When he finished the stranger said nothing right away, but his gaze became distant, his eyes glittering, as if his thoughts were suddenly focused on something else. Kavriel hoped it was only a reflex in the man's memory, and that it was possible he did remember someone from Kavriel's group.

He stared at Kavriel, one gloved hand over his lips in consideration. "I see," he replied after a considerable, awkward pause. "I regret that I have not seen your friends.

What did you say your brother's name was?"

Kavriel couldn't entirely be certain, but for a moment he sensed the guardsman's interest change. "Vaemalin, Vaemalin Soelle." When the stranger didn't react right away he decided to explain in detail who his brother was and what he looked like. The stranger seemed to be eating the words as hungrily as Kavriel had eaten the lamb stew. His unease returned, and he quickly stopped speaking before he revealed that Vaemalin was the son of the Rhyol Overseer. There was something in that little detail that he didn't feel would go over so well in this tavern. Not after what he had heard them whisper about his town, not to mention the server's tirade.

Unfortunately it seemed that he had said too much already. The stranger raised a hand behind his head, motioning with two fingers for the group that had been with him to join them. Within moments Kavriel had gone from the quiet man sitting alone in the corner of a crowded tavern to the focus of dozens of eyes, all watching four large, uniformed men rise from the nearby table and surround him. When they came close, Kavriel was able to recognize what he had heard in the guardsman's voice. He had been speaking with a Rav'agas accent, well concealed when he had spoken the northern tongue to Kavriel. He knew this because the four men who stood solid and motionless around the table wore black and gold uniforms, and embroidered on the chest of those uniforms was the badge of the Patriarch's Ay'vol Force.

The same symbol, Kavriel now saw with the movement of the stranger's arm, was embroidered on the stranger's own vest.

His situation could not get much worse. He should have kept his mouth shut and taken his chances with the angry server instead, Kavriel thought, staring at the red three-bladed cross emblem and struggling to understand this nightmare world he had awakened to as his courage crumbled away.

No one he knew had ever visited the southern nation. The politics were much too volatile, the belief system too rigid, their class system too disparate, creating enormous gaps of wealth between communities. The luxury of Ay'vol City and the Patriarch's Palace itself were legendary. Yet political or financial clout weren't what made Rav'agas dangerous. It was her faith. For hundreds of years The Way had explained the prosperity of Ay'vol Province as due to the Patriarch's direct relation to the Creator himself, whose descendents were placed above the rest of the children of man, enjoying wealth, land, nourishment, and title.

It was also well known that Ay'vol Province sat in a valley containing hundreds of miles of the most fertile ground in the entire nation. The Patriarch spoke of it as part of the Creator's gift but the more cynical Rav'agas, living poorly in the desert, said that was the true reason for Ay'vol's wealth.

It was rare, to say the least, to see a soldier of the Ay'vol Guard on the Quetalian mainland, let alone Nostrac. Yet there were a contingent of five in Kavriel's nightmare, surrounding him.

"What is your name, man from Rhyol?" the stranger asked Kavriel, sitting comfortably in his chair. He must be an officer, Kavriel guessed. Nothing he wore differentiated him from the others, but there was an aura of command about him. Either that, or he was the only one of them able to understand the northern tongue. The four soldiers didn't show any kind of response to what their officer was saying.

"Kavriel Soelle," he replied meekly, noticing that the crowded tavern had become very quiet. Those who had been laughing and drinking earlier suddenly seemed to have sobered up, and many were actually leaving. Kavriel felt the wind as the large door swung open several times, and he wished he could be with them.

"Soelle," the man mused, no longer concealing his Rav'agas accent.

Blood pounded in Kavriel's head, triggering a headache. He felt as if his chair had been moved closer to the fire. He stopped himself from wiping at the beads of sweat that had sprung up on his forehead.

"Soelle. Why do I feel that I have heard that name before?" The man looked away a moment, tapping his lips with a forefinger.

Kavriel glanced up at the four other soldiers, seeing the firelight glinting on the hilts of their blades. They were all watching him, but waiting patiently, as if awaiting an order from their commander. Kavriel had no idea what was happening, but he knew it couldn't be good. The tavern continued to empty out, little by little but with obvious haste on the part of the patrons.

The man looked back at Kavriel, grinning wickedly. "Tell me, Kavriel, where would I have heard that name before?" he asked, his tone hinting that he already knew.

Kavriel swallowed. "I . . . I don't know. If you had been to Rhyol, perhaps you would have heard the name before. We are a small family, but well known in the community." He still didn't want to reveal his father's status in Rhyol. He'd take that information to the grave with him before telling members of the Ay'vol Force.

The man smiled again, cheerfully this time, as if Kavriel had just told a joke. "Well known! Yes, that must be it!" The man laughed again, and lifted his head to speak in Rav'agas to the soldiers.

Kavriel focused on the phrasing, struggling to remember the fundamentals of the Southern tongue. The man was speaking in standard dialect, but much too fast for Kavriel to grasp entire sentences. He caught only words, including Vaemalin, brother, girl, lost, and what he thought was gift . . . or *reward*. He kept his face blank, as if he could understand none of it. The soldiers' expressions suggested that they took what their commander was saying very seriously, and after he finished, they glanced at Kavriel and laughed, as if he had just been the subject of some joke. Kavriel forced out a laugh with them, hoping that feigned ignorance of his situation might help him. It wasn't that far from the truth.

The commander then barked an order to them, ending their amusement. One of the uniformed men moved to the tavern entrance just as the last patron exited. He pushed the door firmly shut, and locked it. Terrified, Kavriel glanced past the men toward the back of the tavern, where he had seen the server go into the kitchen. He must have been too obvious, because the man who had barred the front door then walked in that direction. He disappeared into the rear, and Kavriel knew that he was looking to seal any other exit in the building.

He was trapped in a room with five of the Ay'vol
Force, whose ruthlessness was enough to give any child or
adult nightmares. He wished he was back in the water-filled
tunnel underneath the mines. Drowning would be less
cruel. Looking back to the man seated at the table, Kavriel
saw that he was watching him confidently, like a cat that
had just cornered a mouse.

"When was the last time you saw your friends?" the
man asked.

Kavriel knew the only thing he could do now was
answer as quickly as possible. He had no idea why these
men were holding him, and even less idea what they
intended to do. "This morning," he lied. He had already
said that he had just arrived in Mir Town. He wasn't about
to change his story. Not now.

The officer continued with his questions. "Your
party. How many were with you?" Kavriel had already sort
of answered that question earlier when he spoke of the
others in the group, but the conversation had turned into an
interrogation, and the officer was clearly checking
Kavriel's responses against what he'd said earlier.

"Five . . . including me."

"Are they all from Rhyol, like you and this girl who
supposedly went missing?"

Kavriel replied with a jerky nod. He had never been
very good at lying, and this was clearly not the first time
that this man had questioned people.

The officer noticed Kavriel's hesitancy, and his
finger stopped tapping on his lip. He placed his both hands
on the tabletop and leaned forward, gazing deeply into
Kavriel's eyes. "Are you certain?"

"No," Kavriel replied, feeling broken. "One of them was . . . she was from another village," he tried, but already being caught in a lie, Kavriel found it difficult to resist the officer's questioning.

The man's expression turned smug. He had him. "Not from the island?"

The question caught Kavriel off guard; he paused before shaking his head, blinking too many times.

The stranger smiled. "Then from the mainland?" he almost crooned, and again it stumped Kavriel, causing him to shake his head before he realized his error and stopped. He cursed under his breath as the man's jaw clenched angrily. "Where is she from?" he asked.

Kavriel couldn't hide that secret any longer. "West Point," he muttered

Immediately, the officer's mood changed. His eyes widened, as if he were surprised.

Of course—he wouldn't expect a Rav'agas location as a response. Kavriel felt as if his head was about to explode as the political problems of the southern provinces leapt to his mind. West Point was one of the provinces that had abandoned Ay'vol Province by allying with Quetal, and Kavriel had just said that one of his friends was from West Point while sitting alone with five members of the Ay'vol Force. He might as well have said that he was an assassin hired to murder the Patriarch.

"Is she, now?" the man said with an almost giddy chuckle that lasted only as long as it took for one of his men to circle around the table to stand behind Kavriel.

His head began to pound, and Kavriel felt weak, unable to move.

The man's eyes sharpened, noticing Kavriel's discomfort. "You must truly be having a bad day, Kavriel." He chuckled, but without any humor. "Or be very stupid, to have told me that. You know that it is illegal to leave Rhyol without authorization, and that if you are associated with a treasonous outcast, then you too must be held accountable. I must place you under arrest."

Kavriel finally succumbed to his anxiety. He did not even try to comprehend what the man had just told him. Nothing made sense. "Please," he blurted, holding his hands in front of him. "I . . . I don't understand what is going on. I was hurt, and I can't recall much of anything since I left home. I don't know what you mean—illegal without authorization. I had no idea I was committing a crime."

The officer's expression seemed to soften. He nodded, as if thinking of some other explanation. "Hmm, perhaps you are telling the truth, Kavriel." He smiled almost kindly. Kavriel could barely breathe. "Yet there is one other thing that I must know . . ."

He glanced up at the soldier standing behind Kavriel, who suddenly wrapped his arm around Kavriel's throat while forcing one of Kavriel's hands onto the tabletop by the wrist. Kavriel struggled in terror, but the muscular man was stronger, and he watched in horror as the officer produced a thin dagger from someplace in his vest.

He began toying with it in his hand, waving the blade over Kavriel's fingers as he tried to pull away. The pounding in Kavriel's head became a cacophony of pain, nearly making him pass out. His vision became watery, then blurry. It felt colder in the room, and the flames danced in the fireplace as if caught in a breeze.

The stranger continued with his questioning as the other two soldiers standing behind him grinned in anticipation. "Tell me, Kavriel," the officer whispered, "where is your brother?"

The question was unexpected. Kavriel choked against the arm clamped around his neck, keeping him from responding. His eyes must have given away his confusion, but the officer was not satisfied. His eyes narrowed and he brought the dagger down, penetrating the center of Kavriel's hand and pinning it to the tabletop in a splash of blood. He rocked the blade slightly in Kavriel's flesh and Kavriel screamed, feeling the pain creep up his arm to his head. He choked in his own tears, struggling in vain against the soldier's grip.

The officer smiled at his suffering. "I will ask you the question again, Kavriel. And if I do not like your answer, I will begin removing your fingers one at a time until I have it." He yanked the dagger out of Kavriel's hand and blood flowed from the wound to pool red on the table. *"Where is your brother?"*

For a moment the room became deathly silent. Kavriel was unable to make a sound; he felt himself quickly slipping into the blackness of unconsciousness. He needed air, and he knew it was only a matter of moments before he would black out, only to wake again in blinding pain as the officer made good his threat. He felt as if the room was turning in on itself, circling tighter around him like a bubble of air underwater. He could almost make out the blurry edges of the circle surrounding him, growing smaller and smaller until he was trapped inside it. The bubble vibrated, and Kavriel could almost see the officer in front reacting to something out of the ordinary he sensed in the air.

Yet before he could react to it, a loud bang, like a door slamming, suddenly came from the opposite end of the room, followed by a crash of what must have been dishes and the muffled cry of a man. Immediately the two soldiers who had been smiling cruelly at Kavriel turned toward the sound. The soldier who had earlier gone into the back room flew out into the dining area like a child's tossed doll, crashing into table and chairs so violently, they exploded from the impact. He lay motionless on the floor among the clutter.

The officer stood up quickly. Kavriel was surprised to see fear in his eyes. "Find him!" he shouted.

They simultaneously drew their swords, and the soldier who had been strangling Kavriel released his arm from around his neck. Kavriel choked, gulping air. The bubble burst, and for a moment Kavriel thought that something must have exploded from underneath his table as a loud, deep *blop*, like the sound of a large rock being dropped into a puddle, echoed in the tavern.

The soldiers flew away from Kavriel as if pushed by a sudden gust of wind, the officer rolling over a table several feet back while the two soldiers were suddenly shoved toward the back room. One must have hit a wall . . . Kavriel still couldn't make out much detail, just a blurry shadow as he gasped for air, clutching his wounded hand.

As the soldier stumbled back toward him, Kavriel was just able to jump from his chair and back away before the man's bulky form destroyed it too. He was alive, but his eyes were closed, his face tightened by pain. Kavriel looked toward the wall—or the shadow—in time to see it disappearing into the back room like a living thing. It was all Kavriel could take. Following his fight or flee instinct, he turned toward the front entrance, shoving aside the soldier who had been restraining him, who was now clutching at his head. He fell down in a heap just as Kavriel reached the door and struggled to release the lock with his good hand, slippery with blood.

The door burst open, letting in the cold winter air. Kavriel ran out into the darkness, away from the tavern and the Ay'vol soldiers and the shadow attacker as fast as he could.

CHAPTER 11

Kavriel heard shouts from the tavern behind him as he turned quickly down an alleyway from the main road, running blindly. He turned into another, less illuminated alley, deep in the town, which seemed much larger than he remembered from his many explorations as a child. He couldn't be sure where he was anymore, and as he turned down another dark alley, he didn't see the storage barrels lining the rear wall of someone's home. He stumbled over the first of them, and like dominoes they tipped with resonant thuds, spilling grain and salt over the path as they rolled away.

Groaning, Kavriel sprawled where the first barrel had rested, but the collision seemed to have cleared his head. He rolled over and flattened himself against the wall, listening intently for any pursuers. He heard shouting but it was distant and getting fainter, as if the soldiers had decided to follow the path toward the camp and were moving farther away. He looked around. This was a good place to hide for now, but he knew that wouldn't last; his footsteps in the snow and a scattered trail of blood from his wounded hand would make tracking him easy, once the soldiers shifted from the chase to the hunt.

He stood and tore away the bottom of his shirt, wrapping it around his bloody hand as he thought about where to go. It was too dangerous to stay in the town. The soldiers might have been from Rav'agas, but they would know more about Mir than he would—at least, this new Mir. The dark alleys were a maze to him, and he didn't want to be led back to the main road, which would be suicide. That left Silver Wood, straight through the forest, where hopefully the gloom of birch trunks and darkness would be enough to conceal him. Still, these were trained soldiers, most likely adapted to the terrain. Not to mention that shadow-like thing that had attacked two of them in the tavern. Kavriel had forgotten about that strangeness until now. He wished he still could.

Crunching snow echoed from the alleyway where Kavriel had just been. Someone was running toward him. Before he had a chance to react, the silhouette of a man appeared at the end of Kavriel's alley, and then he was *there*, standing immediately in front of the broken barrels obstructing his path. Trapped, Kavriel leapt forward impulsively, hoping to either startle the man long enough to escape, or knock him down. Kavriel wasn't a fighter, and he knew nothing about self-defense besides the roughhousing he'd done with his brother and Grieg. He could only hope that surprise would succeed against a trained and armed soldier.

It didn't. As he lunged forward with his elbows up the man sidestepped, hooked him under the arm, and spun Kavriel against the building. He cried out as he slammed into it and a gloved hand shot out to cover his mouth. Effectively muzzled and pinned, Kavriel couldn't be sure if his feet were even touching the ground.

"*Be still!*" the man hissed and, realizing that he had no other choice, Kavriel let his body go limp. The man kept his hand over Kavriel's mouth, and Kavriel breathed slowly through his nose, trying to see into the shadows of the hood the man wore. He was not one of the Rav'agas soldiers, at least. He had picked Kavriel out of the air as easily as a bat snatching a flying insect, and now he dropped him to the ground, keeping his hand clamped over Kavriel's mouth as he turned his head toward the entrance to the alley, listening. Kavriel tried to do the same, and heard the rapid beat of the soldiers' boots as they approached, following his trail.

His captor released his mouth slowly without looking at him, clearly certain that Kavriel was helpless against him. Kavriel grimaced from the pain of his back where he had been thrown into the wall but otherwise stood motionless, his hands at his sides, waiting for whatever the man decided to do next—he was no longer in control of his fate, and too frightened to even bolt. But as the hood-shadowed face turned to him, Kavriel tried to move away. The man's arm was up in a flash, one hand holding Kavriel firmly against the wall.

"Xavr," Kavriel whispered, recognizing the man from the ridge and the man who had been fighting both the Wylyn and Saire in the mines, the man who had destroyed the pillars that kept the cavern from caving in, effectively doing just that and trapping Kavriel in the process. Xavr had been following them; he was much more than a traveller from the mainland interested in Highland rocks— he was associated to General Saire in some way. He had been ready to kill Grieg and A'zia; Kavriel remembered vividly his broken and bloody friend stumbling across the cavern with his beloved in his arms toward this man in front of him, who would have done just that if Saire hadn't sent in the Wylyn to attack first. Xavr had revealed himself a skilled fighter, a master swordsman. But Kavriel still could not be sure if he was friend or enemy. He only wanted to be away from him.

"Keep quiet," Xavr answered quickly, but released his hold on him as he turned his gaze away. Kavriel didn't try and escape; at least knowing who had caught him was a plus, despite which side Xavr was on. He studied the man. "Who are you?" he wondered without realizing he spoke aloud, and Xavr again hissed, "I said keep quiet!" His tone wasn't threatening, though, which was enough for Kavriel to think that maybe Xavr had been there to rescue him.

He looked at the man's black outfit, how it made him a shadow amidst shadows. He wondered if Xavr had been the one who'd distracted the Ay'vol soldiers in the tavern, giving Kavriel time to escape.

"You're not out of this yet," Xavr said as if reading his thoughts, still listening to the activity in the alleyway. The voices had become more distant, but they seemed to be directed this way. After another moment of silence, he said, "Now—let's go," and without even waiting to see it Kavriel would respond, disappeared into the darkness.

Kavriel was free, but he cursed, knowing that he was more trapped than ever before. He quickly followed Xavr, trailing him through the turns and twists of the back roads of Mir Town in a northwesterly direction, until the last turn ended at a wall of birch trees—Silver Wood. Kavriel watched as Xavr jumped soundlessly through a thick tangle of underbrush before pushing through himself, struggling past sharp branches and clinging twigs to catch up. A dark horse waited within the thicket, reins secured over a branch; it turned its ears toward the approaching men but made no motion to flee. Xavr grabbed the reins and leapt effortlessly into the saddle, the black horse snorting and slamming its hooves against the hard earth. Xavr held out his arm, and Kavriel grabbed it and was whisked up behind the rider as easily as if he had been a child.

Xavr clicked his tongue, and the animal wove through the woods with surprising speed. They followed no path that Kavriel could see, but Xavr guided the animal with confidence beneath the naked branches of the trees— which was the final proof Kavriel needed to understand that it *was* winter in the Highlands. He had somehow missed three months in the mines.

The dark horse continued into the night while Kavriel watched the moon move slowly across the horizon above the branches overhead. They'd left the sounds and lights of Mir behind them and the only noise was the thud of the horse's hooves on the snow. He had escaped the horrors in town, but as dark green pine trees began to replace the birch he knew that instead of heading toward Rhyol, Xavr was guiding the beast farther north—into the unknown.

"Where are we going?" Kavriel asked, breaking the silence but still keeping his voice low, as he'd been instructed to do.

His guide didn't reply, but instead urged his horse to more speed as they burst from the forest. Without the protection of the trees, Kavriel felt the chill wind cutting across the open ground from the north as the dark horse began to gallop toward a rise on the horizon. The snowy ground turned into bare rock as they climbed higher and the wind became stronger. Turning to look back, Kavriel saw the impressive expanse of Silver Wood stretching to the south. The sea was on their right, several miles away to the east. From this angle the mountainous boulders jutting out of the ocean by Mir camp looked even more impressive, and Kavriel was able to count a dozen more rocks than he had ever seen from the camp itself.

Kavriel had never been this far into Silver Wood before, and he wasn't sure if anyone else he knew had been, either. The woods grew wilder, the farther north one went from Rhyol, and only fur traders and hunters knew the paths that were safe enough to travel without getting lost. They came to Rhyol every other market day, with wolf pets and the occasional bear skin to trade and stories of their life in the wilds. They were interesting, though a little odd from living away from others for long periods of time.

Kavriel wondered if Xavr might be one of them— he seemed to know where he was going. But he dressed like a man from the city, and there was that finely crafted broadsword that Kavriel could feel thumping against his leg—that definitely wasn't for hunting wolf or bear. No, Xavr was more than just one particular kind of person, and yet at the same time, part of everything. It was strange, but sitting near him on the black horse, Kavriel felt that he was somehow more connected to him, as if they were old acquaintances or family members. Yet he also felt discomfort around Xavr, which was easy to explain, after seeing what the man could do with a sword. He was certain that it had been Xavr who had distracted the guards in the tavern, helping his escape. But if that were true, then the man had saved his skin and Kavriel had no need to feel anxious.

The horse circled the rise and slowed as they reached another part of Silver Wood, this section far denser and darker than what they had travelled through earlier. Before they entered the trees Kavriel looked at the moon one last time and estimated that they had been travelling about two hours since fleeing Mir Town. Xavr kept the horse to a slow trot until a wooden cabin gradually appeared, deep in the forest. It had obviously been built for seclusion, with absolutely no clean trail leading to it. It was a hunting cabin, Kavriel realized as they neared it, larger than he'd expected but unkempt, as if it had been abandoned years ago.

Xavr dismounted as if he was familiar with the place, though he approached with a hint of hesitation as he led the horse carefully through the underbrush. Kavriel didn't move from his place on the horse's back, and for a moment considered pulling the reins from Xavr's grasp and kicking the horse out of there. Yet he suspected the animal was fiercely loyal, and that attempt would only result in Kavriel being bucked from the horse.

Moonlight crept through gaps in the tall pine trees to dimly illuminate the cabin against the dark woods, which emitted an astringent scent that, in the cold air, seemed fitting. Kavriel breathed in deeply as he stretched his arms out. It was then that he realized he felt no more pain in his hand. Terrified that he had lost too much blood and it had turned into a senseless blue lump, he brought it up to his face, turning it back and forth while flexing his fingers. Everything worked properly; he peeled aside the makeshift bandage and found that even the puncture in the center left by the officer's thin blade had faded to only a scratch. It

227

was strange, but Kavriel actually expected it to be that way.

"Your hand is fine," Xavr said from the horse's head as he led it toward the cabin. He didn't even look back. "But your head will take a little more time." He chuckled.

Kavriel studied him while absently testing his hand. "What do you mean?" he asked, but Xavr didn't answer, only motioned for him to dismount in front of the cabin.

Kavriel complied, but cautiously, again unsure of his savior. He watched Xavr lead the horse into a half-walled stall adjacent to the cabin and chided himself—Xavr wouldn't have dragged him all the way up here just to kill him. He probably had more vicious plans.

Again it seemed as if Xavr knew what he had been thinking. He wore a smile as he returned from stabling the horse. Kavriel heard it munching away on some food that Xavr must have given him. "Don't worry," Xavr said, pushing back the black hood. His short-cropped, pale blonde hair shone in the moonlight. "You are safe with me." His eyes lit up unnaturally and Kavriel could only hope that was an effect of the moon.

Xavr tested the door's rusted latch before unbarring it and pushing open the large door, the hinges creaking from disuse and the warped wood groaning. "Wait here a moment," he said before disappearing into the blackness of the cabin.

Kavriel crossed his arms around himself, feeling the chill breeze as he stood in the darkness with only the snorting horse nearby. A lamp lit up inside, then several more, the bright illumination of the interior only making the forest seem darker. Kavriel stepped forward just as

Xavr returned to the entrance, carrying a candle. "Alright, come on . . . and don't mind the clutter."

Kavriel entered a surprisingly spacious interior, clearly a giant hunting cabin in its past incarnation but now stockpiled with bookshelves on every wall instead of pelts or traps. Volumes upon volumes of books and manuscripts stuffed the shelves and clustered in chaotic heaps on furniture and floor. Xavr scooped some of those up, mumbling something under his breath as Kavriel stood wide-eyed, taking in all the details of this hidden library in the woods. There was a stove in a corner, with an uncomfortable-looking bed nearby; a table and chair were buried under numerous maps and sketches.

Kavriel approached the table, taking the few moments while Xavr was otherwise occupied to examine the drawings. They were incredible, sketches of buildings, homes, cities, places from all over Quetal that Kavriel recognized from books he had studied, but with more artistic detail. There was a drawing of the Grand Library in Upper Teltraum's political district, the illustrious onion-shaped domes and ornate cloisters making the building the most unique in Quetal. There was the city of Loellen drawn from a distant vantage, the artist capturing the full enormity of the second largest city in Quetal, deep in the Oenes Mountain Range, detailing the stunning masonry of the large perimeter wall that must have been even more extraordinary in real life.

There were many other beautiful sketches of just about every major town and city in Quetal. Kavriel smiled in awe as he fingered through them, until underneath them he discovered drawings of cities and towns that he couldn't identify. They could only be Rav'agas cities, but there were some so strange and exotic that he wondered if they were true sketches of real places, or simply creative fantasies.

"How do you like my drawings?" Xavr asked, startlingly Kavriel.

He looked back to see the man standing behind him and quickly put the sketches back down on the table, fearing that he had been too presumptuous with Xavr's belongings. "They're beautiful," he replied meekly. "What is this place?"

His host looked around the cabin with an amused expression on his face. "This?" He held out his hands. "This is my hunting shed." His lips curved in a smile.

"Hunting what?" Kavriel asked quickly, realizing that Xavr had just attempted humor. It didn't make him feel any more comfortable.

"Information," Xavr replied with a full smile.

Nodding, Kavriel looked at the bookshelves surrounding him, but he was not about to accept his guest's vague response. "Information about what?"

Xavr must have sensed Kavriel's annoyance at his dissembling. He walked over to a shelf and grabbed a book seemingly at random. He flipped through a few pages before tossing the thick tome toward Kavriel. He barely caught it before it fell to the floor. "About history . . . your history, and mine."

Kavriel glanced at the cover of the book that he held, seeing the same symbol that he had seen on his father's map and in the mines. The embossing was so dark and faded by time that he almost didn't recognize it. Yet once he did, he realized also how old the book felt in his hands—older than anything he had held before. He was suddenly nervous, afraid that it might turn into dust under his fingers.

Xavr must have recognized his change in mood. "Don't worry," he assured Kavriel, moving across the room and pulling a chair out from under a table. "You won't destroy it." He turned, muttering a curse, and began picking up several large sheets of paper that had slipped to the floor with the movement of the chair. He sat down, reaching under the table to collect the rest. His reaction to the disorganization of his paperwork reminded Kavriel of Master Femaor, but he knew that Xavr was nothing like his father's friend.

Kavriel's eyes were drawn back to the book in his hands, and he gingerly traced the round symbol with a finger. Unburdened by the headaches he'd experienced in the mine, he was able to study the design more carefully. He opened the book, flipping through the first few pages and seeing that instead of chapter headings, the book was sectioned by dates, like a timeline. The first date was so faint and difficult to read that Kavriel had to squint. When he did, he couldn't believe it. "This is from the Fall of the Temple," he exclaimed, excitedly skimming the first several lines. They were written like a daily log entry, describing mundane subjects like the weather and successful crops.

He flipped through several more sections, reading bits and pieces of the timeline with an insatiable hunger. If this was truly what he thought it was, Kavriel knew he was holding in his hand a rare find indeed. Any books or manuscripts that had been written during the "faith revolutions," as history classified them, were almost all locked away in Teltraum's Great Library for only the most respected scholars to study. This had to be nearly two thousand years old!

Kavriel nearly fainted in shock, remembering how callously Xavr had tossed it over to him. What if he had dropped it! The book started to feel like a block of iron in Kavriel's hands and he immediately wanted to put it down, fearing that his touch might damage it, despite what Xavr had said. He looked up, seeing that the man was watching him carefully—him. Any other loyal collector would have hovered over the book, poised to snatch it out of his unworthy hands.

"Where did you get this?" he asked, delicately closing the cover and handing it back to Xavr.

Xavr didn't reach for it. "I have a rather . . . extensive collection here," he replied, waving his hand around the room in prideful arrogance. He leaned back in the chair, crossing one leg over the other and scratching his face, narrowed eyes on Kavriel. "Tell me," he said, "what do you think?" He pointed at the book Kavriel still held.

Kavriel shook his head, protectively gripping the book. He looked down at it. "I . . . I don't know." He reopened the book, flipping to pages at random. "I've never seen something this old before. I thought all the ancient texts were in Teltraum. I didn't think anybody was supposed to have these."

"Nobody is," Xavr replied with that smug grin.

Kavriel didn't press. It was already obvious, looking at the other old and well-worn texts in the room, that Xavr was either a skilled forger or a thief. There was no other way that something like this book would have left the Great Library. So rare an artifact should have been under lock and key.

"Can you read it?" Xavr asked, and immediately Kavriel thought the question strange. Of course he could read it, despite the faded lettering and the word ordering that seemed a bit archaic; like most from Rhyol, Kavriel was educated. He replied more smugly than perhaps he should have, but it didn't seem to faze Xavr. On the contrary, the man seemed honestly curious.

"Who are you?" Kavriel asked again.

Again Xavr avoided the question by changing the subject. "It seems you have a knack for being in places where you shouldn't be." He smiled.

Kavriel suddenly felt an urgency to escape this cabin and the forest. He had tripped up death several times, but now he was trapped in Xavr's cabin filled with what was most definitely stolen Council property, someplace in Silver Wood.

"I'm not going to kill you, if that's what you're wondering," Xavr said, again astutely reading his thoughts. "What I have here is not going to be missed by anyone— not for a while, anyway." He shifted in his chair and changed the subject again. "The men that you met in the town, have you seen them before?"

Kavriel shook his head, forgetting the book and remembering the surprise greeting he had received in Mir.

Xavr nodded. "But you knew who they were?"

Kavriel sensed that this conversation was turning into something more interrogative. He could only hope that it wouldn't end the same way it had with the soldiers in town, but his nerves were up. "I recognized their uniforms," he replied, and Xavr accepted his neutral response with a shrug.

"Did they ask anything that might have seemed strange to you?" Xavr continued.

Kavriel suddenly felt like he couldn't take anymore; the rage and confusion over everything that had happened to him reaching its limit, now that he was in a place of relative safety and he could actually take a moment to dwell on his thoughts. "Strange!" he nearly shouted. "Everything about this damned night has been strange. What happened with my friends? Did Saire kill them? Did you? Why am I even here? Why did Ay'vol men from the town want to put me under arrest? Why is there a town at all? Mir has been dead for twenty years! What is this place? I want to go home! What do you want from me?"

Kavriel could not control the flood of his confused anger as it spilled over Xavr like a raging torrent. This night, and who knew how many nights before that had kept him shrouded in such an absurd mystery, had tested the last of his sanity and most definitely his patience. He was finished with whatever game he was in, finished with the secrecy and the impossibilities. He wanted answers, and he wanted them now!

Xavr didn't respond to his tirade, and from his relaxed posture Kavriel wondered if the man had even been listening. It infuriated him. "The Creator damn you, answer me! And if you're not going to kill me, then at least tell me *why* you won't!" Now Kavriel was shouting, the sound absorbed by the thousands of books lining the walls of the cabin.

Again Xavr didn't respond. He watched Kavriel curiously, as if he were waiting for something. The blood pulsed hard in Kavriel's head, triggering the painful barrage of arrows under his skull. The rhythm of his heartbeat echoed in his ears, his sight blurred, and for a moment Kavriel thought he saw the thin outline of the grayish bubble that he remembered seeing in the tavern with the Ay'vol soldiers. It slowly began to pull in toward him as the candles on the tabletop nearby flickered as if their flames were teased by a light breeze. When Kavriel noticed this and turned his attention away from Xavr, the bubble seemed to dissipate like a cloud of mist.

Kavriel's rage was gone, and he felt weak in the knees. Before he realized what was happening he saw Xavr jump up to push the chair he had been sitting in underneath him. Dizzy, clutching his head between both hands as the painful arrows gradually dissipated with the bubble, Kavriel tumbled into it. Outside, Xavr's black horse neighed nervously, as if it had sensed something unusual.

"Please." Kavriel surrendered, releasing his hands from his head as he looked up at Xavr standing over him. He felt pitiful and weak, now that the rage and pain were gone. "I don't understand what is happening to me."

Xavr's expression softened as he realized that Kavriel's situation was more complex than he had assumed. He reached over to the table and pulled another chair directly in front of Kavriel before sitting in it, their knees almost touching. "What do you remember?" Xavr asked in a voice that was soothing and kind.

Already weak, Kavriel let go of his inhibitions and explained everything that had happened, from waking up in his home to his rescue by Xavr in the back alley. He spoke quickly and without pause, yearning to be understood by another to make this folly sound believable. He left out nothing, no matter how unbelievable it might sound. Xavr simply waited for him to finish with the occasional nod and smile of understanding, like a patient parent listening to the details of a child's nightmare in the middle of the night. When Kavriel finished the room fell into a deep silence.

Xavr folded his hands under his chin, absorbing everything Kavriel had just said. "So you only *just* escaped the cave-in?" Kavriel nodded, expecting a look of disbelief from the man, but instead seeing something dark and fearful. "So . . ." Xavr almost whispered, "then it *is* time."

Kavriel wasn't sure what the man meant, but he did feel slightly better after relating his tale. "Time for what?" he asked, but his host was already deep into his own thoughts, taking the confusion and terror on himself now, as if Kavriel had simply given it away.

Xavr stared into the space behind Kavriel for a moment before leaning forward to hold Kavriel with an intense gaze. "Listen carefully, villager, for this is important. I'm afraid that you and your friends have found yourselves in the middle of a dangerous and complex situation."

"Where are my friends?" Kavriel asked, not caring what the man had to say, only that he mentioned a concern that had been bothering Kavriel since he awoke in the mines.

Xavr gave him a hard look. "Be quiet, and let me finish," he said firmly. "You must already suspect that I am not entirely what I seem to be." He paused, and despite the urge to interrupt again Kavriel kept his mouth shut. Xavr continued. "I have been following the man you call Saire for some time now, ever since he left the Oenes. I . . . *heard* about his discovery, though I did not accompany him, as you may have believed when we met on the ridge. Your father is right to be suspicious of him." He paused his face seeming to age in the flickering light.

Kavriel couldn't keep quiet. 'You know my father?" he asked.

Xavr shook his head without any visible anger at the interruption. "No, not personally, but I know that he is a very wise man. Saire is manipulative, quick, and very smart. He has more experience in politics than he will ever let on and his penetration into the circle of your national leaders is only a small example of his abilities. He is the most dangerous man alive, and he will stop at nothing to accomplish his goals. Your father suspected as much, but he and many like him are next to powerless against Saire and can only hope to stay out of his way."

"How do you know all of this?" Kavriel asked.

"I know him," Xavr replied quickly, but then he lowered his tone and sounded almost sad. "I've known him for a very long time now, and his ways will never change. He cannot stop what he has begun, but he hasn't realized yet that he will never accomplish what he hopes to. There are greater things than even Saire, and he has forgotten his place." He looked away, his eyes haunted.

"What does that mean?" Kavriel asked, not sure if this revealing conversation was actually helping to explain his situation, or causing even more confusion.

Xavr looked back to him quickly and grinned. "It

means that whatever Saire has now accomplished by finding what was never supposed to be found, he has ignored or possibly forgotten about one thing."

"Which is?" Kavriel asked, already suspecting the answer by Xavr's expression.

"You."

Kavriel felt as if the world had suddenly become very small around him. "Who are you?" he asked again, and Xavr smiled deviously.

"Inspiration," he replied.

That hardly answered Kavriel's question, but he was too tired to try to pick apart the secrecy. There was just too much of it. He decided to try another route. "My friends," he said.

This time Xavr answered. "I cannot say for sure. They were already gone when I engaged Saire."

"What happened to him?" Kavriel asked, knowing from Xavr's earlier words that like him, the general must have escaped the cave-in. Which struck Kavriel as impossible. The exit Kavriel had taken was the only available option. Unless he had been able to get out through the ceiling, but Kavriel didn't think that would have been possible.

Xavr shook his head, looking disappointed, and didn't answer.

Kavriel changed the subject, already hearing what he wanted to hear about his friends' escape. "I must get back home," he said. "I need to make sure they know I'm alive." Kavriel didn't say who he meant by "they," but Xavr's expression revealed he understood he was talking about his friends.

Xavr's forehead wrinkled. "It is too late for that, villager," he said sharply, standing up quickly.

Kavriel rose as well, and looked blankly at him. "What do you mean? I need to get back to Rhyol. I need to see my father and let him know what has happened."

Kavriel tried to move past Xavr, but the man threw his hand up to stop him. "That isn't a good idea. Do you remember what found you in the town?"

Xavr's words struck a chord. Kavriel had forgotten about his encounter with the Ay'vol Force. Xavr waited as Kavriel ordered his thoughts, still unable to understand what had happened. Xavr and Saire's relationship might be beyond his concern for the moment, but the mine, the shed on the beach, the iron gate, the people living in Mir, and the Ay'vol soldiers all were a terrible reality he had awakened into.

He must have looked scared to death, because Xavr put a comforting hand on his shoulder. "How long have I been gone?" Kavriel asked in a quavering voice.

He saw the question burrow deep into Xavr's eyes. He took more time to answer than Kavriel imagined he would. "This will be the fourth winter since I destroyed the cavern under the mines," Xavr said in a gentle tone, as a doctor might, telling a patient that his time was almost up.

Kavriel fell back into the chair. "What?" he exclaimed, feeling the pounding in his head once again. "That's . . . but that's impossible! I would never have . . . I should be dead." He'd known by the weather that he had been away for at least several months, which still would have been impossible, but four years . . . almost five? It was unthinkable. But the camp and Mir Town's revival would require a time frame like that to change so dramatically. And his friends? His family? His town? What had happened? What was left?

Xavr must have sensed Kavriel's desperation. He sat back down in front of him, watchful. There wasn't any kind of confusion on Xavr's face. All these impossibilities were in fact possible for him, it seemed. Who was this man? "You don't think I'm crazy?" he said, starting to feel that he was the only one left in the world who didn't understand.

Xavr shook his head, but Kavriel, struggling for any kind of rationale that might make sense of all this, wasn't satisfied. "The mine," he began, searching his memory. "The mine makes some people sick . . . red-eye. It's caused by the minerals. It's not curable and sometimes can make you delusional." Eyes wide, he looked at Xavr, feeling that he might have stumbled onto something. "I'm sick. It's the only explanation. I must have escaped the mine before, and only remembered it now. My mind is healing itself, and I'm picking apart the pieces of the last four years and only trying to put it together now. Yes, that must be it!" Kavriel wasn't sure if he was trying to convince Xavr or himself.

The man didn't seem to be convinced anyway. He didn't respond, only waited until he was sure that Kavriel had finished with his theory. "Anything is possible, villager," he finally replied, his tone emotionless. "Yet what's important now is that you need to stay away from the towns, yours included. The Guardsmen will not forget what happened. They will find you."

"Is my father or my brother in any danger?" Kavriel asked, quickly remembering the conversation he'd had with

240

the soldiers in the tavern; never mind how Xavr knew about it. Remembering the four-year time loss, he caught his breath. "Are they even alive?" He feared the answer, but Xavr, thankfully, nodded his head.

"They are alive, and they're not in any danger. The Ay'vol Guard knows already who your father is, but they don't know your relationship to him. Names can be erased quickly, if necessary." Xavr displayed another of his smug grins, as if he knew something about Kavriel's father that he wasn't revealing. Either way, Kavriel believed him and he felt relief.

"Tell me what happened?" he asked, and Xavr sighed. His eyes were weary, as if remembering an old problem never resolved. Kavriel wasn't sure what he might say, but he waited silently. He would wait all night if need be, to get at least something, anything that might possibly awaken his lost memory.

"There has been a change in the balance of power between the two nations, Quetal and Ṛav'agas," Xavr began.

Immediately Kavriel began to imagine the worst. He remained quiet, and Xavr looked inquisitively at him for a moment before he surprised him with a question that seemed unrelated. "What do you know about The Becoming?"

The question took several seconds to burrow into Kavriel's thoughts. He shrugged, reflecting on his past studies about the Rav'agas faith. "Only the basics, I guess. The Way suggests that there will be a time when the Creator gifts the people who have proven their devotion with the rebirth of his son. Patriarchs have been preaching

The Becoming for generations, each one suggesting that he will be the one to receive the final blessing by having the Son of Creation reincarnated through him. There seems to be a surge in the belief every few years when some supposed 'miracle' happens that the Patriarch likes to turn to his advantage—strong crops following a tough season, milder weather, star showers and the like. It usually blows over and the Rav'agas people continue to worship in their own way." He finished with another shrug, and Xavr nodded.

"Do you know what happens . . . politically . . . when these 'miracles' happen?" he asked.

Kavriel nodded, becoming interested in the discussion. It reminded him of better times, with his father or with Tess, when they had similar talks. "The bishops come together, by request of the Patriarch, to initiate . . . tests, I think? Yes, something like tests to decide if the Patriarch has actually been chosen by the Creator. I'm not too familiar with what those involve. Not many are, in Quetal or in Rav'agas. It's considered a sacred tradition. Yet usually during those times, whatever minor disputes are going on between provinces are put on hold until the tests are completed."

Xavr smiled approvingly at Kavriel's response. "It sounds like a very powerful strategy to unite a nation, does it not?"

Kavriel also smiled. He was enjoying this discussion. "Yes, it does," he replied, thinking of a theory his father and Master Femaor held about the political games the Rav'agas would play. "Most of the 'callings,' as the tests are called in Rav'agas, come from the Patriarch, but there have been occasions when the provincial powers start the event. A bishop whose people had suffered more hardships for any number of reasons might use the opportunity of the truce for more diplomatic discussions with his neighbors. My father liked to use Secht Province as an example when he talked about this."

Xavr nodded with a smile of his own, and Kavriel figured he knew about the story of the once poorest province in Rav'agas, by unlucky chance being bordered by the Seccacian Desert, that had suddenly become very prosperous with trade from Ay'vol—after the bishop had claimed that he'd had an epiphany that the current Patriarch was the Son of God incarnate. He had been quite persuasive, using extensive examples of the written doctrine to corroborate his dream. The Patriarch was easily convinced, and immediately the elite citizens of Ay'vol began to take notice of their fellow countrymen. The province of Secht suddenly became industrious as the "true believers" demanded Secht goods by the wagonload . . . and the rest was, simply, history.

It had been the last time a "calling" had been initiated, well before Kavriel or even his father had been born. The current Patriarch, who had been ruling for many years, hadn't seemed concerned with this standard ritual of self-indulgence. His strategy seemed more tactical and offensive, directed toward real and feasible concerns—the Temscript Scrolls, the heathen northerners, and the borderland of Ciele. War and conquest.

Thoughts of his studies suddenly made something click in this puzzle. Remembering the Ay'vol Force in Mir Town, he quickly asked, "Has there been a calling recently?"

Xavr nodded as if the question was what he'd waiting for. "Not long after the cave-in." A chill ran up Kavriel's spine. Xavr continued. "The Patriarch has evidently passed the tests, the bishops have united the nation, and for the last four years that you have missed, Rav'agas has been ruled by the Son of the Creator Reborn."

CHAPTER 12

"How is that even possible?" Suddenly feeling restless, he paced, weaving between the scattered books and manuscripts.

Xavr remained where he was, watching him intently. "It isn't," he replied. "Yet the declaration has been made, and more importantly, honored by the people."

"But it doesn't make sense!" Kavriel threw up his hands before rubbing the back of his head, wondering how the night might get any worse. "Look," he said, "don't the tests involve some kind of . . . I don't know, *proof of animation*, I think it's called? Some kind of demonstration of extraordinary powers that only their god might possess?"

Xavr seemed to enjoy his protestations. "You do know a bit about the sacred traditions, don't you. I guess being the son of an overseer has its educational advantages."

Kavriel gave his host a disapproving look. The man laughed as he stood. "I meant no offense," he said with a last chuckle. "Nobody who isn't a bishop or the Patriarch could tell you what those tests are. Not even someone as wise as me."

Kavriel frowned, wondering if the man was trying to be funny to ease his discomfort, or simply just being an ass. Maybe it was his personality. He still had no idea who the man was, but from what he had seen he knew the man was skilled with the blade, intelligent, and well versed in both politics and culture, which placed him in a higher level of society. He was from a wealthy family, probably active in government, for which a quick mind and tongue were beneficial. He had been trained with the sword, and most likely a vast assortment of other weapons, by very skilled masters. Yet his stealth, reclusiveness, and this collection of illegal artifacts suggested an outcast, a fallen son of a noble house, or similar. It would make sense that he'd taken interest in Saire's finding of the Temscript Scrolls. Maybe Xavr was simply a treasure hunter, interested in the thrill of stealing something of incredible value only to those with his status.

He realized he had been staring at Xavr for longer than was polite, but the man was simply looking back at him with that smug grin, watching him with that same "I know what you're thinking" look that Kavriel had noticed earlier. He stiffened.

"You don't trust me, do you villager." He smiled, and Kavriel sneered.

"I haven't had much cause to," he replied, and Xavr shrugged as he walked away from him.

"I suppose that's fair. I haven't been very helpful to you, have I?" Xavr's voice was sarcastic.

Kavriel nodded, understanding Xavr's meaning. "Thank you for helping me out of Mir Town." he replied.

Xavr held up his hands. "There we are! Now, that wasn't so difficult, was it?" He smiled, but it held no pleasure. He solemnly folded his hands as he walked back to Kavriel, head lowered in thought. Only when he was in front of Kavriel did Xavr look up. It reminded Kavriel of his father when he had something important to say; he would fold his hands similarly, as if drawing courage from the gesture.

"I am going to make this fundamentally simple, Kavriel. I do not have the time to explain what you either can't remember or what we think has happened to you. It is important, but it will have to wait." He paused, reflecting on what he had just said. "You should not attempt to make contact with your friends or family. Not until I feel it's safe."

Kavriel couldn't help himself. "Until *you* feel it's safe?" he repeated. "Just what is that supposed to mean? I'm your prisoner here?" He was angry, but not nearly as angry as he had been.

Xavr frowned. "No, of course not. I have a feeling that whatever wise counsel I offered you was a waste of my breath. However, when you *do* decide to figure things out on your own, I suggest you remember what happened in Mir, and that the soldiers will be looking for you. The Patriarch's rule of law over what he considers the 'infidels of the north' is something you have never experienced before and therefore cannot imagine. You have escaped his hounds once already. You would be very lucky to do it a second time, especially if I'm not there to help you."

Kavriel still struggled to put this all together. "What do they want from me, anyway?" he asked.

The question actually seemed to startle Xavr, as if the thought had never crossed his mind. After a long pause he shook his head and shrugged, but in his eyes Kavriel saw something else hidden away. "I don't know," Xavr said.

Kavriel knew he was lying, but there was no way to prove it. There was no way that even a group as notorious as the Ay'vol Force would start poking daggers into people's hands just for fun. Or would they? Kavriel only knew about the methods of the Patriarch's "special stock" from history and the occasional word-of-mouth from Femaor, who had been among the Quetalian defense on the borderlands.

There were skirmishes between the soldiers, but Kavriel didn't know anyone who had actually fought against them. Not even Grieg, whose unit dealt more with the internal relations between the Quetal and Rav'agas alliances. He had been a soldier for only a year, and the Council hadn't sent any direct offense into Ciele to attack the Ay'vol. Any fights that occurred were random and unsanctioned. That didn't mean that the Ay'vol were any less dangerous. From what he remembered reading, the soldiers were not only masterfully trained, but fearless. Every initiate was tested for strength and endurance, and unyielding loyalty to the Patriarch. Yet the soldier who had questioned him in Mir had been crafty and meticulous, and was interested in something quite specific that Kavriel had let slip from his mind until now.

"My brother."

Xavr blinked. He had been caught in his lie. "They were asking about my brother. What do you know about that?" Kavriel pointed a finger at him for emphasis.

This time Xavr didn't try to avoid the question, he simply refused to answer. "I will only reiterate my advice, Kavriel," he said calmly in a fatherly tone. "Do not go home. Not yet, anyway. Wait until I have returned." And he turned away quickly, grabbing a worn leather riding bag from the floor that Kavriel hadn't noticed when he'd entered. He glimpsed several articles of clothing under the fold. Xavr was leaving.

"Wait," Kavriel called, forgetting about what he might have gained. He was confused, and anxious to know why his host had decided to suddenly leave. What had Kavriel caught him with in his question that he didn't want to answer?

Xavr ignored him, moving quickly around the cabin, stuffing other items into the bag. Kavriel followed. "Wait," he said again. "What is it you're not telling me?"

"Much," Xavr immediately replied.

Kavriel wasn't sure how to respond to that. "I . . . I don't know . . . where are you going?"

Xavr merely glanced askance at him. "I have questions that need answering."

Kavriel threw out his arms. "*You* need questions answered?" he began, then fell silent, knowing that anything he said in that vein would only earn sarcasm or argument. He changed tacks. "Then I'll go with you," he said calmly, motioning toward the door.

For a moment Xavr actually stopped, as if considering it. Then he shook his head and continued stuffing his bag. "Too dangerous," he replied, actually looking at Kavriel this time—out of respect, or just to make sure Kavriel wouldn't try to sneak past him?

Xavr moved to the door. "It's not as easy to move in your country as it used to be. I have a long road to travel and a short time to travel it in. You would only slow me down." He opened the door into the first glimmer of dawn, approaching from behind the trees and casting the forest surrounding the cabin into faded black. He didn't move out right away, but waited as if to make sure Kavriel understood that there was no stopping him.

"So that's it, then?" Kavriel asked in surrender, and Xavr nodded and offered a regretful smile, something Kavriel had not expected.

"I'm sorry, villager." He sighed. "I don't expect you to wait for me, but I hope you will remember what I've told you. It hasn't been much, but enough to keep you safe for now." He caught Kavriel's eyes and glared a warning. Kavriel could almost see his reflection in Xavr's light blue irises. "Your home is not what it used to be. Whatever has happened to you in the last several years—the years that you cannot remember—is perhaps for the better. You have been spared the living nightmare of seeing what you once knew and loved ripped apart and remade into something terrible. I can only wish you good luck until we meet again. Your father is safe, and the Ay'vol Force's interest in your brother is not your concern for the moment. Just try to stay out of their way. I will find you again." And with that Xavr stepped through the door.

Before he could disappear into the forest, Kavriel called out to him one last question. Something else he had forgotten and of such strangeness that he hoped it might be enough to keep the man from leaving. It was obvious he wanted to keep Kavriel in the dark, but dependent on him, which only further strengthened his suspicions of who he thought he was. "The urns!" he shouted, and Xavr actually stopped in his tracks. "What was in the urns that Saire found?" This entire event had started with whatever the general had been searching for in the mines. And when he had found it was when Xavr appeared.

Xavr didn't turn to face Kavriel when he spoke, but

Kavriel could sense from the man's posture that he was affected by the question. The urns must have had much more significance than he realized.

"A foolish attempt at changing fate," Xavr answered solemnly. "What is . . . always will be, and there is nothing anyone can do to change that. I only understood too late."

"You knew that the urns were there?" Kavriel pressed, sensing Xavr had some deeper responsibility concerning the urns and whatever had been inside them.

This time the man turned to look at him. His eyes told Kavriel all he needed to know.

"Saire lied to us about the scrolls, didn't he? He knew about the cavern and the urns . . . as you did." Kavriel felt that he had stumbled onto something extraordinary, until Xavr shook his head with a humble smile.

"No, he didn't lie about that," Xavr replied. "Yes, I knew about the cavern, but I cannot say for certain what Saire was expecting to find. Otherwise I don't think he would have acted so . . . impetuously."

"You mean when he sent his man to attack you?" Kavriel spoke of Saire's Wylyn associate. He was remembering more now.

Xavr smiled. "Yes, he should have avoided doing that." Something dangerous lay behind his smile, and his tone suggested he was also starting to understand something beyond Kavriel's reasoning.

"Did you kill him?" Kavriel asked, remembering the amazing agility of the Rav'agas woodsman and how easily he had been able to best both Grieg and the West Point woman. He hoped his friends were alright.

A frown replaced Xavr's smile, but a jesting one. "My dear boy," he said, "you should know by now that it isn't as easy to kill someone as you might have thought. This isn't a matter of simply squishing a bug. Human life is, by its very nature, quite resilient." He pointed at Kavriel's stomach. "Yours is no different."

Kavriel looked down at his stomach, remembering a blade sticking out of his flesh. Yet there was no mark, scar or otherwise. It was like that with his other wounds from his escape from the mines. Yet all of it must have happened four years ago. Time could heal wounds if they weren't too terrible, and maybe the blade that Kavriel thought had killed him had simply delivered a flesh wound, as had happened to Tess. Things had happened so fast in the cavern . . . maybe they happened differently from what he thought. He couldn't be completely sure of anything anymore. The Wylyn's fighting, his wounds, and the red ooze that seemed to disappear into the air almost as soon as it was released from the urns could all be part of some delusion. Maybe only now was he healed completely. Kavriel looked at his hand where the Ay'vol soldier had stabbed it. The mark remained even if the pain had gone.

He heard the door slam and looked up. Xavr had left while he'd been distracted. He rushed to pull the door open in time to see the black horse gallop past him with Xavr astride it. They disappeared into the gloom of the forest.

Kavriel could only watch them go with frustration. He was alone in a strange cabin someplace in the north part of Silver Wood. He stood in the cold for only a moment longer, examining his options, before he returned to the warm interior and closed the door.

There was much that the arrogant swordsman had purposely left out. Kavriel paced around the room again, hands on his head, trying to figure out what the man's intentions were. What Xavr had told him should have been unbelievable. The Becoming, the united Rav'agas, the Ay'vol Force in Nostrac, all were things that couldn't possibly be real. Yet Kavriel had experienced them firsthand when he had been caught by the soldiers, and in the back of his mind Kavriel did believe that he was coming to terms with that. It was like waking up in a windowless room, but somehow knowing that it was daylight outside, without seeing the sun. It only furthered his theory that he had been sick—*or am sick*—and was only just now remembering the last years of his missing life.

Xavr's elusiveness must have been triggering Kavriel's memory. Did the man know that? Was Xavr truly trying to keep him safe, as he said he was? It was entirely possible; otherwise why would Xavr have helped him at all, unless there was something about him that interested Xavr? Keeping him concealed in his cabin until he came back— who did Xavr think he was? And why was he so hesitant to answer questions about Kavriel or his brother? There was still so much missing.

Kavriel continued to pace the cabin, and his anger toward Xavr made him start picking through his things as if they were his own. Not caring if the man would be angry, Kavriel began rummaging through Xavr's belongings, actually hoping that it might frustrate the man. It would be some small satisfaction, at least. He pushed plates and cups aside on the shelves and found a small, sealed barrel that he ripped open to greedily eat the dried meat it held. If he was going to be trapped here, at least he wouldn't go hungry. He started fishing through the books, still upset but growing calmer as his natural curiosity took over. He had already decided that the books didn't belong to Xavr, so there was no point in doing them any damage.

He read a few of the slender ones, the morning sunshine slanting in the windows as he became absorbed in the works of writers he had never heard of. There seemed to be quite a collection of literature from Loellen. Scholarly works on the history and geology of the Oenes Mountains. There was no mention of the Temscript Scrolls in any of the books, to Kavriel's disappointment. Not that he thought there would be; these books seemed much older than those. He put them away, and looked through the newer manuscripts on the table for some mention of the scrolls, suddenly very curious about them, as if they held some importance he had forgotten about. Saire had been obsessed by them, Xavr had obviously been tracking them, and Kavriel had lost four years of memory because of them.

Unfortunately he found nothing, and as Kavriel grew frustrated, he had a sudden urge to see his friends and family. He looked out the window, saw the sun shining through the trees, and went to the front door and opened it wide. The breeze was not as icy as it had been earlier. The sun was stronger than Kavriel had imagined it would be, already melting the snow on the ground. The air smelled fresh, different from the hollow cold of a winter wind, and Kavriel knew that it was a new season.

He shook his head in disbelief. Time seemed to

move outside of his awareness. He had only been in the cabin for a few hours, and it was dark when he had left Mir Town. He hadn't known exactly what time of year it was, but the spring air made him feel more rejuvenated and nostalgic for home. Despite the dangers that Xavr had warned him about, he decided to risk going home. Xavr wasn't going to come back anytime soon, and there was no sense in trying to pick apart the books of the past to understand what was happening now. He would be safer with his family . . . he knew that.

Kavriel turned back and collected his things and a few of Xavr's, including a long knife and a heavier, black coat. He also realized that he had picked up the book that Xavr had thrown at him. The circular sun and star design on the cover seemed to hypnotize him. Kavriel thrust the book into the inside pocket of the coat. He didn't understand exactly why, but there was something about the book that Kavriel couldn't pass up. He was interested in learning what his father had to say about its possible origins, and its worth to the Council.

Thinking of the Quetalian leaders made Kavriel stop in the doorway much as Xavr had done earlier. If Xavr had been telling him the truth, which Kavriel believed he had, it was entirely possible that the Council of Teltraum was no more . . . if the Patriarch had conquered Quetal. What other system was left for him?

Kavriel shook away the thought, looking at the sky through the treeline to judge the sun's height and how long it would take him to get back home. Mir was over two hours on horseback and to the southeast . . . more or less. Rhyol was farther west, but there was more Silver Wood to cover, and Kavriel couldn't be sure how much danger that might involve. He would travel in the daylight, so there shouldn't be any wolf packs to worry about. Yet there were other animals in the forest that were equally dangerous. Bears and bobcats had been seen near Silver Wood's borders; there was no telling what was hidden deeper in.

Clutching the knife hilt tightly for courage, he loosened his coat over his shoulders with the other hand as he started to perspire. It was warmer than he probably needed, but if all went well, and he headed directly southwest all the way, then he should probably reach Rhyol by sundown. If all went well. Nodding as if to convince himself that this was the best idea, Kavriel looked at the cabin one last time, then took off into the trees at a brisk walk. The sunlight glistened against the drops of water falling off the wet leaves.

CHAPTER 13

The forest grew denser, the farther south Kavriel travelled, and the landscape rose and fell in steep hills and bluffs, slowing his progress. Looking at the sky, he noticed that the sun was way past its peak and quickly turning red. He couldn't make out an accurate horizon, but he could feel by the increasing chill in the air that he would be running out of daylight very soon. Kavriel was worried.

He knew he had been moving in the direction he wanted, despite having to backtrack at several impassible parts of the forest, yet there was no trail of any kind that had helped him along, animal or man-made. It was as if this part of Silver Wood had never been explored by anything, ever. Kavriel's borrowed pants hadn't protected his legs from cuts and scratches, and the thick black coat was more of a burden than anything when trying to squeeze through the underbrush. The absence of animal markings on the trees or the ground he took as something positive; at least he wasn't intruding on anything's territory. But he didn't know how far he had to go.

He had figured before that he would be at the outskirts of the forest by now, but he had lost at least several hours fighting through underbrush and he knew now there was no way he would make it to Rhyol before dark. He considered making camp somewhere, but after a moment's reflection realized that with only the heavy jacket and without shelter, that would be a very bad idea. And he didn't want to start wandering off in another direction in search of burrows or hollow logs for shelter.

He continued pushing on, thankful that at least the pine trees had given way to birches again, and he made better progress. The colors became lost in gloom, and without looking at the sky Kavriel knew that evening was fast approaching. He pushed himself harder, tripping and stumbling through the undergrowth and low branches. If anything, the racket of his passage would likely deter any animal that might be curious about him. It was an old trick that Kavriel's father had taught him and his brother when they were young. He knew that they would be sneaking away into Silver Wood when they weren't supposed to, and had decided to at least giving them some sort of instruction in case they became lost. If a child is going to jump in the water anyway, you might as well teach him how to swim first. Kavriel was thankful for that little bit of education now.

He stopped after a while to catch his breath, realizing that his tramping around was wearing on him. He breathed fast but softly, listening to the forest, where twilight had fallen, immersing everything in indigo light. *Time to get going,* Kavriel thought, and resumed his trek.

That was when he heard a branch snap somewhere nearby.

He stopped immediately. Had he heard that, or was he imagining it?

Another sharp snap, much louder, then the crunch of fallen leaves being crushed underfoot. Someone else was in the wood, moving nearby. The steps became more deliberate.

Had he reached a forest clearing where one of the Rhyol woodsmen was finishing up his workday felling trees? If he was heading back to town . . . Kavriel peered hopefully through the trees, cursing the darkness of the forest; only moments ago he could see everything!

More crunching footfalls, closer. Kavriel thought he heard voices from somewhere to the right and left of his location. He'd had enough of the woods. Surely he was far enough away from Mir Town that the soldiers wouldn't be looking for him here. He called out as he stumbled forward, hoping for rescue. Despite the darkness, he noticed faint trails appearing across his route and before him, which further encouraged him. He concentrated on the sounds, moving and stopping, moving and stopping to determine direction.

He crossed over a small hill concealed by the darkness and actually saw the edge of the forest, illuminated by the bright white moon sailing over the sea. Kavriel realized that he had travelled farther west than he'd thought, moving through Silver Wood at an angle. That was probably why it had taken him longer than he had anticipated. He was even farther away from Rhyol than he had expected to be. It didn't matter, though; once he exited Silver Wood he knew the land well enough to get home. He smiled to himself as he moved toward the forest edge.

And then he saw the silhouette of a man—the man whose footfalls he had been listening to. He stood about five feet away, near a large oak tree that looked as out of place in the birches as he did. All relief vanished as Kavriel recognized the uniform of the Ay'vol soldier, and as the man looked back at him with a surprised smile on his face, Kavriel realized that he should have heeded Xavr's advice. He had crossed Silver Wood as far from Mir Town as possible, but it had been for absolutely nothing. Xavr had been right in saying that Kavriel had escaped the Patriarch's hounds once, but he would be very lucky to do it a second time.

Shock and fear made Kavriel feel suddenly weak. His heart racing, he wondered if he should stay and try talking to the soldier, convince him of his innocence, or if he should charge at the man, try to take him on. He was in no better shape than he had been when first facing the Ay'vol, and the hours in the forest had tired him. He gazed at the treeline just beyond the soldier. *So close . . .*

The soldier shouted something in Rav'agas that Kavriel didn't want to understand; he had a good idea what it was.

He took off at a dead run.

The forest came alive.

One moment Kavriel was bounding over the forest floor, seeing nothing but the open grass that was his freedom, and the next moment he was lying on his back, seeing stars that were not in the sky. His jaw ached, and his cheek stung mercilessly as another shape, another soldier, came out from behind a tree adjusting the gauntlet on his forearm that had loosened when he'd used it like a club to knock Kavriel off his feet. He dropped his boot onto Kavriel's chest, keeping him down. Wincing, Kavriel squirmed like a mouse trapped under a cat's paw. Other shapes surrounded him, and the soldier who had been pinning Kavriel with his boot lifted it and pulled him to his feet.

Kavriel swayed, dizzy. The soldier cuffed him across his mouth and shoved him against the oak tree, its rough solidity bringing his mind back into focus. The soldier holding him against the tree stepped away, and Kavriel saw another soldier approaching him. "Keep him still!" the soldier barked, and with horror Kavriel recognized the voice.

The clean-shaven Ay'vol officer, his dark eyes hidden from the moonlight, walked calmly forward, glancing at the larger soldier, who looked at the man strangely, as if he'd never heard him speak before. He did what he was told, though, shoving a gloved hand over Kavriel's throat while pushing his other hand against Kavriel's chest to press him back against the tree. Kavriel wheezed for breath. He understood also that the soldier had looked at his officer strangely because he had given him orders in Kavriel's language, not Rav'agas—this man wanted Kavriel to understand everything.

Behind the officer, the rest of the group that had surrounded him in Mir Town spread out. Kavriel noticed that two had angry bruises on their faces. That had been Xavr's doing, Kavriel thought, suddenly wishing he had listened to the bastard.

He started to plead, just as he had before escaping these men. He knew it would be to no avail and just to confirm that, the dark-eyed soldier only smiled. "So . . ." He spoke slowly and precisely. "You must think yourself quite clever, believing that you might have been able to get away from me?" He sneered. "Where did you think you would go, man from Rhyol? Hmm?"

The strangle-hold that the soldier had on Kavriel kept him from responding, but he didn't think the Ay'vol officer actually expected him to say anything. Kavriel looked past the officer, toward the moonlit green hillsides just past the tree line. He knew exactly where he was; that narrow road running along the edge of woods would turn south before it got to close to the coastal bluffs. It was the same road that Kavriel had taken to Mir Town with Saire and the others. It had been the main thoroughfare between the towns when the mine was operating, and went through the better part of Silver Wood. Kavriel felt stupid, realizing that if the soldiers were after him, they would have been scouting that road. There was no place else he could have gone. Plus he had told them where he was from. It hadn't been luck that let the soldiers find him, only common sense.

Kavriel must have moved more than the soldier wanted, for he felt the gloved fingers squeezing his neck tighter. He stiffened. The officer watched him, smiling, and walked up to Kavriel, close enough that he could smell the man's breath.

"We never finished our conversation the other night," the officer said, letting his accent slip through. Kavriel could tell that he was tired. They probably hadn't stopped looking for him since he escaped, and the line between weariness and impatience was very thin.

He struck Kavriel hard across the mouth with the back of his hand. Kavriel winced, tasting blood in his mouth but unable to move with the soldier's hand still holding his neck. "I asked you a question," the officer growled, as if continuing their conversation from The Backfill tavern.

Kavriel remembered what the man had asked him, because he had asked Xavr about the same thing:

Vaemalin. For some reason these soldiers were obsessed with his brother, enough to track Kavriel through Silver Wood for an entire day and night. It was crazy, but it gave him an idea. "He'll be along shortly," he choked out.

His words had an immediate effect. The grip on his neck loosened almost at the same time as the pressure on his chest. The soldiers behind the officer suddenly forgot all about him; dropping their hands to their sword hilts, they began turning wary circles, scanning the surrounding forest with wide eyes. Even the officer, his lips twitching, stepped back, peering around.

Kavriel didn't understand what the men wanted with his brother, but it was enough to scare them, and that scared Kavriel. These men thought that Vaemalin had attacked them in the tavern. They must have, otherwise why act like this?

Enough thinking, Kavriel thought, and used the momentary distraction to flee. He kicked off of the oak tree, shoving past the cursing soldier, and bolted for the trees. The other soldiers were quicker, however, and grabbed for Kavriel as he tried to get past them. A flurry of fists landed him back on the ground, and the Ay'vol continued to beat Kavriel, screaming and cursing at him in Rav'agas. Kavriel tried to protect his head, trying to ignore the pain of blow after blow. He somehow got to his feet, but another shot in the side brought him to his knees. Before he could move a third time a hand grabbed a clump of his hair, forcing his head back. Cold metal pressed against his neck as someone else restrained his arms from behind.

All he could do was look up into the eyes of the

officer standing before him, holding the dagger at his throat. Kavriel knew he was done for. He could feel warm blood running down the side of his face. His mouth hung loosely to the side. The all-too-familiar thumping started up in his head. He had been beaten more times recently than he had been in his entire life. He looked up at the officer, waiting for him to slit his throat like a sheep for the slaughter, angry not because he had been unable to escape, but because he still didn't understand why all this was happening. It was all some kind of strange, lucid dream. Except the blade on his throat felt real enough.

The officer glared back at Kavriel, hunger and rage in his eyes, but he kept his hand steady. "Come out," he shouted into the darkness of the trees, "or I will bleed this one!" He waited only a moment before repeating what he had said, and a third time, in Rav'agas.

The forest was silent. Kavriel waited with the soldiers for something to happen. It was obvious that they were trying to flush out Vaemalin, believing he was hiding in the trees. Kavriel hadn't thought things through; soon they would call his bluff. He'd gained only a brief reprieve before the officer realized he had been fooled. Kavriel actually saw the moment when realization came to the officer's dark eyes, and they glared at him with the cold certainty of death.

He didn't know why he did it, maybe because he was so tired and hurt that he couldn't help himself, or maybe the thumping of his head had taken his wits, but Kavriel laughed at the officer's frustration. He laughed hard and long, the laugh of a dead man just before the axe falls. Kavriel forgot where he was and why he had come here, he stopped worrying if any of what he was trying to do would make sense at all. He had been trying to understand a four-year-old world in yesterday's time. He was tired, and he would sleep and this would all be over. Let the blade take him before dementia. To the Creator with all of them.

The officer scowled as he either blessed or cursed him in Rav'agas, Kavriel couldn't understand which. Then he tugged Kavriel's head up and pulled the blade across his throat. Strangely, Kavriel didn't feel any kind of pain, but only a slight pressure on his neck that suddenly became very warm. He must have stopped laughing, or simply couldn't make the sound any longer, but his eyes remained focused on the officer's satisfied smile. The trees around them began to spin; he had a hard time keeping his eyes in one place. Before he knew it he was on his back again, hearing a strange bubbling sound coming from just below his chin while the stars and moon gradually lost their light until all became black.

CHAPTER 14

Kavriel stood over the body that lay crumpled in a heap at his feet like a discarded towel. He listened to the wind that breathed softly through the tree line, coming off of the distant sea illuminated by the moonlight. There were no other sounds in the forest, not one creature stirring. Neither was there any movement from the body below him. It was as if everything had suddenly frozen. All life, suddenly imagined.

Kavriel raised his head, slowly at first, feeling a resistance in his neck, as if a rope had been tied around it. He rubbed it with his hand. It was still tender to touch but otherwise intact. The memory of the blade opening his neck was very clear in his mind, but he couldn't be quite sure that it had been an important memory or not. It was simply distant. His hands, coat, and the entire front of his shirt were stained with a wet blackness that was extremely uncomfortable in the chill night wind. He realized belatedly that it was his blood . . . or was it?

Around him were other bodies, pieces of bodies, scattered about the clearing like the remains from a vicious wolf attack. Kavriel couldn't tell how many bodies there were. It was too . . . disturbing, as if the men had been ripped apart by the force of intense shaking, as a dog might shake apart a cloth toy in play. Only by their eyes did Kavriel recognize who they had been before this slaughter, those already clouding in death. They were the Ay'vol soldiers who had captured him twice already. There was not going to be a third time.

Kavriel realized that he was in shock. He looked at

the piles of red meat and sinew that had once been men and knew what he was staring at, but he couldn't think how it had been possible. He wanted to scream and cry at the same time. Bewildered, confused, and dizzy, he stumbled backward until he tripped over the Ay'vol officer. Well . . . tripped over part of him.

There was a great amount of blood spilled around Kavriel, as if it had been dumped over his head. As the smell of the dead soldier's excrement crept up through the salty breeze, Kavriel fell over, sick and shaking and convulsing until he'd emptied every last bit inside his stomach onto the black leaves. After what felt like an eternity the spasms passed, and Kavriel rubbed his wet eyes over and over again with the back of his hand, unable to keep them focused. He wiped his nose and smelled the iron scent of blood and it almost renewed his sickness, but he pressed his hands quickly to his sides and closed his eyes, breathing slowly through his mouth.

Through great effort he managed to climb to his feet, and walked unsteadily a dozen paces out of the killing grounds before he opened his eyes. Once away from the carnage Kavriel's mind began to reconnect him with reality, but he still had absolutely no recollection of what had happened to these men.

As before, when he had awakened under the mines in the basin chamber, nothing made any sense. He had been killed. His throat had been cut by the officer now lying in pieces behind him. He had not imagined that. That meant that he must be dead, but why could he sense everything so sharply? The air, the cold, the sounds of the ocean, the blowing leaves and the smell of death behind him . . .

surely dead men could not do these things? That meant that Kavriel was still alive—impossible, but true.

Something swaying in the branches above him caught his eye. Kavriel looked up, and saw one of the Ay'vol soldiers, unlike the others only in that he was still in one piece. He was still quite dead, suspended on the thick oak branch that had gored him which now looked like a bloody spearhead sticking out from his chest. His arms and legs dangled from the lifeless body like some ghoulish string-puppet; it was the breeze, not animation that had moved them, catching his attention. Kavriel turned away from the horrible sight and left the forest, moving toward the Rhyol road.

CHAPTER 15

Twilight came like the sigh of a waking infant, the moon gradually drifting off to the west while a blanket of yellow and pink reflected off the morning mist hanging over the ocean. The road cut through fields of tall grass that slowly became farmland, and the gravel road Kavriel followed became wider and more level as he ran.

Moonstone Shrine appeared to Kavriel like the fallen remains of a pure white beacon, glowing in the advancing daylight. He paused, leaning against one of the upright slabs to catch his breath. A memory of the basin chamber hidden under the mines, with its forest of white pillars so similar to those of Moonstone Shrine, flashed into his mind. Here, too, a shorter, cylindrical rock sat in the center, a mirror of the subterranean basin. He didn't understand how, but Kavriel knew that the two places were connected.

This thought didn't last long. His eyes strayed past the circle and he saw the outermost houses of his home town, and Kavriel sprinted away from the shrine and down the ridge, ignoring the pain in his chest from the exertion of running for the past few hours. His only thought was to reach his house.

When he passed the first stone building and entered Rhyol, though, despair overtook his exhaustion. Mir Town had received a new breath of life, but what had once been Rhyol had been taken away. All the homes that he passed, the stables, the barns and the storehouses, all that had been sturdy and sound seemed to have fallen in on itself, neglected and left to the elements. The road he walked on was almost as difficult to navigate as the deep forest of Silver Wood, littered with rocks and the paving stones jutting up at jagged angles, unrepaired for who knew how long. There was not a soul around. He heard yipping and a moment later saw a pack of feral dogs roaming the town, snapping and growling at each other as they scavenged for something to eat. The mutts barked and scattered as Kavriel approached, trotting down the once busiest road in Rhyol. Kavriel couldn't fight back the tears.

Voices startled him, suddenly erupting in the oppressive silence, shouting somewhere farther down the road where the dogs had headed. A moment later a figure chased them away from something, hollering and cursing in a language that Kavriel immediately recognized as Rav'agas. He ducked off the road, backing up behind a high stone wall. He poked his head around the wall, and saw three men dressed in heavy jackets walking in timed precision down the road. They were still too far away for Kavriel to make out much detail, but he knew already what kind of men these were as they jibed and chattered with each other like bored guardsmen everywhere.

He turned and made his way down the same alleyway he had taken what seemed like yesterday, when he'd left his father's house in search of Vaemalin and Tess, four years ago. He ducked down several crossing alleys, moving quietly, listening to the Rav'agas Guardsmen as they passed by him on the main road, unaware of his existence. He rounded one last corner and there was his house, waiting like a nightmare, an image from his memory warped and twisted by time and despair.

For a brief moment, Kavriel thought he had

confused his home with another. Yet as he approached it cautiously, he knew by the window frames and the wooden porch that it truly was his. He crossed the porch to the oak door, and lowered the handle, thankful that no latch had been set as he slipped into the softly lit entryway of his house and closed the door quickly but carefully behind him.

The salon was like a crypt, cold and vacant, without the usual noises of residents going about their chores. For a moment Kavriel felt that he was the only one here, until a faint shuffle of movement came from the opposite corner, and a spark lit up the room, blinding him momentarily. The flash gave way to the softer glow of an oil lamp, held by someone whose face remained in shadow behind it. As the figure raised the oil lamp, Kavriel sensed movement behind him and turned just as something blunt and heavy struck him across the head. The room vanished in a flash of white, and Kavriel stumbled forward as the floor of the entryway rushed up to greet him.

* * *

Kavriel awoke in what seemed like only seconds. He recalled somehow being forced into a sitting position while he had been stunned. He felt something cold and wet on the back of his head, but he was unable to reach back; his arms were tied to the arms of the chair he slumped in. He arched his neck, and a thin white dishcloth dropped down into his lap. Kavriel focused on it while waiting for his surroundings to stop revolving like bed spins after an overindulgent drunk. When he felt as if he could see straight, he looked up. Candles now burned in the corners of the room, and he recognized his home with a pang of familiarity. He also saw that he was not alone.

271

Standing quietly and motionless by the dark and empty fire pit was a person he did not know. The young man glared distrustfully at him. Forgetting the restraints, Kavriel tried and failed to stand, the heavy chair creaking underneath him. "Who are you?" he snarled up at the stranger in his home.

He studied the young man. He was slightly shorter than Kavriel would have been if he could stand to compare, but with wide shoulders typical of a Rhyolian. He was dressed in a loose brown shirt and pants and a long, light jacket, as if he had just come in from the yard. His dark, curly hair, wooly as a sheep's, hung past his ears. He had a beard, or at least the beginnings of one, sparse as most found on boys on the cusp of manhood. It poorly concealed several bruises on his jaw and cheek. His dark eyes stared at Kavriel with sharp interest.

The young man definitely had the look of someone from Rhyol, but Kavriel had no idea who he was or what he was doing in his home. Seeing a broken fence post gripped in his hands, Kavriel knew what had struck him when he'd first entered his home. Caught by surprise by this would-be thief, now Kavriel sat roped to a chair, wanting very much to break free and toss this youth out the door. He shouted at him again, but the stranger remained silent, as if waiting for something else. Kavriel realized that was exactly what he was doing as he saw the stranger's eyes drift away from him to another person in the room who was standing behind the chair.

Kavriel didn't quite understand how he knew, but as he felt the presence of the second person pass around him, he felt suddenly reassured, as if he knew who it was. The sensation surprised him a moment, but as the person moved in front of the chair, Kavriel knew that his instincts had not been wrong.

Overseer Cyr Soelle, Kavriel's father, stood there in the flickering candlelight like a vision of hope, but he looked at Kavriel like he wasn't quite sure what he was seeing. and as Kavriel became more aware of the changes in his father, he imagined that he must have a similar expression on his face. This was the same man, that was for certain, but faded into a thin reflection of who he once was.

Cyr Soelle had always prided himself on his posture despite his gimped leg, but this new Cyr Soelle stood slightly hunched, and his once thick and neatly trimmed head of grayish brown hair was long and matted, as if he spent his days working in the fields. His clothing had been modest but still always well-kept and clean, but now a worn, moth-eaten robe hung from the overseer's shoulders like a funeral shawl, and he peered at Kavriel with narrowed eyes full of mistrust and pain and suppressed rage, something he had never seen from his father before. Like everything else Kavriel had seen in Rhyol, his father had changed into a terrible manifestation of what he had once been.

"Father?" he whispered. The overseer paled. "Father, what is going on?" he strained against his bindings, yearning to touch his father, to comfort him and take comfort from him. The overseer made no move, only stared strangely back at him. "Father!" Kavriel called out again.

It was the young man with the wooden post who spoke, in a voice that was deep beyond his years. "Master

Soelle, do you know this man?" Kavriel stared at him in surprise.

His father nodded. "This is unexpected," he said dryly, without turning his gaze away from Kavriel. "Who are you?" he asked.

Kavriel, not at all expecting that sort of question, replied in a voice that was weak with sadness and fatigue. "Father, it's me," he choked out, and the overseer looked hard at him, moving closer to get a better look. Kavriel felt as if he were being torn apart from the inside. "Father, what's going on!" he shouted as he fought back tears.

The overseer held an open palm toward him. "Be still," he said softly, "I don't mean to cause you discomfort if you are who you say you are. But you must understand what seeing you here is doing to me."

"Seeing me here?" Kavriel gasped. "What in Creation are you talking about? This is my home—this is *our* home! Damn it, Father, untie me!" Kavriel struggled against his bonds, his sight blurred by tears. He looked pleadingly at his father as his limbs began to shake. The flames on the candles flickered all at once, but all were too distracted to pay any attention to them.

"Don't you recognize me?" Kavriel's voice quavered, and he knew that in a moment he would be a slobbering mess. Yet it would be with good reason. Kavriel had travelled a nightmare ever since reawakening in the mine, and having to confront the father who no longer knew him crossed the limit of his sanity.

As if sensing his distress, the overseer changed into the father Kavriel remembered. His face softened and a slight smile tugged at his lips. "Of course I recognize you, my son," he said, laying a hand on Kavriel's own. "I am so sorry . . . I am so sorry." Cyr grunted out a laugh of disbelief that was hiding behind some deep sadness, and Kavriel choked one out in response, still baffled by this odd greeting but ever so happy that his father had finally seen him for who he was.

As his father bent to untie the ropes that bound Kavriel's wrists to the chair, the younger man at the fire edged closer, his frown disapproving. Kavriel didn't care; when he was finally free he grabbed his father and the two came together in a tight embrace. In his father's arms, Kavriel finally released his sorrow and heartbreak. He had struggled too much, over *so much*, and now, in the warmth and familiar smells of his home, he had finally reached a place of peace. He still knew nothing of his lost life, but for the moment he didn't care. It was a painful yet wonderful feeling, and when he let his father go he almost felt as if he had awakened yet again, but this time into someplace that he knew well.

Cyr Soelle pulled back and held Kavriel away from him to study his son. He was not a man to show his emotions so openly, and Kavriel knew he was still struggling to control them. He also knew just from his father's reaction to his arrival that whatever had happened in the last four years, Kavriel had not been with his father. As far as he knew, this was the first time that his father had seen him since his disappearance. He could only imagine the emotions overflowing in his father's own thoughts, and envied the man his ability to control himself.

"Oh Kavriel," Cyr said, "what have you gotten yourself into."

It wasn't really a question; his father's sorrowful tone suggested disappointment in something that Kavriel had done. He wasn't sure how to respond, but he followed his father's gaze down to the front of his shirt . . . the blood-covered shirt. Kavriel suddenly understood his father's confusion and concern. Behind him the stranger, still wary, leaned back to rest his makeshift weapon against the wall with obvious reluctance.

"My dear boy," Cyr said, shaking his head, "what have you done?"

"I . . . I had some problems with some men. I'm not hurt." Kavriel felt foolish. It was the same response he probably would have given at ten years old, after scuffling with the neighbor children. He shook his head, then quickly stopped when the throbbing from the blow with the wooden fence post intensified. "I mean, I don't know what happened, exactly. After the mine collapsed, everything was so complicated . . . I was trapped, but I found a way out. There were guardsmen, or soldiers, who tried to put me under arrest, said I was a criminal. . . . something about who I was associated with, I think. I've forgotten . . . I had to hide in the woods. Xavr thought it would be best."

He was speaking in fragments, trying to understand while at the same time explaining it to his father. His father was patient, smiling kindly as he motioned for Kavriel to sit back down in the chair. Kavriel didn't right away, but stood flushed with embarrassment at his rambling. He seemed more lost now than ever before, here in front of the man he loved and respected far above anyone else. It felt awkward and wrong to be having this meeting with him. Finally he sat back down in the chair that had constrained him, rubbing self-consciously at the front of his shirt as if he might be able to brush the blood away.

Cyr frowned in concern, looking studiously at Kavriel as if he truly did want to understand. "My son, I can see that this is . . . difficult. But please, you must try to tell me where you've been." His father dragged over a second chair and sat down in front of Kavriel, steepling his fingers and placing his chin on their tips as he waited. This familiar trait of his father's calmed Kavriel, who nodded, feeling slightly more confident as he began his story.

He told his father the exact same thing and in the same detail that he had with Xavr, only adding the more recent events in the forest that ended with him seeming to awaken on his feet in a circle of death.

This detail concerned the overseer the most. "Kavriel," he said softly when he was certain his son had finished his tale. He spoke with a modulated precision meant to be calming. "Did you kill those men?"

Kavriel blinked in surprise, feeling sick to his stomach as he recalled the memory. "No!" he said quickly, and with a volume that made the strange man ease back toward his weapon. His father hadn't moved, but concern still shone in his eyes. Kavriel forced himself to calm as he shook his head. "I'm sorry . . . There are so many holes in my memory of everything that happened since I left here. I don't know what happened, but I couldn't have killed those men. I just couldn't have!" Kavriel wasn't sure about many things since his escape from the mine, but he refused to believe that he could have killed anybody! Let alone tear the Ay'vol men to pieces like they . . . No, he felt nauseous just thinking it.

His father must have sensed his unease. He patted Kavriel's arm as if to relax him. Behind him, the young man stood poised against the wall with a gleam in his eye, as if he was about to pounce. "Alright, Kavriel, it's alright." He changed the subject. "But why did you go back to the mines? With the patrols, it's impossible, not to mention dangerous. What were you searching for?"

Kavriel blinked in confusion. Was he serious? Had his father been listening at all to what he had just finished telling him? And who was the most confused? He actually felt a little hurt. "Searching? No . . . You knew what we were in the mines for. You sent me there to keep an eye on Saire." His father's expression was blank, as if he'd never heard the name before. "General Saire, Father! Remember? He came to explore the caverns, to see if they had any connection to the Oenes Caverns. You told me to watch him when I went with the others—Vaem, Grieg, Tess."

"Tess!" the stranger leaning against the wall echoed, drawing Kavriel's attention back to him.

Overseer Soelle didn't take notice, instead finally digesting Kavriel's story. He leaned back in his chair and his eyes went wide. He too whispered the names to himself before addressing Kavriel. "I . . . we will need to take this one step at a time. We all are in need of some answers, I think." He turned his head slightly to address the stranger. "Seth, could you boil some water for tea, please?"

The young man responded immediately. "Of course, Master Soelle." He moved into the kitchen.

His father continued to study Kavriel, who wondered why he paid no mind to the stranger bustling about in their home as if he had been doing it for years.

Kavriel sensed that whoever this young man was, he had been. The name that his father called him also seemed to nudge a memory that Kavriel couldn't quite grab, but he decided to focus on his more immediate concern.

"Why do you seem so surprised to see me?" he asked casually, and the overseer grunted as if he had just got the punchline of a joke.

A moment later he met Kavriel's eyes. "You're serious, aren't you?" he asked, and Kavriel could only nod solemnly, already expecting the worst. "Kavriel . . . I thought you'd been killed when the mine collapsed. I haven't seen you in—"

"Four years," Kavriel finished for him, nodding in resignation, remembering what Xavr had told him yet hoping he had imagined it.

Now it was his father's turn to become quiet as he blinked in confusion. They sat in silence for a moment. He shook his head dramatically before continuing. "I am just . . . I am just glad that I was mistaken. But Kavriel, where have you been this whole time?"

"I . . . " Kavriel shook his head and closed his mouth, realizing that the only response he could give would be the impossible. *I was under rock and stone for four years, Father.* There must have been someplace else that he had been, regardless of his memories. There just had to have been. He let his gaze stray to one of the nearby candles, staring at the dancing flame, feeling the calmness in its sway. His memories would come back in time . . . they must!

"He said that you were buried with the others, Saire, his associate, and another man," his father said softly.

Kavriel turned to him. "Who said?"

"Your brother."

Kavriel was still feeling like he had been cut adrift, but the mention of his brother offered hope. "Vaemalin got out," he said, addressing his father but confirming the statement more for himself.

His father nodded.

"Then he's alive, thank the Creator." Kavriel looked around the room curiously. "Where is he?" he asked, and wished he hadn't when he saw the strange, distraught expression that suddenly appeared on his father's face. The small noises coming from the kitchen also went quiet. The young man had stopped what he was doing to listen.

"Kavriel," his father replied sadly, "your brother is . . . well, I am not certain where your brother is now. He couldn't stay. I'm sorry, but I have not seen or heard from him in a very long time, either. I am so glad that you are here now."

His father's response and the doubt in his eyes before he looked at the floor told Kavriel that something was seriously wrong. "What about the others?" he asked, hoping to get a different reaction, but his father only shook his head, repeating in silence the same response. He smiled, regarding Kavriel lovingly, and Kavriel sensed that there was much more that had happened to his family and friends, something that went beyond the politics of Rav'agas and the Patriarch. He thought about it for a moment, then spoke more on the recent events, hoping that might shed some light on everything.

"Father, when I was in Mir, the Ay'vol soldiers questioned me about Vaemalin."

His father immediately looked concerned. "Did they hurt you?" he asked, ignoring that Kavriel had mentioned they were Ay'vol in the first place.

Four years seemed much longer to someone who hadn't lived them, and Kavriel decided not to assume his father was as ignorant as he was about everything. He merely glanced at his hand, seeing that even the scratch mark he had noticed in Xavr's cabin the other night had disappeared. He shook his head. "No, they didn't. I was able to get away from them before that."

The overseer nodded silently to Kavriel's response, but his eyes fell down over Kavriel's bloody shirt once more. Kavriel didn't mention that the men he'd "had trouble with" were the same group that had interrogated him in Mir Town. There was no use picking out those details. They'd been asking him about Vaemalin, and they had chased him through Silver Wood for answers. That was the point. He sighed.

" I . . . I can't remember anything that has happened to me since the cave-in. I know it sounds strange and probably impossible, but I don't know where I have been and what has happened to our home and Quetal. It's like I've been asleep for four years." Kavriel paused, letting this sink in as he continued to wonder if anything like what he had just said was feasible.

Thankfully his father seemed to understand, and nodded while taking the cup of tea that Seth had finished brewing for him. He offered it to Kavriel, who declined, not needing anymore stimulation for the night. He needed to clear his head on his own terms.

"It's alright, Kavriel," his father said. "I think I'm

starting to see things now. Your condition isn't the first case I have encountered. Delusion and memory loss are common symptoms of the illness. I'm just glad you haven't fallen completely into dementia. Just by talking to you now I can see that you seem to be healing on your own. It's fascinating, actually, your situation. I don't think there have ever been two cases alike, but yours is quite unique. I can't tell you enough how surprised and grateful I am that you are alive!" His father had switched his mien to the more serious town elder and the change came as a relief to Kavriel who nodded, understanding what his father suspected. He had thought the same thing.

"I don't know how I must have caught red-eye. Yet it seems the only rational explanation, doesn't it?"

Again his father reassured him with a nod, even though they were still talking about a strange and complicated sickness that had never been fully understood. Unlike the propaganda initiated on the mainland about the illness, Kavriel and certainly his father knew that it wasn't the death decree the politicians made it out to be. There were rare cases of death in those who had fallen ill. Memory loss was the most common symptom and seemed to be expected. Yet Kavriel had never heard of anyone simply losing all of his memory for such a long period of time. His father was correct to assume that his was a very unique case.

His father seemed to be thinking the same thing. "Look, Kavriel, I don't want to frighten you. The caverns had been sealed off for a reason when Saire went against what I asked of him. I blame only him for what has happened to you all."

"All?" Kavriel repeated, startled.

His father paused and looked intently at Kavriel before nodding. "I'm sorry, Kavriel; I haven't been clear with you. Maybe it will be best if I explain what has happened in the time you can't remember. If anything, then perhaps you might begin to recall certain parts of your life that were lost." He took a moment to collect his thoughts, sipping from the teacup while Kavriel waited anxiously.

The other man had decided to finally join them, but took a chair a bit farther away and behind Kavriel. Kavriel only eyed him silently, knowing that the man was still expecting him to do something rash.

His father spoke. "We assembled a team quickly after it was known that there had been a collapse in the caverns. It was the two Loellen men, actually, who notified us as they tore into Rhyol on their horses. Grieg and his Rav'agas woman-friend came with them. He had been badly hurt, and she as well. We were grateful for the Loellen for helping them back home, but the others were not with them. They said that Vaemalin and Tess had stayed behind to try to find another way into some kind of chamber that you had found?"

His father looked at Kavriel for confirmation, and he nodded. His father frowned, and Kavriel didn't have to hear the words to understand how frustrated his father must have been that they had gone so deep in the caves and so carelessly. If something like this had ever happened while Kavriel was a young boy sneaking off to Mir, his father would have had his legs removed just to make certain he couldn't run back to the mines.

"I went with about a dozen men from the town,

riding as fast as we could so that we might help," Cyr said. "Kair and Femaor stayed behind to help with the others. Strange, but I never wanted to go back to the mine so much more in my life." He actually smiled. Kavriel knew that his father would rather have leapt into a burning house than return to that place that had been responsible for his mother's sickness and his handicapped leg.

Kavriel nodded. "How did you find them?" he asked, remembering the caved-in route that he hadn't been able to use. His friends must have escaped through another passage that he missed.

"They found us, actually," his father said, which surprised Kavriel. "By the time we arrived Vaemalin and Tess were sitting outside the adit, covered in dust and grime from the caverns. They were alright, but devastated . . . especially Vaemalin. Your brother felt personally responsible for letting you become trapped." Cyr paused to control his emotions. He looked earnestly at Kavriel. "I never blamed him, Kavriel. I promise you."

"I . . . I would never think that," Kavriel replied softly, wondering why his father would feel it needed clarification. He wouldn't have accused his family. It was the mine that he hated. He always had. His father shook his head, gazing down into his cup. 'Were they injured?" Kavriel asked, sensing that his father had drifted away from the interest the Ay'vol seemed to have with his brother but not wanting to bring the conversation back to that for fear of missing something important.

"No, thank goodness," Cyr said. "Yet they refused to believe that you were lost to us. It was days before we had to accept the inevitable truth. The caverns were weakened by whatever had caused the collapse, and many of the passages were blocked." He looked at his son with genuine shame. "I'm sorry, Kavriel, but there was nothing more we could have done for you."

He paused, and Kavriel took the moment to reflect on the fact that his father had just told him that they'd conceded that he had been killed by the cave-in. It was strange hearing about one's death while still being alive. Not wanting to dwell on it, he changed the subject. "What about the general and his men? And Xavr?"

His father shook his head. "I'm sorry, but I don't know who this Xavr person is." He said, brows puckered in confusion. "Vaemalin and Tess mentioned another man who had fought Saire and his associate. They didn't know who he was, but he seemed to know Saire very well. Is that the man you mean?"

Kavriel nodded. "Yes. He helped me out of Mir Town and kept me safe in his cabin until this morning."

His father's brows rose. "Was it possible, son, that this man might have been taking care of you longer than that?"

Kavriel knew that he was testing his memory. He understood why, but as he thought about the bizarre rescue Xavr had executed, he was certain that he couldn't have been with him for such a long time without remembering more. He shook his head.

His father nodded, accepting his reply. "How do you know him?" he asked, and Kavriel could tell that the question dealt more with Xavr's relationship to Saire than with who he was as an individual.

"I met him at Moonstone Shrine the morning we

left. I had never seen him before. I believe he was Loellen, now that I think about it, but he looked more like Saire than any Loellen that I've met." His father nodded thoughtfully. "What happened to Saire?" Kavriel asked, and his father shook his head.

"We don't know. Vaemalin and Tess were alone when we found them. They mentioned that the soldiers Saire had brought with him had escaped together, but they never returned here. It's entirely possible that they headed to Port Dior by another route."

"Saire went with them," Kavriel assumed.

Again his father shrugged. "I thought he had been killed. I didn't leave the camp for several days while . . . searching for you. We never saw anyone else leave the area. If Saire escaped, he must have been desperate not to be seen." Cyr paused, watching Kavriel carefully. "Was it something to do with the fight?" he asked suspiciously, and Kavriel nodded, knowing that whatever reservations his father had about Saire before the event, they had been confirmed, if Vaemalin and Tess had explained what had happened. He believed they had, but it seemed as if his father needed to hear Kavriel's story. He told him, with the detail that he remembered about the general's odd behavior and the conversation with Xavr, including his attack against him, something Kavriel painfully remembered.

His father scowled. "I knew it, the bastard." He looked over to the young man, as if he was an advisor. The stranger nodded in agreement.

"Is that why you wanted me to watch him?" Kavriel asked, wishing he knew more about the young man Seth and his relation to his father.

The overseer nodded. "I'm sorry again, Kavriel, to you and to everybody. I rashly put all of you in danger. That man is deceitful and untrustworthy. I should have heeded Femaor and Councilman Richart's advice. Damn it! I have caused all of this."

Kavriel suddenly was ashamed, seeing his father trying to put all that had happened on his shoulders. He put a hand quickly atop his father's. "No . . . Father, it isn't your fault, what happened. There was something that Saire was looking for in the mines, something that he must have learned about from the Temscript Scrolls. He didn't care about anything else. I think if it wasn't for Xavr, none of us would have escaped." This last remark surprised even Kavriel, to hold Xavr in such high regard even though he must have been involved in Saire's quest at a deeper level. Yet as he thought about it from a different perspective, he knew that it was the truth. Xavr had saved them.

His father pondered Kavriel's words. "Tess said that there were golden containers of some sort in the cavern, that he was after those . . ." he mused, brow furrowed as he struggled for the memory. That particular conversation had taken place four years ago.

It only heightened Kavriel's concern for the whereabouts of his friends. He nodded, but until he could be certain he knew what he was talking about, he decided that his other concern was more important. "Yes, urns that were hidden away."

"With some kind of liquid inside them?" his father interjected, focused on the reason for Saire's treachery, now that he seemed to be remembering more of it.

Kavriel still hoped to get back to his point. "Yes, I

think so. I don't remember too much about them, other than that Saire was very interested in them. Where is Tess?" he asked quickly.

The question caught Cyr off guard. His face sagged and the young man behind them lowered his head. "Tess," he repeated slowly. "Tess is dead, Kavriel."

It took a moment for Kavriel to truly comprehend what his father had just said. "No!" he said, not wanting to it. "No, that's impossible. You told me she escaped with Vaemalin!" Kavriel glared at his father for saying such a poisonous thing. Tess was his friend . . . she couldn't be dead. "No," he said more firmly, glancing over to the other man, who had not yet looked up. "You're wrong. Where is she, Father? Where is Vaemalin? Tell me now!" Kavriel knew in his heart that he had no right to speak to his father so. His anger was unjust, but he couldn't stop himself.

His father quickly replied, "Kavriel, this is difficult for all of us. I will not—"

Kavriel interrupted him. "No!" he shouted. "You're lying! This—"

"Kavriel!" his father shouted, and instinctively Kavriel snapped his mouth shut. But the damage had already been done, and he could feel tears trickling from his eyes. His father waited a moment, a firm gaze on Kavriel to make sure he was ready to listen before he began again.

"I'm sorry to have to tell you, Kavriel, but I assumed you already knew. Forgive me. Tess was arrested by the Ay'vol and sent to Teltraum for trial and execution. She was one of many. I didn't realize . . . I'm sorry." Kavriel didn't reply. He was still trying to keep himself from falling apart.

His father continued with the events following the cave-in. "After we returned home, I immediately began sending reports to the mainland about what had happened. Saire had clearly manipulated me, the Council, and who knows how many others in order to fulfill a private agenda. Again, I wasn't sure if he was even alive, but both Femaor and Richart from the Council of Trade in Teltraum advised that I report the event. None of us could prove any wrongdoing besides what Vaemalin and Tess told us, but my mind was . . . I was angry. Vengeful. I needed blood."

His father paused, and Kavriel saw the old rage that had taken his father all those years ago return to his eyes. "Saire was gone and his men had disappeared. The Loellen men stayed in Rhyol for several weeks, helping us with the information they'd gathered already, pertaining to Saire's interest in the mines. They had been with him for over a year already, working as part of a joint Loellen and Council collective to keep an eye on him, not much different than I asked of you." Cyr smiled grimly. "I'd assumed that I was alone in thinking ill about the general. I was wrong. The Council had been keeping an eye on him for longer than I thought, and his 'interests' had been under close observation."

"Why?" Kavriel asked, simply curious.

His father shrugged. "I cannot say, definitely. That kind of information was restricted to the Council Nine only, and I was lucky enough to have a contact in one of the other committees. Yet it didn't stop what happened, and we found out too late that all of our secretive efforts had been for nothing. Saire must have been suspecting us all along, and his reach went further than any of us had imagined."

"You mean to Ay'vol?" Kavriel asked, and his father's smile was tight, as if he were remembering a past defeat that he had to accept. Kavriel wiped his eyes, becoming focused on the story. "Then why didn't the Council stop him, arrest him or something?"

His father shook his head. "It was too late for that. By the time all of our reports had made it to Council, the Rav'agas had already come across the Viliros." He grimaced, baffled. "I still don't fully understand what happened, but one moment the Patriarch seemed satisfied to pick at Quetal near the Ciele border, and the next moment he'd been declared the Reborn." He lifted an eyebrow at Kavriel, most likely uncertain if Kavriel knew something about what he was talking about.

Kavriel nodded quickly. "I know a bit about that," he said. "Xavr told me about the declaration of the Patriarch's Becoming. He said that the provinces united and the Ay'vol Force had come to Quetal." Cyr nodded, probably relieved that he didn't have to go into that. Things were strange enough already. Kavriel imagined that the details of what had happened baffled more people than just him.

"Alright, then," his father said. "But you don't remember that yourself?" Kavriel shook his head. "No matter, what's done is done. The Patriarch must have had some other agenda he was working on while he bided his time in Ciele. I don't think Quetal would have been able to stop him, regardless. Rav'agas is so much more powerful than us, even more so now."

"Is it true then, that Rav'agas has taken Quetal?"

Kavriel asked, already knowing the answer.

His father nodded reluctantly. Kavriel thought he heard a snort from the young man. He was still looking at the floor but it was evident that he was pleased about something.

The overseer noticed it too and allowed a tiny smile. "Officially, yes. The Council has been disbanded and replaced by a man named Zoren, who is some kind of chancellor to the Patriarch. A second, if you will, to try to keep us 'heathens' in our place."

Kavriel was intrigued. "Try?" he repeated, and his father's smile grew.

"Quetal may not be as powerful as the Patriarch's Ay'vol Force, but we are not ready to bow down to the so-called Son of God, either. Our contacts remain, and we keep fighting the good fight, despite the occupation."

"What does the Patriarch want?" Kavriel asked.

"Domination, clear and simple," his father responded matter-of-factly. "He has always been a mad leader in Ay'vol, and now his methods are only proving him more so. However, he hasn't been as preoccupied with Quetal as we imagined. It wasn't a long war, after the declaration had been made." His father sighed in remembrance. "In all honesty, Quetal was finished from the beginning. We had never prepared ourselves for an all-out attack from Ay'vol. It just seemed too impossible. We were wrong, of course, and now these Ay'vol Guardsmen occupy every village on the mainland and here in Nostrac."

"Have they been here long?" Kavriel asked, wishing something would click in his memory to remind him of all of this, but there was nothing.

"About three years now. Once the Council had been taken out, it wasn't long before the chancellor declared his rule over Quetal and sent out his wolves." His father wagged his head from side to side. "It's better that you don't remember that, son. It truly is. For a man who has declared himself the Son of Creation, he has certainly forced many unholy things upon our people. It's a wonder we're still around at all." Anger, outrage, sadness, all tugged at his father's face.

Despite what his father said, Kavriel wished he could remember. "What do you mean?" he asked.

His father waved away the question. "No. I will not go into that horror with you now. The Cleansing is something that I wish to forget and I will not relive that experience for your sake. What is done is done."

They sat silent for some moments, as if waiting for the threatening memories to fade. Whatever this Cleansing was, Kavriel didn't want to pressure his father about it. His concern was still on the whereabouts of his friends. The thought of Tess dead still stung and he needed to get back to that. "About Tess, Father?" he asked softly.

His father nodded, coming back to the subject. "Yes, of course. As I said, it wasn't long after the declaration that we were already seeing Rav'agas soldiers in Quetal. Nostrac was most likely the last, but they came, near the end of the harvest, about a year after what had happened. We'd been expecting it. Femaor had taken Grieg and his friend back to Teltraum once their wounds had healed, and he was working nonstop with his friend and my contact Richart on trying to stop the Rav'agas control from getting out of hand. It was strange, but whatever madness was happening outside of the capital, Teltraum seemed to hang onto its tradition of bureaucracy quite easily, as if it came with the country. Last I heard, Richart had become the Chair of the Council while still under the Rav'agas rule."

"How would that be possible?" Kavriel asked.

His father shrugged. "I'm not certain, son, but maybe the Patriarch bit off more than he could chew by having the chancellor rule in his stead, and needed a Quetalian icon for the people he had conquered. I don't know. After the previous chairman was murdered, things seemed to get only more complicated."

"Murdered?" Kavriel exclaimed, realizing that he was only helping his father drift away from his original concern.

His father nodded, but his expression showed that he wished to avoid that subject as well. So much horror had occurred in the world that Kavriel once knew that he wondered if he would ever completely understand it all.

"Yes, and that . . . well, that brings us back to the subject of your brother, and why the Ay'vol might seem to be concerned with him," Cyr said.

Kavriel leaned forward. "What? With Vaemalin? How is that—"

His father waved his hand, frowning as he seemed to be calling forth memories. It was the stranger, Seth, who answered. Kavriel turned to him in surprise; he'd forgotten he was even there. The young man's voice was deeper than one would expect from someone with such a youthful face, as if the events of the last several years had aged him internally. "Tess and your brother had fallen ill with red-eye."

"Damn." Kavriel exclaimed with a sigh. He had feared as much.

His father nodded with a sigh and took over the conversation. "It's true, son. Only we didn't realize it until several weeks after." He scratched his chin, and his face grew haunted. "Tess's condition was less apparent. She would become lost, or confused about where and who she was at times. I considered it quite normal after all that she had been through, but her mood became more . . . erratic and at times dangerous for her. She would go days without eating, hiding away in her home without seeing anyone. We were all concerned, her father especially."

"And Vaemalin?" Kavriel asked, feeling helpless.

His father's face became taut. "You brother had been taken with the sickness at a level none of us had ever seen before. He was angry and violent, fighting with everyone who tried to help him. I was the only one he seemed less hostile towards, but there was such a deep sadness in him whenever he was near me. He had changed into someone I didn't recognize. We didn't know what we could do for them; despite what was happening on the mainland, they needed more skilled doctors than we could provide on Nostrac. Femaor and Richart thought it would be best if they were sent to Teltraum, where they might get the care they needed. The physicians of the Council are the most skilled in all of Quetal, and Grieg and his woman had been cared for already in that place. It only made sense that we should send the others.

"I was hesitant, of course; the Rav'agas coalition had begun and the Patriarch was already amassing his soldiers in the south. Not to mention all the credibility that the Highlands would lose with the Council, having the overseer sending his son who had been afflicted with the disease they so readily demonized. It would be a public nightmare for Nostrac, yet I didn't see much other choice.

"Still, the preparations took longer than I had hoped. Teltraum was already on the defensive, and months passed before we heard anything from Femaor or Richart. Unfortunately, the Patriarch had moved much faster than anyone could have expected. We were now at war."

His father paused, letting the memories settle. "Grieg and his friend returned to the borderlands in the chaotic assembly of defensemen once the Ay'vol began to move, but by then it was too late. The Rav'agas had come, wiped clean all of the Quetalian and allied defenses, and were already in Teltraum before the year was over. The chancellor arrived with his minions, and the Cleansing order was issued." His father stopped talking and his gaze grew distant for a moment, as he recalled the Cleansing that Kavriel still didn't understand but was reluctant to ask about.

"We lost complete contact with the Council, and we were left in the dark about what was happening on the mainland. The soldiers arrived in Port Dior by spring, and moved into the Highlands not long after. There was a large number of Rav'agas settlers with them, moving farther north into Mir, for the mines."

"The mines?" Kavriel repeated.

His father nodded. "Yes, apparently the chancellor had done his research, and the resources in the mines were of great importance to the new rule. I suppose it was ironic that, for all these years, the clansmen had been hoping for the Council to reopen discussion about the trade, but it took Rav'agas occupation for it to happen." His father chuckled ruefully. "Not that it mattered. The Rav'agas were now in control of Nostrac, and the clans were scattered. I am in contact with only a few of the leaders. The villages emptied to the hills and Mir Town became the new Highland capital. So strange, how things happened." His father paused again, reflectively, as if what he had just said was as much for him as it was for Kavriel.

Kavriel nodded, beginning to understand why Mir Town was the thriving place he had found. It still didn't answer the question about his friends, though.

As if he had been reading Kavriel's thoughts, Seth began speaking again, and he spoke of them. "Tess took care of me and my family after I lost my sister. We didn't know she was sick then, but she was like another member of my family. I don't think we would have made it without her."

Kavriel looked at the young man for a long moment after he'd spoken with such feeling about Tess. Finally he realized who this person was. "Seth." The young man looked up at his name. "You're Seth Kessor, the boy who was found on Poldr's farm. Your sister was Millie . . . wasn't she?" The man paled and he nodded. Kavriel hadn't put a face to the boy Seth when Tess had spoken about his disappearance, but looking at this man now, he could truly understand the amount of time that he had forgotten.

"Yes," Seth replied. "My sister had gotten lost in the caves when we were playing. I only remembered it later, but by then it was too late."

The overseer reached over and patted the young man's shoulder affectionately. Seth responded with a soft smile. Kavriel began to understand their relationship. Both had lost someone dear to them in the mines at almost the same time. The Kessors were neighbors to the Taloes but Cyr was a good overseer to his people and took all the townspeople's pain for his own. It was the Highland way.

"I'm sorry for your loss, Seth," Kavriel said sincerely.

Seth nodded calmly. "Thank you. I'm sorry for knocking you over the head earlier. It's gotten kind of dangerous around here with the Guard, and I was only protecting Master Soelle."

Kavriel wasn't expecting an apology from the man, and had forgotten how they had first met, even though he felt the tender knot on the back of his head. He smiled, knowing that he would have done exactly the same thing if their roles had been reversed. "There is no need, Seth. Actually, I should be thanking you for looking after my father."

Seth grunted, accepting the gratitude shyly and with youthful disregard. Kavriel took the opportunity to study him, now that his expression had softened, and he was struck by a strange sense of familiarity; he reminded Kavriel of something or someone he had seen recently. The image of a girl smiling at him in a dark room suddenly flashed into his thoughts, and Kavriel blinked and leaned quickly back in his chair.

His reaction did not go unnoticed. "Kavriel, are you alright?" his father asked, peering at him with concerned eyes. Seth too had suddenly become more focused.

Kavriel knew already what they were thinking and he nodded firmly. "Yes, I'm fine. It was just . . . just something that I might have remembered, is all."

His father and Seth shared a look. Cyr nodded. "That's good, son. That means your memory is improving. I don't know how long it will take before all of what you have forgotten has been restored, but I think you're moving in the right direction."

Kavriel nodded, feeling strangely anxious about something. He calmed himself with a few deep breaths. The other men waited patiently. "You said that Tess had been arrested," he said, trying to put all this new information together in his head like the pieces of a jigsaw puzzle. He needed to concentrate on one thing at a time.

"It was when the Ay'vol came to Rhyol," Seth said, and Kavriel got the impression that the young man felt responsible for whatever had happened to Tess. She was clearly important to him, and that eased Kavriel's uncertainty of him. "It was after the Cleansing, when the villages had been pretty much wiped clean of any pride or rights by the southern dogs."

"Guard your tongue, Seth," the overseer said, quietly but firmly. "You know the policies for disrespect to the Ay'vol."

"They're not here," Seth retorted, but his voice still carried an underlying respect for the man. Kavriel watched the interplay between the two with interest.

"That doesn't matter," Cyr replied. "You are too quick-tongued, Seth, and even if you think we're safe here, it doesn't mean you will remember that in more public places. It's best to simply banish those thoughts

298

completely. We all think the same of the Ay'vol, but keep it to yourself."

Seth nodded, ducking his head.

Kavriel's father continued where Seth had left off. "A unit of soldiers came with the Mir Town workers, about a dozen men altogether, with their commanding officer. The soldiers didn't seem to be of Ay'vol stock, but the officer certainly was. He was a mean, hard man clearly handpicked by the Patriarch to establish new laws and regulations for Nostrac. Apparently all the other villages had the same laws of the land laid down. There must have been an army of Rav'agas on the island at that time, like nothing we have ever seen in our entire history. We were frightened and unsure what to do, after hearing what had happened on the mainland.

"White-robed priests of the Patriarch and black robed deacons of the chancellor came with the men, insisting that because of our misinterpretation of The Way, we would have to prove our worth to the Creator through struggle and sacrifice. We weren't entirely certain what that meant, but it seemed to begin with our educational and governing systems. The elders, including myself, were no longer in charge; the town was to be 'overseen' by the deacons. The schools were supplied with lessons of the Divine, and a strict law of worship was prescribed that took precedence over all other activities. It was strange, for a community of people who worshipped if and when they chose to now be assigned times of prayer. It was like the day suddenly being declared night and night being declared day. It was difficult, and the Rav'agas ruled that noncompliance would be met with strict enforcement, either through detainment or reassignment, as they called it."

"My father was sent to the mines as punishment for not attending service one day," Seth interjected. "My mother and I have had to survive on our own for months now. The damn—" He stopped, remembering what the overseer had said, and glanced over to him. "The Ay'vol Guard does not allow criminals to have an income, so we are beggars." He looked away in shame.

Cyr shook his head. "You are doing what you can, Seth, both you and your mother." Eventually the young man nodded.

The overseer turned back to Kavriel. "With your brother and Tess's condition, it was difficult to get them to comply with the Rav'agas demands. In their sickness they seemed almost unaware of what was happening, or they simply didn't care. They continued to remain isolated from the community and even from each other. It was as if they had become complete strangers, even to themselves." His father sighed. "It was inevitable, what would happen to them. They would be arrested and sent either to the camp or some other place. It was important that the Rav'agas not know that they were sick, or they would be seen as useless and killed. We . . . we were terrified of what to do when the priests came to evaluate the citizens one at a time."

His father shook his head. "It is so impossible to believe, what we had become. I almost envied Vaemalin and Tess for not being aware of it." Kavriel swallowed with difficulty, listening intently. "Something happened that none of us ever expected. Tess seemed compliant with the priests and the Guardsmen in their questioning, almost as if a moment of clarity had come to her. It was a blessing."

The overseer turned to Seth, who nodded in confirmation. "I was there, and it's true. I almost believed that she wasn't sick anymore."

Cyr nodded, but quickly stopped, and his face paled. "Vaemalin wasn't so accepting of the demands of the Rav'agas. It was almost too much, his behavior toward the regulations. We were a free society that was now under strongly religious rule. Of course I understood his and others' feelings about what we could and could not do any longer. But we are also survivors, and we would bide our time until we would knew exactly how to combat this oppression. Yet Vaemalin . . . Vaemalin seemed to take it much more personally, as if the demands of worship touched him specifically. He was defiant, unruly, and confrontational against the Ay'vol.

"Under any other circumstances, Vaemalin's behavior toward the deacons would have been met with either containment or death, as Rav'agas law stipulates. Yet his extensive knowledge of Rav'agas doctrine was absolutely bizarre, and his argument against the deacons fascinated them enough to stay the blades of the Guardsmen."

"Vaemalin?" Kavriel exclaimed, suddenly unsure if the man his father was talking about was indeed his brother.

His father's face mirrored his bewilderment. "I know, Kavriel; I couldn't understand it either. Vaemalin must have become obsessed with The Way after the mine incident and became some kind of scholar. The deacons were impressed; they wanted to send him to Ay'vol. His viewpoints on the Rav'agas faith were oddly precise, and if he was to be condemned a heretic, then they felt it should be done by a higher authority in their order. Vaemalin's knowledge surpassed even their own!"

"I . . . I don't believe it!" Kavriel shook his head, actually feeling a bit jealous of his brother. Kavriel had studied Rav'agas doctrine like any other Nostrac youth during his school years, while Vaemalin's interest in education never extended past practicality and fixed issues. Why study religion when there were buildings to be built and wells to be dug? It made absolute sense, actually, as Vaemalin was preparing himself to be a town elder, if not the future overseer, while Kavriel was still playing around with senseless ideals about beliefs and unproven theory. Yet if he had known more than a deacon . . .

"I don't understand," he admitted, trying to think of a practical reason. "Were they true deacons of the order, or just soldiers dressed like the Ministry?" he asked sarcastically, and his father responded with a grudging grin.

"I don't know, Kavriel. As I said, it was as strange to me as it is to you. Yet that wasn't the worst part. Vaemalin might have been hiding this knowledge from the rest of us, but he had become much more volatile emotionally. He . . . he attacked the guards when they tried to take him from Rhyol."

"No," Kavriel whispered, feeling the same despair he'd felt when his father had said that Tess was dead.

Quickly his father shook his head, knowing what Kavriel was thinking. "No, Kavriel, it wasn't like that. It was more . . . it was—" His father was unable to continue; the emotion of the retelling had taken his voice. He shook his head.

Seth picked up the thread, although Kavriel wasn't sure if that was for the best or not after what he had heard. "Vaemalin slaughtered them," he stated.

Kavriel gaped at him. "He what?"

Seth nodded. "All of them. The deacons, the soldiers . . . only the officer was able to get away, and that was because we'd restrained Vaemalin. He tore them apart like they were dolls—I've never seen so much blood. It was as if he had the strength of ten men as he smashed them against walls; their heads burst like clay pots."

"Seth," the overseer warned, casting a disapproving look at the young man, who was actually grinning. Seth immediately took the hint and the grin vanished. He turned his eyes to the floor again.

Kavriel suddenly felt dizzy. He had a horrible vision of what he had awakened to in Silver Wood; Seth's description of his brother's actions made him realize that those Ay'vol soldiers had been killed in the same way. He suddenly understood why the soldiers had asked about Vaemalin. "By the Creator," he whispered. How could his brother have turned into such a thing? The red-eye must have taken all his morality. Kavriel actually felt afraid for and of his brother, just from what his father and Seth were telling him.

"The men in the forest," he said, thinking that it would be best to say what was on his mind, "they were also killed brutally. I thought it might have been some kind of animal. They were asking about Vaemalin. Do you think . . . ?" He turned to his father, who was looking again at the front of his shirt and not at his face.

"I don't think so, Kavriel. Vaemalin killed those men four years ago, and he fled Rhyol afterwards." Cyr looked into his son's eyes. "We had to send him away, for fear of what the Rav'agas would do to him. He . . . he actually seemed to understand and said that he would find a way to cure himself. I finally recognized my son, after thinking I had lost him for so long." He paused, and Kavriel saw the tears well up in his father's eyes. "At least I had a proper chance to tell him goodbye. He has not been seen in the Highlands since."

"Where did he go?" Kavriel asked, knowing immediately that his father wouldn't know anymore than he.

His father shook his head. "The only place I assume he would go—Teltraum. Yet before we had a chance to send any information to Femaor or Richart about what Vaemalin had done, word had already spread through the Ay'vol army in Nostrac. It was . . . it was terrible, what happened. The soldiers were enraged at the deaths of their colleagues at the hands of a northern heathen, and they took it out on the villages."

His father looked downwards and rubbed his forehead with his palm. "I . . . We lost so many. The animals . . . the Rav'agas killed innocent men, women, and children just to satisfy their rage. The officer who survived, Bellon was his name, he was mad with power like the Patriarch had been. He burned and killed without thought, releasing his men like a pack of hungry wolves on a flock of scared sheep. So many died. Rhyol was hit the hardest. Those who weren't killed were arrested to be sent to Teltraum for judgement by the higher order of the chancellor. There was still some precedent to follow." His father laughed bitterly.

"Tess was arrested?" Kavriel asked.

His father nodded. "Yes. Somehow her relationship to Vaemalin was discovered, either through interrogation or simply pleas for mercy. The officer personally took her from us to take her to the chancellor."

"Were you taken for the same reasons?" Kavriel asked.

"Not like that, no," his father replied. "I was to be made an example of. I was still a high official of a fallen regime, and even the Ay'vol wouldn't have simply strung me up as they did the others. No, I was meant to live and make sure I understood what that rule was." A fire lit in the overseer's eyes.

Kavriel could not imagine all that his father had been through. "The elders? Master Kair?"

His father shook his head slowly. "They, along with Tess, were taken to Teltraum for trial. I found out through Femaor that they had been judged as 'resisters to the True Way,' a weighty judgement with a penalty of death by hanging. I had lost everything, and the officer had succeeded in making an example of me. There was little trouble in Nostrac after that, and whatever efforts we make are small and insubstantial compared to the tamed attitudes of the rest of the island." His father looked to the floor as tears began to streak down his face.

Kavriel stared at his father in silence, realizing that he too had been crying as he wiped wetness from his face. Depression weighed heavy in his heart and he wished he could have been killed in the mine.

Seth seemed to be the only one who was thinking of the retelling differently. "No, it's not insubstantial, Master Soelle. We are still fighting." Kavriel and his father looked over to him. "We haven't lost everything, and Vaemalin is still out there."

"No, Seth. You will not say such things," the overseer said.

Seth wasn't listening this time. "It's true, Master Soelle. You can't deny it. Vaemalin—"

"That is enough, Seth!" the overseer shouted, then glanced at the front door to make sure his voice hadn't carried. He returned to Seth, who was clearly steaming. "That is enough," he said more softly. "There is nothing that can confirm what you want to believe. I too wish for heroes to save us from all of this, but the man you and unfortunately the Ay'vol think is my son has been murdering both Rav'agas and Quetalians."

Seth shook his head. "No, that's not true. Chairman Olenson was a traitor to the Quetalians, he was the one to sign the declaration for the Cleansing."

"Under duress, Seth; you know this," Cyr retorted.

The young man stubbornly shook his head. "No, there were plenty of other options that he could have taken. Councilman Richart—"

"Richart could have done no less. He is a gifted speaker, but the Patriarch's rule is final and the chancellor would have executed Olenson if he'd acted otherwise."

"Vaemalin executed him anyway, and he deserved it!"

"That's enough, Seth!" Again the overseer raised his voice, but instead of looking over to the door he watched the young man rise and pace around the salon, muttering.

Kavriel could only imagine the details of what they had been arguing about. He waited a moment for the tension to ease before he spoke. "Olenson Tavrick, the chairman?" he asked, remembering the name of the leader of the Quetalian nation, and high voice in the Council Nine. "Is that who was murdered?" His voice wavered. "Vaemalin killed him?"

His father turned to him and shook his head. "No." He looked quickly over to Seth, who had apparently left the conversation and was angrily clattering things around in the kitchen. "No," his father repeated. "Vaemalin's actions against the soldiers had been reported in Teltraum and I suspect Ay'vol City, but the Patriarch has never been able to capture him. Since then there have been . . . incidents throughout Quetal, against the Rav'agas and their Quetalian supporters, those who have acknowledged the new rule. There have been strange and violent deaths, up to and including the murder of the chairman in his bedchambers. Femaor sent me the information from Teltraum. The city was up in arms.

"There were many suspects but the wave of terror that was directed at the Ay'vol over the last several years seemed to draw attention back to the story of the villager who destroyed the officer's unit here in Rhyol—Vaemalin. He had become some kind of inspiration to those of us still surviving, a leader of a nameless resistance, if you will. Yet whenever the Ay'vol succeeded in capturing another person suspected of rebel actions, they would always deny any knowledge of Vaemalin. He was a ghost only, but a powerful one."

"That didn't cause any problems for you?" Kavriel asked, feeling a mixture of pride and shame for his brother who had become this iconic figure.

His father shook his head. "None, though I suspected that I wasn't off of the Guard's watch list, even if they didn't bother me." He glanced down at Kavriel's shirt once again. "If what you told me of what happened in Silver Wood is true, however, I don't think it will remain so for much longer."

Kavriel caught his father's meaning, and without knowing why looked to Seth, who had calmed down and was leaning on a cutting table, his hands splayed on the wooden surface. His eyes were full of fear. "This is bad, Master Soelle," he blurted, suddenly back on the overseer's side.

Kavriel looked at his father, who nodded. "Indeed." He began to scratch at his chin, something Kavriel knew was an old habit whenever his father was deep in thought.

Feeling that he had betrayed his family, Kavriel spoke quickly while touching the black stains hardened on his shirt. "What happened in the forest, even if I don't remember it, will be traced back here?" He already knew the answer.

Seth cursed. His father nodded.

"Then the soldiers will come to you asking about Vaemalin . . . like they asked me," Kavriel stated, fearing the worst for his father. "We have to get out of here!" he nearly shouted.

His father held up a hand, motioning for Kavriel to stay calm. "Easy, Kavriel. I have been here a long time, and this is the first direct attack on the Ay'vol in four years. They will question me, but they have been watching me closely. If I'm not here to answer their questions, that will cause problems for the families that have stayed behind." He looked deeply into Kavriel's eyes. "I will not allow that to happen again. But you, my son, cannot stay here."

He paused in thought. "Was there anyone who might have recognized you in Mir?" he asked.

Kavriel shook his head, recalling that of all the people he had met, there was no one besides Xavr that he remembered from his past life. "No, but they knew where I was from. The people in the tavern seemed to have a dislike for Rhyolians."

His father nodded. "Yes, there are issues between the towns in the Highlands now that didn't exist before the arrival of the Rav'agas. Still, Mir was mostly repopulated by them, so it would only make sense. Either way, knowing where you are from will only tell the Ay'vol where to start asking questions, and if what I hope you have told me is true, then only Seth and I know of your existence."

He sighed, and looked over to the young man, who seemed to have perked up at such dire information. "That means you will have to go with him, Seth." The young man grinned.

Kavriel wasn't sure what he should say. He understood everything that his father had said, and even if he couldn't remember what his place in all of this was, he knew that his father was right. He nodded, feeling anguish again as he looked into the sad eyes of his father, who was forcing a smile. "Alright. But where am I supposed to go?" he asked.

Seth answered. "Teltraum," he said with a smile.

CHAPTER 16

Kavriel was anxious to leave Rhyol. It had been his dream since he was a child to travel to the mainland, to visit the sites of Quetal and the great city of Teltraum, yet under such odd circumstances, being home with his father pulled at his heart. He felt unsure what to do, being part of a world that was known but still so unfamiliar to him now. It was as if he had left already. Being with his father made him at least feel peaceful, even though that peace would be temporary—the soldiers would be discovered in the woods, if they hadn't been already, and madness would descend on his home. He wanted so much to be with his father to protect him from it, but he knew in his heart that his being there would only ignite the flames of Ay'vol's sense of justice.

Teltraum was the most reasonable decision. There was little else Kavriel could hope to accomplish elsewhere in Quetal. Femaor was still there, which would be a blessing, to see another familiar face. And his father's friend and contact in Teltraum, Councilman Richart, had recently been designated as the Chairman of the Council Nine . . . well, what was left of the Council—the committee was only a figurehead now, kept in place simply for the image of unity for this "new" Quetal. Still, having a friend in such a high position was nothing short of luck. Kavriel would need Femaor's help to reach him, now that he was virtually under the chancellor's nose.

Kavriel painfully remembered the elders and clansmen who had been taken from Nostrac to Teltraum, Tess and Master Kair among them, from his father's speech, but Grieg and his West Point friend still had been part of the struggle against the Patriarch in the beginnings of the war. There was little chance that Kavriel would find them in Teltraum, let alone alive, but there had to be someone who knew something about what had happened to his friends, if not Femaor then one of the other committee members—and most definitely Richart.

As for Vaemalin . . . there was no telling exactly what he would find out about his brother, but the most important thing that he would have to remember was to deny that he *was* his brother. Kavriel would hold onto his name, as Seth would, but they would need to travel anonymously if they were to keep safe. The Ay'vol Guard rarely pestered small groups of Quetalian peasants on the road, as long as their papers were in order. That was his father's task; he had a surprisingly large number of forged identity parchments hidden away in his house.

When the overseer had said that they continued to fight the good fight, he wasn't joking, Kavriel realized. He still had a hard time coming to terms with the man that his father had become, but he knew it was a logical result of the situation. Still, he laughed at the irony of his father helping him plan for a trip that he'd always tried to deter Kavriel from taking.

Cyr was thorough in the detail, even somewhat excited about it as the three men planned while kneeling between maps that had been rolled out onto the floor. They were worried, all of them, but the planning seemed to have given them a jolt of determination. Kavriel started to see more and more of the father he remembered as map pages were folded and lines drawn coarsely over the colors denoting old borders. The overseer would tap his cane rhythmically on the floorboards when he was deep in thought, and Kavriel smiled like a fool when he should have been paying attention.

The arrangement seemed uncomfortably straightforward. Seth was to lead Kavriel safely out of the Highlands, since he knew the routes and checkpoints of the Guard with frightening accuracy. They would make their way via a southern trail over the bluffs, following the coastline to Port Dior, where Kavriel would buy passage on a trading ship heading for the mainland. They would be travelling on foot, since the Guard had forbidden any unwarranted horse travel between the towns. Still, Port Dior was quite a journey already. Kavriel also worried about the expense of booking passage on a trade ship. The overseer was confident, though, revealing that he had some money tucked away, and assuring Kavriel that following the coast was faster and safer than the road.

Yet even if all of this planning was successful, complications would arise once Kavriel landed in Port Sai. He would be on unfamiliar ground, unknown even to the overseer, and he would be on his own. Seth wouldn't be able to come with him, since the Guard kept track of villagers. The overseer had reminded Seth of this during their planning, which had set off a whole new heated argument that Kavriel had waited through.

Seth's reasoning seemed sensible, though the excuse for his disappearance to the Guard, while quite believable, was extremely risky. The soldiers in the village would be searching for a suspect in the attack on the Mir Guard in Silver Wood. Since there were no survivors, who was to say that Seth Kessor, already a troubled young man, didn't have something to do with it? He was allowed into Silver Wood for work, and if he suddenly went missing after the murders . . .

It seemed reasonable to Kavriel, but his father was adamant in insisting that Seth return, if for nothing else, then his family, who would be subjected to harsh interrogation by the Rav'agas. He could be lost in the woods as easily as he could be a murderer, but dead men could not protect the family they loved. Seth had thrown up his arms with a dramatic outcry, but in the end acceded to the overseer's wishes. Kavriel started to like the young man, whose fiery attitude and lack of tact around respected officials reminded him somewhat of Tess.

As for Kavriel alone on the mainland, his father had no recent information about new regulations or forbidden areas, the number of Rav'agas patrols and checkpoints, and so on. It would be a challenge, but as long as Kavriel could keep his head on straight and stay off the main roads, he should make it to Teltraum before the next winter.

The capital would be a whole new hive of problems, every one of them bearing a Rav'agas standard, but he would need to cross that bridge when he came to it. Hopefully Femaor would have received the overseer's coded message about his arrival by then. But who was to say for certain about anything in the city, his father warned. Still, Kavriel's optimism rose as he traced the lines on the map to the great city he had always dreamed of visiting. His chances of passing unnoticed would improve; Kavriel would be just another face in Teltraum, his relationship to Vaemalin unknown. The soldiers would not be expecting him to knock on their front gate, declaring who he was. You didn't look for the fish on your plate when you still hadn't found the sea yet, as the old saying went.

Once in Teltraum, Kavriel would have to locate an inn called The Stray Moon, just west of the Upper city, near the Council buildings but in a rundown area referred to as the East End. Kavriel wasn't optimistic about his prospects there, remembering vividly the clientele in Mir's Backfill tavern, yet Femaor liked the place, and it was there that his father would ask his friend to meet Kavriel.

* * *

The planning done, the route established, and the bags packed and ready to go, Kavriel stood in his bedroom in his father's house just as the sun lightened the horizon on Kavriel's third morning in this new world, ensuring that he'd not forgotten anything. Seth had left moments before to confirm the positions of the Guard before they embarked on their journey. Despite the four years he'd been gone, his father had kept his room undisturbed since he'd left it, as if it were a shrine for the son killed in the mines. Kavriel didn't go check, but he wondered if his brother's room was kept in the same fashion.

His father had been in his room for some time while Kavriel was adjusting his items in his own, and he was caught off guard when his father's voice announced his arrival.

"Kavriel, I need to have a word with you."

He turned. His father stood behind him, resting on his cane, his expression solemn. An old sheet swathed something long that he had tucked under his arm. "Take this with you." His father let the sheet fall, and Kavriel's

315

eyes widened when he saw the sword in its scabbard that his father held.

His father had wielded it as a soldier during the bloodiest and most violent years of struggle in the borderlands. Kavriel had seen it many times before, and he and his brother had often tried to play with it, but his father had been quite adamant about respecting the battered steel. It had meant a great deal to him, a symbol of the time he served protecting loved ones during the early years of the war, and he regarded that charge with high esteem. Kavriel and Vaemalin had been allowed to touch the weapon only when their father was around, and they'd been warned to touch it carefully. They'd never had been instructed in the proper use of a sword; it was never an educational requirement outside of the military.

His father's feelings for the sword were a complicated issue that Kavriel could never quite understand. His father was an avid pacifist ever since leaving service, hating everything about devices created for the sole purpose of taking someone's life. He had declared he would support Kavriel and Vaemalin in every endeavor they chose to pursue, as long as it wasn't with the military. Kavriel had often wondered what his father had seen during his time in the field that left him with such animosity toward arms and armies.

If his father was offering Kavriel his blade, that meant that he was worried.

Both shocked and touched by the gesture, Kavriel immediately tried to refuse the gift, even stepping away from it, shaking his head. "I can't take this from you. I don't even know how to use it! I know how important it is for you and I don't want to lose it or break it. I would never forgive myself it I did."

His father laughed. "Good! Then lose it! Or better yet, cast it into the sea when you cross the channel from Dior! You might get lucky and have it strike a giant predatory fish on its way to the bottom, saving the sea from underwater tyranny." He laughed again, and Kavriel squinted at him, wondering if his father might have experienced one too many surprises recently. Noticing Kavriel's concern, he stopped laughing and nodded, again serious. "Yes, Kavriel, the sword is important to me. I've had it for many years, since it was first issued to me when I was even younger than Seth." He looked down at the sheathed blade and sighed. "I know it's not special to look at or even comfortable to hold, but it's sound, and it will help you when you need it."

Cyr took a step forward and said earnestly, his voice low, "The world is not the same as you left it. I wish only that you could stay here with me, but we both know that that is impossible." His eyes became very sharp. "You must be very careful, Kavriel. A new darkness threatens this land, and even the people you thought you knew might not be as you remember them. You must learn that."

What a strange thing to say, Kavriel thought, but before he could respond his father moved slightly to his side, lifting his cane from the floor. Fearing that he might fall, Kavriel quickly reached out to grab him. Instead the sword moved into his hand, and his father stepped back, smiling.

Kavriel frowned at the deception and his father grinned. "Now it is yours."

317

Capitulating, Kavriel examined the coarse leather scabbard, the crossbar guard and the metal grip covered in smooth shark skin. He remembered holding it with his father's supervision when he was a child. He was older and stronger now, but the weapon still felt awkward in his grip. He pulled the steel from the leather throat, and a splash of sunlight seeping in through the bolted windows glinted off the length of metal. The blade was nicked and worn, but it still looked quite beautiful, even if it had been created for un-beautiful things. Kavriel looked at his father, seeing the sadness in his eyes.

Seth came into the bedchamber, dressed for travel. He nodded at the two men. "It's time, Master Soelle. The guards are rotating shifts."

The overseer nodded back. "Then you must leave." He looked one last time to Kavriel. "Please be safe, my son." He gripped Kavriel's shoulder tightly.

Kavriel nodded, feeling ready to cry, as if he were still a child. "I'll find him, Father, and I will come home."

His father's smile was strained, and his eyes glittered. "I know you will, son. I'll be waiting."

CHAPTER 17

Captain Geav Bellon was a man distracted. Clad in red metal plate armor, broad shoulders straight, he sat rigid at his work table, itself covered in the paperwork his officers brought him nightly. Referring to one of the parchments that he had finished interpreting, he jotted notes in a small ledger next to it. He was not required to be in full uniform while doing this tedious office work, but he was a proud man and his armor did not restrain him.

Lately his officers had become lazy, and were scribbling down nonsense that was unnecessary to his report. He had been away from his soldiers for too long, trapped in this post playing the bureaucrat in this barbaric town of undisciplined and rowdy heretics while his officers had become simple watchdogs. It was near time to change things, before they all became toothless old men remembering the good old days.

Cursing as the quill snapped under his strong fingers, Captain Bellon rose from his wooden chair and marched over to the blazing fireplace, where he tossed the useless pen into the flames. It was extremely warm in the little room, and the one and only small rectangular window did nothing to carry the heat outside, where the air was what he considered sharp, even if this was what the heathens referred to as spring on this cold, wet island. Yet he didn't feel the cold or the blazing heat when he was absorbed in his duty. He was far too disciplined for that.

Bellon tapped his fingers on the three-bladed golden symbol of the Ay'vol Force etched into his leather breastplate, then delicately touched the numerous medals of command on his uniform as he stared into the fire, forgetting his paperwork. He was troubled by the recent orders he had received from the chancellor that morning and had spent the rest of the day and evening searching for any hidden tricks that might have been contemplated by his Patriarch's second in command. He didn't feel comfortable, and although feeling discomfort at an order from the chancellor was something he was used to, it wasn't something he particularly enjoyed.

Captain Bellon had served in the Ay'vol Force for over thirty years and had surpassed all of the Patriarch's expectations. He'd been a dirty-faced boy in the slums of Ay'vol City, scrounging for food like a rat along with his equally pitiful siblings, who would steal from him just as often as they would from others—until his skill with improvised weapons and his survival instincts were recognized as potential by those in the Ay'vol Force. He had been recruited as a cadet at an age when most children were still looking to their parents for guidance and security; instead the military forged his mind into a disciplined and proud follower of The Way. His fighting ability, already established, was further honed amongst seasoned soldiers, and he rose to rank quickly, leading and winning victories for his command against drifting armies of unregulated provinces that blighted Rav'agas like a disease.

He was one of the lost children of Mother Rav'agas, reconstructed by their father, the Patriarch, to see the light—to recognize that their leader was the one and only Son of God. Captain Bellon was his champion, and he would continue as such throughout his life.

Chancellor Zoren was a man that caused him

suspicion, and his shaky regard for the second of his master suffered further after he had been assigned to this post on this worthless rock in the northern sea, when he should have been on the mainland with his men.

Bellon truly missed the Cleansing. The Quetalians had been surprisingly livid fighters, refusing to accept the truth of The Way and needing to feel the wrath of the believers to understand. They had been no match for the Ay'vol, of course. Nothing could match that massive power led by the Son of Creation himself, and his fellow Ay'vol had bathed in the glory and bloodshed of the hundreds of Quetalian heathens they had sanctified by blade and fire. He had been drunk with invincibility; there was no stopping them from completely removing the stain of nonbelievers from all the northern lands.

Those days were gone. *When did it go wrong?* he wondered with a sigh. The Cleansing decree had been the last true Ay'vol command issued regarding this occupied nation. It had been—what?—three years since Bellon's sword had last tasted heathen blood. Now the mighty had certainly fallen, into the painful, inevitable next phase of occupation: bureaucracy.

Bellon shook his head, wondering where his Patriarch had found this man Zoren to lead the new world into The Way. The chancellor was powerful, and a true believer of the Order, yet his methods were tame, in Bellon's opinion. He was more of a bookkeeper than a ruler, and should have been kept in Ay'vol with the rest of the elitist gentry who considered themselves worthy to live in the house of God based on blood ties alone. There was only one true Son of Creation, and Zoren could not even be considered a distant cousin to him. Still, his master knew much more than he could ever hope to, and who was he to question his god?

Bellon still hadn't decided exactly how to follow his orders.

Despite being a well-trained and loyal member of the Ay'vol Force, Captain Bellon still retained certain . . . faults, flaws that he could still recognize in himself. One of those was his pride, most likely rooted in his childhood. He, born as a piss-poor urchin, had become a man whose victories for the Patriarch outnumbered many times over the errors he had committed, and he could count on one hand the number of times he had been bested by an adversary. He was smug about his success, and though his fellow officers teased him for it, they could not deny his determination and his will. One had tried, many years ago—his commanding officer when he was still green in the Force. Bellon had defeated him in a fair Rav'agas duel and ended all doubt about his possibilities when he had tossed the head of his superior on the stairs of the Patriarch's Temple House, as tradition dictated. On that day, he had become a captain.

Yet then he had experienced his most shameful defeat. Bellon stared into the burning fire pit, reliving his memories. It was a stupid defeat, and one that should have called for his execution. He had run from a fight. And yet he had been spared.

He should have been on his guard when he learned that this young villager from some no-place Highland town had been able to lecture the Ministry about what they were born into. Maybe he had been caught in the same

322

fascination as they had. It was so unusual, and in a strange way magnificent, how the young villager fought so well against such superior numbers. Unfortunately, it had not been so magnificent for the men who were killed by this strange force of nature. Who was he, this young nobody from a forgotten rock, and how had he been able to best a contingent single-handedly?

Bellon frowned, unconsciously stroking the arm that the villager had snapped like an old branch. The Ghost, they had called him now, that cursed man-child who had killed his soldiers and fled like a coward. He would never forget that day. Maybe that was why he had received the orders from the chancellor this morning. A chance to redeem himself. That they had come directly from the chancellor, however, were what he found so difficult to comprehend.

There had been an incident several nights ago in a part of the forest that the locals called Silver Wood, involving the Mir Guard. What they were doing away from the town and how the events had bypassed his knowledge to go directly to Teltraum first was unknown, which was why Bellon could not be entirely sure the information was credible. He was still acting commander over the island, and Port Dior was the hub of his so-called territory, which meant anything that occurred here must go through him first. Yet it hadn't. Why hadn't his own people notified him first? Bellon scratched at his white goatee. Did the chancellor have doubts about his reaction?

It was true that many in the Ay'vol Force knew what had happened to him; it was why he had struggled much harder to retain the Patriarch's respect. Yet his personal defeat in the same place where this new incident had occurred should not have hampered procedure. He was still a loyal officer of the Son of God, and that went above any personal desire he might have for revenge. Still, the similarities were undeniable, and so was his urge to perhaps take the opportunity to right a past wrong against him. That must have been why he hadn't been informed first. The decision of whether he was capable of putting his personal feelings aside to do his duty according to Rav'agas law had been referred to the chancellor.

He spat into the fireplace, cursing Zoren's name under his breath while wondering what else the man thought of him. He would do his duty, go to the Highlands and find out what exactly had occurred there. If anything, it would give him and his men a chance to escape this dismal port town of beggars and whores for a few days. He knew that whatever he might find would likely be unrelated to the incident with the Ghost. That blasted defeat had caused a run of inspiration in the Quetalian heathens who still believed that their way would save them, not the Patriarch's.

The Ghost . . . If only he might have a chance against him again.

Bellon unclenched his fists, realizing that his thoughts were exactly what Chancellor Zoren was testing. He forced his feelings aside, wishing more to defeat the chancellor's opinion of him than destroy the villager who had shamed him. He was a disciplined and loyal disciple of the Patriarch. He must never forget that.

Deep in his thoughts, Captain Bellon hadn't noticed the messenger who entered the room until the man nervously cleared his throat. He turned quickly and glared at him in irritation. "What is it?" he growled.

The man twitched to attention. Bellon noticed that he'd dared not cross the threshold. "Captain Bellon." The man bent in a formal bow, one arm across his chest.

Bellon did not acknowledge the greeting and only waited, feeling his patience slip away.

"I have a message that just arrived from the mainland, Captain." The man extended his hand, showing a many-folded bit of parchment.

Bellon didn't move to take it, until he recognized the seal. Not wanting his excitement to show, he walked over to the man with trained precision. The messenger cleared his throat again and shifted his feet as Bellon approached him, actually taking a step back when Bellon snatched the parchment out of his hand.

"When did you say it arrived?" he asked, his eyes boring into the young man's.

He blinked rapidly. "It arrived just after sundown, sir—by pigeon." The man gulped.

Bellon's interest rose. "You don't say . . ." He turned away from the man, who had most likely just given him everything he knew about the message. The seal was untouched, whatever secrets it protected still safe for his eyes alone. Captain Bellon waved his hand at the messenger behind him. "You may go."

He heard the quick thud of retreating footsteps as the man left, in such a hurry to be away that he hadn't closed the door behind him. Captain Bellon's reputation made him used to that, however. He broke open the red seal and read the words quickly, suddenly feeling that all his worries about the chancellor's order had not been without reason. He tossed the message into the fire as soon as he had finished reading it, and adjusted his armored uniform. "Guardsman!" he shouted to the wall of his office.

Within moments another soldier appeared at his doorway. "Yes, sir!"

Bellon turned to him, a man closer to his own age, and when Bellon offered a triumphant smile, he responded with one of his own. Sergeant and captain had fought together for many years. "Your orders, Captain?" he asked, already sensing Bellon's excitement.

"We move tonight." Bellon answered evenly. "There has been an incident in the mining town and we are requested to investigate."

His sergeant nodded without losing his smile, already suspecting. "The men are at ready, my captain."

Bellon couldn't help himself, he let out a dark laugh. How well he knew his men! "Then we ride north," he declared, and grabbed the broadsword that had been lying unsheathed atop the scattered heap of paperwork. Bellon looked hungrily along the blade's length, the edge a shining line in the firelight. He nodded to the man at the door, who quickly turned to relay the command with Bellon following, feeling in a most triumphant mood.

In the hearth, the creased white parchment had long since turned to blackened ash, but the red seal was slow to melt. The sun icon encircled by six stars was still visible, though gradually losing definition. Soon no one else would know who had sent the message, if they even knew that the emblem was used by one of the Patriarch's favorite pets, the man who called himself Saire.

CHAPTER 18

What is he thinking? Why is it so hard not to let things be? Everything he wanted has been accomplished, more or less. We have let things run their course and now they have become exactly what was expected. Why has he decided to test them? What is the point? Is he angry with them? Is he angry with us?

He hasn't spoken in so long, and I am not the only one who is worried. Kai'sa thinks I'm overreacting. She would. But Tondal and Dar don't agree with her optimism. Father has never gone this long without contacting us. These quakes, the storms and eruptions—is this his way of getting our attention? Well, he has it, but what's the point?

The mortals are learning to adapt . . . and they are learning quickly. Damn, how did they grow so strong! Sa'rire knew this would happen, but what do we do now? What is Father waiting for? Sa'rire thinks he is waiting for nothing, that he is acting only as a spoiled and wrathful child. Yet what did he expect? Eventually man would move away from him—and us—but this will end badly for everyone, I can just feel it. The mortals will find out the truth, it is inevitable. And then what? Will we be destroyed, our purpose fulfilled?

I don't know. I don't like Sa'rire's idea any more than Dar does, and I've been talking with Faythe about it in private. She seems to be the most reasonable, but I think she might be too influenced by these mortals instead of the other way around. She thinks Sa'rire's plan is worth a try, though; if anything we may get some real answers. If Father won't talk to us his way, then maybe he will talk to

327

us our way. If Sa'rire can do what he believes he can, and those writings Tondal found are accurate (why would Father have kept notes?), then we will know for certain. Who knows, maybe the test is for us.

Either way, we can't stay here much longer whether this summoning works or not. Our influence is not as subtle as it used to be. Damn politics; whose idea was that, anyway? Dar's, probably. Anyway, I don't think we should be seen together. People are becoming suspicious of us; we are too . . . different from them, I suppose; we were never truly able to become one of them.

This experiment of Sa'rire's will need all of our involvement, and using the temple as . . . anyway, it only makes sense. We need a focal point that is strongest in his faith. Especially nowadays, there doesn't seem to be many of those places left anymore. Except in that southern kingdom, perhaps, where Sa'rire likes to "fit in." The Cieleans seem to be devout . . . if perhaps a bit too primal in their traditions. Yet who am I to judge. I was there when all of them were like that. It will be interesting to see what they all become in another thousand years. I hope to see that, but I doubt I will. Something tells me this plan of Sa'rire's is going to be disastrous.

I am more worried what Father will say than if the experiment will even work at all. I trust Tondal's expertise and he is more than ready for this, just out of curiosity. Sa'rire seems to be thinking other things he is not letting us know about. I am not sure why, but he seems to be on the defensive. Is he frightened? It's hard to say. I know I am. Still, there is more preparation to be done, and I need to leave soon if I am to make it to Ciele before the next moon, when the conduit is at its fullest. Kai'sa is waiting for me.

"Aye! Watch your footing, boy! Or you'll be scraping my skiff to pay for my catch."

Kavriel looked up in confusion from the book he had been reading. A heavyset sailor stood beside the hull of a large fishing boat, screaming obscenities and shaking his tattooed and muscular arm like he was trying to free it from barnacles. Kavriel backed up quickly, not realizing that he had been walking while he read (two very complicated tasks that should never be attempted at the same time), and looked down at his boots. White stones were scattered over the wharf where he had been walking. He lifted his foot and realized that they were not stones at all, but shellfish, spilled from the large fisherman's torn net. He had been walking on the man's trade! Kavriel quickly apologized to the red-faced fisherman as he tiptoed over the shellfish to a clear area, holding up placating hands, one still clutching the book he had appropriated from Xavr's cabin.

Seth, who had been surveying the moored boats nearby, ran over in response to the shouting. "Is everything alright?" he asked, glancing at the fisherman, who was collecting the shellfish into a bulging sack.

Kavriel nodded. "Yes. I got distracted, and didn't watch where I was going."

Seth nodded, giving the fisherman a frown as he guided Kavriel away by his elbow. His eyes fell to the book Kavriel had been reading. "It's that good, huh?" he asked curiously, and Kavriel smiled and nodded.

He had started reading the old tome during the breaks in their journey from Rhyol to Port Dior during the past week. "Yes. I still haven't figured out exactly what it is, a novel or a memoir."

Seth quirked a brow in interest. "Whose memoir?"

Kavriel shook his head, frowning. "I can't figure that out. It's old—I mean *really* old—and there is no way one person would have been able to kept track of such a timeline, unless he was immortal."

"Really?" The young man's eyes lit up.

Kavriel smiled at him, seeing a little bit of himself in Seth's reaction to a good tale. "Probably not, but the content suggests it."

"What's it about?" Seth asked as they walked slowly off the wharf and into the busy port town, whose locals reminded Kavriel of Mir Town denizens. After what his father had told him, he couldn't be entirely sure the place was safe, but they could only conceal their nervousness and behave like two young men going about their daily business along with everybody else.

"History, mostly," Kavriel replied, hiding the book inside his coat as several Rav'agas guards strolled by. They didn't pay them any mind. "But I can't tell if it's real or just based on real things. I recognize a lot in the book—the names of towns and cities, and several characters, like Dar."

"The first Chairman of the Nine?" Seth interrupted.

Kavriel nodded, happy to have a learned person as his travel companion. It had made the journey more enjoyable. "Not the true chairman, but maybe a namesake, I think. It also talks about Ciele, and the temple, but there isn't a lot of detail; it seems like something written by somebody just jotting down thoughts." He frowned, tapping the hard cover concealed in his coat. "It also seems to talk a lot about the First Faith, about the Fall of the Gods and such."

Seth leaned close to him. "Keep your voice down about that," he warned.

Kavriel nodded, remembering where they were. "Of course," he whispered. He'd forgotten momentarily that any talk of religion that wasn't The Way had been outlawed in this Rav'agas-occupied territory, even if The Way was actually a faction of the First Faith, as it was called in his studies. "Still . . . it is interesting."

"I'll read it when you're done with it." Seth looked ahead. "First we need to find someone."

Kavriel nodded, remembering their priorities. They'd walked the principal road into Dior that morning. The port town was mostly just rows and rows of wooden wharves lining a harbor full of fishing rigs and trade ships that trawled back and forth to the mainland. The rest of it was inns and eateries. It wasn't as extravagant as Kavriel had expected the main port of entry to Nostrac Island to be. The entire town was built along one main road and the harborfront; behind that was farmland and pastures. Kavriel had a print of Dior's harbor in his room back home that Femaor had brought him once as a gift. The vibrant colors had been highly exaggerated, the details blurred, and Kavriel felt disappointed that it was nothing but a simple crossroads village that had been romanticized in his mind as a place of beginnings for adventures. He hoped that Teltraum wouldn't be a similar disappointment. He didn't think it would be, even with the Rav'agas occupation. You couldn't simply erase the majesty of a city that large.

They stopped in front of a shabby building with a rusted metal sign swinging over the doorway. Seth moved in close to whisper, "I know a man who runs coalfish between here and Port Sai. His rig is docked past that cove." He nodded in that direction. "Unfortunately there is a patrol station around the corner, but I should be able to find him if he hasn't set off yet."

Seth glanced at the sky, judging the time. The sun had been up for less than an hour. "He tends to sleep in, so we should be alright." He looked to Kavriel, then nodded at the building. "This tavern is owned by my cousin. The soup is good."

Kavriel began to salivate at the thought of eating real food. They hadn't rationed their meals correctly, and the last night they had been forced to forage for nuts and berries that had survived the winter. "Alright then, I'll wait for you in there."

Seth adjusted his travel bag over his shoulder. "Try not to look…obvious."

Kavriel smiled with a nod as Seth turned toward the cove he had indicated, pushing his way through a crowd of men and women who were heading to the harborfront to ready their boats. Kavriel glanced up at the rusted sign with a shellfish emblem etched into the metal before pushing open the heavy wooden door below it.

The smell of the interior went directly to Kavriel's nostrils as he stepped inside, and his stomach growled in response. The tavern was large, with a dozen or more tables, nearly all vacant. The place must have just opened its doors for breakfast. Kavriel moved over to a stool near the corner, as he had done in Mir Town, but he didn't feel the same tension he'd felt in The Backfill as he sat down. He was admiring the peculiar sea-themed pieces that decorated the walls of this more hospitable establishment when a pretty woman with dark hair and a long white apron appeared from the kitchen. She was wiping her hands with a cloth when she noticed Kavriel in the corner. Putting it down on a nearby table, she moved quickly over to him with a friendly smile.

"You're just in time, good sir. I've finished preparing the soup. Will you have some? I'm sure you'll realize you've had none better." Her smile was bright, and Kavriel couldn't help but relax as he returned the gesture.

"Yes, please. That sounds wonderful."

The woman nodded before he'd finished, already knowing his answer, and was off to the kitchen. She came back carrying a rather generous bowl of thick, creamy white soup. She dressed it with a couple of rolls and returned to her chores of straightening chairs and moving tables, giving Kavriel a passing smile each time she came near. Kavriel appreciated her service, but he barely noticed anything else—his face had been in the bowl as soon as it had left her hands. The soup was as delicious as she claimed, fish and shellfish that had been boiled in cream, mixed with potatoes and carrots, and spiced with herbs. Kavriel knew the dish, and had a similar recipe back home for it, but it was not as good as this. He finished it quickly.

The woman returned. "Would there be anything else?" She eyed the bowl, probably wondering if Kavriel had even had a chance to taste the soup before gulping it down.

He shook his head. "Not for the moment, thank you.

I'm waiting for a friend; he should be arriving shortly."

She took up the bowl with a shrug. "You from Mir?" she asked, and immediately Kavriel's unease returned. He hadn't prepared himself for any questions.

"Yes . . . well no, not exactly," he stammered.

Her expression didn't change despite his confusing response. "You a miner?" she asked, lifting one of her thick dark eyebrows.

Fantastic, Kavriel thought, wondering if he should order another bowl of soup simply to be rid of her. She seemed genuinely curious about him, and normally he wouldn't have minded having this conversation with a beautiful woman, but he knew that these weren't normal times and he could very well be heading in a dangerous direction if he said too much. He decided on a smoother way out . . . taken directly from a page of Vaemalin's book of charm. "When the work is there, but if your soup tastes this good each time you make it, I think I need to find a different trade nearby."

The compliment worked; she beamed down at him before heading back to the kitchen with a girlish giggle. Kavriel hoped that Seth would get there soon, and as if in answer he heard the outside door open. He honestly believed his wish had been fulfilled, until he looked that way.

He broke into a nervous sweat as a pair of uniformed men entered the tavern and took a table between him and the door. He cursed softly to himself, trying to remain inconspicuous, as Seth had suggested. The soldiers were not Ay'vol, thank the Creator, but they didn't strike Kavriel as Quetalian either, if that was even possible anymore. They must have been some provincial unit, he decided, unable to recognize the designs as they began talking to one another in Rav'agas, seemingly unaware of anyone else in the room. Kavriel hoped it would remain that way.

The woman returned from the kitchen with two bowls of soup that she pushed toward the men. He noticed that she hadn't given them any kind of greeting, or stuck around to ask them where they were from. Kavriel assumed by her behavior that she already knew them, and the way they rudely ignored her and simply ate the soup without any reaction confirmed it.

The door opened again. The smells of the tavern must have begun to waft into the street. A small group entered. They were not soldiers, but swarthy fishermen who began to talk loudly as soon as they came in. Kavriel thought that they seemed rather lively for early morning, but their mood quickly softened after seeing the two soldiers, who themselves went silent and glared at them. After a moment they returned to their conversation. The fishermen looked over to Kavriel, gave him friendly nods, which he returned, and took a table that was situated between his and the Rav'agas'. He almost said thanks.

Kavriel still hadn't been able to remember what had happened in the five-year gap in his mind, but he seemed to be familiar with the attitudes between the fishermen, who were locals, and the Guardsmen from the south. There was clear hatred between them, but it had been worn down to the nub after the war and it seemed to him that they merely accepted one another like old neighbors who had gotten tired of each other's company. Kavriel wondered what kind of regulation the Ay'vol had over Port Dior, but the thought made him realize that since he and Seth had arrived, he hadn't seen any Ay'vol stock. They all seemed to be provincial. Kavriel tapped his fingers on the table before he reached into his jacket to pull out some coins for the soup. He couldn't just sit there looking bored without drawing notice.

The door opened for a third time, and two more soldiers came through the door. Kavriel kept his eyes down, pretending to count his money. The air seemed to become thick in the tavern. One of the soldiers passed uncomfortably close to Kavriel on his way to the seated soldiers. It was clear that he was studying the occupants while the other soldier remained at the entrance, speaking Rav'agas to someone outside. The group of fishermen hunched over their table, their conversation falling to whispers. They weren't necessarily frightened of the soldier passing by, Kavriel thought, but they were clearly unnerved, even as they continued to laugh and joke, putting up a good front. Kavriel, on the other hand, felt as if he was swimming in his shirt.

"Well, aren't you handsome and generous! I hope you do come back more often, if you keep paying for twice as much as you eat." The woman had surprised him with her quiet approach, and he heard a snicker from the table of fishermen.

The soldier who had been wandering around was now in front of the two seated men, engaged in conversation. They didn't notice as the woman shot the fishermen a wink and they returned to their conversation in a soft burst of laughter.

"For the kind service, is all," Kavriel whispered, trying to look calm, even though his fingers continued to tap on the tabletop.

She didn't go away this time; on the contrary, she leaned over suggestively, putting her elbows on the table and her chin in her hands so she could look straight at him. "Don't you have the most stunning eyes," she remarked.

Shocked by her candor, Kavriel leaned back in his chair, feeling the tavern heat up even more. "Um . . . thank you," he mumbled. "They're my mother's . . . she doesn't know I took them."

His quip was overheard by the table of fishermen, who responded with another burst of laughter. The soldiers looked disdainfully in his direction before returning to their own conversation. Kavriel very much wanted to be away from this place.

The woman continued to smile at him. "Well, I might think about returning them if I were you, sweetie," she whispered, but not too softly. "Pearls are hard to come by; ask these fishermen." She nodded over to the adjacent table; the men simply smiled at her. Kavriel should have been flattered, but he wasn't quite sure what she had meant. "Tell you what, honey. Since your friend doesn't seem to be coming, why don't you head into the kitchen with me and I'll fix you another bowl if you help me clean up." She smiled coyly as she turned away and began to sway back to the kitchen.

Kavriel stared at her, frozen in his seat and not entirely sure what he should do. He wondered if it was some kind of trick, but the table of fishermen seemed to have the answer for him already. "You better get going, boy, she don't ask twice!" The laughed again, and before the soldiers might turn another time, wondering what all the racket was about, Kavriel stood quickly, nodded to the locals, and walked toward the kitchen door, feeling like a target.

He drew a deep breath and went in, the door swinging shut behind him. He was in a cramped room fitted with two small fire pits over which hung black cauldrons. A worktable in the center was covered in dishes and utensils. A wash table was in one corner near a small window, and next to that was a door leading to the outside that stood halfway open, allowing the heat in the room to escape. Kavriel wondered if he could make it through the door before the woman, who had her back turned, filling a satchel with soup, realized he was gone. He took a step and she glanced over to him with her smile. He still needed to be polite.

"Listen . . . um, lady," he said, trying not to sound too ungrateful. "Thank you very much for the soup, I appreciate it, but there is no need and I really should be looking . . . "

The door swung open, interrupting his speech, and to Kavriel's horror a large, red-bearded man entered the room carrying a net in one hand and a fish hook the size of his torso in the other. The man was a giant, nearly as wide as the door, his head brushing the archway as he passed under it. He looked at the woman for a brief moment before seeing Kavriel in the room. His gaze narrowed. Kavriel actually thought about taking his chances with the Rav'agas in the other room as he felt for the door behind him.

"What do we have?" the bearded man said in a

voice that was surprisingly soft for his size, but powerful all the same. His eyes remained on Kavriel.

"Three inside and two at the door; the captain took the others north," the woman replied quickly, and with a strange tone of command that Kavriel had not expected from her. "He had a whiff of something pretty appetizing, I think. They left two nights ago and I don't think they'll be back for a few more days."

The red giant hummed. "There is another shift that just left the dock; the harbor's clear till evening."

The woman nodded, and Kavriel noticed that she had placed the satchel on the table and was beginning to fill another. She smiled warmly at the large man, who must have done the same, although it was difficult to tell through his thick beard.

He walked up to the table, throwing his net and hook on top of it. Kavriel backed up quickly, thinking that the man was going to run him through.

"So." Red beard finally addressed Kavriel directly as he stood up tall, his chest thrust out and his hands on his hips. "What do you have to say for yourself, bringing trouble into my home?"

Kavriel felt his throat close up.

"Jassar, don't scare him," the woman said, flashing the big man a disapproving look. "He's just got in from Rhyol. Give him a break."

Kavriel stared at the woman, who seemed to have changed into a completely different person before his eyes. "How did you know?" he asked, not about to try hiding the fact with that large man still standing over him.

The woman pursed her lips as if he had insulted her.

"Know!" she exclaimed. "The better question is how everyone else *didn't* know. The way you tensed up and nearly broke apart my table with your shaking, I had to make it look like you were nervous about something else, *sweetie*." She smiled once more at him, but Kavriel saw now that the seductive posturing she had shown earlier had obviously had been a ruse. "You must be in some kind of mess."

Kavriel's eyes went wide. Then he noticed another man trying to push his way through the door behind the red-bearded giant.

"Get out of the way, Jassar, you big oaf!" the man said, and Kavriel saw Seth's head pop out from behind the giant when he squeezed himself aside. "Sorry Kavriel, I tried to get back sooner," Seth said, looking up at the man named Jassar. "But this lug is slow on his feet. Thanks, Ella." He nodded to the woman, who gave an exaggerated curtsy before handing a bowl of soup over to him. He drank it quickly.

With Seth's arrival, Kavriel felt a bit more at ease. Jassar held out his hand, a smile barely visible under his red beard. Kavriel took it reluctantly, still not entirely sure what was going on, and the man nearly shook Kavriel's arm out of his shoulder.

"It is a pleasure to meet you, Soelle," Jassar said politely, despite his gruff appearance. "Your father's a good man." Kavriel was in shock. He could only nod as if he understood everything. "Seth told me that you need to get to Teltraum quietly. Said it's important. I can take you to Sai, but you'll need to keep close and we need to move now." Jassar turned without another word, and two long

340

strides took him out the door.

Seth, pushed boorishly out of the way, responded with another insult that the large man ignored. He moved over to give the woman a warm hug, which she returned. "Thank you, cousin," he said, kissing her cheek before turning to Kavriel. "You heard him," he said, and quickly followed Jassar out of the kitchen.

Uncertain what to say, Kavriel thanked the woman before following his friend. As he turned she gave him a slap on his rear that made him jump. She was smiling playfully when Kavriel turned to look at her oddly as he rubbed his behind. He hurried after the others, his cheeks hot with embarrassment.

They followed red-bearded Jassar down an alleyway back toward the docks, making sure to avoid the tavern's front entrance. He hadn't seen the soldier that must have been waiting at the door, as the woman Ella had mentioned, but even so he didn't want to raise suspicion if he was seen leaving out the back.

Seth, walking next to him, spoke lightly in his ear. "Ella and Jassar have been keeping an eye on the waters since the soldiers first came to Dior," he explained as if Kavriel's questions had been drawn on his face. "They pass information along to those who need it, and help out when they can."

"How do they know me? Or my father?" Kavriel asked.

Seth smiled while answering under his breath. "Remember when we said that we were still fighting the good fight?" Kavriel nodded. "Well . . . I'm from a large family, probably one of the largest in Nostrac. The Kessors have a clan-stake."

Kavriel nodded again, already knowing a bit about the Kessor Clan and how they had been one of the remaining supporters of the overseer, even after that political mess about the mines. "Yes, of course," he said quickly. "Your father has been very helpful to us, and I remember him and my father being almost friends." He looked over to the young man, hoping he hadn't presumed anything.

Seth merely nodded. "Not almost," he answered. "Anyway, the overseer helped out my cousin about a year back, when the chancellor was issuing orders to shut down all Quetalian-owned businesses. Occupation is tricky business when the wolves can't simply eat all the sheep." He smiled. "Your father was actually able to get Chairman Richart to convince the chancellor that it might be best to keep changes to a minimum. We already know that we've been defeated, and there's no use shedding any more blood than necessary. Keep the locals happy, and keep their businesses open. Change titles over if that's what politics demand, but don't stir up too much resentment. There is no undermining going on here."

Seth shot Kavriel a sarcastic look and he nodded, catching the man's reasoning. The war was over, and now the adjustment had simply become the natural order of things. Still, there must have been some horrible events before these things were realized. Either the Patriarch had a heart or he was very tactical. No use stirring up any more trouble—it was something he had learned from his father each time the overseer had met with the clans, if only on a miniscule level.

They skirted the cove that Seth had headed toward earlier, southwest from the town proper, and near the end of a pier Kavriel saw a fishing trawler rocking gently on the waves. Several men were hoisting large nets from the pier to the deck, and they gave only a passing glance to Jassar as the three of them approached.

"How soon?" Jassar asked the closest fisherman. Kavriel had already figured out that this giant man was not one for long conversation. Direct and to the point was all he needed.

The barebacked man on deck wiped the sweat from his brow as he replied in heavy sea-born slang, "Near r'dy, Cap'n." He spoke behind his teeth, his eyes squinting in the strong sunlight. "The blanket's been-a dressed down, and we've need only to-as stock up."

Jassar grunted in what Kavriel could only assume meant approval. "Don't bother," he said, causing the other man who had been working the nets to stop what he was doing and look at their boss questioningly. "We're not dragging, we carting." He nodded in Kavriel's direction. "I need to get this one to Sai . . . promised the wife that I would help her cousin out."

The men only shrugged, pulling the rest of the netting onto the deck with more vigor than they had earlier, probably since they wouldn't be using them today. One of them leapt down and untied the trawler from the dock. They were loyal to Jassar, Kavriel could see that, and didn't seem unaccustomed to sudden changes of plans.

As Kavriel jumped the narrow gap between the pier and the boat's deck after Jassar, he made a mental note to ask the man how things had been since the Ay'vol came.

He was, after all, the son of an overseer, and he felt personally indebted to the man, even if he might have been doing this only as a favor to his "wife's cousin," as he'd said.

As crewmen came up on deck to guide the boat out of the harbor, Kavriel felt excited, realizing that he was about to start his voyage to a place he had always wanted to go. It was easy not to think about the occupation. Then again, he hadn't been there to see it happen—or remember it.

Soon they were in the rough waters of the channel, sailing toward the mainland, and as the waves crashed relentlessly along the sides of the small trawler, rocking her back and forth as gracelessly as a drunken dancer, Kavriel's excitement was soon taken over by the reality of sea travel. He huddled over the rail, doing his best to keep the soup that he had eaten that morning from making a return visit up his gullet. Despite the marvelous view of the sea in all her glory, he didn't see himself embarking on another open ocean voyage anytime soon. The wind sometimes kicked the water of the nearby Glen Lakes into waves, but they were nothing compared to this.

Noticing his nauseated scowl, Seth sat down next to him. He looked quite comfortable, smiling up at the sunshine as the chill ocean breeze danced in his hair. Despite mild resentment, Kavriel was happy for the company.

"The channel's pretty rough today, don't you think?" Seth asked, a smug smile tugging at his lips. Kavriel gave him a rueful look and Seth laughed before becoming serious.

"Listen Kavriel, I spoke with Jassar and he mentioned that there've been some incidents near the mainland waters." He looked over at the red-bearded man, who was himself looking out over the water toward the western horizon.

"What kind of incidents?" Kavriel asked suspiciously.

Seth frowned. "Not sure. Pirates, he thinks, old tradesmen gone bad after the Rav'agas came. They've been hitting the cargo liners and deep sea trawlers. Probably for the catch or the hold, I don't know. He hasn't seen any himself, but he has a bad feeling about the sea today. I didn't tell you this, but he is a bit superstitious."

It was Kavriel's turn to frown, and as he looked at the large man he regretted the rumors he had forgotten, about men of the sea and their strange customs. His father had sailed in the Quetalian Fleet in his military days, and had told Kavriel stories about how life at sea tended to play with your mind when you'd spent too much time away from hard dirt under your feet. Feeling his stomach turn in circles, Kavriel happened to agree for the moment. "Is he still going to take me to Sai?" he asked.

Seth shook his head. Kavriel should have known that things were moving much too smoothly so far. At least Seth had decided to come with him for the trip, otherwise he wouldn't know how to proceed with the fisherman while fighting his nausea at the same time.

"I don't think so." Seth grinned. "The man's a stubborn child when he wants to be, but there's plenty of shoreline nearby. We'll be close to the mainland soon but chances are you'll have to use the rowboat." He motioned over to the hollowed-out tree trunk that he had called a "boat," strung up to the side of the trawler, and Kavriel felt the soup tickle the back of his throat. His reaction must not have been discreet, because Seth laughed out loud. "Still better than swimming!" he joked, poking Kavriel in the ribs.

Kavriel let the humor attempt to change his mood, but he realized that soon he would be on his own. He was frightened at the prospect, realizing that he would honestly miss Seth. They had only been travelling a week together, but already they had bonded as if they had known each other for years. He could only hope that Seth would make it back to Rhyol safely.

"Will the ship return to Dior right away?" Kavriel asked, his concern obvious in his tone.

Seth shrugged, looking at the deck a moment. He seemed to sense Kavriel's disappointment and was feeling the same thing. Clearly he too had wanted to keep travelling, but they both knew that it would be too risky. His father must have known what he was talking about, if the Rav'agas would start asking difficult questions about Seth's disappearance.

During the voyage, Kavriel had time to piece together certain things that he had heard and seen. Specifically the lack of Ay'vol in Dior and how the woman Ella had mentioned to Jassar that some "captain" had left to the north with most of his men. That could have only meant one thing: the word was out on the dead Guardsmen. Was it Xavr who had killed them, Kavriel wondered, refusing to believe that it was actually his brother, after seeing how well the book collector could fight. Kavriel considered himself lucky to have avoided any problems since then, but he was becoming worried for his father.

Seth answered his question about the ship's destination.

"Yes, but not right away, and the channel patrols will probably stop us." He smiled coyly. "Jassar has that all figured out already."

"He wants the Rav'agas to catch him?" Kavriel asked, confused.

Seth hummed out an arch "yup." He waved a negligent hand. "He will explain some kind of broken cord, or ripping the net, had caused him to lose his catch, and he was trying to reclaim it before having to go back in, losing the day. The patrols don't like to see ships out of dock after curfew, but since there will be nothing to loot but destroyed fish nets, they will probably only fine him. It wouldn't be the first time. Plus, better the patrols than the pirates."

Kavriel nodded, understanding the point of the ruse. "But what if the patrol talks to you?" he asked, remembering what his father had said about keeping track of the locals. "Won't they wonder who you are?"

Seth shook his head. "Not one bit. I'm too stupid to be considered a threat." He smiled deviously. "And the patrols don't care about who is working the ship as much as they do about the captain. They know Jassar already, but they will leave him be, even if they have to ground his ship for a week."

Kavriel nodded, convinced that Seth would be alright, but still sorry for the problems he might have caused. "I don't want your family to be in any trouble because of me, Seth," he said. "I will honestly try to repay whatever Jassar needs to pay in fines."

Seth shook his head. "Don't worry about it. Jassar wouldn't even have this boat if it wasn't for Master Soelle. He might seem a bit rough and angry, but he knows what your father did for him and he wouldn't even think about asking for any favors." He gave Kavriel a cunning smile. "Now, before he throws you overboard, let's figure out where you're going."

He dragged his large travel bag from where he had stashed it behind some crates to keep it dry and pulled out one of the maps that the overseer had given them before they left. He rolled it out in the sunlight, and shoulder to shoulder, the two looked at the detailed drawings of the northern Quetalian coastline. Kavriel's head began to spin while trying to read the fine lines during the rocking of the ship, but he concentrated anyway.

"This is where we are . . . more or less." Seth glanced at the sun and horizon several times, pretending that his assumption might be reasonable. Kavriel thought it was, since he had meanwhile estimated about the same thing, despite having only minimal knowledge of sea navigation, from his father, of course. "And this is probably that stretch of rock out that way." Seth pointed at a coastline on the map before pointing out to the horizon, where indeed a thin trace of dark color was visible.

Kavriel couldn't help but smile, seeing the Quetal mainland for the first time in his life. Seth continued pointing at several places on the map. "Here are the villages and . . . ranches, maybe? I think it says that there. The overseer didn't know much about the mainland, but luckily we have Jassar, and according to him, the Guard pay little mind to the small inland communities and keep mainly to the port towns. That means that you should be able to find help along the way. Maybe even buy a horse to shorten your trip. How much money do you have on you, anyway?"

Kavriel shook his head. "Not enough for that, and anyway, I want you to take most of it back home with you. We didn't need much of it so far, and it doesn't belong to me. You need it for your family, if your father hasn't been able to work."

Clearly surprised by his generosity, Seth nodded graciously. "Thank you, Kavriel, but I'll go through the overseer first."

Kavriel agreed, happy that this young man was a respectful individual and a good help to his father right now. He felt sorry for not being more involved with the Kessors, but that was the past.

Suddenly a shout from one of the fishermen stationed in the bow of the ship caught Kavriel's attention. He was pointing and saying something to Jassar in such a rough sea dialect that Kavriel couldn't make out what he was saying. He looked to Seth, who returned an equally confused expression. Together they stood and moved over to Jassar, who was still staring over the sea in the direction the other man had been pointing.

And there in the distance, they saw with crystal clarity a galleon warship, flying the colors of Rav'agas, coming up to meet them. Jassar cursed, and Seth echoed it back loudly as the red-bearded man turned to Kavriel.

"Go below deck, Kavriel." He spoke with calm precision, despite the fishermen running around the deck, putting things in order. "I'll take care of this."

CHAPTER 19

"Damn," Jassar growled as he strode from the stern toward the bow, motioning to his men. "Drop the sails and put all our stock in sight; we don't want to look like we're making a run for it."

The crew leapt to his command, and in moments the trawler had slowed to a crawl, helpless to the stronger sea currents. Kavriel grabbed a railing as his legs went weak under him. He tried to pull himself over to the bow, curious to see what was happening. Seth had already begun helping the other men, moving with a confidence bred of familiarity—he must have had worked on these kinds of boats before. The larger Rav'agas patrol ship was nearly on top of them.

"Why are you letting them catch us?" Kavriel asked Jassar when he was close enough.

The man gave him a discouraging look. "I thought I told you to get belowdecks," he repeated before moving toward the center of the rig.

Ignoring the order, Kavriel trailed behind Jassar, watching as he released the trawling mechanism, letting the netted hook drop into the water with a splash. He immediately began turning the crank to bring the net back up above the waterline. *Making the trawl look like it had been used during the day,* he realized. Jassar was planning on attempting his ruse with the Rav'agas earlier than planned.

"Jassar?" Kavriel asked again, and the man cursed as he turned and saw Kavriel.

"We don't have a choice," Jassar replied, still

growling in frustration. "That's not a patrol ship, it's a battleship, twenty-five oars to a side, by my count. We'll be lucky if they don't simply ram us for practice."

Instantly worried, Kavriel looked to the Rav'agas ship again, watching the wooden oars rising and sweeping like the legs of some giant sea spider. He decided then that it was probably best to head belowdecks, as Jassar had suggested, although he wondered if drowning under or above the deck would make any difference.

He caught Seth by the arm as he moved past him, more for balance than anything else. "What's a battleship doing out in the channel?" he asked, wondering if his question made any sense, since he still wasn't used to the idea of Rav'agas in Quetal.

Seth shook his head. He too looked worried. "I don't know. Maybe Jassar was right about the sea today. Just keep calm and do what I do. He'll handle this." He moved past Kavriel, determined to keep helping the fishermen.

The activity was less chaotic as the Rav'agas ship pulled up alongside them. Kavriel had a new appreciation of the sheer size of the ship, which dwarfed the trawler like a shark swimming alongside a minnow. The three square-rigged sails must have stood over a hundred paces above the Rav'agas deck. Several uniformed soldiers stood on the long bowsprit that jutted out from the bow, their crossbows aimed at those on the deck of the trawler. There were several large crossbows also fixed to the deck, loaded with arrows thick as tree trunks, ready to fire.

Realizing that it was too late to duck under, Kavriel did as Seth, waiting calmly with the rest of them. Until his eyes fell on his and Seth's travel bags, and he realized that they had carelessly left them in plain sight. The pommel of his father's sword just barely poked out below the flap of his bag. He quickly looked away from it, wondering what the Rav'agas would do if they found it. He hadn't mentioned the blade to Jassar, and he hadn't seen the fishermen carrying any actual weapons on them beyond the usual belt knife. *They're probably forbidden,* he thought, and wondered if he should try to kick his bag over the side of the ship. His father had suggested as much, and he didn't care about losing his clothes and maps as much as he feared getting them into anymore trouble.

He slowly moved toward it, but froze when a man dressed formally in a long gray jacket with a conical helmet upon his head called down to them in a Rav'agas-accented voice, "Who is the captain here?"

Jassar stepped up to the railing. "I am."

As the uniformed man looked to him, Kavriel stepped closer to his bag, keeping an eye on the soldiers who were watching at all of them over their crossbows.

"Fisherman!" the soldier commanded, his nasal voice making him sound arrogant. "Prepare to be boarded and searched. Failure to obey will result in your immediate destruction."

Jassar nodded without a glance to his men, and several started forward to comply. Kavriel watched as ropes tumbled from the higher deck of the other ship to be secured to the trawler's bollards, while the anchor dropped from the battleship and hit the water with a large splash before sinking, its heavy chain slipping after it like a waterfall to stop after only a short time. The water must not

353

have been very deep here, which possibly meant that they weren't far from the mainland. He didn't know all that much about ships, but from occasional conversations with his father, Kavriel knew that this particular vessel was not large enough to be an open water frigate, though *too* big to be a coastal rig. He didn't remember seeing any other kinds of ships like it in Dior, so he assumed it must have sailed from one of the local harbors. He wondered if that was good or bad for Jassar.

The large man now had several papers in his hands. Behind him, Seth leaned calmly against the trawl, his arms crossed, and the others were scattered about the deck. A gangplank slammed down onto the deck from the Rav'agas ship, and the fishermen nearest moved away as two Rav'agas soldiers tramped onto the trawler, crossbows aimed. Kavriel instinctively backed away as well. Jassar held his ground, calmly awaiting the commander of the Rav'agas ship. Kavriel noticed that Seth also didn't seem to be fazed by the Rav'agas soldiers and their weapons; he regarded them with a calm rage simmering in his eyes that made Kavriel wonder what the young man had seen in the last several years, to take all the fear out of him.

The man in formal dress stepped down the ramp onto the trawler, glancing around before walking straight up to Jassar. Only the conical helmet made him as tall as the large, red-bearded fisherman. As if sensitive to this discrepancy, the commander snatched the paperwork out of Jassar's hand and studied what Kavriel assumed was identification. The large man didn't react.

The commander looked up. "Quetalian," he snapped, as if he had not just learned Jassar's name from

354

the document, "you are authorized to fish only in Dior waters. What are you doing here?"

Kavriel swallowed hard, fearing he'd be betrayed. But Jassar claimed he had ripped his nets, and had been trying to restock his load before returning home. No mention of passengers.

The commander responded with several other questions relating to that, and reiterated the regulations involving "water zones" that the Rav'agas had apparently allotted to those of Dior on Nostrac and Sai on the mainland. At the moment they were in Sai waters, and it was illegal for Jassar to be fishing there. He was looking at a stiff fine, but likely no more aggressive penalties. Already the Rav'agas soldiers on the ship were starting to release some of the mooring ropes, and the crossbows were lowered. After handing Jassar some kind of citation, which the big man took reluctantly, he turned and began walking to the gangplank.

Kavriel drew a relieved breath, then held it as one of the soldiers who was still on the ship with them called out in Rav'agas. The commander stopped and turned, and to Kavriel's terror, he realized the soldier held his father's blade!

The commander carefully strolled back onto the trawler. Jassar's face turned red. Kavriel didn't need to see the big man's eyes to know that he had just gotten them into serious trouble. The fishermen were quietly whispering among themselves, casting sidelong glances to their captain.

Seth had moved to the far rail and still seemed calm and uncaring, but Kavriel noticed that one of his hands had disappeared over the side of the ship, and he could only imagine what sort of weapon the younger man might have found and now concealed. Behind him, out toward the mainland, Kavriel saw a second Rav'agas patrol ship approaching. The situation was rapidly going from bad to worse. He only hoped that Seth wouldn't try anything stupid before this second ship arrived.

The commander took the sword from the solider, unsheathed it, and held it up for examination. Then he walked over to Jassar. Kavriel saw sweat beading on the big man's forehead now. "What is this?" the commander asked.

"It's mine," the big man replied, not exactly answering the question.

The commander didn't seem to care. "Having a Quetalian blade in your possession is a serious offense. You are now in violation of more than the sea charter." He returned the blade to its scabbard and handed it to the soldier who had found it. "You and your crew are under arrest. You will be held aboard my vessel and your ship will be confiscated. Move up the plank, Quetalian, or you will be killed where you stand." Though the Rav'agas was simply doing his job as a patrolman, Kavriel thought he detected glee in his tone. Jassar looked as if he had already been run through.

Kavriel couldn't just let these soldiers destroy all that the man had, because of him. "The sword is mine," he blurted, and immediately, all eyes fell on him. Jassar looked dumbfounded, while Seth's wide eyes seemed to be urging Kavriel to keep quiet.

The commander smiled smugly, as if amused, and

slowly walked over to Kavriel. "You?" He looked Kavriel up and down. Kavriel nodded, his throat too dry for words. "Where did you get this blade, boy?"

The commander didn't believe him, and most likely wouldn't believe anything else he had to say. Jassar was still going to be punished for having the sword, even if it wasn't directly in his possession, and Kavriel had jumped into the stew along with him. He decided to be honest. "My father gave it to me."

The commander lifted an eyebrow. "Why would he do that?"

"So I would get rid of it for him, toss it into the sea." For a brief moment Kavriel thought the commander was going to laugh. He didn't believe him, but he seemed to be enjoying the conversation.

"Did he, now?" He glanced over to the soldier holding the sword.

Kavriel noticed that the man wasn't listening to the conversation, instead watching the second patrol ship that had come up from the mainland, and was now slowly circling the two. Most of the fishermen were doing the same. The commander snatched the sword from the soldiers' hand, causing him to stand quickly to attention as if he had been slacking in his duties. The commander looked irritated, but he too was more concerned with the second patrol ship that had joined them. He eyed it carefully, and Kavriel took the opportunity to do the same.

It was larger than the trawler but not nearly the same size as the other Rav'agas vessel. There were no oars pushing it along, but three sails like those of a standard merchant ship. Despite being painted with Rav'agas colors, no crewmembers were visible to confirm nationality. The ship turned and went farther out to sea after circling them once more.

The commander frowned before returning his attention to the crew of the trawler, but remained distracted by the other ship, because he seemed to have forgotten about Kavriel and his sword. As he moved quickly up the gangplank, Kavriel glanced over at Jassar, who was watching the water where the second ship was headed. He too didn't seem to understand what was going on, but his expression had definitely softened.

Kavriel and the rest of Jassar's crew were forced to follow the commander up the gangplank. He found navigating that difficult, the plank no more than two feet wide, but once he'd stepped onto the black-painted deck of the frigate, Kavriel's nausea lessened. The larger boat made the rocking of the waves less pronounced, and the height from the water made it easier for him to keep his balance. A group of Rav'agas soldiers forced them back against the railing while a team of about a dozen descended to Jassar's trawler. Kavriel watched the commander staring out at the ship in the distance, which had turned once again and was heading back toward them.

"What's going on?" he whispered to Jassar, standing next to him.

The large man shook his head, also watching the approach of the other ship. It seemed to be coming in very fast. "You better hold onto something," Jassar whispered back, a twitch of amusement tugging at his lips.

Kavriel looked at the others. All of the fishermen, including Seth, were now gripping the wooden railing behind them. The merchant ship was on their port side. As its bow leapt out of the water, cresting a large wave, Kavriel saw a long extension from under the bow of the ship, like the beak of a bird.

The commander shouted something to his crew who had all been watching, and they sprang into action.

For the next few moments, Kavriel could barely comprehend what was happening. The large crossbows attached to the bulwark swung quickly toward the merchant ship on its collision course toward them, and he heard another shout, and recognized the Rav'agas word for "fire."

Too late. Kavriel fought and failed to keep his feet as the ship lurched heavily to the side under the assault of the ram. He heard a loud crack and the hull of the Rav'agas patrol ship shuddered. The force of impact shoved the large boat into the trawler still moored alongside, and the red-bearded man growled an obscenity as the smaller trawler seemed to be kicked off the sea before rolling onto its side.

The ram having effectively impaled the Rav'agas patrol ship, masked men started leaping aboard with swords and knives drawn. That was when everything became strange.

The Rav'agas men engaged these mysterious fighters with a roar of vengeance, and soon about thirty men were brawling on the black deck in a deadly melee that Kavriel had only seen depicted in battle illustrations during his studies. Yet unlike the artists' obvious representations of one side versus the other, this fight was impossible to understand. All the men seemed to be dressed the same, as if the merchant ship had been another battleship disguised as something less threatening. Yet why were the soldiers attacking their own side?

Kavriel scrambled away from the fury of the fight on his hands and knees. Screams and shouts filled the air. He had no idea where Seth had gone, or Jassar and his crew, but he wasn't about to stand up and call out for them. The fight had stayed mainly up near the bow, where the other ship's ram had penetrated the Rav'agas patrol ship, but as more masked fighters boarded, the Rav'agas soldiers had been forced back into more open areas of the deck to defend themselves. He pushed to his feet and crouching, dashed for the protection of several crates that had tumbled across the deck with the ram's impact. Peering around the corner of one, Kavriel thought he saw Seth in the confusion, swinging a long spear at the Rav'agas. The red-bearded Jassar was easier to spot; he too seemed to have found a weapon and had joined the masked strangers.

It was obvious that the Rav'agas were being defeated. Even the oarsmen who had dashed up from the lower levels of the ship, a sweaty, shirtless group equipped with only knives and clubs, did little to swing the fight in their favor. The masked fighters took care of them easily enough. Yet the commander seemed to be holding his own quite confidently, dispatching two foes with several swipes of his thin blade. He still clutched Kavriel's father's blade in his other hand, as if he had forgotten what it was. He turned toward Kavriel, then ran toward him, snarling. Kavriel scrabbled desperately backwards, wondering why the officer had taken a sudden interest in him. The man swung at his head with his blade. Kavriel had never been attacked with a real sword before, and with his lack of experience, he didn't try to evade it strategically but simply fell away, trying to keep his head low.

The officer must not have been interested at all in Kavriel, for if he was he could have run him through while he sprawled against the cabin door behind him. The commander had been trying to move into the cabin, and Kavriel had simply been in the way. He understood this as the man's boot hit his chest. The door crashed open behind him and the kick propelled Kavriel off his feet and indeed, off the deck. For a few seconds Kavriel became light as a feather, before smashing onto his back halfway down a stairwell, the impact driving the air from his lungs. Momentum kept him thumping down the staircase like a much-battered sled until he slammed against another door and lay there, feeling as if his back had snapped in two. He inhaled with a groan, his neck and shoulders throbbing from his collision with first the door, then the staircase, then pushed himself slowly, carefully, to his feet.

Blinking bleary eyes, he peered up the staircase— and saw the commander of the Rav'agas patrol ship charging down the stairs, his blade drawn. Kavriel's head was ringing but he was still able to get the gist of the curses the commander was hissing through his teeth. By the worst coincidence in the world, this man was still desperate to reach the door behind Kavriel, and Kavriel was still in his damn way. A frustrated rage burned in the commander's eyes, and Kavriel knew that this attack wasn't about him at all, but about losing the ship to the attacking pirates. Kavriel was simply an obstruction in his path. Kavriel could only concentrate on keeping out of the way.

The first jab missed, somehow, but as Kavriel moved against the side of the stairwell the commander turned with him, lifting his blade with the intention of slashing Kavriel's throat. Kavriel grabbed the commander's wrist and instinctively reached for sthe man's other wrist as his hand came up. Kavriel's fingers closed on the hilt of his father's sword, still held tightly in the commander's left hand.

The Rav'agas spat in Kavriel's face and he twisted aside, slamming his heavier body against Kavriel, driving them both back against the door and then into the cabin beyond when it burst open under the impact. Kavriel backpedalled into a spacious cabin, illuminated by large windows that were half underwater and beginning to crack from the pressure. The Rav'agas patrol ship was sinking.

We're all going to drown, Kavriel thought in a flash, until he hit a large worktable and fell halfway over it, knocking several documents and books to the deck. Scowling, the commander raised his blade and threw the empty scabbard in his left hand to the floor. It was only then that Kavriel saw what he was holding: his father's sword. He must have inadvertently drawn it from its sheath when the commander shoved him.

The man came at him fast, taking advantage of the open area of the cabin to fully swing his blade, and as Kavriel parried awkwardly, he realized that he had just entered a duel with the Rav'agas officer. But then he felt the sharp edge of the commander's weapon slide across his wrist and he screamed, dropping his blade to clutch his arm. The commander slashed diagonally across his chest. Kavriel felt as if he had been kicked again as he fell over the table and landed on his knees on the other side. He knelt there, panting with pain, helplessly watching the commander rounding the table to finish him off.

A crack like breaking ice swung Kavriel's head toward the large windows in time to see them burst. Water gushed in, knocking the man to the wet floor. Partially protected by the table, which was fixed to the deck, Kavriel watched wide-eyed as it somehow rose upward. Then he realized, as the floor seemed to drop away from his feet, that it was the ship itself that had lurched. He started sliding as the floor tilted. His chest burned and had felt wet before the sea had entered, but Kavriel was more concerned with his wrist; he clutched it tightly with his free hand while trying to get to his feet.

The room became a pool, the cold ocean water rising a foot every few seconds. Holding his arm tight against his chest to protect the damaged wrist, Kavriel crawled toward the canted stairwell, its lower steps already underwater.

A hand grabbed him from behind and flung him onto his back. Kavriel sputtered as he was momentarily submerged, then the commander wrapped his fingers around Kavriel's neck and pulled him up to his face. Forgetting his injury, Kavriel clawed at the man's fingers, trying to pull them free of his throat, but the man was too strong. He hissed obscenities in Rav'agas that Kavriel didn't even try to understand; the savagery of the delivery conveyed enough of the meaning.

The commander smiled, more a rictus of hatred. Already defeated by the pirates, he was about to have his final vengeance. The smile widened as he pushed Kavriel's head under the water, and Kavriel choked and struggled to free himself, hampered by his injuries while the commander kneeled on his chest. His eyes rolled back in his head as the sea water again entered his lungs. Yet just as Kavriel again faced his death, something seemed to burst away from him, a bubble released from his pain that pushed the commander off of him in an explosion of water.

The man smashed into the table and Kavriel was on his feet, somehow, and a breath later armed again with his father's sword. Feeling like a puppet with his strings being pulled, Kavriel watched his arm move skillfully around the commander, who had also found his blade, and the two men whirled in a strange dance of death—until Kavriel's blade cut through the commander's torso. The man looked up, dumfounded, at Kavriel as he fell to his knees, holding his gut to prevent his insides from spilling out.

Equally dumbfounded, Kavriel returned the man's gaze, suddenly feeling as if he had just regained control of his body. He was breathing hard, and the sword seemed to have gained another twenty pounds.

Uttering one last word in Rav'agas that Kavriel actually was able to understand—"Impossible"—the man fell over dead. Kavriel blinked as the corpse was carried away out the cabin window, wondering what had just happened. He felt frozen in place, the water already up past his waist now as the ship continued to sink. He saw the blood dripping off of his father's sword and quickly dipped the metal into the water to clean it off. The ocean inside the cabin turned red.

Fearing more what had happened than drowning, Kavriel turned toward the stairwell and headed up to the deck of the sinking ship. Repeating the Rav'agas word for "impossible" in a whisper, he desperately went in search of

Seth.

CHAPTER 20

The sea had finally calmed its ferocity with the setting sun, and now the swaths of purple and red in the sky reflected off the water as if it were glass. Standing on the deck of the merchant ship, Kavriel gazed at the horizon in silence. He hadn't moved from the spot in hours. He wasn't concerned about where he was or who had saved him. Something had happened in the Rav'agas ship. Something that he didn't quite understand, and he had needed time to reflect on all the possibilities.

The fighting had ended by the time Kavriel had escaped the commander's cabin, and in what seemed more like a hazy dream than reality, Kavriel had been escorted by masked men dressed as Rav'agas onto their ship. Seth, Jassar, and Jassar's surviving crew were there, and as the trawler was cut loose the two vessels moved away from the sinking patrol ship and into deeper waters, away from the mainland.

Kavriel didn't care. He felt strange; dirty—as if he had been part of something that went against everything he believed in. He had killed a man. He knew that for certain, but the worst part of it was, he didn't understand exactly how. It had all happened so fast. He was thankful he hadn't needed to explain himself to this strange crew of men who had saved them from the Rav'agas.

It was obvious that they were on his side, and that Jassar and even Seth, to some extent, knew who they were. A few hours ago Kavriel might have been dying to know more, to put this aspect of this dangerous but exiting new world he was trying to remember into perspective, but having discovered something about himself that he never would have imagined possible, he felt more comfortable being alone.

His father's sword rested against the railing about a foot from where he stood, as it had for the last few hours. He hadn't the nerve to throw it away, but he hadn't touched it since he'd boarded this new ship. It may as well have cast a barrier around him, for no one approached. He understood. He had overheard the whispers that this stranger had killed a Rav'agas officer in a duel. That meant he was interesting, but since he didn't understand how or why, and turned away rather than explain this strange skill he had acquired sometime in the last years to these men, he preferred to keep his distance. Kavriel had felt their eyes on him since he'd thrown his sword down and huddled against the railing. Even Seth hadn't come to see him.

Kavriel was still able to hear the voices of the crew, however, and he had already figured out who the captain of this pirate ship was by his loud voice and gruff tone, not much different from that of Jassar. Indeed, the two of them conversed with a familiarity that made Kavriel wonder if the attack had been planned. Jassar seemed to be genuinely upset, though, shaking his head while looking elsewhere whenever the captain tried to make a point. If the attack had been planned, Kavriel decided, Jassar clearly hadn't known anything about it.

He was older than Jassar, Kavriel noticed, but not by much, and while Jassar had a thick mass of hair on both his head and face, the captain of this ship was as bald as a new-born, his sunburned pate supported on a bull-thick neck. The only hair that Kavriel could see was on his bare shoulders, which were covered in tattoos that extended in sleeves down his wrists and in a tattooed collage of shapes and figures down his torso. Physically, he was a slightly smaller version of Jassar, with his barrel chest and tree trunk arms, all muscle. The man reminded him of a wild boar. He called himself Kell, and his cool demeanor suggested a dangerous level of experience in fighting Rav'agas.

Later on the conversation seemed to lead to Kavriel, and he cursed under his breath and focused on the horizon, uneasy being the center of attention. He wondered if this was what Vaemalin felt like all the time. After what seemed like an eternity under Kell's dark-eyed scrutiny, Kavriel finally turned to acknowledge him.

The man stood nearby, noisily crunching on an apple. He continued to eat his apple under Kavriel's gaze, looking at Kavriel occasionally. Finally he tossed the core over the side of the ship. "What's your name, boy?" he asked around the last mouthful, so casually that he seemed bored and disinterested.

Kavriel gave his first name only, remembering what his father had told him. His throat was dry from the fresh sea air, and he needed to clear it before he spoke. He hoped his distrust didn't sound too obvious in his tone.

The man named Kell didn't reply, but simply strolled up to stand near him at the rail, snatching up the sword on the way over. Kavriel tensed up, turning to face him. Kell was shorter than Kavriel, but his shoulders were easily double his own, and the sword looked like a stitching pin in his huge mitts. He studied the blade with analytical eyes that seemed strange in such a boorish-looking individual. The light of the red sun halfway below the horizon caught the flat of the blade, clearly defining the Quetalian markings. Kell seemed to be reading them.

"This is quite a weapon you have here, boy," he said, and the tanned skin above his eyes where eyebrows would be rose appreciatively. "The commodore who gave it to you must have thought you deserved it. You don't see folded steel outside of the officers' quarters too often." He smiled at Kavriel, showing a mouthful of pearl-white teeth that contrasted with his sunburned skin.

Kavriel nodded without revealing any surprise. Obviously Kell knew more about standard-issue blades than he realized, despite the man's appearance. "It was my father's."

Kell nodded as if he already knew. "You could get quite a bit of money for this . . . if you could ever find a willing buyer." He smiled smugly. "These swords are not too popular among the Southlanders. It is very dangerous item to have. Yet that doesn't frighten you, does it?"

Kavriel knew there were questions hidden in that comment. He wasn't ready to answer what he could not, not just yet. So he tried to change the conversation. "Are you a pirate?" he asked, using that label to sidetrack the man's inquisition.

Kell smiled, but before he could answer, Jassar and Seth joined them. Seth nodded politely to Kavriel, but he seemed a bit reserved.

Jassar moved next to the railing. "Kell runs . . . deliveries between Dior and Sai."

Kell grunted a laugh, turning toward him. "Thank you for thinking so highly of me, old friend." He turned back to Kavriel. "I have a broader job description than that."

Kavriel smiled. "You're a smuggler."

Kell nodded as if he considered the title an honor. "I'm not breaking any of your laws, am I, boy?"

Kavriel reluctantly shook his head. He should at least repay the man with his respect. He smiled, offering his hand. "Not at all. Thank you for helping us out. I was stupid to keep that blade with me. I didn't realize—"

Kell interrupted him. "No need. I have about half a dozen crates of these on board right now. They are important things to have." He shook Kavriel's hand. "Jassar was delivering you to the mainland, so I hear?"

Kavriel nodded. "Yes. I need to get to Teltraum. There are some questions that I need answered," he replied, willing to be honest, but only just.

Kell seemed to sense the missing information, but he didn't pry. "Well then, it's your lucky day. I happen to be headed that way—to the mainland, that is. I have some shipments to deliver to Misam. I could give you passage." He handed Kavriel his father's sword as he spoke, which Kavriel accepted after a moment's hesitation. Kell noticed. "It's a shame," he said. "It's not often that I find a skilled swordsman on my ship. Well . . . one not wearing an Ay'vol uniform." He smiled, and Kavriel sensed that he was still prodding. Maybe it was because he continued to smile.

Kavriel wasn't sure what he could answer, so he shrugged. "I'm not, as far as I know," he replied truthfully, seeing that both Jassar and Seth were watching him carefully for his response. "I seem to have forgotten a bit of my recent past. I figured I just got lucky, is all." He shrugged again, picturing the commander of the Rav'agas patrol ship as he had died under Kavriel's blade. He felt that dirtiness again.

"Perhaps," Kell answered softly, "but still. I have a business to run, and people that need me. I don't often have the time or the interest to smuggle fugitives to the mainland."

Kavriel understood the man's meaning, but he became defensive nonetheless. "I am not a fugitive," he replied, maybe more gruffly than he should.

Kell didn't seem offended. He opened his large hands wide. "Neither are any of us," he declared " . . . to ourselves." He rested his hands back on his hips. "Yet the chancellor's descriptions of us tend to be a bit different. Still, I am not a greedy man and I can offer my service to a fellow man-at-arms in need." His smile became sly. "For a price."

Kavriel nodded with a sigh, thinking of his conversation with Seth before they'd encountered the patrol ship, how he had been hoping to give him the money that his father had loaned him. "I'll give you all the money I have," he declared, not caring so much about having to relinquish his funds as much as being unable to help out the Kessor family back home.

Kell surprised him by shaking his head, still smiling. "No, young man, no. Money isn't important to me. I have more than enough to keep my little . . . operation . . . going. No, what I need is fighters, and skilled ones. These are dangerous times and the Rav'agas seem to be getting more numerous every day. I need men."

His smile disappeared when Kavriel looked over to Seth, who merely shrugged. "Oh, don't worry about your friend," Kell said, also looking over to the other man. "He is welcome to join me. He's young, but he can handle himself against the Rav'agas well enough for me." Seth nodded, smiling; he must have accepted Kell's offer sometime earlier.

Kavriel suddenly felt responsible. "Seth?" he asked, and the young man had a hard time looking at him directly. "You need to go back to Rhyol. You heard what my father said."

Seth waved away Kavriel's lecture. "Look, Kavriel. I know what he said," he pleaded, looking over to Kell as if he'd found a brand new toy, " . . . but you've seen what these men can do!" he exclaimed, and his eyes lit up. "They're fighting what your father and I have been fighting. What your friends have been fighting. Kavriel, this is my chance! This is our chance!"

Kavriel shook his head. He knew Seth, but not well enough to understand what the young man had been through in the last few years. He had seen his town destroyed by the Rav'agas, seen their friend Tess taken and learned of her death. He had more reason to hate the Patriarch than Kavriel did, and he knew that he wouldn't be able to change Seth's mind even if he wanted too. The only thing Kavriel could do, then, was support him, but he still felt responsible.

"Fine," he said to Kell, who had been listening patiently to their conversation. "I'll go with you to Misam." He pictured the northwestern town at the edge of Quetal, known more for its hustling and gambling than for the wood resources the port town exported. He felt that he needed to look after Seth, and he gave Kell a disapproving scowl with the admission that he had been beaten.

"Splendid," Kell replied, and grabbed Jassar's elbow, jerking his head to one side in a signal to leave. The two men strolled off down the deck toward the swarthy-looking bunch who had rescued them.

Kavriel cursed, turning to the sea, dangling his father's sword over the railing.

Seth hesitantly joined him. "I'm sorry, Kavriel. It's for the best."

Kavriel didn't turn to him, but he nodded reluctantly. "If it's what you want," he said, feeling as if he had just lost a friend.

Seth must have sensed it. He touched him on the shoulder and Kavriel looked at him, seeing the justification in his eyes. "Listen, Kavriel. I don't want to go back to Rhyol. There is nothing there for me anymore. I want to fight. I want to make a difference for our people. Times are changing, you heard your father. The chancellor is losing control and the Quetalians are breaking through the occupation. Kell is just another of those under the Patriarch's heel. We need this."

He paused, but continued when Kavriel didn't react. "Your brother might have gotten sick, like you, but he has become something more for the resistance. People like Jassar, Kell, and my cousin Ella all believe that the time will come when the Patriarch will have to leave Quetal. Vaemalin is a figurehead, and you're looking for him. Well, so are we all, in a sense."

Kavriel frowned. "Is it true that he killed Chancellor

Tavrick?" he asked.

Seth blinked quickly. He knew he had understood his meaning. The conversation they had in Kavriel's father's house was still fresh. "I don't know. Lots of people think so, including the Rav'agas. Maybe I do too. "

Kavriel thought about this, wondering if Seth's loyalty to his father had affected his opinion. He glanced over to the cluster of Kell's crewmen. "What about them?" he asked, wanting to know more of what Seth had told them.

The young man shrugged, not taking the hint. "They've heard of the Ghost like everyone else and where he might be from, but I don't think they've made the connection to you. I know Jassar would keep his big mouth shut, at least."

"What does *he* know?" Kavriel asked, glancing inconspicuously towards Kell who was now at the far end of the ship.

Seth replied quietly. "That you got mixed up with the Guard somehow. He didn't ask, but he seems to be more interested in what you can do with that." He nodded toward the sword in Kavriel's hand.

He pulled it back over the railing and slid it under his belt. He didn't know what had happened to the scabbard during his fight with the commander, and figured it was at the bottom of the sea . . . where he should be. Still, he understood what Seth was trying to tell him as he saw the obvious distrust in his eyes. The secrets seemed to go both ways. "Alright," he said. "I know you're wondering what happened, but I swear to you I don't know!"

He had raised his voice, and Seth held out his

hands. "It's alright, Kavriel," he said quickly. "I believe you. Your memory is no good . . . I get that. Yet you can't deny what happened."

Kavriel shook his head. Seth nodded. "Then let's make the most of this," Kavriel said.

Seth nodded over to Kell and Jassar. "Kell is heading to a town called Gelod's Stream to collect some kind of Rav'agas documentation—a book or a report or something. Apparently it contains some nasty secrets about the chancellor's stations in the north. I think they're planning a pretty big raid."

Kavriel gave Seth an incredulous look. "They told you all of this?" he asked, not sure he believed him. Seth nodded. Kavriel sighed, discouraged that his friend had been so easily caught up in this rebel quest. If what they had told Seth was true, that meant that he had been recruited into their cause. There was no way he would be able to get out now. He wondered if all the discretion that he had been forced to live with while biding his time in Rhyol had taken its toll. It was believable. Seth was hungry, and wanted to make a difference. Kavriel sighed and smiled. He shouldn't be too tough on the young man. He probably would have done the same, in his place. In a way, he already was.

Kavriel nodded, not wanting any more bad blood between them. Seth was still the only friend he had now. "Alright. What do we do?"

Seth rubbed his hands together, frowning as he tried to think strategically. "We go with them to Misam, like he wants. Something big is coming, and if anything, whatever we learn will be more than we would have on our own.

These guys are fighting the same fight we are."

Kavriel nodded, wanting so much to remind the young man that he simply wanted to find out where his memory had gone. Still, the idea appealed to his sense of adventure; he did feel a bit curious about this kind of life. Yet he needed to remember their priorities. "And about Teltraum?" he asked. "Father will be trying to contact Femaor, and his friend Councilman—I mean *Chairman* Richart," he reminded Seth. "We can't let them down, otherwise my father and your family might think something has happened to us."

Seth nodded, clearly having forgotten that part but struggling to shove it into his plans. He bit his lip, and his youthfulness showed as he pondered the problem. "Right . . . That is still to our advantage. We're all on the same ship here, either in Teltraum or Misam. The northwest is actually safer than the capitol, and we can send word home from there, maybe to the overseer's friend Femaor. If we have an army on our side, it's even better for the chairman, right?"

Kavriel forced a smile, wondering what had generated such hatred against the Rav'agas in Seth. "I guess so, yes," he replied, still not sure he could even trust these rebel "smugglers." Yet what choice did they have? Ditch them on the mainland and try heading into Teltraum on their own? Kavriel had already seen how the patrol ships worked; he could only imagine how the Rav'agas would be on the mainland. He had the forged papers, but he would need to avoid the main roads. But he wasn't a frontiersman; he couldn't survive in the wild. Sure, there were certain things that Kavriel was learning about himself that he must have forgotten, but that didn't mean that he had become a full-fledged ranger, did it? He sighed again, unable to find the options, fingers absently tapping the sword hilt sticking out of his belt. It had felt strange in his hand, *hadn't it*?

"Then we go with Kell," he announced, turning his attention back to Seth, who was smiling like a child discovering what a sweet tasted like for the first time. "Then we go with Kell," he repeated, and they moved toward the crowd of smugglers, who seemed to be waiting for them, hiding the grins on their faces

CHAPTER 21

*Forgive us Father, we had no choice. You have
been too long away from the mortals, and you have not
understood their progression as you once believed you did.
They are strong, and they are resilient. There is nothing
that I can see to stop them from becoming what we are, in
time. Isn't that what you wanted? Why you changed your
theories while watching their evolution? Isn't that why you
brought us to them? Created us as a medium between your
intuition and our direct association? I thought so once, but
after you spoke . . . I wasn't so sure what had become of
you.*

*I am sorry it had to come to this. Kai'sa thinks it is
too late for forgiveness. Dar and Faythe think much the
same. I haven't seen Tondal since we brought you down
from the heavens, Father. Since Sa'rire did . . . what he and
what all of us thought we needed to do. I am sorry. We are
all responsible, and we accept that.*

*I know you must have sensed this coming. Were you
ready to go, Father? You could have stopped all of us, and
all at once, if you had wished it. Erased us from existence
as you did the other, all those eons ago. Had he sensed the
same thing, I wonder? When you realized that his
reasoning was not for those that he had helped to create
but for his own sense of greatness? I wish I knew . . . but
now it is too late. There is no way that you could have told
us, even if you wanted to. I am not sure even we, your
second gift to this world, would be capable of
understanding.*

We are not much different from the mortals, in that

378

way. They think the same way we do, they understand and accept the mysteries of the world and make their own theories about it. The only difference between us is that they seem to use their limited lives as strengths, and not as weaknesses, as you suggested the last time you spoke to us. I know you were angry, disappointed maybe, with them or with us, but you must have understood that this was never about you. It was about them. Tondal knew that, otherwise he never would have gone through with this. You had become too erratic in your subtlety. No one understood what you expected of them any longer, not even us.

The mortals adapt, as they always have, but they separated themselves from The Word when they saw that the differences they made in their lives to please you did nothing. I and my brothers and sisters know that your appreciation doesn't necessarily work that way, yet how were they to know? We cannot simply tell them about us . . . cannot tell them directly who we are and why we were sent to them. Sa'rire thinks we should, but his opinions are based only on the mortals of the southern kingdom. They are more traditional in their ways, and he thinks they would understand.

I know that is what you wanted in the end, to bring the lost sheep together. That was why you sent the sky and earth against them. Yet why couldn't you understand? They had become fragmented because of the ability to reason that you gave them. You could not expect them to go back to the way things were simply because you had changed. It was too late for that.

I wish you could have understood that. Then maybe we wouldn't have had to do what we did. Again I am sorry, but I still think that you wanted it to end this way. You must have. We will see what our decision creates for your children. We will do what we always have. We will watch.

"Welcome to Quetal!" Kell whispered loudly as the rowboat struck sand, and Kavriel stepped onto the mainland for the first time in his life. Unfortunately the merchant ship had arrived sometime in the middle of the night, and heavy fog had hidden the landscape from Kavriel's eyes.

The crew moved quickly and quietly, transferring the crates of smuggled goods from the rowboat to somewhere in the hilly gloom. No one spoke, and Kavriel worked with the men in silence, the only sounds being the thud of their feet on the beach. Men were waiting for them, and the sound of horses galloping away was the final signal to Kell that the delivery was complete.

Darkness gave way to sunrise, and Kavriel watched with Kell and his men as the ship sailed off into the morning mist on the horizon. The trawler had gone with the merchant ship, Jassar with it. Kavriel had thanked the red-bearded man for his assistance, and had given him nearly half of the money he had planned to give to Seth.

His young companion from Rhyol had almost choked up as he hugged Jassar rather awkwardly before he left. Kavriel didn't want to ask if everything would be alright for Jassar as he returned to his trade and to his wife with her soup. It would only make Seth uncomfortable. No one could be certain about anything anymore. The only thing they knew for sure was that their leader was now Kell, and they were part of his crew of smugglers numbering nearly two dozen.

When Kavriel asked him where they were, Kell responded with a shrug, explaining that they had landed about two weeks' voyage from Misam, and twice that to Port Sai, where Kavriel had originally thought they were heading. Kell gathered everyone into a huddle to look at the map he'd brought. Kavriel asked about Teltraum, just out of curiosity, and how long it would take to reach it.

"One month with a fast horse and an open road, neither of which you have," Kell responded with a grin that irritated Kavriel. The answer was meant to discourage him from leaving the crew, if he was contemplating that.

That had been a week ago. Since then they had travelled fast along the north coast.

"Stay here, and wait for my signal," the scout, Ulin, instructed before ducking around the hedges where he and Kavriel had been waiting for the last few hours.

Kavriel nodded impatiently, tired of being told the same thing for the hundredth time. He watched his smuggler companion adjust the dirty coat over his shoulders before hobbling down the hillside toward the village, where stone houses breathed thin streams of smoke from their chimneys into the cool spring morning.

Kavriel started counting, timing the smuggler's absence, as had been his duty over the last several days, whenever he was scouting with Ulin. Kell had introduced both Kavriel and Seth to him while they were concealing their tracks on the beach when they had arrived in Quetal. He was a scout and an informant, among his other responsibilities in Kell's strange company. He was a studious-looking individual, his blonde hair cut short and clean, his face clean-shaven, and his clothes well-kept. He didn't have the usual sailor piercings or tattoos, and reminded Kavriel more of a city politician than a smuggler pirate.

There was pain in his dark blue eyes, remorse or possibly fury, that did well to disguise his true age; Kavriel thought he was older than him by ten or so years, but he might be even older, for all Kavriel knew. He had a long white scar down the side of his cheek that Kavriel conjectured was the result of a blade or a hot flame. He didn't say where he was from, or how he came to be with Kell, but then, Kavriel didn't push too hard to get personable. Ulin's cool demeanor and more precise manner made Kavriel cautious around him. Plus he carried more weapons on his person than all the other crewmen together.

Still, despite his initial feelings about Ulin, Kavriel liked him. He was reserved, and did not come off as vulgar like the rest of Kell's crew. His voice was clear and refined when he spoke, as if he had been educated, and when he watched the crew spar in practice he seemed to have a haughty air about him, which could have just been arrogance, but it was far from volatile. He was obviously dangerous, but less so than the rest of them, so Kavriel didn't really mind having to work with him.

As an added benefit Ulin, being a scout, had an extensive knowledge of the geography of northern Quetal, which Kavriel was hungry to learn about. He had jotted many notes on his maps whenever Ulin explained where they were in relation to everything else. He also seemed to know a lot about the culture of mainland Quetal—the ways of the people, the economies of the villages and towns they passed, and local politics. Kavriel was curious what kind of background gave Ulin all this knowledge, but their conversations were limited to the practicality of their assignments.

Ulin also seemed to harbor some kind of animosity toward Kavriel, as if he'd wronged him in another time that he had forgotten. He seriously hoped not, but Kavriel couldn't be sure of anything that had happened in the last five years. So they continued to do what Kell required of them.

Kavriel had learned from Ulin that the villages in the region they scouted were unoccupied by the Rav'agas in comparison to the other districts of Quetal. The coastline between Sai and Misam was practically ignored, with only random sea patrols that were manned by the least experienced soldiers and those too old or too young to be regarded worthy of deployment in other companies. Ulin seemed to stress that last point, as if to remind him that whatever he'd accomplished on the patrol ship that Kell's crew sank might not have been nearly as spectacular as the others had thought. Kavriel actually felt better for that remark. He had feared that he'd become an expert killer during the last five years, but Ulin's remark helped confirm that it had been sheer luck that had saved him.

Kavriel had also learned that a very important assembly was about to take place in Misam in the next several days, something that both invigorated and worried Kell's crew. The villages that they had scouted were for reconnaissance mostly, ensuring that the Rav'agas kept to their routines so that Kell's party could pass undetected.

Kavriel had accompanied Ulin, both of them

disguised, as he visited several of these villages, letting the well-spoken man lead the conversations. The locals took to him quickly, considering him some fallen noble or former overseer that had lost his status after the Rav'agas occupation, and they were helpful. The meetings were brief, and generally covered the same subjects—how difficult the winter was this year, when the crops would be in, and how the animals were too skinny—the same kind of talk Kavriel might hear back home. It made him feel more relaxed, despite being so far away from home. Villagers were still villagers wherever you went. If not for the apple orchards instead of the fragrant blackberries and silver birches that he was used to, Kavriel might believe he was still in Rhyol.

A gust of the chill morning wind from the drizzly North Sea brought Kavriel back to his task and he scolded himself for letting his focus drift as, still counting, he squinted west of the village toward the small cluster of dark dots that were the rest of Kell's crew. This was not an ordinary reconnaissance mission. This was Gelod's Stream, the village that Seth had spoken of as the location of a Rav'agas document that the crew needed. It also held a permanent posting of Rav'agas soldiers commanded by an Ay'vol Corporal Commander. This was by far the most dangerous assignment Kavriel had been given since entering Quetal, and he couldn't help feeling excited, as well as anxious.

He glanced at the sun. *He should be back by now.* He wondered exactly how much time had to pass before he signalled to Kell that the mission had failed. *Not yet,* he hoped. It would require a quick withdrawal, leaving Ulin on his own to either rejoin them later or face Rav'agas justice. Another look confirmed Kell's crew were still moving along the coastline toward Misam. Kavriel was just as dead as Ulin if things went bad. No loose ends.

His knees were stiffening up. Kavriel shifted his weight. *Something's wrong,* he thought again, looking up at the sky, as he had done only moments ago. Several more minutes passed with Kavriel nervously glancing from the village to the sky. Then he made probably the stupidest decision he could. He removed his sword belt and concealed the weapon in the tall grass before standing and stepping around the hedge to start down the path to the village. He was going to find Ulin himself. Kell had never told him directly not to.

The village was tiny, but the locals ignored him, remaining focused on their chores. Kavriel didn't like that; it confused him. Villagers normally would say hello or at least nod in goodwill, especially in the smaller towns. But the people of Gelod's Stream kept their heads low, their eyes on the ground. Pulling his collar higher around his neck, Kavriel kept walking, surreptitiously searching for Ulin.

He approached a workshop where an older man was binding the staves of a wooden barrel together with iron hoops. Kavriel stopped to watch for a moment, using the pause to memorize the layout of the village, in case he needed to disappear fast. The cooper suddenly cursed, and Kavriel, seeing a chance to be helpful, instinctively approached and grabbed the loose staves in a hug. The local looked up at him in surprise, then nodded and put the iron rings in place, using a small hammer to tap them securely.

When the work was done the cooper straightened and gusted a sigh, wiping sweat from his forehead. Kavriel stood up next to him. "My thanks, stranger," the cooper said. "My strength seems to have gone away with my youth." He grinned, revealing a mouth missing a few teeth.

Kavriel smiled back. "You're welcome, sir." He glanced around. "Where is your apprentice?" he asked, hoping to win the man's trust before asking the real questions.

The old man frowned and shook his head. "He left along with the others."

"Left?" Kavriel repeated. "Where did he go?"

The cooper's eyes narrowed and he looked askance at Kavriel, who realized too late that maybe he should have acted as if he knew what the man meant. "To the camp with the soldiers." He tilted his head, still eyeing Kavriel. "You aren't from the garrison?"

Kavriel cursed mentally, remembering why Ulin did all the talking with the locals. He needed to find him. He shook his head, moving in a bit closer to the cooper, who didn't move back. "No," he whispered, pretending to be looking at something else. He was assuming much from the man, who could just as easily be a Rav'agas ally. "I'm looking for a friend of mine. Have you seen any other strangers besides me this morning?"

The old man placed his hands on his hips and seemed to think for a moment. His behavior didn't strike Kavriel as suspicious. "No, young man, I haven't, but thank you kindly for your help. I should be able to finish on my own now."

Kavriel nodded his welcome, feeling disappointed that he hadn't been able to get anything more from the man but relieved that he hadn't done something that might have gotten him caught. He turned back to the street, then stopped when the man suddenly said something more.

"You might try asking at the stationhouse."

Kavriel looked back at him. The man hadn't looked up from the barrel. "Maybe one of the guards saw your crippled friend." He raised his head and winked.

Kavriel smiled, knowing that he hadn't mentioned anything about Ulin's disguise. Nodding his thanks, he walked slowly across the street, looking at a larger building decorated with an Ay'vol banner, gold on black—that had to be the place. It only made sense that if Ulin was seeking Rav'agas documents, he would likely find them there.

There weren't any guards at the front of the building but that didn't mean he should be less cautious. He ducked behind a home beside the stationhouse and approached the building from the rear, scanning the back wall for potential access points. A window on the second floor was open, reachable by a nearby tree. After a quick glance around to make sure he wouldn't be seen, Kavriel climbed up the tree and into the building with minimal effort.

The room he entered was empty. He crossed to the door and peeked out onto a railed gallery overlooking the lobby area below. Looking right, then left to make certain he was alone, he crept over to the railing to gain an understanding of the interior layout. Two uniformed soldiers stood facing the entrance. And there was Ulin, speaking to another person directly below the gallery.

Kavriel could see only the person's gray hair and thin shoulders and masculine hands, one holding a book as the other wrote something in it. Ulin who was already well into a conversation.

"...Twenty, armed with bows and blades, moving east on the coastline directly north of the main road."

The gray-haired man continued to write. "From where did they arrive?"

"Port Sai on a merchant ship. They destroyed the Rav'agas patrol." Ulin seemed comfortable, and Kavriel became suspicious.

The gray-haired man grunted angrily, and the two soldiers nearby shifted uneasily. "Do you know where they are headed?"

"No, My Lord. Teltraum would be my guess."

Kavriel sensed trouble. He had no love for Kell, but if Ulin had decided to shift his loyalties, it was not going to help his situation, either. Kavriel struggled to remain calm. There must be a reason for this!

The gray-haired man barked a laugh. "Teltraum! Then they are fools."

Ulin showed no outward reaction. "Yes, My Lord, but they are en route to meet with others. It would be better to stop them from continuing now, before things become too complicated."

The gray-haired man stopped writing and lifted his head to look curiously at Ulin. "Indeed. What do you know of this company?"

"Smugglers," Ulin replied. "They are planning to deliver their shipment to a second contingent arriving from the southwest."

"Impossible." The gray-haired man closed the book and moved out of sight. Kavriel heard what sounded like a drawer opening, and a moment later close. The man must have stashed the book in a desk.

Ulin seemed to be watching this intently, and Kavriel suddenly understood what was going on. Ulin had been using his silver tongue on more than just the locals. Apparently he was regarded as some kind of informant for the Rav'agas. It would only make sense; otherwise how would he have gotten unhindered into the stationhouse? Still, how did he plan to retrieve the book, which must be what Kell and his company considered the important document, surrounded by soldiers? Perhaps this was simply a ruse to find out where the book was, and Ulin would return to Kell's party and tell them where to find it. Yet why had he given away their location, despite lying about the reason they were there? Was Kell planning an ambush?

There were two guards in the room besides the gray-haired man at the desk. Kavriel hadn't seen any other Rav'agas in the village, but that didn't mean they didn't exist. He thought it best to leave before things got complicated, as Ulin had suggested. Yet when he backed away from the railing, he realized the conversation wasn't finished.

"Whatever plans these heathens have, they will be stopped, as you suggest," the gray-haired man stated, moving away from the desk and giving Kavriel a full view of him. He was older than Kavriel had imagined. *A relic of the Ay'vol Force*—Kavriel almost smiled at the thought of him being one of the Patriarch's handpicked. He must have had his reasons. "Round up the men," the man called to one of the soldiers at the door, who snapped to attention. "We will roust out these . . . smugglers . . . ourselves."

"The men are ready, at your command, My Lord," the soldier responded.

"Then I *command* it, soldier," he declared, and he and Ulin both moved toward the front door.

Kavriel knew that this might be the last chance he'd have to escape unnoticed. Yet . . . he knew where the book was hidden, but no one knew he was here. *He* might be able to retrieve the book for Kell while Ulin distracted the soldiers. It was risky, but it might work. Yes; he'd try it. He'd wait in the room behind him until they left, then snatch the book from the drawer and be back on the hillside before anyone realized it. Feeling a heightened sense of importance, Kavriel turned from the rail. And froze.

He stood face to face with a large Rav'agas soldier standing behind him, dressed in full uniform, his short blade in his hand. He swung fast, the blade arcing upward to open up his neck under his chin, but somehow Kavriel sensed it coming and leaned back, avoiding the blade but slamming into the banister.

The Rav'agas soldier, angry at missing his target and seeing Kavriel nearly dangling over the rail, leapt at him, using the full weight of his armor to shoved Kavriel over.

With a loud crack, the wooden railing separated. Astonished at the sudden disappearance of the floor, Kavriel passed gently through a cloud of dust, a bird again, gliding gracefully in the open air in a moment of simple, limitless freedom.

Then he slammed into the desk below, and

paperwork flew into the air as the desk exploded beneath him. Kavriel lay stunned by the force of impact, until he heard surprised shouts and the hiss of drawn steel. He made it halfway to his feet before falling back down again, wiping dust and blood from his eyes as blurred images of men fighting came into view. One of the shapes approached, pulling him upright through a haze of wood chips. His legs struggled with their given purpose as he dumbly watched the face that was shouting at him. The words didn't make sense at first, but as his vision cleared he recognized Ulin.

"Fool!" Ulin was shouting. "What were you thinking?"

A soldier came at them from the bottom of the staircase, the same one that had knocked Kavriel over the railing, swinging his sword above his head. Seeing Kavriel's gaze directed over his shoulder, Ulin dropped him back to the floor and spun to face the attacker.

Kavriel couldn't see exactly what the man did, but one moment the Rav'agas was storming toward them, screaming Rav'agas battle cries, and the next he was gripping two metal hilts that had appeared in his throat. He gurgled something incomprehensible before falling to the floor, and Ulin rushed over to retrieve his throwing knives before coming back to Kavriel.

"Get up, stupid boy!" he shouted, and Kavriel finally did manage to make his limbs work. Ulin reached into the pile of shattered desk remnants and pulled out the dusty, but still intact, book. Slipping it inside his coat, he guided Kavriel out a second door that he had not seen, hidden behind the stairs.

Daylight blinded Kavriel and he tripped, momentarily slowing them down and earning another insult from Ulin, who was dragging him along as if he were a drunk. A horn sounded from somewhere nearby. Hearing the hooves of galloping of horses among the confused cries of locals, Kavriel forced himself to sobriety. Ulin urged him into a run and they left the homes of Gelod's Stream behind, sprinting toward the hills and the hope of escape.

Kavriel slipped as they neared the top of the hill, his knees giving out, and he landed on the grass just as a something whistled past his ear. He stared at the arrow buried in the ground just ahead of him and realized that had passed where his head had been. Several other arrows followed, decorating the green meadow with feathered sticks. He willed his knees to work and regained his feet.

Looking back, he saw four soldiers on horseback, no more than thirty paces away, close enough that he could see triumph in their faces. Like a startled deer staring at the hunter, Kavriel was unable to think and unable to run.

The soldier came in hard, swinging his sword—then suddenly jerked to the side, pulling the reins of his mount with him. Neighing in fear, the horse reared, throwing the rider off. He landed in the grass near to Kavriel, and he saw an arrow lodged deep in his chest.

"Kavriel!" a voice shouted behind him.

Regaining control of his body, Kavriel turned, right into his father's blade. Tossed to him by Ulin, it nearly knocked him down before he grabbed the hilt in midair. He saw the scout desperately trying to nock another arrow on his bow as he shouted something else to Kavriel.

The sounds of the horses, the shouting soldiers, and

the sea wind triggered something in Kavriel's mind. The world seemed to slow, like a faded memory gradually remembered, and a large beast passed by Kavriel's shoulder, a soldier mounted on its back slashing his blade toward Kavriel's head. He crouched instinctively, feeling the cold metal dance through his hair like a lover's touch as he turned, swinging his own blade to hamstring the horse as it moved toward Ulin. The beast screamed and slammed into the hillside, snapping its neck instantly. The soldier flew from the beast onto the hill.

Kavriel thought he saw Ulin drop the bow and stab the arrow into the man, but he couldn't be sure. He was concentrating on the two other horsemen who had been coming up behind the other, with less haste. They were bowmen, and working as one, they lifted their loaded weapons and fired two feathered arrows in his direction. Kavriel couldn't be sure, but he thought the arrows might have been launched prematurely, because they came at him so slowly that he thought they might simply fall into the grass long before they reached him. He was wrong; they flew true, but the air seemed to have become dense as water. Kavriel swung his father's sword when they came close, snapping the two arrows into four as they spun past him, and they dropped to the ground.

The world came back to life again. Holding the blade at his side as if nothing had happened, he saw the startled expressions on the soldiers who had shot at him. One of them suddenly tumbled off his horse, a pair of silver objects buried in his chest with magnificent accuracy.

Ulin brushed up alongside him, reaching into his coat for another pair of throwing knives, but the remaining

Rav'agas kicked his horse, sending it and him back down
to the village before Ulin threw his knives. Turning to him,
Kavriel noticed the strange design of the solid metal
weapons; they looked like flattened stakes. He was more
concerned with what had just happened, though, as he
watched the rider disappear. Ulin cursed loudly.

"What was wrong with their bows?" Kavriel asked
looking at the fallen soldier who had taken the first two
metal stakes full in the chest.

Ulin ignored him as he walked down the hill to
retrieve his knives. Kavriel turned to see the soldier Ulin
had run through with the arrow, and the horse he had killed,
and felt suddenly ill. He dropped his sword and
immediately vomited. He was shaking, as if wrapped in
cold air. It was the same sensation he had felt when he'd
fought and killed the commander of the Rav'agas patrol
ship. Fearing he'd pass out, he breathed deeply and slowly.

He didn't think that they were in any immediate
danger. The rider had not returned yet, and the village
seemed quiet. He heard Ulin approach, and he got up
slowly to face the man, who was regarding him with an
expression that he could not read. They stayed like that for
several seconds, staring at each other, before Ulin began
walking down the hillside. Kavriel sensed that whatever
rage the man had for him for blowing his cover in the
village had changed into something deeper and more
personal. He didn't understand how he knew this, but he
suddenly felt as if he didn't want to be left alone with the
man any longer.

He had made a mistake in the village. He
understood that, and would probably hear about it when

they rejoined the crew. Who knew how much danger he had put them in by flubbing up whatever plans they had made, and more especially, having one of the Rav'agas escape. Kavriel thought he could actually see the rider on the west road, heading away from Gelod's Stream as if death itself pursued him. He wondered what he would say to the others.

Yet what was important was that Ulin had been able to retrieve the book that was their mission. As he watched Ulin walk away toward the crew along the coast, Kavriel called out to him about it. "Did we succeed?"

Ulin turned slowly, giving him a look full of arrogance and irritation. He spat into the grass before continuing on his way, not caring whether Kavriel followed him or not. Kavriel noticed his hand touch a shape in his coat pocket where he had put the book, and it was all the confirmation he had needed. He also saw that Ulin still clutched one of his metal stakes. It didn't look bloodied, so it hadn't been one of those recently used. That could only mean one thing, and Kavriel kept his distance as he followed the man back to Kell's crew, his eyes on the naked blade that he was certain had been meant for him.

CHAPTER 22

"You were asked a question, wench. You will answer any and all questions posed to you!" The soldier spat at the woman, who had fallen back against the table after he'd backhanded her.

She glared defiantly up at him as the young soldier reached down and pulled her back up, drawing back his hand to slap her again. She flinched and closed her eyes, anticipating the sting of his gloved hand, but it never came. Timidly opening her eyes, she saw that his arm was being held in check by one of the others. He was older than the motivated soldier, his goatee dusted white by age and experience. Watching the young soldier back away from her with humble respect, Ella felt more unease about this Ay'vol commander than any other Rav'agas dog that had given her a hard time in the past.

The commander didn't even bother to reprimand the soldier. He didn't need to. Yet he breathed out a strange sigh of contentment, as if things were going in his favor with or without the need for violence. He dressed formally in full captain's regalia, though the soldiers with him looked more road-worn than the typical swarm of southerners that had moved into Dior after the war. She hadn't met Gael Bellon of the Ay'vol Force since his arrival on the island, but she knew his reputation and after recognizing the uniform, knew that this man was him.

Other Rav'agas had stormed into her kitchen from the dining room, complaining about supposed conspiracies or simply that the food that was too "drab" for their tastes; she would simply acknowledge them with smiles and nods, like she cared what they preferred. They were lucky she hadn't fed them poison! Yet with this Ay'vol, she wasn't sure how to react. He had such control over his face! But she saw a shadow of rage in his eyes, like a brewing storm, and she was afraid.

Ella moved back against the wall, looking irritably at the other five Rav'agas crowding her small kitchen with demands to know who she had contacted in the last several days and what connection she had to Mir Town, of all places. She had been overly coarse with them, before the captain arrived; she was accustomed to rowdy individuals in her place, even if they were soldiers. She had her dignity, and she didn't like to be bullied. Yet now she was silent, shaking with fright, and she did not enjoy the feeling at all. Being questioned was not the worst situation she could find herself in, and she crossed her arms tightly across her chest.

Moving slowly, like a man with nothing to do the rest of the afternoon, the captain delicately picked up several of the utensils that had fallen from the table and began wiping them clean with a rag he had pulled from his sleeve, as if this was his kitchen, and he was simply doing mundane chores. Ella watched his movements closely as he placed the items back on the table. When he was done he lifted her eyes to his, as he looked upon her with gaze as cold as a dead coalfish.

"My dear." His voice was like sharp ice, and Ella arched her back, standing up straight despite the terror drifting off of her like a perfume.

Do not cower, she told herself. *Oh please . . . do not cower.*

Captain Bellon looked at her calmly. "Several days

ago, two young men came to your . . . establishment, and left shortly after."

She swallowed. "People come into my establishment all the time, My Lord." Her voice was hard, as she had trained it to be, but maybe she had put a little too much arrogance into her tone. He seemed to find it amusing. *Do not cower!*

"These two men came from the north that morning, and left by ship with your husband to the mainland." The captain held her eyes, not welcoming her wit and not about to let her distract him. She recognized this right away.

"I . . . I don't remember," she replied, twisting a damp towel in her hands as if hoping to squeeze out courage. "My husband takes many to the mainland, dockhands mostly, looking for work. I know he doesn't always follow procedure but I can assure you that he is not doing anything against the chancellor." She swallowed nervously, refusing to wipe the beads of sweat from her forehead.

"Indeed?" The captain nodded, but with a flash of tension in his eyes that suggested to Ella that she had said something he didn't like. He twitched a grin. "The chancellor is not one to concern himself with heathen savages from this island. I can assure you of that." He stiffened, then his cold control returned. Ella wasn't sure if the man was troubled or simply insane. He continued. "These men you would remember, my dear. One of them was your cousin."

Ella blinked and her throat suddenly became dry. This captain knew more than she had thought, much more. She rubbed a damp palm along the side of her skirt as she desperately tried to think of something to say. "My cousin?" she replied, forcing herself to sound innocent. "I'm sorry, but my cousin could not have come here. His village is under retention edict, and it's difficult for Highlanders to receive travel documents."

Ella breathed a bit easier, hoping that her reference to Rav'agas law would deter the captain from further questions. Another thing she had learned was that all Ay'vol officers were a bit pompous about regulations, and felt pride when they heard one of the locals parrot that dribble back at them.

The captain didn't fall for it. "Where did your husband take them, my dear?"

He would not let it go. Ella began to wonder if he was pretending not to know anything to let her fall into his trap. She had to answer very carefully so she wouldn't put her family in any danger.

She sighed, schooling her expression into one of submission. "Yes. Of course he was here, and with a village friend of his. They had not been authorized. I'm sorry to have lied to you; I was just so happy to see him. It has been so long . . . They needed work, and my husband knows a fisherman in Sai who is always looking for young men who aren't afraid of water. My husband will be back in the next few days to answer any questions; that will confirm what I've said."

The words fell out of Ella's mouth like well-rehearsed lines in a play, and once Jassar returned from the channel he would be able to jump into her excuse immediately, as he had so many times before. The deception would work, and there would be nothing this

Ay'vol captain or his men would be able to force upon them besides a fine for abetting illegal travellers. The Rav'agas were a brutish people when it came to discipline, but they were also strict on regulations when they didn't have a Cleansing order issued. Ella didn't fear for her life any longer. Just the paperwork alone that this captain would have to fill out for his chancellor would make him hesitate.

Captain Bellon frowned, his fingers tapping on the flour-dusted tabletop. He seemed to be analyzing everything she had just said. Ella was becoming worried that this man was far more intelligent than the typical Rav'agas. "Tell me more about this *friend* of his," he said smoothly. "What do you remember about him?"

In the back of her mind Ella had actually suspected that was why the captain of the Ay'vol Guard was questioning her himself. Overseer Cyr Soelle's son had looked too nervous in a room with Rav'agas soldiers; he must have had a story to tell. She hadn't asked. There hadn't been time for that. But she knew that something had happened in the Highlands important enough to send the Ay'vol captain and his hounds galloping north. They had only returned this morning, and she was relieved that they had missed her cousin and the Soelle boy by a few days. Yet the attention had come much too quickly for her liking, and the captain must have connected something to have him so interested in a man that no one had actually thought existed.

Vaemalin Soelle was the son that the Rav'agas had on their wanted list, for what he had done to a company of Rav'agas. Kavriel, on the other hand . . . Well, Kavriel was supposed to be dead. How had Captain Bellon found out otherwise? Who had given him away?

He waited patiently for her response. An act quite unusual for a Rav'agas, let alone an Ay'vol captain. Ella wondered if she was being tested again.

"Nothing out of the ordinary, My Lord," she replied, still acting humble so she didn't seem suspicious. "He was just like any other young man that might come have a meal, only he was from the same town as my cousin, is all. I don't know who he was."

Ella could see that she was pushing her luck. The man seemed much too calm as he moved closer to her, nodding. *Do not cower!*

"Did he introduce himself to you, perhaps? His name?" The captain asked, and Ella shook her head quickly. Too quickly, she realized.

"No," she said. "He hardly spoke. He was rather shy, and only wanted more soup." Ella motioned to the cauldron behind her, shifting the focus of the group of Rav'agas. The tension in the room actually seemed to lessen as the soldiers eyed the cauldron hungrily. Bless her grandmother's recipe for shellfish soup; it could woo any man, regardless of uniform. "He was polite." She spoke to the ladle in her hand, stirring the broth. "That's all I remember." She turned back to the captain, knowing that she had taken an extreme risk by turning away from him in the first place, but she needed to ground herself and was unable to do that under his gaze.

"So you were not aware that the man associated with your cousin has a bounty on his head, and that anyone who assists him can be arrested for conspiracy against the

401

Patriarch and Rav'agas?"

The captain's voice was becoming strained, even if his face didn't show it. Her time to get out of this situation was running short, but at least she didn't have to dance around what she had already assumed about the young man who had come with her cousin. Damn these stupid Rav'agas regulations! It was a surprise that there was anyone left in Nostrac who didn't have a bounty on them.

She spoke up quickly, starting to find her confidence. "No, he did not tell me who he was. If he's a criminal then it's his own fault and it does not concern me or establishment. I can only hope that my cousin didn't do something foolish with him."

"My dear." The captain's voice was theatrically affectionate, as if he pitied her, knowing something that she didn't. She wished she had the ability to disappear into the air like the steam coming from the simmering broth behind her. She had neglected her soup for too long, and she would need to start this batch over . . .

The captain was going to tell her something terrible, she could sense it. He smiled, moving close enough that she could smell his breath. "A Guard was killed in the north by your cousin and his friend several nights ago, and I have just found out this morning that a patrol ship was sunk off the mainland." His voice became hard. "Your husband was, unfortunately, unhelpful concerning the attack on Rav'agas men in the north of this savage island, but he was quite helpful when he confessed to his involvement in the patrol massacre. For that, he was hung for treason from the mast of his rig this morning."

The world swung and Ella's eyelids fluttered.

Whatever confidence and self-assurance she had built into herself was now being tested. Tears filled her eyes and she struggled to keep them from streaming down her face. She told herself that the captain was telling her lies to break her. *Damn southern dogs, all were the same, and the Ay'vol worst of all!*

Hatred suddenly surged through her, and she spat in Captain Bellon's face. "Get out of my kitchen, you bastard," she growled, knowing that she was now facing a penalty worse than a fine for her actions. Yet if what this animal had told her was true, then she would fight all of these men in her kitchen with her bare hands. She reached back quickly, grabbing for the steaming cauldron of broth. The metal burned her hands. She didn't care; she would throw the liquid into this man's face for what he had said, and do worse if he had told the truth.

Another pain stopped her before she could lift the pot, and grabbing quickly at her chest, Ella felt something cold and sharp underneath the knot of her apron. Her eyes opened wide in confused wonder, watching the officer casually lift the dish rag that she had been squeezing to wipe her spit from his face. Ella wasn't sure why she couldn't feel anything below her waist.

The captain's other hand pulled back forcefully, making her lurch toward him as something was yanked out of her. Her apron became warm around her trembling hands, and she saw the red stain blossoming over her apron. Weariness overcame her, and her eyes fluttered again as she wished for sleep. Such agonizing pain . . . Why hadn't she dropped to the floor yet? So tired . . .

She looked at Captain Bellon's hand and saw that

he held her boning knife.

Her legs finally gave out. Ella thought of the young man who had come with her cousin. She thought of her husband, the man she wished would soon come back to lift her up, scolding her that she'd get dirty.

Her head dropped forward and her wide brown eyes stared blankly toward the floor.

* * *

Captain Bellon waited until her breathing stopped and her eyes had glazed over in death. He smiled, knowing that it always took several moments of incredible pain from that sort of wound, just inside the waistline, through the stomach. He had applied it numerous times, but he didn't remember enjoying it so much. It was the satisfaction of penetrating such a lovely woman, perhaps. Yet his enjoyment did not last long, and his lips curled in frustration. He turned to his men and nodded.

One of them pulled out a black notebook and began writing down what he had witnessed. It was a report of the interrogation—who the accused was, what information she had given, and why she'd been dispatched—a common detail for any "sacrifices" that had to be made, for future reference. The captain and his men had no fear of scrutiny from higher authorities, as long as the papers were in order.

Finishing his entry, the soldier held out the book for Captain Bellon to sign before he turned to leave the room. Yet another report that he would have to prepare for the chancellor, just as he had done for the man that morning.

The Rav'agas soldiers lifted the dead woman off the floor, careful to avoid the pool of blood that would stain their uniforms. They placed the body in a cloth bag that had been brought in and carried it out through the back door to a wagon driven by a heavily cloaked soldier dressed all in black—the local collector of unfortunate souls. Inside the carriage were several other white cloth bags that held several others. As the carriage slowly rolled away from Ella's tavern, a soldier nailed a sign on the front door, marking the place closed for reasons of security.

The villagers who frequented that tavern watched mournfully, understanding all too well what that sign meant. They quickly lowered their heads and continued on their way, not wanting to be caught watching for too long.

The wagon headed past them toward the harbor, the jarring from the cobblestones jostling the bag carrying the body of Ella. A bump as the wagon hit a pothole, and the body rolled over to rest against another bag, one containing the body of Jassar, as if in death, the couple still strove to be together.

Captain Bellon cursed as he walked to a washstand and rinsed the blood off his gloves. He had been anxious when he had taken his most trusted with him to the north. Too anxious, hoping that he'd have the chance to redeem himself by not just eradicating a Quetalian menace who had murdered the Mir Guard, but also the man who had shamed him all those years ago. It had been a mistake, he realized, and a foolish one at that, to think that the man who had committed the crime would be stupid enough to wait for him. He had acted unprofessionally, creating a window for the murderer to disappear to the mainland and destroy a Rav'agas patrol ship in the process, instead of securing the harbor. He cursed again, shaking his gloves dry in the cool afternoon air.

He had been set up from the beginning by the damn chancellor and his message. How the man might have come across such valuable information from the mainland when even he himself had not heard a breath about it until too late was unforgivable. The Highlands might not be under his direct authority, but he was still the ruling magistrate over the island. Everything that occurred *had* to pass through him. Otherwise, why would he need to do all of those needless reports, if the chancellor and his minions were running the system behind him? The bastard.

Fuming, Captain Bellon wondered what else the chancellor was scheming. It was no secret that Chancellor Zoren did not trust him, but there was still the matter of respect. Bellon pondered how and if he should try to contact the Patriarch about this affair. Surely he would be understanding, maybe not enough to throw that overzealous second of his from the Teltraum throne, but enough to offer compensation.

He massaged his arm under his shirt, as was his habit whenever something bothered him. It was a pitiful reminder of what the cost of failure felt like.

Looking up at the flags of Ay'vol waving on the masts of the half-dozen patrol ships that he had ordered back to the harbor, Captain Bellon thought again about the symbol to which he had dedicated his life. The Patriarch was his life, and he trusted and believed in the Divine Son of Creation. The chancellor was nothing but a bureaucratic deacon who had charmed his way into the Patriarch's favor; by the grace of God, he would receive his just punishment for toying with the Creator's most dedicated—those like Bellon.

Bellon was not alone in thinking this. Many other Rav'agas would agree, and not just the hounds of war that had been united under the Patriarch's will, but also commanders of the Ay'vol Force; older and more experienced men like him, who understood corruptibility. The chancellor had buried himself too deep in the past ideals of this savage nation and their former Council of Nine, who had been innately corruptible in themselves, and spread their leadership capabilities too thin. It had been their downfall, this party organized to decide the well-being of the people—an *elected* party, for that matter! Of course their leaders brought division into the Council, being chosen by all of the classes together. It was asinine, the confusion chosen by the confused. No wonder that foolish country fell so easily to the Patriarch, who proved that the children of God must be guided by God himself—*one* leader, *one* voice—with no disputes, no arguments.

The Quetalians mocked every belief, and look where their system of democracy had led them. Captain Bellon smiled smugly. The chancellor had been too easily manipulated by those beliefs, keeping the Council Nine alive and allowing for a chairman simply to appease the occupied nation and prevent disruptions. Yes. See how well that turned out, Bellon thought, shaking his head, thinking of the bodies of his former colleagues, ripped apart. He wished he could have taken the heads of those men that had been killed, so he could toss them at Chancellor Zoren's feet as a display of his failed system, but the wolves, or feral dogs, had gotten to them first. Who knew what kind of savage beasts hid in those blasted lands?

"Captain!" a man shouted from the deck of a ship

being secured to the pier, distracting him. He waited as the soldier jumped over the side of the ship to land with a thud on the dock, then ran over to him, bypassing the others waiting to descend the gangway.

"What is it, Ensign?" Bellon asked nonchalantly, eyes surveying the men tramping down the gangway.

"Activity has been reported from the mainland, Captain." The sunburned young ensign swayed slightly on sea legs not yet reaccustomed to dry land. Bellon looked at him and lifted a questioning brow. "A regional officer was killed, Captain, along with several Guardsmen. In the northeast region. Again."

Bellon tightened his jaw. The young ensign waited in silence, still catching his breath. Bellon didn't know who he was personally, but his insignia said he was one of Bellon's own, so whatever news he provided would have merit. He still felt like strangling him, however, and any other man unfortunate enough to be in front of him this moment. He kept his anger in check. This wasn't the time for needless violence against his own, but he needed to release his anger, and soon.

This wasn't the first time a report like this had come to Dior from his watchmen. The surge of recent rebellious attacks in northeastern Quetal, more violent each time, confirmed Bellon's belief that the area was undermanned and unmonitored, complications solely due to the chancellor. The man should be hanged. "What else?" he growled.

The ensign nodded and continued hesitantly. "The port authorities in both Sai and Misam have been assigned to the coastline, and since you are the official in Dior, you are required to follow the same order."

"Assigned by whom?" Bellon scowled, already knowing exactly who had given those orders. The ensign shifted nervously and proffered a letter bearing Chancellor Zoren's seal. Captain Bellon did not take it. He was not about to place his neck in the chancellor's noose again. Instead he looked steadily at the ensign, who immediately returned the letter to his pocket in silent understanding. "Tell me what *you* know," Bellon said.

The ensign nodded. "Yes, my captain," he replied formally, before moving surreptitiously closer to his captain.

Bellon hid a smile at the young man's spirit. He recognized himself in the ensign, another young Rav'agas hardened by the monotony of security life, when he'd rather be out in the field, spreading the Patriarch's justice his own way. The young man would be grateful when he was told the plans that Bellon was formulating in the back if his mind.

"The Sai Guard has reason to believe that this group is the same rebels who destroyed the Fourth Division's patrol, and the chancellor . . ." The young man paused and glanced carefully at Bellon. Bellon didn't respond. He recognized that this young ensign felt the same way about their leader as he did, just from that pause. Seeing that he was not to be reprimanded for his assumptions, the ensign continued. "The chancellor thinks they might return to Nostrac, from what I have heard, sir."

If Captain Bellon hadn't been insulted by the chancellor's doubts about him before, then he certainly was now. Such blatant deception! "So he believes that patrolling the channel with the other commanders would be the best place to keep us, is that it?" Bellon mused aloud, knowing that the ensign wouldn't answer him, even if he knew. There was still protocol, despite their mutual feelings about Chancellor Zoren.

Bellon was beginning to understand the game being played in Teltraum. The man who had slaughtered the company in the north four years ago had returned. The chancellor, knowing Bellon's involvement in that event, understood all too well what his reaction would be. Chancellor Zoren had informants in the north, keeping an eye on the new community established by the Rav'agas who had migrated there for work. He knew that Bellon was volatile, and sensed his hunger for revenge, but he also assumed that he would not be as useful anywhere else in Quetal. The Patriarch had assigned Bellon to the chancellor, and the chancellor had decided to find a place to keep him. Dior seemed to be the most reasonable location, just out of reach of whatever had wronged him and far enough away from Teltraum not to be a nuisance.

Yet he knew that Bellon was still a commander handpicked by the Patriarch, even if that was a long time ago, and couldn't simply brush him under the carpet when Quetalian uprisings flared up. So he had sent the message about the attack . . . only a few days too late. It had given the murderer, the *Ph'oe-an'tam* as the Rav'agas had named him, a chance to escape to the mainland where, in all perfect reasoning, the chancellor had set some kind of trap to catch him. The Ghost had been at large for four years, and if Chancellor Zoren could capture the legend that inspired the Quetalian rebels, his station would be secure, despite all ill feeling toward him.

Captain Bellon breathed out his anger in a low hum as he began putting the pieces together. He had gone to the mining town and the adjacent towns, hoping to gather information about the murders. He'd listened to the frightened gibbering of the stupid locals, who only wished to go back to their hills and crops. He had even spoken to the man that had once been considered the overseer, some old and decrepit fool too ruined by sickness to say anything rational. He had met the overseer before, when he had first come to the town where his soldiers had been killed, and he knew this was not the same man. Apparently he had died of fever shortly after Bellon and his second company had burned that cursed village to the ground. He didn't believe it, and he didn't care either who was in charge of the place now, but whether anyone had heard more about the murders.

Not surprisingly, the locals had suggested that wolves had attacked and killed the men. Bellon was from Ay'vol City, and despite never having seen or dealt with wolves himself, he knew that wolves hunting in packs never attacked groups of men, let alone armed men. No, there'd been a conspiracy there, but he had realized that too late, and missed his target. He should have hung the inbred hill folk as an example to the rest Quetal, rather than leading his men back to Dior . . . and the news about the patrol ship and now an attack on the mainland.

His reputation would suffer for this, and all because the chancellor had conspired to lead the Ghost to Teltraum and into his arms. Now the chancellor was keeping Bellon occupied with some menial task, thinking that he was too stupid to understand what was truly happening. Bellon had to admit that so far the chancellor's plan had worked.

Then there was that second message from Saire. Had the general been working as a double agent for the Patriarch the entire time he had been in the Quetalian army? It was possible, Bellon thought, remembering the message warning him to *watch every direction.* He had promptly ignored it by rushing into the Highlands.

Saire had also given him something that he hadn't had before: the name of the Ghost. He had his suspicions before, of course, from eavesdropping on local gossip about the outlaw. But why had Saire sent him such a message . . . unless the message had hidden meaning? Bellon had memorized the short phrase that the general had written, even though he trusted the man less than he trusted the chancellor. Seccacian Desert tribes were nothing but thieves and tricksters by nature, even if Saire had been raised by Rav'agas.

The Patriarch held him in high regard, though Bellon smiled, knowing that the only reason for that was the man's unusual fair hair and features, common only in those with Cielean bloodlines. The same place where the Patriarch had announced his receiving the gift from the Creator. Oh yes . . . the general might have deceived every other fool in Quetal, but the Ay'vol knew where that man had been born, despite his claims to the desert folk. Bellon knew as well. It didn't matter how the Patriarch felt about Saire; if anything, he had used him to gain entrance into Ciele, behind those damned Quetalian lines.

Besides his knowledge of the world (which Bellon found impressive), there was nothing particularly special about General Saire except his association to the Patriarch. Yes, he was a formidable tactician and an exceptional fighter, not to mention his ability to convince an entire nation to believe in his cause—though there were those who suggested that in that he was only doing the same as the Patriarch. The chancellor was one of those, and had been quite outspoken in his feelings about Saire, which the Patriarch had ignored.

It made Bellon wonder if perhaps the message sent to him by Saire had been communication from the Patriarch, warning him to be wary and confirming what he'd always suspected. Strangely, the thought filled him with hope, knowing that through all his issues with the chancellor, he wasn't alone in fighting this political war.

Inspired by this idea, Bellon turned to the young ensign who had been waiting patiently the entire time Bellon had been lost in his thoughts. He was a good soldier. "Commanders Failon and Janick," he said, mentioning the two men who, like him, were experienced Ay'vol commanders who had been assigned port jobs in Sai by the chancellor. He knew it would be them the chancellor would give the same orders to, orders that he hoped they'd ignore, as he would. The Misam commander, Bellon had never met. "How many ships are at their command?" he asked.

Straightening his shoulders, the ensign replied quickly, as if he'd expected the question. "Four armed galleys with seventy-five men apiece. All equipped with forty arbalests mounted on the bulwarks and six fire bolts, and one thousand missiles."

Captain Bellon smiled, thinking of the nearly four hundred Rav'agas soldiers included on his own four warships, docked and ready to set sail at the pier. "Where are they now?" he asked.

The Ensign turned and pointed to the horizon. "There," he said, and Bellon indeed saw the shadows of ships on the horizon. The ensign turned back to him. "Ready and at your command, Captain Bellon." He smiled, and Bellon could not help but do the same as he scratched his goatee.

He looked curiously at the young man. "You are one of mine, are you not?" He already knew that was the case, but he didn't know the man's name.

The ensign came to attention. "Pa'ul Janick, sir," he said proudly.

Immediately, Bellon understood everything. Ensign Janick was indeed under his command in the Rav'agas Dior Company, but his kin was Commander Janick of Sai. He must have been sent by him. That could only mean that they were all trying to keep this arrangement to themselves. None of them trusted the chancellor. Bellon wondered if his two colleagues had received similar messages from Saire, and they were simply waiting for him to decide what to do, since he was the senior officer in the region.

There was still information that he was missing. He looked solemnly at the young ensign. "There was a regional officer killed." Ensign Janick nodded. "Who was he?" Bellon asked.

The young man replied immediately. "Captain Relt."

"Gelod's Stream, then?" he asked, knowing the region where Captain Relt had been assigned. He cursed under his breath as the ensign nodded.

"Very good, Ensign," Bellon said after several moments of thought. "Go to your ship and await my orders."

With a quick nod of acknowledgement, the junior Janek strode briskly back to the ship he'd come from.

Bellon suddenly felt as if he had swallowed a rock. *Relt,* he repeated, *the old recorder.*

He suddenly understood why, of all the garrisons in the northeast, Commander Relt's unit had been targeted by the Ghost and whoever he had allied himself with. Though a most vigilant officer, skilled on the battlefield and in his command over his soldiers, Relt's greatest strength had lain in his incredible reports. His eye for detail, from battles, company divisions, and regional populations down to the number of cows in each Quetalian village, had made Relt a valued commander despite his age. *He should have retired by now,* Bellon thought. Instead, like so many others, the fine officer had been humbled by the chancellor, assigned to a backwater, out of the way. His death was a loss to Ay'vol, and while Bellon would give his respects when time allowed, now he understood what the chancellor planned.

They intended to ambush the Ghost, and his allies. It only made sense. Relt would have had detailed information about the command posts that the Ghost would probably target, those most important to the chancellor, such as Misam, or even the mountain prison the locals had named the Crypt; intel valuable when planning an attack. The chancellor had made sure that the Ghost had obtained this information, sacrificing his own men so that he might have the chance to capture the outlaw himself.

Bellon felt sick, thinking how low the chancellor would stoop to boost his own reputation. Failon and Janick must have been thinking the same thing, and were now wondering what they should do—follow the chancellor's indirect orders to stay out of the way, or do something more worthy in the Patriarch's eyes, what Saire might have been suggesting in his strange note.

Stroking his chin in satisfaction, Captain Bellon walked briskly to the office building that he had been chained to these last few years by the chancellor, knowing that he had only one more message to write—not to the chancellor, but to his colleagues waiting outside the harbor. Enough of the chancellor's deception of both him and the Patriarch! There was a man on the run in northeastern Quetal who had taken both his men and his pride, and now he was targeted to be taken by the chancellor and his priests. Bellon could not let that happen. He would get the Ghost first, and if he needed to burn his way along the coast to do it, just like in the old days, then so be it. If he could not answer to the Patriarch any longer, then he damn-sure was not going to answer to the chancellor. Maybe that was what Saire had meant when speaking for the Patriarch.

Captain Bellon had been granted his revenge.

CHAPTER 23

It has been almost five hundred years that the children have lived without their true father, and nothing has changed in their faith. Not truly, anyway. The belief has fragmented into dozens of meanings with hundreds of perspectives, but that was bound to happen with or without Father . . . or us, for that matter. It is what their scholars call "evolution." I actually like that word. It sounds circular, a word that is only proof that the mortals have come one step closer to understanding how close they truly were to their creator, despite never being given proof of his existence. He was the spark that lit the tinder, but he did not try to control the flames. He was more interested in seeing if the forest would burn . . . and burn it did. Now he is gone, and I wonder why we continue to think our involvement will have any significance.

We were the whispers in the mortals' dreams, the visions in their creativity, and the inspirations for their beliefs. We were The Watch. Yet what can we possibly do any longer that they cannot figure out for themselves? They have grown beyond our influence and it is by chance alone that their lives have stricter limitations than ours, otherwise who knows what might become of them.

Was this what Father was trying to show us? Was he flaunting his mistake or his brilliance? He must have wished us to remain for some reason I do not know, otherwise he could have easily destroyed us. Still, maybe Sa'rire and Tondal were right . . . maybe Father wasn't as strong as I feared. We certainly are not as strong as I believed.

I haven't communicated with Dar or Kai'sa in many years now. Faythe has become distant. She cannot see the good in people anymore, and sees only the desperation and the suffering. She has been listening to Sa'rire. They are like the light and the darkness, those two. Like our Creators. But ever since we killed our father she has become more . . . clouded. They have all but forgotten about me already. I am grateful that at least Tondal still speaks with me when he is not so preoccupied with Father's remains.

I still don't understand why they have been kept— what remained of them. Time has turned the bones and tissue into nothing, but for some reason the blood remains, like the water of the ocean long after it has reduced mountains into islands. It is strange, yet how are we to know anything about what should or should not happen to a god once you have killed one?

Maybe it is simply the fact that we have kept his blood that unnerves me the most. Why did we do it? To understand him? To understand us? Where we came from? I am not certain, but Tondal believes that there is s significant connection. When Father was destroyed and he . . . split the body that had summoned him into six sections . . . was that why he created only six of us after he had killed his own brother? Were we created from his remains? Are we a more direct connection between the mortals and the Creator, as Sa'rire's southern kingdom constantly preaches about with their Patriarchs?

It is possible, but all of this is well beyond me. I am not as clever as Tondal or Sa'rire. They must know something more about the blood than the rest of us, and

418

why they have kept it in six separate containers. We are too afraid to pour them into one for fear of his possible return, even though Sa'rire has assured us, based on his studies, that it is not possible to resurrect a god in that fashion. I don't know. I just try to stay away from the room where Tondal is keeping them.

Sa'rire has come up with a suggestion, but I do not believe it's a good one. I am not ready to drink anybody's blood, regardless of the possibility that it will make me stronger than I am. I have no need for such nonsense. If Sa'rire wants to test his theory so badly, then let him have all the containers, if he wishes . . . But maybe that too isn't necessarily a good idea. He is much too ambitious. Father told us all many times how Sa'rire reminded him of his own brother. Maybe that was why Sa'rire hated him so, why it was his blow that destroyed Father. Simple vengeance?

Anyway, I am not worried so much since Sa'rire is convinced that he cannot simply take the power of Creation so . . : deliberately. Or maybe he is simply afraid. He suggested yet another possibility but he hasn't come out and discussed it fully yet. He said that he wants to speak to us in private first. I think that is very strange, but seeing how Faythe and Kai'sa have become like ghosts already, and Tondal has been too obsessed with his writings, then perhaps I will go and see him. Still, I have a bad feeling about all of this, that our island sanctuary will not be safe for much longer.

Kavriel closed the book as Kell called, "Load up," as he had said at least a dozen times now, since they had left Gelod's Stream. They were now into the fourth day of rugged travel since, and Kell had allowed them only a few moments of rest at a time, hurrying them along with determination, unwilling to risk staying in one place for very long. Kavriel knew that his lack of judgement in the village was most likely the reason for that. He had tried to speak to Kell many times since he and Ulin had returned, but the man seemed to be more concerned with the book they had taken, which Kavriel found out later was a very detailed Ay'vol command log similar to a captain's log on a ship. There was very specific information about Rav'agas command posts and garrisons that would be especially important to have, if one were thinking of going against the Rav'agas directly.

Seth, clearly excited about the news, had been pestering the crew about where they thought they might strike. He still discouraged Kavriel's suggestions, but he could only support his friend's thirst for battle—his heart was in the right place, at least.

He wasn't sure why he thought Kell would tell him anything. The man had been quite secretive about his motives since they met, and it was rare that he spoke to them seriously. He reminded Kavriel of a politician from the Pasav Lake District that he had once read about, whose easygoing and open personality had succeeded in winning the love and support of his constituents, but hid his true agenda of lowering trade taxes on products that he had interests in. He was crooked and even looked the part, dressing much too richly with too many accessories, but he was still loved by the people of his district. If his actions didn't necessarily aide the community directly they certainly didn't harm them, so it was accepted the way it was, and the overseer was only another man looking out for his own skin.

Kavriel wondered if Kell was just like that. It was possible, but maybe he was being biased in his opinions. Being the son of an overseer did tend to generate certain opinions about the citizens who led questionable lifestyles, such as smuggling.

At least Kell hadn't reprimanded him for his stupidity, as Kavriel thought he would. He still looked at Kavriel as if assessing him, something that had become more frequent since they'd returned. It was obvious that Ulin had told the man everything, even if he didn't seem to care, but he still hadn't tried to hear Kavriel's explanation yet. He kept his distance.

Ulin, on the other hand, was clearly still angry. He hadn't approached him since they'd left Gelod's Stream, and not surprisingly, Kavriel was no longer needed to scout with the man. Kavriel wasn't quite sure how he should react to that. He was being guarded more carefully now. He had killed those Rav'agas . . . he had killed more men. Any other man might consider it fateful luck, but Kavriel didn't like to believe in luck, fate, or even coincidences. He had become something else in the last five years that he could not remember, and unless he would remember, he feared for his future. That was why Kell avoided him and it was probably why Ulin was ready to kill him.

At least Seth had remained faithful, Kavriel thought as he moved quickly to follow his friend, who had already started walking into the wet forest. Seth saw him coming and waited, grinning.

The change in landscape had come like a quick

thunderstorm over the ocean—one day they travelled through orchards of apple trees scattered across the rolling hills of the north coast, and the next day they had entered the greenest and dampest forest Kavriel had ever imagined. The trees were thirty to forty paces high, covering them with a canopy of thick leaves the size of a man's head. The ground below was a green carpet, a mirror of what was above. Kavriel couldn't be certain which direction they were headed. He kept close to the others, who seemed to know where they were going, even though there was no indication that anybody had ever come through these woods.

There was plenty to eat. Deer, rabbits, and squirrels were everywhere, and the streams hid fish of all colors and sizes. Their pace slowed, and during the next week they were given more time to relax while the scouts set out ahead of them and returned with nothing interesting to report. Kavriel didn't think they were being tracked by the Rav'agas, and he wondered how far they actually were from their destination.

On the fourth afternoon since entering the forest the ground suddenly rose to a ridge overlooking a large bay with the buildings of a community clustered on its eastern shore, and his question was answered. They had made it to Misam. Kavriel knew very little about the place besides the fact that the town was the youngest settlement in mainland Quetal, whose history only went back a couple hundred years. Their story was still being written.

It was a renowned sanctuary for people in Kell's line of work—illegal traders, smugglers, and fugitives from the regulations of the Council. Out of politeness or simple nostalgia, Kell became more talkative once they came in sight of Misam, even giving them a brief explanation of the town's origins and the land around it, as if he had a personal connection to it.

During that first afternoon, Kavriel and Seth listened intently to the man finally speaking about something that didn't seem duplicitous, and Kavriel was more than grateful to learn about Misam, about how the economy was primarily wood-based thanks to the tall and plentiful redwood trees surrounding the bay. Apparently Misam red-bark was extremely workable, more so than any other kind of wood. It was pulped and formed into parchment, fashioned into stylish furniture for the wealthy, and provided rich tone when used to make musical instruments. Kavriel was especially impressed when Kell mentioned that the Misam wood was used to construct the ten thousand shelves of the Great Library in Teltraum, and after hundreds of years had never lost its luster. He wondered how a smuggler might know something about the library in Teltraum.

As in the other towns and villages of Quetal, the residents of Misam had been quickly suppressed and put under the control of an Ay'vol overseer. Its shady history was known to Ay'vol, and instead of trying to assimilate the community as the chancellor had done with the others on the mainland, he simply cleaned Misam out. The Rav'agas had no interest in establishing territory here. The climate was too damp and they saw little potential in this fishing hamlet far away in a remote corner of the world for any really ambitious plans. The first Cleansing had effectively reduced the population by over half, leaving no reason to keep an Ay'vol overseer or a detachment of the Guard in the town.

Kavriel had finally learned what a "cleansing" involved, and he still had a difficult time believing that trained soldiers, when given an open order to deal with the northerners any way they felt necessary, seemed the most barbaric. It was like releasing your guard dogs on the neighborhood children . . . for just a little bit. Kavriel was glad he didn't remember that terrible ordeal that had lasted, according to Seth, over a month. The Rav'agas had effectively tamed the Quetalian populace through terror. It was disgusting just to think about and terrifying to believe that a man could allow such a thing, let alone issue an order for it.

Whatever had happened during those black days, Misam had become what the chancellor wished it to become, a wasteland. The Rav'agas had withdrawn afterward, and the townsfolk left to fend for themselves. In a way Misam became the only true "free" district under Rav'agas control, but what was this freedom? To the north was the sea, which Rav'agas patrolled; lands to the west and south were garrisoned; and the east was nothing but the Oenes Mountains. Why station a man to watch the closet when you had the rest of the house surrounded? Either way, the town hadn't become much after the war but it was still a relatively safe haven for the smugglers and now, factions rebelling against the Rav'agas occupation when they could.

Kavriel didn't think he could imagine a smile so large that it completely overran a man's face, but he saw it on Seth once he had learned of all of this. In a way it made Kavriel feel good too, knowing that he had somehow become part of a greater cause when he still couldn't remember how it all had happened. Misam was probably the safest place that he could be right now, and Kavriel wondered if it might be a lead to finding Vaemalin. He wanted to believe it, but something inside him told him the opposite, as it he had some kind of internal sense that flared if he was getting close to his brother.

Seth had become part of a new order now, and a full-fledged member of Kell's crew. Kavriel watched him from the hillside where he sat, watching evening settle over the bay town in the distance. He was alone, but once his fellow Rhyolian neighbor noticed him he ran up the hillside to join him. He looked down at Kavriel's hand, and saw the sun and stars icon on the cover of the book. "Still reading that?" he asked with a smile.

Kavriel nodded, suddenly remembering that he was holding the book. He had been reading it so much lately, whenever he had a moment's break, that he was beginning to fear that he was becoming obsessed. He had already read through it once and was going through the sections that seemed to be more relevant to his situation. He wasn't sure how any of it could be possible, but the passages were written so intimately that they seemed to be speaking to him directly.

"Yes," he replied when Seth continued to watch him with an uncertain expression. Kavriel let it go for now, still partly involved in the pages that he had just finished. "I'm not sure, but I think whoever wrote this might be more of a historian than just somebody with a wild imagination."

Seth shrugged, sitting down next to Kavriel and looking down at the lights starting to illuminate the town.

"What do you mean?" he asked, more out of politeness than interest.

Kavriel didn't care. He was too stuck in his own thoughts. "I'm not sure. Have you heard of a group called The Watch?"

Seth shook his head. "No. Who are they?" He nodded to the book, assuming that the question stemmed from something Kavriel read.

Kavriel frowned. "I'm not sure, but I think they might have something to do with The Way. There seems to be a lot of correlation with Rav'agas scripture, The Fall and so on."

"You mean when the God of Light destroyed the God of Darkness?" Seth asked, obviously having been schooled in at least the basic fundamentals of The Way.

Kavriel nodded, recalling what he knew, as well. "Yes. I think this is some kind of journal kept by a group of serious believers who called themselves The Watch. Apparently they lived outside of mortal society but only did as they said they did: they kept watch. I just finished with a chapter, or a timeline, that suggests that they were created out of the remains of The Fallen."

"Mortals?" Seth repeated, catching that reference. He looked skeptical. "Sounds like a book for the Patriarch, if you ask me. Isn't he also supposed to be created from the remains of The Fallen?"

Kavriel shook his head. "Descendant, actually. The Patriarch is a descendent of the God of Light and The Fallen was *his* brother, or his father or his son . . . I think it depends which book you read. The end is the same. The God of Darkness was destroyed for the betterment of mankind, and the God of Light gave the blood of his only son to the mortals so that he might lead them, etcetera, etcetera." Kavriel mentally flipped through his studies of Rav'agas doctrine, learned as a child years ago. The sun-icon book seemed to have triggered those memories, which he thought he'd forgotten, thinking that they were irrelevant.

Seth was right, the book seemed more appropriate for a believer in the divine rebirth than a typical Quetalian philosopher. Still, there had been things that seemed to be too closely related to what he had experienced. He remembered the mines, the urns, and the strange liquid that had dissipated in the air after striking Vaemalin and Tess. He remembered the strange, unnatural battle between Xavr and Saire, and even Xavr and the Wylyn. This book seemed to be talking about these things . . . but from the perspective of someone who had been witness to all of it. How could that be possible?

He pulled out some of the names he had read, asking Seth if he had heard of any of them. He hadn't, except for the name Dar, which also had been the name of the first Chairman of the Council Nine when it was established about two thousand years ago.

"Who wrote it?" Seth asked, nodding at the book again.

Kavriel shook his head, having wondered the same thing since first opening the book. "I have no idea," he admitted with a shrug. "He or she was a follower of The Way, but also someone with more practical reasoning, maybe one of these Watch-people. I don't know."

Kavriel was beginning to feel uncomfortable

speaking about the book, and he couldn't understand why. He wondered if it had something to do with his missing memory. Maybe there was more to these "memoirs" than he could know. He set the book aside, and Seth, noticing his change in mood, looked back over to the group of Kell's men at the bottom of the hill.

"Have you spoken to Ulin yet?" he asked, effectively changing the subject.

Kavriel shook his head, his eyes finding the fair-haired scout in the group. He was currently shaving the stubble from his face with one of his flat-bladed throwing knives, his movements quick and certain, almost fluid.

"What do you think?" Seth asked.

He didn't have to elaborate. Kavriel had told him all about his interactions with the man. "I have no idea. Maybe he knows me somehow . . . or maybe my brother."

Seth frowned. "I don't see how. They don't know you're a Soelle, and not a lot of people outside of Nostrac know who your brother was, either." Kavriel must have looked surprised, because Seth chuckled. "It's true!" he said quickly, as if he needed to defend his point. "Only we Rhyolian know who he is, and what really happened. Everyone else think he is a *Ph'oe-an'tam*." Seth looked at Kavriel uncertainly, as if for confirmation of the word.

Kavriel nodded, knowing at least that much Rav'agas. *Ph'oe-an'tam* meant 'wandering spirit'. A Ghost.

"So they don't even know his name?" he wasn't convinced, and Seth looked troubled, reassessing his thoughts.

"I am sure there are some, the Ministry maybe, the

chancellor or obviously that Ay'vol officer you said you met in Mir Town. Still, most of these mainlanders have invented their own things to call him. Vaemalin isn't a common Quetalian name to remember and it is easy to mix up. Anyway, I've heard the Rav'agas in Rhyol talk about capturing all sorts of names."

Kavriel resolved to keep what Seth told him in mind, wondering if it was really true. He certainly hoped so.

"What kind of name is Vaemalin, anyway?" Seth asked, back to the subject.

Kavriel couldn't help but smile. "It's a Cielean word. My mother's family was from the southeast, Plains People. She studied a lot about the ancient cultures of the area. Ciele was part of those studies, being so near the border, and she came across it, so that could have explained it. My father said that she thought it was pretty, and so she gave it to her firstborn son." Kavriel paused while a sudden urge to laugh overtook him.

Seth noticed and started to smile. "Why is that so funny?" he asked.

Kavriel chuckled aloud. "It's not a name." he replied. "Vae-malin in Cielean means *absent of light*, or *without light*. Simply put, Darkness. I don't think my mother ever knew that."

Seth looked confused. "And how do you know that?"

The moment of amusement suddenly fled Kavriel's mood, quickly replaced by unease and a near sense of shock. shook his head. He had no idea, but he must have come across it somewhere, maybe in the book, or from someplace in his missing memories.

Seth shrugged, but Kavriel still felt uneasy. He realized that he had been staring at Kell's party gathered around the small fire as he spoke. He sensed Seth was doing the same.

"Well, Ulin isn't a local name either," He said with a smirk. "It's Loellen."

Kavriel perked up. "How can you be sure?"

Seth nodded to the group in general. "The others told me. They said he was from one of the Houses, one of the rich ones with lots of vineyards or holdings or whatever." He scratched his chin in thought. "His family lost their lands and titles after the chancellor came. I'm not exactly sure about the details. Only Kell knows the truth, maybe, besides Ulin. I don't think he would tell us anything we didn't need to know."

Kavriel nodded, watching the yellow-haired man down in the camp below and suddenly understanding him. It made sense, what Seth said. He had already suspected that Ulin was a nobleman, or had been. He was much too fastidious and arrogant to be anything else—coin tended to create well-bred asses. Still, he had never met a Loellen high-blood before, and he didn't want to become too biased based on what others had said. His father didn't seem to mind them, although he did say that they were a special breed that needed to be dealt with more delicately than your normal elite. His friend Richart, now the new chairman, held Loellen titles, as had his predecessor, Olenson Tavrick . . . the one who had been killed. Kavriel wondered about Ulin's connection.

They fell quiet for a while as both Kavriel and Seth

looked back over the bay, watching the sunlight dancing over the water. The repetition of the patterns soothed, lessening Kavriel's worry about the world, and as he listened to the susurration of the waves and the whisper of the wind he tried to picture himself the year before, and the year before that, hoping for something that might seem familiar. There was nothing, and Kavriel sighed in frustration, wondering if he had even lived those years, or if he had simply been removed from existence.

CHAPTER 24

"Who are they, the men Kell is with?" Kavriel asked.

Ulin raised his head and spoke without actually addressing him directly, his tone flat and the end of one of his blades his pointer. "That one is Dillon Tyne from Sai. He keeps watch over the Rav'agas that travel westbound. The ugly one next to him is Fras Beallor, who is an inlander who watches the south garrisons, and that distinguished-looking gentleman over there is Robart Stoal, who was once the Overseer."

Kavriel nodded silently and leaned back on his bench seat, trying not to be bothered by Ulin. The man was sitting in front of him with his boots hanging over the next row of pews in the Misam town hall, a bored expression on his face while he danced a knife over his knuckles. Seth was leaning against the wall nearby, while the rest of the crew seemed to have disappeared into the town as soon as they entered. He wasn't sure what he was doing there, but Kell had made himself quite clear when he told Kavriel that morning that they were to go into town. Kell still wanted to keep an eye on him, he supposed, because Kavriel had no idea what this meeting was about; he would be told, he imagined. His focus wandered, eyes touching on his surroundings.

The hall, centrally located in the bayside town like most town halls, was similar in structure and design to Port Dior's, if emptier. He hadn't seen many of the locals, and those that he had seen kept out of the way of Kell's men as they walked briskly through the town to this triangular

wood building that had obviously been a temple at one
time, like Rhyol's town hall, only without any renovations.
The altar remained, as did the rows of pews and even the
Rav'agas religious icons on the walls and windows; Kavriel
felt as if they were in the southern kingdom itself and not
some forgotten community hidden away in the corner of
Quetal.

The men that Kell was arguing with were
apparently the reason for this visit, and by their whispered,
but heated discussion, Kavriel assumed it was a meeting of
great importance. "They seem uneasy," Kavriel said to
Ulin.

The man only chuckled. "You could say that." He
turned to face Kavriel with a coy look in his eyes. "You
should feel at home, villager. This is a momentous
argument that you have been invited to witness. It doesn't
get much more political than this."

"Why have I been invited, if I'm only to be put in
the back?" he asked, not hiding his irritation. The man
obviously knew more about Kavriel than he'd let on, and
keeping that from him only quickened Kavriel's temper.

Ulin didn't reply, only chuckled again as he looked
around as if interested in the others wandering around the
hall, all of local stock and of all ages and sorts, from well
dressed to ragged. They nodded at Ulin as they passed.
Kavriel was surprised when several of them actually shook
his hand before leaving the building, seeming to be happier,
now that he was there.

Hoping to pull something out of Ulin, Kavriel
observed quietly, "You seem to have friends here."

Ulin nodded without looking at him. "It is good to

have friends."

Before Kavriel could ask anything more, Kell walked over to them, quietly fuming as he sat heavily down next to him. Ulin turned as Seth pushed off the wall to join the party.

The smuggler looked as if he had been reprimanded. "Fools," he spat, not specifically addressing anyone but making sure he was loud enough to be heard by all. "Overzealous fools."

"What is it?" Ulin asked as Kell clenched and unclenched his meaty fists.

"The committee has sent two hundred to the gate. They didn't even need to wait for me, it seems."

Kavriel wasn't sure what he was talking about, but that didn't stop him from listening.

"Two hundred is not a bad number," Ulin remarked, defending the decision by the committee that Kavriel understood had been the three men still standing around the altar, deep in discussion.

Kell cursed, his face red with barely suppressed anger. "It's not enough and you know it! They knew we were held up in the forest until the patrols had changed shifts. They could at least have waited for me."

Without thinking of the consequences, Kavriel spoke up. "Where is it that they sent these men?"

Ulin glowered at him, but Kell was too distracted to show offense, if indeed Kavriel had said something that he shouldn't have. He still didn't know what was going on.

Kell sighed and answered reluctantly, "They took them to the Crypt."

Seth surprised Kavriel by uttering his own curse.

Kavriel looked curiously at him. "And that is what?" he asked them both, intrigued. "...some kind of stronghold?"

Kell grunted and nodded, looking at Kavriel as if he had just asked if the sea was wet.

Seth leaned over to them and said quietly, "Kavriel hasn't been remembering things clearly."

Kavriel frowned, not entirely sure he wanted Seth to defend him. Kell and Ulin exchanged a quick look. Seth continued, speaking to Kavriel directly this time in a strange, ominous tone. "It is the Oenes Caverns, Kavriel. After the war the chancellor turned the camp into a place for the Quetalian prisoners of war. The caverns are numerous and nicely isolated in the Oenes. Actually the Patriarch had ordered the camp remain operational, hoping for more discoveries. He hasn't abandoned his interest in what Saire discovered there."

"You mean the Temscript Scrolls?" Kavriel interrupted, recalling the story of General Saire's accomplishments in the mountains and the reason he had come to Kavriel's island town. Finally, there was a connection here.

Seth nodded. "Yes. He has the prisoners digging away in the caverns. The Council had thought the place was some kind of *library*." Kavriel nodded, remembering the same thing from his own past. "Well, the Patriarch thinks the same."

"I envy you, Kavriel," Kell interrupted, bringing himself into the conversation. Kavriel turned quickly; he'd forgotten for a moment that he was still there. "The eastern realm holds many secrets. Some even say that an ancient civilization might be hidden away deep in the Oenes. It's good that you haven't seen how our new rulers have exploited us to pursue that theory."

Kavriel truly felt the emptiness of his memory, seeing the dark pain hidden away in Kell's eyes. He looked at Ulin, and saw the same thing as he nodded, keeping his eyes on the floor. "I'm sorry," he said. "I don't mean to bring up anything uncomfortable, but I really don't remember what has happened here. I know about the caverns from what Saire had discovered, and what the Council had been studying. I had no idea that the place had been changed into something so . . . terrible."

Seth and even Kell seemed to recognize his honesty. Grunting, Ulin got up from his seat and strode out of the hall. He clearly didn't want to reminisce. Kavriel gave Kell an apologetic look and the large man nodded.

"It is true, what your friend has said, isn't' it?" Kell asked, motioning to Seth, who seemed to catch a bit of Kavriel's discomfort as he looked away. Kavriel smiled slightly, answering Kell's question without the need for words. The man grunted. "Well then, it seems that you have even more secrets than the rest of us, little man." He smiled, showing off his pearl-white teeth. "How does it feel, not knowing *why* someone might want to kill you?"

Kavriel quickly responded. "What do you know about me, Kell?" He looked quickly toward the door Ulin had stepped through. "And Ulin?"

Kell's smile remained. "I don't know anything about you. Expect that you are intelligent but still stupid enough to think that you might be able to do better without us." He paused, and Kavriel felt his face grow hot in embarrassment. "I agreed to take you along with me because I needed men, and even though you might think of me as a criminal, I still keep promises made to my friends." He glanced at Seth, who looked down as if shamed.

Kavriel held his tongue, wondering how transparent he had been, travelling in this black company.

Kell nodded, sensing his weakness. "You are a child of a powerful man. I knew that when I first saw you. Obviously a Highlander, even if you don't look the part." His eyes roamed over Kavriel.

"So what?" He replied. "You think that I'm a Rav'agas spy, or something?" His question sounded mildly arrogant, not to mention ridiculous.

Kell kept his smile. "That would be interesting, but no. You are the son of an overseer by the name of Cyr Soelle, who in his own way has played a very helpful role in my cause against the chancellor and his southern dogs."

"Shit." Kavriel whispered regretfully, casting a glance to Seth who shook his head in denial. He nodded his head. "Ok. So you know my father." he admitted, curious about the rest of what he said now that the little armor he had was suddenly gone. "What does that mean for you?"

"Oh, don't worry, boy. Your secret is still safe with me." Kell chuckled while leaning back on the bench, letting his words sink in with the same stress as his thick bulk in the thin bench. Kavriel felt naked besides him. "Still . . ." Kell continued, scratching at his chin and studying Kavriel, sizing him up as if he were a prized catch, "I heard that you were dead. How did you manage that?"

For a moment Kavriel thought the man was being serious. He shook his head. "I . . . I don't know. Like I said.

I don't remember anything after what happened to me and my friends."

Kell raised his large hand to silence him. "No need, I know your story. I too have spent some time on Nostrac, even before the Rav'agas came, and for what it's worth, I never believed all that nonsense about the mines getting people all sick and forcing them to shut them down." He sighed. "I actually made decent money during that time, and I'm sorry to say I miss it." He grinned smugly, and Kavriel suddenly remembered what kind of man this was. In another time and another place, he was sure people like his father would have sent Kell to the Council for judgement.

His cover gone, Kavriel decided to risk questions. "What kind of people did you smuggle for, Kell?" he asked.

Kell quickly turned humble, even if it was obviously feigned. "Not the Rav'agas, if that's what you're implying," he said with a laugh. Kavriel only glowered at him. "No, no. I was simply keeping the districts from falling too far behind in their taxes to the Council," he assured Kavriel, as if he believed what he was doing was for the good.

"Which districts?" Kavriel asked, more curious than angry.

Kell replied with a word: "Bairn."

Kavriel raised his eyebrows. Bairn was the westernmost district of Quetal, and the poorest. Its populace was by no means destitute by Rav'agas standards, but Kavriel had heard that the overseer of Bairn was a worthless drunk, whose leadership and office was corrupt.

The people of Bairn had a hard time as it was, and since the district was hugely diverse (it was a haven for Rav'agas refugees), the overseer was criminally oblivious to the needs of the people regarding the strict tax laws, which kept a people already without means from ever bettering themselves.

For years the Council had tried to force the overseer to resign, but it being a democratic system, the people kept the man in charge. Kavriel could never understand that. He remembered talking to his father about it once; Cyr had explained to him that since the majority of the people of Bairn were not Quetal natives, yet still given all the rights and accommodation of the Quetalian people, they had not truly come to understand how the democratic system worked. If they kept the overseer in power it was because they truly believed he was doing the best for them. If the Council got involved it would have shaken that belief, and the system would fail.

Kavriel's father had also explained that the true way of Quetalian rule was through her people, and the Council understood this. Unfortunately it could be misguided or manipulated, as when propaganda about the red-eye sickness reached mainland ears, leading to the closing of Mir Town's mines. The people had decided, and the leaders had needed to listen. The Council and its representatives, Cyr Soelle declared proudly, were not actually leaders, but only spokespeople for the citizens of Quetal.

With this in mind, Kavriel looked at Kell from a new perspective. He hadn't just been a smuggler and a criminal to the chancellor and the Patriarch, but to the Council and the overseers in the Quetalian government. Yet in all of this, he had still remained a "people's champion" even if they might not have understood all of his motives. Kavriel understood why his diverse crew was so loyal. They loved him because he was a human first, and a criminal second. And with that understanding came respect.

Kell was watching Kavriel put all of this together in silence. Kavriel knew he wouldn't have to come out and say that he now understood why the man was who he was; Kell already saw it on his face.

"Now, as for Ulin," Kell suddenly resumed, bringing out that grin again as if he was enjoying twisting Kavriel around like this. "I can't tell you why he has an itch for you. Maybe you should have listened to him? Or maybe he's just jealous."

"Because I am the son of an overseer, and he's a noble of a fallen house?" Kavriel responded, bringing out an arrogant smile of his own to see how Kell would take it.

Kell seemed to take it well, because he laughed boisterously, loud enough for the three men at the altar to shoot him disapproving glances. Kell ignored them, although he lowered his voice to something more conspiratorial. "Oh, Ulin is a bit more than that." His smile turned devious. "But yes . . . essentially." He shrugged.

Kavriel couldn't help but laugh. He was starting to become more comfortable with Kell, which was probably the point. "Alright, then." He decided it would be best to move away from the subject and nodded at the men by the altar. "So what was that about, with this business with the Crypt? I know what was in the book that Ulin took from the village, and what it keeps. I imagine that you . . . or those like you . . . have been planning some kind of raid on this prison."

Immediately Kell's mood turned gloomy as he looked at the three men. "Yes, the fools. Six months, I've dragged my men across the north, looking for clues to the place. It's a stain on the face of Quetal, and many good men have been kept there."

"Yet wouldn't a strike against the place set off the chancellor in Teltraum, prompt him to send out his Rav'agas to hunt you down?" Kavriel asked, not knowing much about the present situation, though he'd learned enough when studying the tactics used in previous wars to know that any rebel attack in an occupied territory couldn't be good.

Kell gave him an irritated look. "If they knew what we had done, yes." Kavriel must have looked confused, because Kell shook his head and leaned closer. "Listen. That book was a full report of not only the locations of all the Rav'agas-occupied zones, but the names of the commanders, officers, and even the bloody soldiers. That Ay'vol officer in Gelod's Stream was probably the best thing that ever happened to Quetal. We were going to go in, liberate the prison, and place our own people in the Crypt, all under the chancellor's eyes. They wouldn't know the difference, and we would have had a sanctuary for freedom fighters until we could finally storm Teltraum herself and put that damned black-bearded chancellor into the ground. If we move fast enough, we can do it all before the chancellor has time to warn all the outposts listed in that book."

Becoming more animated, Kell glared at the men by the altar, his face turning red as his dissatisfaction exploded from him. "Those fools decided that they didn't need this information; they think they can do what we've been planning for six months with a couple hundred villagers armed with pikes and cleavers. It will be a slaughter, and it will all be for nothing!"

Kavriel blinked, thinking hard about all this new information. He felt Kell's anger and frustration, even if he still didn't truly understand what had happened. It was as if he were reading a book about a failed military operation in one of his history books back in Rhyol. He shook his head.

Seth leaned in to speak. "Is it true then that the Crypt is very close to us?"

Kell thought a moment, then nodded. "Yes, but not next door, if that's what you mean. The Crypt is still about a week's journey along the Oenes Range."

"Then there is still time to catch them?" he asked, and Kell smiled at him, obviously having thought the same thing. "That's the idea, yes, but they're already two days ahead of us."

"Still," Kavriel interrupted, picking up on Seth's idea, "a company of two dozen travels faster than two hundred."

Kell nodded. "Yes, it does, but we can't leave tonight. I'm waiting for a ship carrying another hundred fighters before we can go. They should come in sometime before dawn, and then we set off." He looked curiously at Kavriel a moment, possibly thinking about all that he had told him. "So where does that leave you, Soelle?" he asked. "I've answered your concerns about me, and I know all about you. Can I still count on you to fight with us?"

Kavriel looked over to Seth, saw the excitement

shining in his eyes. He felt as if he had just been swallowed up in that history book, and with each page he turned, he wouldn't be able to put it down until he'd finished it, even if it wasn't what he had intended to do in the beginning.

He wasn't entirely sure what he'd do. He knew that he needed to get to Teltraum—Femaor and Chairman Richart would have received news by now that he was coming. Yet could he abandon this cause for his own selfish reasons? He knew the answer. In his mind he could see the look his father would give him if he answered incorrectly, as if he were being tested.

He nodded, offering a hand to Kell, which the smuggler took. "You can count on me, Captain," he said, and the large man's contented laugh echoed through the hall.

CHAPTER 25

Night came, and with it a stifling humidity that Kavriel thought was only possible during the summer months. When he thought about where he was in the world, he realized that it must be the norm year round; he doubted it even snowed in this part of the world. Though the frequent rains weren't uncomfortable, Kavriel was growing homesick for the dry Highland nights and the cool sea air of his home. He smiled, remembering the night fog rolling over the harbor like a gray blanket, the smell of salt air, the leaves on the silver birches and the green and pink shrubs near his home with their little blue berries named Blackhearts.

He had left the temple-turned-meeting hall several hours ago and come to the building close to the water that Kell's crew had taken as theirs. After eating and a hot drink, he'd been assigned to keep an eye on the bay for the ship that Kell was waiting for, or any Rav'agas patrols that happened to be particularly ambitious this night. It was not an assignment he particularly enjoyed and he was hoping that one of the other crewmen would replace him soon.

"We are trapped. Have you noticed?" The voice in the darkness startled him, and Kavriel turned quickly to see that of all the crew, it was Ulin who had come to join him from the shelter. He was balancing one of his knives on his hand while he leaned against the wall, looking out over the harbor as if he had been there with Kavriel for hours.

"What do you mean, trapped?" he asked.

Ulin began pointing in different directions with his knife. "The Rav'agas are closing in from the North Sea,

444

and the soldier that got away must already be back with his company. We won't make it a day before they catch us."

Kavriel didn't let the implication or the man bother him any longer. "Then what should we do?"

Ulin laughed softly, pointing his knife blade at Kavriel. "Give them *you*." His voice was angry. "It's what they want anyway."

"What difference do you think that might make?" Kavriel growled, no longer caring about the knife as Ulin glared at him. "I would think that a Loellen noble might be a bit more appealing to the chancellor than some simple overseer's son."

Ulin's reply surprised him. "Possibly." He grinned. "Yet my brother isn't the Ghost."

Before Kavriel could put his thoughts together Ulin twirled the naked blade skillfully and made it disappear into his cloak. He turned and returned to the building before Kavriel could say anything, leaving him furiously assimilating that.

Suddenly fearful that Ulin knew more about him than Kell had let on, Kavriel left his post to follow the man into the building. He needed to speak with Ulin, find out what else he knew.

The atmosphere inside the building was lively, the men and women seated at ten tables arranged end to end along the walls eating and drinking and hooting and shouting at one another in deafening good humor. There were about a hundred people in the place, but Kavriel saw Kell right away, speaking with the three men that he had been arguing with earlier in the meeting hall across the room. Turning his head, Kavriel found Seth, speaking with a rather buxom woman. He felt fleeting good cheer for his friend, but he couldn't concern himself with that for the moment.

Ulin had moved quickly into the crowd and was now standing near an area where the tables had been pushed back and a circle of cheering onlookers watched two men, shirtless and sweating like field hands, strike at each other with wooden swords. The mock battle drew Kavriel closer, and though he saw Ulin in the corner of his eye, he forgot his anger as, swept up in the excitement, he found himself shouting and clapping along with the other onlookers.

They moved with surprising skill, dancing in then out, their wooden blades thrusting and parrying until one man caught the end of the thick blade on his chest and went flat on his back. The crowd cheered as the grinning champion threw up his arms, slick with sweat. Stepping over to his fallen opponent, he extended a hand and pulled him up to his feet, giving him a slap on the back as they laughed and applauded together with the crowd.

Clapping at the victory, Kavriel watched as the champion called a challenge, and another man stepped in to replace the loser. The game continued, the winner of each round remaining in the circle until he too was defeated and replaced by another. He laughed as one champion fell to an opponent wielding a broomstick like a jousting lance. Wooden swords changed to practice axes, or small knives, and even bare hands. No one was seriously wounded, Kavriel was happy to see, and even those who fell sometimes came back to try again after having rested for a while. The crowd grew larger, as those at the tables moved over to enjoy the show, too.

Kavriel was surprised when Seth stepped into the circle. He saw the young man's lady friend smiling at him from the sidelines and realized he was most likely trying to impress her. Seth grabbed up a wooden blade and smiled at the crowd, the spectators clapping furiously, eager to see how this young newcomer would fare. Wiping the sweat from his brow, Kavriel frowned, worried when he saw that Seth's opponent was a green-robed man who looked way too amused to suggest any inexperience in fighting. But Kavriel was again surprised when Seth moved the sword with a calm ease, as if he had been fighting with a blade all his life.

Seth actually proved a worthy adversary. Kavriel's worry changed to pride as he cheered on his fellow Rhyolian. After a bit of play, however, the green-robed man decided enough was enough and kicked Seth's legs out from under him. Kavriel groaned as Seth landed hard on his back, then covered his eyes in mock shame, laughing. Seth, still on the floor, laughed too, and the green-robed man smiled and yanked Seth to his feet, then pushed him into the crowd with a slap on his shoulder. The crowd cheered, and Seth waved as he limped back to his lady. Kavriel could tell from the look in his eyes that he was ready for another chance, when his turn came again.

Looking back to the circle, Kavriel felt a moment of terror when he realized the green-robed man was pointing his wooden weapon directly at him. He instinctively glanced at those around him, to see that they had stepped back. It was too late now to back up and disappear into the crowd. Strong hands gripped his shoulders and arms and

447

shoved him into the clearing. Someone else tossed a wooden sword to him, and he caught it awkwardly, setting off a roar of laughter. Kavriel saw that it was Seth, grinning, who had relinquished his weapon, and he realized that he had been targeted.

Sighing, Kavriel reluctantly bowed at his opponent, who was waiting patiently for him to ready himself. However, as Kavriel positioned himself in what he thought was a reasonable defensive stance, the crowd suddenly booed as a man stepped up behind the green-robed man and tapped him on his shoulder. This was going against the rules. As soon as the green-robed man saw who had tapped him, he smiled and stepped out of the way. Kavriel gaped at the replacement.

Ulin.

As the nobleman lifted the long oak staff he had chosen as his weapon, Kavriel actually smiled. This was what both of them wanted.

Ulin threw the cloak off his shoulders in a flash of gray, tossing it at Kavriel. *Dirty move,* Kavriel thought as he fumbled with the heavy fabric. It only took a moment to tear it from his face, yet as he did he felt the end of the staff pop against his forehead. Half of the crowd laughed as he fell while the other half hissed at Ulin, who continued to smile, holding his weapon out toward Kavriel.

Shaking his head to clear the stars from his vision, Kavriel grabbed Ulin's staff and pulled himself to his feet. If they had been following the rules, Kavriel would have known that he had just been bested, but he wasn't ready to quit. He leapt forward, trying every kind of attack he had learned from the crew. Within moments the staff had knocked Kavriel's sword from his hand and banged against his head. The crowd heckled, disappointed.

Kavriel did not fall this time, but the blow was still painful and would be considered a "death blow." Still angry, he nevertheless had enough dignity to admit defeat. He nodded to the crowd, who had already begun separating to look for a new challenger.

The end of the staff jabbed him in the shoulder. The crowd hissed again, and Kavriel turned slowly toward Ulin.

"So soon, child?" Ulin taunted. "And I thought Highlanders were made of stronger stuff."

Kavriel glowered, and curled his hands around a staff similar to the one Ulin had that someone tossed toward him. Kavriel looked into the crowd, and saw that it had been Kell. The big man nodded his bald head in approval. Kavriel felt his confidence grow as the crowd cheered.

Ulin let out an amused laugh and came at him with more precision, but slow enough to give Kavriel a chance to defend himself. He kept himself from getting "tagged" with the wooden staff and as their faces met, Ulin dropped his arrogant smile and nodded respectfully. Kavriel knew that this time it was going to be for real. So the dance began, slow at first but gradually moving faster, until Kavriel started getting the hang of it. Ulin called out his errors and shouted his approval whenever Kavriel did something that he was supposed to, and he realized that the man was teaching him.

Ulin moved around him more skillfully, using movements that Kavriel recognized from earlier fighters, and he was able to stop or dodge them successfully. He actually felt more comfortable with the staff than he had holding the sword, and he brought the attack to Ulin occasionally, giving the crowd something to cheer for as they watched this lesson less boisterously than they had earlier.

The firelight scattered against the dark wood walls of the room, soothing. The noise of the crowd melded into one steady pulse. Kavriel became drawn into it, the beat of noise and the rhythm of his heart together, spellbound. He focused on his breathing, keeping it even and relaxed as he danced with Ulin, hearing only the *tuck, tuck, tuck* of wood striking wood. The crowd disappeared completely for him. It was only the staff and his heart that he could hear now, and he realized that Ulin had actually started moving slower. Yet he was struggling to keep up, and the sheen of sweat on the man's face fed Kavriel's confidence. He let himself go.

Putting all the anger and spite he felt toward the man into his attack, Kavriel pushed him back with each blow, as if he were ten instead of one. Time slowed, and the *tuck* of the wood started to echo eerily, as if Kavriel were fighting in a cavern. He could feel the hair on his head dampen, but he wasn't tired. On the contrary, he felt he could move faster. He spun around his opponent, mimicking the same style that Ulin had used against him as his staff came down. Ulin vanished from his vision, only to be replaced by another man who had come to fight him.

Kavriel didn't care any longer. He had become the fight. He had become the battle. Ulin had been defeated, and soon so was this other man. They were trapped in mud while he could fly above them. Others came, older one moment and younger the next, long hair becoming short, green robes to red, beards to clean-shaven chins. Sometimes there was more than one . . . two . . . three! Kavriel didn't notice details, only the direction that he had to go.

He felt the blood surging through his body, the beating of his heart, and the pulsing in his temples as he continued to dance with the changing shadows. He used it, used their anger, their love, and their skill, their energy to feed him, to keep him going. It was all his for the taking!

"Kavriel!"

Thrust and parry, strike and dance, stick to stick. The room echoed, the lights flashed around him.

"Kavriel!"

Kavriel drew from the sudden rush of emotions pouring through him. He wasn't sure if he controlled them or they controlled him. He wasn't sure of anything except that he seemed to actually see the motion of his attackers *before* they struck, like the shadow of a backlit man before he entered a room. He didn't need the staff any longer. He didn't need anything anymore. He let the weapon drop and simply walked between the attacks, taking the balance from his opponents when they overextended themselves. They were not fast enough for him. They could not even touch him!

Feeling the energy of the room surround him, he drew it all in and laughed like a madman as he danced in the circle.

The water was ice cold, and the dull echo of the room suddenly left him as every sound rushed into his awareness. The crackle of the fire, the shouts of the men, and the cries of the women surrounded him, and when Kavriel opened his eyes (he didn't remember closing them) he did not see Ulin or any of the subsequent opponents, he only saw his friend Seth holding an overturned bucket in his hands. His face was pale as a sheet of snow, his eyes terrified.

Kavriel felt his clothing, realizing that he was soaking wet. Seth dropped the bucket noisily to the floor. The room had become quiet as a grave. There was no cheering or laughter, no hollers of support or insults, only soft whispers passing between the people around him. They were looking at Kavriel much as Seth had. As if Kavriel had turned into a ghost.

"Kavriel." Seth spoke calmly, holding his hands up defensively. There was a horrible expression on his face, and he nodded when he spoke, almost as if to make sure Kavriel understood him. "Kavriel, it's finished. Please stop this."

It was the strangest thing Seth could have said, and Kavriel nearly laughed as he stood there, scratch at his drenched head. "Seth, why did you pour water over me?" he asked, chuckling.

Seth responded with wide eyes.

Kavriel looked around the room. And saw why his friend had done what he had done. He went cold with fear.

Men littered the floor, men that he had fought and beaten. They were everywhere, about twenty in all, most still conscious but a few yet to awaken. Kavriel stumbled back, and his hands went to his head as a jolt of pain shot through his brain. He had a memory of Silver Wood, when he had awakened to the carnage of the Mir soldiers, and he recalled the commander of the Rav'agas patrol ship as he had been sliced nearly in half by his hand.

A moment of clarity came, and Kavriel suddenly remembered doing all of those things he thought he had forgotten. He saw himself pulling the Mir Guard from his throat after his neck had been slit. He should not have lived, but he did. He had shoved the Guardsman, tossing him back, and grabbed the soldier who had been holding him, ripping his arm from his shoulder. He had not stopped. He continued to tear the man apart as his screams rang terribly in his ears. The other Guard tried to escape, his face a rictus of horror, but Kavriel had taken up the blade of one of the Rav'agas and had cut through him and another before they'd even moved a foot. He remembered the last man, how he'd looked at him with such hideous terror when Kavriel picked him up from the ground and hurled him into the trees. He remembered the sickening sound of the tree branch impaling the man. He remembered the sickening snap of the Mir Guard leader's neck as he spun his head around almost enough to wrench it free. He probably could have done it. He could have sliced the Ay'vol commander of the patrol ship from balls to chin if he'd wanted to, but he had chosen a quicker attack to finish the more experienced fighter.

He remembered everything now, and yet he did not want to accept it. He looked at the men starting to move off the floor around him, and he felt the confusion, saw the looks of terror from the people in the room. He saw his friend look at him with horror, and Kavriel, in a moment of horrible clarity, turned and ran.

He ran from the building and into the humid night,

not caring about anything except escape. He had killed men, and now he remembered. What had become of him in the time that he had lost? The Creator save him!

CHAPTER 26

How could this happen? How could he have done this?. Sa'rire is lost. He has become the thing that he hated most and it is inevitable, what he will do next to the rest of us. I don't know why . . . I don't understand how he could have done such a thing. His own brothers!

He must have tricked Dar. It was the only way. Dar was always too loyal to the family and Sa'rire used that for his experiment. Damn him. Damn him for doing such a thing. Dar was our rock! He was the most honorable of us! How could he? And Tondal . . . poor Tondal. He was working so hard with Sa'rire in order to understand why we are who we are. Why we were created, and our purpose. It was all for nothing. Sa'rire destroyed him and he would have done the same to me, if I hadn't escaped.

I damn myself for fleeing once Tondal was struck down, but what would I have been able to do? Sa'rire has become something powerful. I did not fully understand how that could even be possible, but since leaving the kingdom I believe I have come to terms with what has happened. My time is limited, I fear, for once Sa'rire has discovered where I have gone, he will certainly come for me. I can only hope he has not decided to go after Kai'sa or Faythe first. They know nothing of his treachery, and it is my responsibility to warn them. Maybe together we can . . . I don't know.

I didn't think it was possible, all those years ago. Yet Tondal had discovered something important. He called it a "Shift," some kind of transfer of our souls to one another. It sounded too odd when he and Sa'rire were explaining it to me. Yet by then it had been too late. Sa'rire had decided to test his Shift theory by destroying Dar. He must have succeeded in acquiring his soul. It would be the only explanation for how he had become more powerful than Tondal and me together.

Father had created all of us from one being, and both Tondal and Sa'rire believed that through one of us it could be possible to harness that. Yet why would he want to? What purpose could it possibly have? I think Sa'rire had become too involved in the southern kingdom, listening too much to the mortals' take on this supposed "resurrection." I believe he is trying to become what he destroyed all those eons ago. He wants to become Father. The resurrection is false, but Sa'rire believes he can become what the mortals desire. He is mad! The power must have taken what was already corruptible in his soul and augmented it.

He is more dangerous now than ever before, and I am not sure even the three of us who remain will be able to stop him. That is why I have decided on another option, and I am writing this down now in the hope that, in future times, if I am still here, what I have done will not be forgotten. The mortals must never know the truth of their existence and Sa'rire must never be allowed to become their god. It is a desecration to everything the mortals are, even if they might not understand. It is their life, not ours!

We have no place here any longer. Our work is done and it would be best if all of us could simply disappear into the wind. It is too late for that, and Sa'rire has become exactly what we were all created from— darkness eternal. Once he has succeeded in destroying all of us I believe he will then take Father's remains unto himself. He has not done that yet and I can only believe that it is because he is not yet strong enough. Otherwise, why wait? What is he intending?

Anyway, I cannot dwell here much longer. Sa'rire is again distracted by the southern kingdom and he has left the temple. My advisors have told me this and since I cannot trust my own brother then I must keep my intentions to myself. He must never catch me, otherwise all is finished.

This might be my only chance. I have written and already sent the information to the Hielias Kingdom. The mountains will bury the secrets of my actions until the time comes when I will need to reclaim them, if ever. Sa'rire should not suspect that, but he will most likely search for me or the scrolls in time. I truly hope he never finds them, otherwise he will find the urns of Father's remains. I will immediately claim them. I have already decided where to hide them, since I cannot simply destroy them.

If ever he should destroy me or our sisters, then at least he will never be able to complete his quest to take Father's soul. He will never become infinite. I will not allow that.

Again I ask my father for forgiveness for what I have done and what we have done as your children. We have betrayed our cause and we should be taken from existence. All of us.

Kavriel knew where he needed to go, even if he didn't completely understand why yet.

As he pushed open the elongated wooden doors and crossed under the wooden archway into the seclusion of the

Rav'agas temple, all the pain and guilt he had been feeling seemed to wash away. He breathed calmly, felt a new-found peace as he stood in the vacant temple, smelling the wood burning in the roaring fire in the fireplace, left to burn unattended. Alone in the temple, he felt more at ease, knowing that there was no one present who might question why he was there. He had no other place to go.

Kavriel moved slowly down the aisle, stopping halfway along the rows of benches. He sat down heavily, placing his head in his hands. The throbbing in his mind slowed as his eyes closed in concentration. He did not know how long he sat there, listening to the quick beat of his heart and the crackle of the fire as it warmed his body, but after a time the pain in his head disappeared and he could now bring his thoughts together. He wondered if it had something to do with being in the temple, as so many followers of The Way had believed, that being in the house of their Creator brought inner peace.

Kavriel studied the temple, looking up at the wooden walls and the icons of that faith, trying to forget what he had just recently remembered about himself. He had killed men, and he wondered if even the Creator could forgive him for such atrocities.

The acoustics in the temple were excellent, and Kavriel could hear every shift and hiss and crackle from the fireplace as the sounds climbed into the steep arches high above. His eyes followed the curves down behind the altar, then the windows in the wall above it, stained with lustrous colors and designs that depicted important events in the scriptures of The Way. They were beautiful, and the story they told was one of reward for the dedication of those who followed The Way.

It was not a linear account. Not exactly. Kavriel noticed the two outside pictures followed each other, and then the scenes moved inward, guiding the observer toward the center frame, located directly above the altar. Kavriel read the windows, starting from the two outermost and moving to the center, and he understood the meaning immediately.

The first two windows depicted the two gods who created all that the Rav'agas believed in, and to some extent, those in the rest of the world. They were depicted not as men, but more splatters of colored shapes, one bright and illustrious and the other dark and oppressive. "The Brothers," as they were known in Ay'vol; "The Father and Son," as they were known in the northern provinces and in Quetal; even "The Sisters" by the female warriors of West Point. Whatever they were called, they were simply the Light and the Darkness, and together created man.

In the next windows the two shapes clashed together in what was called The Falling, when the two gods battled one another over spite or simple arrogance (in Kavriel's own interpretation), the God of Light overthrowing the God of Darkness and shattering him in the mortals' realm.

Kavriel followed the story as it was continued through the next pair of windows, the colors more joyous, more vibrant, representing peace and harmony. The God of Darkness had been destroyed, and the mortals revered the decision their one Creator had made.

Kavriel realized that these windows must be retelling a very old version of the doctrine, when the people of ancient times had thought the battle between the gods was a simple case of good versus evil. Subsequent believers had pulled that theory apart into fine threads, deciding through endless arguments and irrational proof that the war was started for much more selfish reasons. Kavriel saw that too being depicted in the next set of stained glass windows. They showed the people of the world, the mortals. Those on the right window continued to rejoice to their god, while those on the left looked much too preoccupied with their pursuits for such reverence. Their expressions were not content like the others', but distracted and irritable, as if they sought the truth of their creation through other, more meaningless methods.

Kavriel couldn't help but smile at the depiction, and its partner showing the faithful ideal in all of its grandeur. Those that still rejoiced to their Creator were smiling, surrounded by strong homes, temples, and children; gardens, rivers, and animals filled every corner of the glass. The artistic propaganda, continued on the centerpiece panel, which depicted a male figure standing alone, dressed in a long white robe and draped with a scarf of gold and black. It was the Patriarch, or one of them. He was the icon of the faith, and the leader of Ay'vol through the bloodline of the God of Light, who had blessed his house with his seed.

Kavriel had seen pictures of Patriarchs before, unchanged through hundreds of generations of faithful. His pristine white robe symbolized simplicity and purity, yet a solid gold mask covered his face, hiding his mortality, and the rather humble shepherd's crook he held had a handle carved with the image of the sun, the ancient symbol for the

God of Light. The scarf was also covered in icons and symbols that were too precise to be simple imagery; Kavriel knew that they were letters of the Temscript language, the language of the gods, the language that was etched into the cavern walls in the mines of Mir Town.

He remembered what had happened there, and how Saire had deceived them all in his secret, self-serving search. And he suddenly thought of a connection to passages he'd read in the book of "memoirs"—the urns containing the metallic red liquid. That was what Saire had been after. Kavriel suddenly felt uneasy. He still didn't understand what the writer had been trying to say, but could the urns be the same containers that held the remains of "Father"? Could those urns in fact hold the remains of the God of Darkness, or the God of Light? Kavriel couldn't be sure. Rav'agas doctrine never spoke about what had happened after the god was "shattered against the mortal realm." It was as if the story had ended with him, it was no longer of importance.

And yet this other group of followers, this *Watch,* seemed to believe a different version, or simply a continuation of the story. Sa'rire, Tondal, Kai'sa, Faythe, Dar . . . .these were the names of The Watch. Yet who had been the last? Who had been the author of these memoirs and what had happened to him? What had happened to all of them, that no written records existed besides what was in the book Kavriel had? Two had been killed, murdered by this Sa'rire person who had wanted to become a god himself, resurrecting the power to assimilate into himself. It was crazy, Kavriel thought, it was blasphemy that might even be considered too extreme for the Patriarch. Or was there a deeper connection, and the Patriarchs might have descended from this Sa'rire?

This new Patriarch had passed the tests of The Becoming, from what he had learned from Xavr. Was it true then, that perhaps Sa'rire had succeeded in his quest? Was General Saire conspiring with the Patriarch with his quest, or was he simply another book collector like Xavr, who had been convinced of the stories' truth and went looking for his own glory?

What was he missing? Kavriel stared at the image of the Patriarch in the window, trying to put the puzzle together, wishing he had more information. He didn't understand how, but he knew there was some kind of connection to him, and Xavr seemed to be the only person that might know. He wished he'd stayed with him longer. Would he have understood what he learned? Probably not. Kavriel sighed. He had only recently finished the book, long after he had left Xavr's cabin. He had not been ready. Strange, though, that Xavr had purposely shown Kavriel the book of memoirs, as if it was something the man felt he needed to read. He tapped the shape of the book, still hidden deep in his coat pocket; it had never left his person.

He didn't hear the door to the temple open or the person enter until he was standing directly behind him. Kavriel nearly jumped from the pew when he spoke.

"Quite a beautiful portrait, wouldn't you say?"

Kavriel spun around to face Kell, who quickly held his hands up to show that he was no threat. Kavriel realized that he would need to get used to that reaction, knowing now what he was capable of. He wouldn't want to sneak up on him, either.

"Easy, boy." Kell said in a calm voice.

"I'm sorry," Kavriel replied meekly. "You startled me."

Kell nodded, and the tension in his shoulders eased as he let his arms drop to rest his hands on his hips. "Then I apologize. Am I disturbing you?" He looked around the temple with curious eyes.

Kavriel watched him carefully, knowing the man well enough now to know that he hadn't followed Kavriel to the temple simply to apologize for doing so. He wanted answers, and Kavriel had no right to keep his secrets from the man whose crew he had scattered across the floor like spilled grain from a broken barrel.

"I have wronged you and your men," Kavriel said quietly as Kell turned back to him. "I let myself lose control. I didn't mean to harm any of them, I promise you."

"Harm them?" Kell exclaimed more brightly than Kavriel expected. It put him off guard. The man showed his pearly teeth in a smile. "By the Creator, son, you gave them a lesson that they needed to get months ago! Still, it might be best if you could avoid Ulin for the next several days." He chuckled. "You gave him a rather justified humiliation. Served him right, to speak to you about your brother like that."

Kavriel didn't reply right away. Kell was being sincere, and seemed genuinely happy about what had happened in the makeshift tournament. Kavriel was relieved that his actions hadn't killed anyone this time, but it didn't answer any of his questions about what he had become. It also didn't answer why Kell would bring up the subject of Vaemalin, but he had an idea.

"You think I'm the Ghost, don't you. Or you think my brother is."

Kell seemed to have expected the question. He smiled and shook his head. "No son, I don't. Your brother is simply another victim of the bastards occupying my homeland. Oh, I believe that he attacked and even killed Rav'agas when they came to his home. It wouldn't have been the first time that something like that happened. I myself actually put an Ay'vol captain's head through the wall when he came to Sai trying to put me and mine out in the streets. But I don't believe he could have done all the things the Rav'agas wet their beds over." He laughed, crossing his large arms in front of his barrel chest.

Kavriel could easily believe that Kell had done that, but he wasn't convinced that he was telling him everything. Seth and his father might be the only ones left alive who had witnessed what his brother supposedly did, they and the Ay'vol commander he had chased out of Rhyol, but he didn't think Seth would have said much else.

Kell waited a moment, watching Kavriel with an odd expression before sitting down on the bench beside Kavriel. He sat down as well, turning slightly to face the big man.

"Kavriel." Kell began, then paused, scratching the side of his face. Kavriel waited, knowing something important was coming. "Do you know what the Ghost really is?" Kavriel kept still. Kell continued anyway. "The Ghost is a symbol, like that crook that fellow is holding in the picture." He waved toward the window depicting the Patriarch. Kavriel had to smile. "And like it, the Ghost has become a legend among the Quetalians like me, and Ulin, and even your father. Everyone who has made it the purpose of their lives to end the Patriarch's control over our homeland." The man glanced at Kavriel to see if he was paying attention, and Kavriel nodded to show that he was. "People like us need to have something to believe in, like the Rav'agas have their god and the Patriarch has . . . well, he has himself."

Kavriel couldn't help but chortle. Kell smiled again, and Kavriel knew he was trying to make him feel better about what had happened. "At any rate, we've spread word of the Ghost around Quetal so the Rav'agas have something to fear, since they no longer fear us."

"So there is no man terrorizing and murdering Rav'agas in their sleep?" Kavriel asked, relaxing in the knowledge that the frightening story had all been fabricated.

Kell shrugged. "There has been terror and murder, yes, but it hasn't been done by any particular person, or Ghost. It's been done by people like me, against the occupation. We are not the cleanest of fighters, but we do what we must. Maybe we're no better than the dogs we fight, but when you have no arms to swing or legs to kick, you have to bite with your teeth. He smiled again, showing his.

"Then what has that got to do with my brother?" Kavriel asked, wishing he'd been able to speak more to Ulin.

Kell shrugged again, but his mood seemed to have darkened. "Unfortunately nothing, but the Patriarch needs to have symbols to believe in besides his staff and mask. Your brother has become a target, and every high commander in the Ay'vol Force has his name written someplace on his blade. They need him as a sacrifice, proof to us 'rebels' that if the Patriarch can destroy the Ghost, then we stand no chance."

Kavriel cursed. It made sense, then, why he had to remain in hiding from the Rav'agas searching for his brother—or him, as Ulin had mentioned. The Guard in Mir had been after Vaemalin, and there was a good chance there were others. Kavriel had lost his home, his family, and his friends to the general, whose involvement in all of this he still did not understand. And now the Soelles of small Rhyol seemed to be entangled in the politics of warring nations. He felt as if his head was about to explode with the implications.

He must have looked perplexed, because Kell cleared his throat before saying gently, "I don't know too much about you, Kavriel, and neither does Ulin." At Kavriel's questioning look, he elaborated. "He doesn't have ill feelings toward you in particular, despite your reluctance to do as he asks." He smiled again, but Kavriel could tell it was forced. "You don't know about him, however, and he tends to keep his secrets to himself."

"What are you getting at?" Kavriel asked.

Kell sighed as he continued. "Ulin isn't a new friend of mine, but he has only recently left his home to fight by my side, after what happened to his family and his titles."

Kavriel remembered what Seth had said to him earlier. "He's Loellen, isn't he, from one of the noble houses in the wine valleys?"

Kell nodded. "Yes, but more than that, Ulin is from

House Tavrick. His father was Olenson Tavrick; perhaps you have heard of him?" Kell asked sarcastically.

Kavriel suddenly felt sick as understanding came. "Chairman Olenson of the Council Nine," he whispered. "The one who was murdered by—" He couldn't continue, remembering what his father, and Seth, had told him about the stories that followed his brother once he'd become the Ghost.

Kell nodded. "I'm sorry, Kavriel, but you must understand that Ulin's feelings are misplaced. He knows that the Ghost does not exist, and I have explained to him what I believe truly happened to his father once Chancellor Zoren took power. The Ay'vol murdered him once he'd done what he was ordered to do—issuing the Cleansing order—and the name of your brother was used as simply that, a name to chase. Unfortunately he is stubborn and needs to direct his revenge at something tangible. When you showed up on Jassar's boat, I knew he wouldn't take it well. That was why I sent you two out together on those scouting runs. I was hoping you could resolve things between you.

"Nobody believed that you lived, Kavriel. When you showed up again it brought up old theories about the Ghost. It didn't help that you'd lost your memory. The red-eye, was it?" Kell asked, and Kavriel nodded. Kell let out a grunt. "Anyway, I thought that Ulin might have let go of his old hate. Then he told me what you could do in a fight."

Kell's tone became very serious, and Kavriel felt a chill run up his spine. "I had a hunch when we first met, to tell you the truth, but I wasn't ready to believe it. You are clumsy. Yet you have skills that I would never believe in one so young and inexperienced. By the Creator, I never thought I would see a man fight like you, and I have fought with many!" Kell's compliment did nothing to ease Kavriel's mind. If anything, it made him feel worse. "You have a certain ability to defend yourself that I have never witnessed before. Don't get me wrong, you are still clumsy in your attack, but you have speed and an ability to sense the danger around you. I don't know where you learned to keep yourself alive so skillfully, but we need people like you in our cause. I need you."

Kell spoke genuinely, and for a moment Kavriel felt less tense. Kell was a good man, despite his shady methods against the Rav'agas.

"Yet after seeing what you can do tonight, I know that even I wouldn't be able to stop you from leaving if you chose to go right now," Kell admitted. "That was why I followed you. I know you're looking for your brother. He is a part of your life that was taken from you and you don't even remember why! I get that. If my daughter was ever put in your brother's situation, I would travel to the Patriarch's Palace in nothing but my skin to find her, if that's what it took."

Kell had grown flustered, distracted by the mention of his daughter, and Kavriel wondered what the rest of that story was. Kell sighed again. "That's why I think it would be best if you stay with my crew, Kavriel. You can travel to Teltraum as soon as I finish speaking, if you want. I won't even try to stop you. Yet I don't believe you will find what you are looking for there. You brother, if he still lives, would not be in the capitol. I can't believe that the chancellor's most wanted would be hiding in his bedroom."

He snorted. "I don't know if you have been to Teltraum
since the chancellor arrived—or remember if you did.
Either way, the place is more secured by the Rav'agas
Guard than the Crypt itself. There is no way Vaemalin
Soelle would remain hidden in such a place."

He paused, and Kavriel reflected on what the man
had said. He seemed genuine; he didn't think Kell would
lie about his brother just to keep him around. "Are you
suggesting that Vaemalin is being held in the Crypt?" he
asked.

Kell shook his head with that irritated look in his
eyes that suggested Kavriel had again said something
stupid. "Of course not. The chancellor would have had his
head on a stick on the highest peak of the Oenes for all to
see, if that was the case." He glanced at Kavriel. "My
apologies," he muttered, but Kavriel didn't mind. Kell
shook his head. "No, I think that your brother has
disappeared into the wind. If he lives, then he is smart and
would most likely be doing what the rest of us are doing:
surviving."

He nodded, and Kavriel did the same, but he still
wondered what he should do now. He wanted to help
Kell—and Seth—simply for the sake of it being the right
thing to do. Yet he had obligations to his father and to the
friends that he had lost. And there was still a piece to the
puzzle that went deeper for him than any political issues.
Kavriel wondered if he should focus his efforts elsewhere.
On himself, for one—try to find out what exactly had
happened to him in the time that he had lost.

He must have been considering for a while, with
Kell watching the entire time. "So," Kell finally asked,

"what do you think of my proposition?"

"Do you think it will work your plan, to attack the prison?" Kavriel asked, and for a moment Kell looked uncertain.

Frowning, the big man looked away, toward the Patriarch in the window. "I don't have a choice anymore," he replied almost humbly. "I never intended to be the leader of a cause. I was only doing what I thought I should, but now I have responsibilities to those that have decided to join me. I can't let them down."

Kavriel nodded, seeing not the smuggler but a wise fatherly figure. "You're a good man, Kell," he said, causing the man to turn to him with a smile. "I will help you."

Before Kell could reply, the double doors of the temple burst open with a rush of fresh air. Kavriel and Kell turned together to see what had interrupted their conversation, and immediately ducked down behind the benches when a contingent of armed men entered. Kell whispered a curse, and when Kavriel recognized the gold and black uniforms, he echoed the captain.

CHAPTER 27

Kavriel fought panic, realizing that the company of Rav'agas soldiers had trapped them in the temple. From what Kavriel had learned in the past, in other occupied towns and villages, the best thing to do was *not* what he and Kell had just done. Yet Kell's reaction had been the safest choice, since these soldiers, drawing swords and nocking bows, were here with a purpose—they were after something or someone.

"What are they doing here?" he whispered to Kell while peeking under the benches.

Kell didn't respond. His eyes flicked quickly over the half-dozen men who had entered, and Kavriel knew Kell was sizing them up, inventorying their weaponry. He was trying to determine which man he could kill the quickest.

"Kell!" Kavriel whispered, and the man gave a venomous hiss that shut him up.

The doors swung open again and another six soldiers entered, making their chance of escape even more unlikely. Kavriel heard screams and the sounds of fighting coming from the village proper. He glanced at Kell, whose jaw tightened at the sounds.

Kavriel turned his focus from the doors, searching for some other exit. He tried to see behind the altar, the wall under the stained glass windows; if this temple was similar to the town hall back in Rhyol, there would be a sacristy someplace in the back. He found it in an alcove to the left of the raised platform holding the altar, but the chances of getting to it unseen were nil.

The invisible arrows began pricking at his skull in time with his agitation. He thought about the men and women outside that he had heard, how many were fighting and how many were dying. As Kavriel suddenly remembered Seth, he heard one of the Rav'agas soldiers in the temple shout, and his words chilled Kavriel to the bone.

"Heretics, remove your weapons and step out into view!"

Kavriel did the opposite, pulling himself underneath the pews and wondering if he could somehow slip into the cracks in the floorboards. As Kell drew two long knives that could pass for short swords from somewhere under his jacket, Kavriel cursed, realizing that he had left his father's blade in the other hall when he had joined in the tournament. It was entirely possible that the Rav'agas had already discovered it, but he hoped that maybe one of Kell's crew or even Seth might have taken it up to defend himself. Either way, he was of no help now. He thought about trying to slide under the pews toward the altar, but Kell was much too large to be able to follow, and he would not leave Kell to the Rav'agas.

The man must have been reading his thoughts, because he motioned to the space underneath the long rows of seats. Kavriel shook his head furiously, but Kell looked pointedly up to the ceiling, and when Kavriel followed his gaze he saw the large wheel of candles hanging above the entrance, a long cord used for raising and lowering the rustic chandelier running off at an angle. He followed the cord to a winch lever no more than a foot beyond the first row of benches, near the altar. He looked quickly back to

Kell, seeing the excitement in his eyes, and nodded.

Pulling himself along on his belly, Kavriel squirmed under the benches as fast as he could. The Rav'agas soldier was still shouting for whoever was hiding to reveal themselves, and Kavriel began to wonder why they were reluctant to come farther in, or even start turning up the pews one by one to flush them out.

Kavriel pulled himself free of the last bench and crouched in front of it, eyeing the heavily decorated altar. He suddenly understood why the Rav'agas remained overly cautious. This was their house of God, and the amount of wealth that had been pumped into the building for the sake of their belief was enough to keep them from trashing the place. Kavriel had heard about the Temples in Quetal, and how extravagant they had remained despite the minority population that still worshiped in them. It was as if they had to buy their way into the "modest" flock of The Way with gilded candelabras and linen altar cloths. Kavriel wondered if the Rav'agas soldiers had even taken off their boots before entering as he peered back under the pews at Kell's face and signalled that he had made it.

Kell opened his hand wide, and then closed it twice in rapid succession. Kavriel nodded, understanding the gesture for a ten-count. Count to ten, then drop the candle wheel. He looked up at the windlass, a mere three feet from him. The lever was upright, held in place by a balancer; all he had to do was release it and the chandelier would fall.

Kavriel counted, staring at the winch as if he might be able to move it with his mind. He reached ten just as the Rav'agas sounded as if their patience had just run out. Kavriel leapt up, hand outstretched for the lever. Something hissed through the air as he got to his feet, and when his hand hit the winch, a burning sensation ripped through his side.

Kavriel looked down, then up. A soldier was scrambling to reload his crossbow. He must have fired as soon as he caught Kavriel's movement, because the bow had been hastily aimed and the bolt had missed Kavriel's vitals.

Ignoring the pain, Kavriel slapped the winch and the lever spun out of control. The chandelier dropped. But the Rav'agas reacted quickly; only the last three soldiers to enter the temple, were caught in the metal and wood web of lit candles. It came down directly on their heads, and while their helmets might have saved them from splitting open like melons, they didn't do much to protect the men's necks; they snapped under the weight of the massive wheel.

The house built for prayer and humble worship suddenly became a vulgar battleground as the soldiers shouted and cursed as they spread out into the temple. *So much for their affinity to the God of Light*, Kavriel thought as he heard a loud grunt from Kell, only to see the entire long bench lift up from the floor. Nearly ten paces long and solid wood, Kell hurled it directly into the crowd of Rav'agas while they were still in a state of shock. Several more of the soldiers went down.

"Get out!" Kell shouted as the remaining soldiers charged forward, a handful of them throwing themselves on him, piling over him like a pack of dogs over a dropped leg of lamb. Kavriel heard the man curse as he fought, but there wasn't anything he could do without a weapon. His only chance was to find the others.

As Kavriel sprinted toward the door behind the altar he wondered if he had just witnessed Kell's death. He didn't have time to dwell on the terrible thought, for as he reached the door it smashed open into his face, pushing him back into the waiting arms of two Rav'agas soldiers. The two who had pushed the door immediately threw themselves on him.

The armored men smashed him around the head and chest to bring him down. He fell to his knees, instinctively throwing his arms up to protect himself as the onslaught continued. With each blow from a gauntleted fist, something seemed to grow inside him, overwhelming his fear. It was anger—anger at being attacked, anger for seeing the man he had confided in taken down by these soldiers who should not even be here, anger at the attacks on his friends. His past had been erased, those he had loved before vanished or killed. His father had hidden away in his home, dreading the truth of what his son might have become, and his friend Tess had been murdered by the righteous rule of the Patriarch, whose men would soon destroy him.

Something else grew inside Kavriel, like a faded circle of gray stretching out from him like an air bubble that was neither seen nor felt. When he reached a point where he could no longer feel the blows or feel the blood on his broken skin, the bubble had grown to its fullest—and this time Kavriel made it explode.

CHAPTER 28

It was a moment that would have either earned Captain Bellon a medal from the Patriarch for his loyalty, or the headsman's axe ordered by the chancellor for his direct disobedience. Either-or, it made no difference. The battle had been joined, and that was all that mattered now.

He drew his immense sword to engage a young man recklessly swinging a hammer, removing his head from his shoulders before the assailant came close. As he stepped over the corpse, he listened to the thunder and lightning crackling in the night sky. Symbolic—he had brought the storm to this village of heathen savages and pirates and his god was rewarding him with a show of brilliance and power that penetrated his soul. His men, four hundred strong, howled like wolves as they swept through Misam.

It hadn't taken much for Bellon to persuade Captains Failon and Janick to follow his command when he had notified them of his plans. Yes, he had ignored the direct command of the chancellor, but if so many others had been ready to fight this cause, then more than just he alone believed it was time for a change in the realm. Secluded Misam was not a secret well kept by the Quetalian savages who still refused to believe in the true order of things, and it was shameful that the chancellor had been sitting on his hands for so long while the rebels continued to nip away at the Patriarch's heels in this land that was and would always be his kingdom to claim. That would end tonight. Captain Bellon would make sure of it, even if he had to burn Misam to the ground. Enough was enough.

476

His armada of ships and army of Rav'agas pulled from the patrols had been hungry for the blood of nonbelievers, and he had opened up the pantry so they might feast. He understood that there would be repercussions to his actions, so he had ordered his men to take as many men alive if they could, since it was still against the Patriarch's regulations to completely eradicate a Quetalian community without formal advisement.

The Quetalians were fighting back, meaning he would be able to justify his actions here simply in his report of the resistance. Already the number of weapons he had seen on these "tamed" citizens of Quetal would be more than enough to persuade the deacons that his decision had been the right one. Who knew, maybe even the chancellor would understand what he had done and forgive his actions just to save his own face—not that Bellon cared. Once he had explained his discovery to the Patriarch and the Ay'vol Command, the chancellor would not remain on the throne for much longer. He had been a stain on the Patriarch's robes as dark as that of the Quetalian resistance, and his lack of initiative would not go unpunished.

Captain Bellon wiped the blood from his weapon, listening to the cries of the women in the falling rain. His men were ravenous, and would take as many opportunities as they could. He felt the old yearning for the freedom he remembered during those beautiful days of the Cleansing, when all was right with the world. It had been far too long.

The brutal attack the Misam people had launched on his men when they arrived in the harbor had now become a scattering of terrified peasants, running for their lives as the storm passed its peak and the wind began to die down. An ensign approached as he paused to think of his next strategy. Dark red blood stained the man from head to toe, and he was grinning. Captain Bellon listened as he made his report with pride in his voice.

"Captain, the counter-attack has been successful. Most of the unblessed have fallen or are captured. We are victorious."

Captain Bellon smiled as he listened. Beyond the ensign he could see the shadows of his men, moving along the road that was now lined with kneeling Quetalian prisoners or Quetalian dead.

With a sudden shout, a small group of Rav'agas ran toward the temple in the center of the town, their weapons drawn. Immediately Bellon's anger flared. Had the Quetalian heathens no limits to their savagery? Taking the battle to the house of God. . . He pushed the ensign aside and ran to the steep-roofed building.

There, he quickly sensed some kind of danger of unnatural origin coming from the sacred place. He pushed open one of the doors, the other hanging crookedly from one hinge, and stepped warily into the desecrated temple. The interior was lit by a growing fire that centered around the scattered candles of the wrecked chandelier, which lay atop several dead Rav'agas soldiers. The pews had been overturned, the vases and priceless ornaments had been toppled from their stands around the altar, which itself lay on its side. Yet that wasn't what startled Captain Bellon the most.

He stared in fury and horror at the man standing in a circle of Rav'agas corpses, standing like a butcher among mounds of mangled meat—a man who might have seen half a dozen years since his first growth of beard, standing like the vanquisher of trained Rav'agas with an empty look in his eyes, as if death too had reached him but had not yet decided what to do with him yet. His eyes were light and his hair almost fair, with a reddish tint like that of a demon Wylyn *Jag-wa-ru.* The firelight shining through the red background of the stained glass window behind him made the fiery highlights even more pronounced.

Captain Bellon gripped the hilt of his sword with a painful uncertainty, and as a second . . . or third group of Rav'agas soldiers came in to face this stranger, he realized why he felt as he did. The memory of the man in that Highland town who had ended the lives of a dozen trained Rav'agas soldiers rose in his mind; the memory of the horror that had led him to flee . . . This was like a dream of retribution he had wished for and wanted for so long, come to fruition.

He had found him. He had found him as he remembered, Bellon realized, watching the overconfident Rav'agas soldiers falling or being thrown aside as the man danced and struck like a cobra. This fight did not trouble him as it had in his nightmares after the first event. Perhaps he had prepared his mind for too long for this. Even so, he was hesitant to engage the man. He had trained with the best from Ay'vol City, and he knew every fighting technique, from those of the Seccacian Desert tribes to the *Gar'i'or-Fe'oam* women of the west peninsula. This man seemed to be using all of them together. He turned aside soldiers stronger and larger, using their size and power against them. They struggled to keep their feet while the man in the center pivoted and maneuvered.

He was fast, Bellon noted as he slowly approached, testing the weight of his broadsword in his grip. knowing that despite his own ability and dangerous skill, he would still not be quick enough for this young adversary.

He leaned the weapon against a bench, seeing that there was another Quetalian nearby. He was on his knees, held there by three Guardsmen who watched the man fighting, focused more on him than their prisoner. Not that it mattered. Bellon saw that the men were frightened, but their prisoner was far from ready to attack. He was barely conscious, one eye half closed while the other was already lumped out and red from the beatings he had received. He was a large man, and for a moment Bellon seemed to recognize him as some kind of outlaw on the mainland. There was certainly some reward for his capture, which was probably why the soldiers were guarding him so closely. Yet Bellon could see in their eyes that they would rather be anywhere but here in the temple. Bellon certainly understood why as the last of the soldiers went over the altar like a tossed sack of potatoes.

Bellon took the initiative and moved up closer, reaching for his twin daggers. He tossed one quickly at the man, who seemed to be regarding something more distant than Bellon or even the temple. His hand blurred upward and caught the dagger in mid-flight, tossing it aside without even a glance. Bellon was not surprised. This man had very precise talents, and he would not be easily bested.

Nearer now, Bellon studied him. The sudden realization came that this might not be the same man who had been in the village. That man had been larger, and darker haired. He had hoped too much; his own fear when he had faced the man before must have affected his memory. He paused, to which the man didn't react; he swayed on his feet like a drunk.

A dozen more Rav'agas soldiers flanked him. Bellon held them off with a raised hand, lifting up his dagger to show his opponent what he was planning. The man didn't seem to notice, but his eyes seemed to be struggling against their vacant look, blinking repeatedly. Bellon had seen similar things in the battlefield before—soldiers who had been wounded or fallen to infection losing all lucidity despite their ability to breathe and sometimes even walk. This man must have been suffering similarly. Yet there was an air of readiness about him, like a lion lying in wait as its prey trotted closer. That was something Bellon remembered about the other man, who must have had the same master, or perhaps was the master himself. The "wilders" from Wylyn had similar ways, but this man was no Wylyn, despite his reddish hair. No, there was something different about him. Bellon felt the excitement building in him as he licked his lips hungrily.

He took one step closer before rushing at the man in full attack. The Rav'agas soldiers in the room must have been waiting for that signal, as they all moved against the man together.

At first it was exciting, the soldiers hanging back while Bellon wielded his dagger against the quick-moving man, though Bellon didn't think they stayed beyond striking distance out of respect for his seniority. Several of them still had their crossbows locked onto the man, a target too close to miss, but Bellon was not interested in killing him. He needed him to find the one who had shamed him.

481

So he used techniques meant to maim and hinder an opponent's attack, a slice to the inner arm, a stab in the leg, and so on. But not one of his blows landed. His excitement turned to respect, then to actual fear as the man moved like a shadow, his hands darting out in a blur to clutch Bellon's knife hand. He pulled him in close, and as Bellon looked into the eyes of his opponent he felt something that he never would have expected. Horror.

With a twist of his grip, Bellon's dagger fell to the floor. A punch picked him up and sent him crashing back into the pews.

The soldiers attacked. Three separate crossbow bolts pierced the man's flesh at three different angles, all passing completely through flesh and bone and out the opposite side of his body. The man cried out and fell to his knees. A swordsman came at him, ready to end this madness.

Bellon was still on the floor, his lungs burning from the blow that took him directly in his breastplate. He wouldn't have believed that the armor could be dented by a bare fist, but it had. If he hadn't been wearing the breastplate, the man's fist would have gone through his chest.

What he saw next would haunt him till the end of his days, trying every ounce of faith that he had.

The man had not been killed by the crossbows, nor did the blade remove his head. He seemed to split himself out into sections just as the blade came down, only to smash onto the empty platform. Bellon could see that the man was still there, but at the same time he was several paces back, as a ripple in a pond might look, radiating out from a thrown rock. He lifted a candelabra from a point near the altar and thrust it like a spear into the soldier with the sword, then lifted the screaming man a good foot off the floor before tossing him aside. The other soldiers came in, and blood flowed.

Bellon struggled to his feet, wanting to help his dying soldiers, and grabbed his broadsword. He swung erratically at the man, who had just torn through a dozen men of his company. He did not know what he faced, just that this was not simply a well-trained fighter, but some unholy creature that had been banished from the Light.

The temple shook, as if absorbing his rage, and all air seemed to be sucked out of the room. The man continued to kill, attacking in a frenzy with his bare hands. Just as Bellon thought he might actually become pulled into the man like a hooked fish, the man leapt behind them onto the altar to escape the onslaught of swords and spears wielded by Rav'agas mad with fright. Bellon stepped back as if he had been pushed, and he saw the surviving soldiers move as if the same had happened to them. The man waited only a moment, gripping his head in his hands as if he had been struck there by one of the soldiers, but Bellon couldn't be sure.

Then the man did something unexpected. He turned toward the stained glass depiction of the Patriarch, about a man's height from the floor and four paces from him, and jumped. The window shattered as he hurtled through it.

Bellon and his men could only stare at the empty hole in the night that had once been the Patriarch's image. It was no coincidence that this creature of darkness had chosen that particular window for his escape.

CHAPTER 29

Blood ran from the shards of glass sticking out from his flesh, but Kavriel couldn't think about that right now. As a matter of fact he couldn't think of anything that mattered except to escape this place and get as far away as possible. He ran, unaware of the direction and not even sure if he was running at all. He could not feel anything but a tingling burn from his chest down to his legs and his eyes refused to focus clearly. The world was a muddy gray, and then it was a bright haze. The only thing that Kavriel knew for certain was the pain from the invisible arrows in his skull, pricking relentlessly into his mind. He thought he could hear himself screaming from within the cavity of his own head as he stumbled and fell, no longer able to see the ground below his feet, weary beyond measure.

He struggled to crawl out of the mud, and he could actually feel his blood and guts spilling out of him as if he were a split sack. He had been cut, stabbed, beaten, and shot and pain became the only reality. The hazy light became black, and Kavriel let his head drop to the mud as he exhaled his final breath.

He did not know how long he was in the darkness, how long he had been in the shadows of death, but he could not seem to completely surrender to it. It was as if he was in a deep sleep, but with nothing to dream. He wanted to stay there, stay *below* everything, in the silence. There was nothing for him in the nothingness, but he would not will himself away from it. He had the strength, a certainty that he could do it if he chose to leave, but he would not. It was an odd sensation, to have the power to either return to

484

existence or simply dive down deeper into the darkness. He was above the calm surface of a black ocean with neither land nor ship to save him from drowning. Yet he didn't need either. He was able to walk over the water forever, if he so desired. He was locked in absolute limbo, neither here nor there.

He realized he had been in this place before; everything seemed comfortably familiar. He couldn't think of when but he knew that it had been recently, and that he had been in this exact state of limbo for a very long time. *What is it, exactly?* He thought as he shifted the blackness around him with his mind.

The sky opened up to a bright blue and the sounds of life rushed in as he awoke, and for a second time in his existence, Kavriel pulled himself out of finality.

A reminder from the gentle breeze to begin to breathe reached a point of urgency, and Kavriel gulped the air in with heavy gasps. He coughed, taking in the world much too quickly, and rolled onto his side to vomit onto the grass. He was soaking wet, but not from his bleeding wounds or from the rain of a storm, but from the dew of a misty morning. The grass was wet, soft, and bitter cold. Kavriel pushed himself to his knees and saw that he was surrounded by shards of broken glass, all around where he had lain, like an outline. His cloths were in shreds, and as the cold morning air reached his flesh he started to shiver.

He rose, testing his legs, and stood running his hands over his body. The wounds he had taken in his fight with the Rav'agas were gone, not a scratch on him, his body healed completely as he slept. It was as if he were no longer a human man, but some kind of puppet controlled by an unseen master who pulled his strings when he was required to fight and repaired him when he had been broken. Kavriel could think of no other answer to his state of being.

He could remember everything that had happened in the temple when the Rav'agas had attacked, and he had given himself over to some other part of himself when he could no longer tolerate the attacks. That was when he was somehow pulled back into the shadows of his mind while another came and assumed his body. It had happened in Silver Wood, it had happened on the Rav'agas patrol ship, it had happened in the tournament, and it had happened against the Rav'agas soldiers in the temple. Kavriel had forgotten who and where he had been in the last five years, but someone had not forgotten him.

This was not simply a matter of a sick mind any longer. There was another soul in him who was dangerous and unstoppable. By the Creator, what kind of darkness was this? Kavriel looked at his hands, slowly ceasing their shaking, and he couldn't be entirely sure that they were his own or if they were that *other* person.

Clouds passed over the sun, and the world around Kavriel became sullen and lifeless. He looked up to the sky and nearly fell back in shock, seeing immense mountains of rock rising up above him into the heavens toward the east. He had never seen such a range in his entire life. It continued endlessly to the north and south, as if the world had suddenly thrown up a giant wall of jagged rock. The black and gray peaks rose through the clouds as if to prove that nothing was safe in this realm. It was the most frightening and at the same time the most majestic landscape Kavriel had ever seen. He realized he was standing before the Oenes.

As the clouds passed, the bright sunlight illuminated the crevices and crags of the towering wall, streaks of shining white crisscrossing the highest peaks. Kavriel shivered just thinking about the kind of cold that was at the top. He smiled like a fool, thinking that this must be what an ant felt like when he looked up. The world was so much larger than he could ever imagine.

Dropping his gaze, Kavriel began to notice his surroundings, and the unfamiliarity of them brought back his fear. He was no longer in Misam, that was for certain. The humid forests surrounding the bayside village were nowhere near where he was standing now. As Kavriel turned in circles, trying to find his bearings, he realized that he had no idea where he was. He was lost in a new wilderness, colder and rougher than he had ever known before, with nothing to protect his skin besides clothing that had been shredded by the window he . . . or the other. . . had jumped through.

How long ago was that? he wondered, thinking that he had dropped from exhaustion sometime during the night outside the town. Yet that would have been impossible, the Rav'agas would have found him. Even with the abilities he seemed to have, he would not have been able to hold off the Rav'agas forever. At least two dozen men had come at him, including a higher-ranking commander who seemed have a strange interest in fighting him. Kavriel frowned, remembering that he had witnessed all of this as if he were an outside observer, looking in from a set of windows that were his own eyes.

He focused on the present, knowing that whatever had occurred, he was clearly not in the vicinity of Misam any longer and therefore must be safe for the moment. He might not understand the strangeness around him, but whoever this other person Kavriel might be, his sole purpose was protecting him—or them—from harm. He could only hope that he had merely been gone for a night, or at the most several days. He shook his head, wishing that he hadn't forgotten his father's blade, or at least not his father's maps. All of his possessions were gone. He would have to make do with what he found where he was now.

Yet where was he, and how had he gotten here? He looked at the impressive range long and hard, recalling the maps in his mind from years of daydreaming of visiting the Oenes. He knew that the mountains were like a solid barricade stretching the entire eastern edge of Quetal. Those to his right would go directly north into the North Sea, passing close to Misam. He might not be as far away from that as he imagined, but there was something itching away inside him that seemed to be urging him to follow the Oenes south. If he did he would eventually reach the Viliros River and the border of Ciele. Rav'agas was beyond that, but he had no intention of going there. He would reach Loellen long before that, but he knew from the geography of the land that Loellen was at least a month distant from Misam.

He wouldn't reach *that* without any clothing besides the torn shirt and pants that he wore. He was thankful for the jacket that he still had on—well, what was left of it, he thought as he reached into one of the pockets. His fingers touched the old book from Xavr's library; despite all that had happened, he still had that. He pulled it out, letting the sunlight dance on the worn leather as he looked at the cover for a long time without actually opening up the book. He studied the symbols, the six stars circling the sun. Kavriel suddenly realized what they meant. They represented the group of followers that believed they were neither gods nor mortal men, but something in between—The Watch.

Kavriel mouthed the names of the members as he gently touched each of the six stars, as if they were tiny life forms. He was still missing one name, but he understood who the sun represented: the God of Light. Even a child in the first years of study knew that icon of Rav'agas faith. Yet the stars were something different altogether. Not children of the earthly realm, but a power in the heavens, a being almost equal to the Creator, perhaps slightly less powerful. Who were those people, and why had no one ever have heard of them before?

Rationality told him that it was only a story, but another part of Kavriel believed something different. Was that the other Kavriel? The Kavriel who could fight and kill like a master warrior? He didn't know how he could possibly answer that question on his own, but he must have already known the answer . . . somehow.

He looked into the Oenes Range with a heavy heart, and focused on a part of the mountains that seemed to be slightly different than the others. It took a moment for Kavriel to understand what he was looking at, and he started walking up a small incline in front of him. When he reached the top he suddenly understood where he was, and why that section of the mountains had looked different.

There were man-made structures, some kind of

camp-like settlement, built directly into the face of a mountain. The camp was still a good day's walk away, but he thought he could see the tiny dots of what might be people moving around the structures. It was definitely too small to be the mighty city of Loellen, and Kavriel actually breathed a sigh of relief for that small fact, since that would have meant he'd travelled a month without being aware.

Still, he did not feel safe when he realized what he was seeing. It was the place that Kell had been planning to attack before the Misam leaders had sent the fighters before him, the place he had been planning to reach before the Rav'agas attacked. He was looking at the former camp used during excavation of the famous Oenes Caverns, where the Loellen Scrolls had been discovered by Saire and his team. Yet now it had been transformed from a place of science and research to a prison of suffering and denial. Kavriel was looking at the Crypt.

As he realized this, Kavriel also noticed that he was not alone. He stood in a small glen, and from it, about two hundred meters from him, a dirt road rose and cut along the side of the range. On that road was a moving black blanket, flocks of crows and vultures, agitated and noisy. He was surprised he hadn't noticed their screeching and cawing before, but now that he saw them he could hear nothing but the thousands of ravenous creatures as they fought over a feast. Kavriel did not wish to investigate further but he had a dreadful suspicion than the creatures were feasting on human corpses, dozens of copses, buried underneath the rolling blanket of black. He knew there were murdered people under the birds, and knew somehow that they were the same group that Kell had planned to lead into the Crypt to liberate and at the same time repopulate it with his own people.

Months of preparation had been wiped out in a single battle that the Rav'agas had won. By now the Southlanders would be bringing things back to normal, forgetting that this attempt had ever happened. Kavriel swallowed as he thought of Kell and Seth, whom he had abandoned back in Misam, wondering what had become of them—and, strangely, how he'd somehow "materialized" in this exact location.

He felt something stir behind him, and a voice whispered inside Kavriel's head, *Turn around.*

He spun to face a man he'd never expected to see ever again. Standing ten paces away, he was pulling back a bowstring nocked with an arrow aimed directly at Kavriel's head.

"Ulin!" Kavriel cried in recognition.

The blonde man, dressed entirely in black, did not lower the bow; he barely acknowledged that he had been identified.

Kavriel looked straight at the arrowhead pointing at him, and he raised his hands slowly out from his sides to show that he was no threat. Ulin looked him over with one eye, the other still closed to sight his target more accurately. He didn't let the arrow fly, and Kavriel hoped that was a good thing.

"You." Ulin's voice was neither affirmative nor certain, just tired.

Kavriel nodded, blinking rapidly. He'd been staring at the arrow for too long. He let his eyes drift over the man who had been one of his crewmates, and saw that the outfit was black because it had been burned recently. There was a nasty red scar over half of Ulin's head, the blonde hair seared off. The rest of the man's face looked exhausted. Kavriel wasn't sure how long he might have been standing there with his taut bowstring, but by the way it wavered Kavriel knew that the man was about to let go. Kavriel waited patiently in silence, hoping Ulin would drop the weapon entirely, yet there was another part of him that actually hoped that the man would let the arrow fly . . . if only to prove his theory about what he had become.

Fortunately Ulin slowly lowered the weapon to his side. The struggle to have kept it up was obvious in his expression and for a moment Kavriel thought that the man might actually fall to his knees. He did not, instead walking up to him with a strange look on his face that Kavriel couldn't be quite sure was rage or relief.

As he came within arm's reach of Kavriel, who still had not moved a muscle, Ulin forced a grin. "Well, well." He snorted. "I should have figured it was you."

Kavriel blinked, swallowing the ball of tension that had formed in his throat. He watched Ulin walk casually past him to the ridge to study the Crypt, leaning heavily on one leg, which reminded Kavriel of his father's limp. Ulin must have been hurt badly in the attack from the Rav'agas, but there was a powerful will emanating from him, like an odor that mingled with the smell of his burnt clothing.

As if realizing this himself, Ulin suddenly dropped the bow and removed his blackened jacket, letting it too drop to the ground. "We cannot be found like this." He spoke almost dreamily, as if he had not yet come to terms with finding Kavriel. Kavriel had the same thoughts, but only waited patiently. There was an air about him that Kavriel couldn't identify with certainty—fatigue, or insanity? He must have been through horror. "They will kill us on sight if they find us," Ulin continued. He looked back to the blanket of crows on the road. "We should be able to find some armor."

"Ulin, what happened at Misam?" Kavriel finally asked. This strange show had gone on long enough. Only a moment ago, Ulin had been about to kill him.

Ulin continued to gaze out over the road, but he spoke. "I have been tracking the soldiers for days. I was right about what was going to happen, but I was too late. To late to warn them. They were trapped in the middle. Even the guardians of the Crypt knew what was happening; they had been warned ahead of time. The soldiers went out to meet them." He now looked at Kavriel, dangerously angry. "They didn't have a chance, you understand. They were slaughtered like animals and when they tried to retreat to Misam, they were felled by the arrows. I have been searching the hills for other survivors." He glowered. "Where in the name of Creation did you come from?"

Kavriel suddenly understood the man's behavior. He wasn't insane, but he wasn't too far away. He had escaped Misam with his life when countless others had perished. Ulin had already suspected something bad was going to happen, but he'd gone along with the plans anyway. Now he was trapped by the Rav'agas along the Oenes Range like the two hundred fighters who had thought they might stand a chance against the Crypt. Kavriel also understood Kell's frustration, for if the men had waited, there would have been a greater number, if only to defend themselves against the Rav'agas who had surprised them on the bay. Kavriel had no idea how many Rav'agas soldiers had attacked, but he could only believe their numbers were greater. Who knew what had happened to the people of Misam proper, if they were taken or simply killed.

That the Crypt had been forewarned was terrifying news; he knew now that Ulin had been hoping to find survivors who had fled the attack. But why was Ulin watching him so carefully? Kavriel became uneasy under Ulin's scrutiny; he looked at him with the same expression the Rav'agas soldier had given him in the temple. He remembered what Kell had told him of Ulin's history, and he wondered if the business with his brother wasn't all that settled yet. He decided to come straight out with it.

"I'm not who you think I am, Ulin, and neither is my brother. We had nothing to do with what happened to your father and if—"

"I don't care what you claim to be, villager," Ulin interrupted in a menacing tone. "I believe what I see with my own eyes, and what I have seen is a man who claims to be one thing but is obviously something else. I cannot trust you, and I refuse to believe anything you say to try to convince me. You are like a plate of fresh meat set out in a forest of wolves, and every which way you go, death seems to follow." Grimacing, he took a step toward Kavriel. "You are something different from the rest of us, that is clear. I'm not some fool peasant who has decided to pick up a rake and strike at the Rav'agas, and neither am I some criminal of Quetal, using this occupation to justify my actions. I am nobility, from a family of respect and honor that was sacrificed to the chancellor for his chance at capturing the wind. Don't you understand anything yet, boy?" he growled.

Kavriel thought to step back, but was afraid that if he did, Ulin would lose whatever control he was clinging to.

"You are the Ghost," Ulin went on. "You, me, and everyone involved in this god-forsaken fight that we continue to wage. The Rav'agas murdered my father, my mother, and all of my cousins after the Cleansing order was issued, and that order was issued because of people like us, who believe our freedom is worth more than our families that we sacrifice. You just happen to have a target painted on your back that might make a difference to the Rav'agas. At least that's what I believed . . . until I knew what you could do."

He paused, narrowing his eyes. Kavriel couldn't find anything to say. As if expecting that, Ulin nodded, a twisted grin on his face. His eyes fell to Kavriel's shirt, shredded by glass and crossbow bolts. "You have a different kind of secret that you are hiding. No man should be able to fight like you do, and every man can die." His face became more somber, as if he were a child who had just discovered that the world was not as fair as he believed. "I don't think things are quite so simple for you."

He turned before Kavriel could reply. He was stunned at what the man had told him. He'd known some of the man's history from Kell, but he'd had no idea how much it tore him up inside. The man had nothing left. His nation, his home, and even his family had all been taken from him, and the only person he might have considered a friend had been either killed or captured in the temple fight, while Kavriel escaped. No wonder the man seemed so distant, yet so angrily focused at the same time. Kavriel might be able to relate, but nowhere near this level. At least he knew that some of what he had been in the past had survived. Ulin was a corpse.

"I don't know how you managed to get here before me." Ulin spoke more to the mountains than to him. "You weren't captured with the others, and you can't fly." He cast another glance at him, just to make sure Kavriel understood that his flip remark wasn't meant to be humorous. "Yet you are here, proving my point." He grunted, and Kavriel suddenly felt very cold. "Still, perhaps we can make some use of this."

He reached for his belt, unbuckling a scabbard that had been one of three the man wore, not including the double harness under his vest that had been stocked with those flat-bladed knives. He tossed the weapon over to Kavriel, who caught it with a grim smile, recognizing the hilt. He pulled it half out from the borrowed scabbard just to make sure he wasn't dreaming. "This is my father's!" he exclaimed, and looked at Ulin with grateful admiration. "How did you find this?"

Ulin turned to him as if he had said yet another stupid thing. "You left it behind, foolish child. Didn't your father ever teach you to respect his weapons?"

Kavriel shook his head. "No, he thought they were too dangerous for me to be around." He was being honest, but his words must have sounded humorous to Ulin, who started laughing as if that was the funniest thing he had ever heard.

"Indeed," he chortled when the laughter died down. "Your father sounds like a smart man." He chuckled again, and Kavriel smiled before buckling the scabbard at his waist.

He must have looked quite odd, he reflected, ragged and half torn apart, with an officer's blade strapped at his side. "So," he remarked when he was done, "what do we do now?"

Ulin looked at him, his expression devious, and Kavriel wondered again if perhaps he had been too hasty, thinking that the man hadn't fallen into madness yet. "We follow the plan," Ulin hissed through clenched teeth. "We break them out."

CHAPTER 30

Kavriel couldn't get near the corpses, even if the birds hadn't been there protecting them. The smell was too terrible. He wondered why the Rav'agas had simply left them out to rot in the mountain sun and not put them to fire, at least for the sake of their health if not out of respect for the dead. Mercifully, there weren't nearly as many dead as he imagined but even one Quetalian body that lay scattered across the hard-packed road was one too many. Ulin had been right; these must have been the workers-turned-soldiers, who had tried to flee when they'd realized that their plan had been compromised. The massive number of crows and vultures was simply due to the lack of anything else to easily eat. Or at least Kavriel assumed.

They moved on, keeping above the road by a western ridgeline that seemed to form a smaller incline along the mountains like a receding wave. They weren't completely hidden from any eyes on the road, but it was safer than trying to approach the camp directly. They reached the camp in late afternoon, as the sun painted the snow-covered higher elevations pink and purple while it crept toward the horizon behind them. Kavriel and Ulin lay on their bellies, watching the activity in the camp. They had not found any usable clothing from the dead, and they were forced to lie on the cold ground in what they had. Ulin had not reclaimed the burnt jacket that he had removed earlier, but the growing cold did not seem to be affecting him as much as it was Kavriel. He had another kind of heat warming his body from the inside, and Kavriel listened anxiously to the man steadily tapping on his knife blades while it was all Kavriel could do to keep his teeth from chattering.

Below, armored Rav'agas moved repetitively around a bulging half-moon barricade that had been recently constructed out of sharpened spears and pikes. The Rav'agas had been expecting an attack, but it had already come, so there were few Guardsmen outside. The camp had been cleverly constructed out of a dozen habitable homes and sheds circling a larger work facility. Kavriel wasn't sure what he'd expected the place he had read about many times to actually look like. It was about what he'd pictured in his mind, only like most other things, it was a bit smaller in real life than in his imagination. It was so far away from anything else, an insignificant point along the road that looked no different from the hundreds of miles stretching north and south of the Oenes Range.

He knew that the cluster of caves that dotted the mountains were why it was important, although if they were there, Kavriel couldn't see them from this ridge. *Possibly near the road I might,* he thought. It would have taken a keen eye to discover them unless you knew where to look. How Saire had done it, Kavriel would never guess.

"One hundred, thirty-six," Ulin whispered, disrupting Kavriel's focus as he handed the spyglass over to him so he could count for himself.

Kavriel could hardly believe it. "In all?" he asked, beginning to count the black and gold uniforms below.

"That I can see, yes," Ulin answered with a discouraged grunt.

Kavriel had come close to that number when he put the instrument down. "There will be no place for them," he commented, recalling their conversation on the ridge about the Crypt. The soldiers were temporary, having come in from Misam with prisoners of their own after crushing the Quetalians between them. They would soon leave, but Kavriel and Ulin couldn't just sit outside in the cold until that happened. They would have to find a way into the camp for shelter, if for nothing else.

He needed inspiration. "Do you think Seth and Kell are in there?" He asked, remembering with a surge of hope what Ulin had told him, that there was no trace of the crew when the Rav'agas had moved south, but there were quite a few prisoners to add to the camp, including those two.

Ulin considered it. "I'm not sure about your friend. He's not young enough to avoid death, but I don't think they would have just slit his throat someplace on the road, either." He looked to Kavriel for his reaction, and Kavriel gave him a frown. Ulin only chuckled. "The Rav'agas are animals, but they are efficient when it comes to their protocol. The prisoners are considered a single entity rather than individuals. They will be tried together, forced to the caverns together, or killed together. Yet it is still too early. Messengers have not arrived back from Teltraum and the chancellor would want to know about this. Kell, on the other hand, has enough bounties on his head that he should be kept in almost kingly fashion by the steward himself."

Kavriel nodded, looking at the Oenes back deeper into the camp. He made out structures built high into the bluffs, like watch turrets linked together by rope bridges. One in particular was larger than the rest and constructed with stone from the mountain. Or maybe he was just looking at one of the cavern entrances and hadn't known what it was before. It was strange, but by looking at the camp from another perspective, it seemed as if the wooden homes and sheds were not the first community to be there, as if the mountainous alcove had sheltered similar camps for hundreds of years. It would make sense; if the scrolls had been found in the caverns, then obviously there had been people living there before.

One of the passages in the memoirs he had been reading suddenly popped into his head: *The mountains will bury the secrets of my actions until the time comes when I will need to reclaim them, if ever.* He shivered at the thought that this could be the place the writer had been referring to. Were the Temscript Scrolls part of those *secrets of my actions* that were being kept hidden from the Sa'rire person? He wasn't certain why, but Kavriel suspected that he was getting closer to understanding a great many things.

"How do we get in?" he asked, keeping his eyes trained on the large central turret, avoiding the nagging similarities between his life and the book.

Ulin nodded toward the Guardsmen. "We will need to be disguised, at least long enough for me to find out where they are keeping the others, and set them free."

He was serious. Kavriel wasn't sure he was entirely comfortable with what they actually were planning to do, but he knew that he owed his friend enough to try to save him. "You think that this can still happen?" he asked, not needing to elaborate.

Ulin understood well enough. He scowled. "Everyone needs to fight."

Kavriel frowned, feeling that inside chill again.

"How many Quetalians are here?" he asked, remembering a little of what Kell had told him.

Ulin shrugged. "I don't know, one hundred—maybe less, maybe more. It was never intended for this."

"Why does the chancellor even bother?" Kavriel wondered

Ulin laughed heartily. "It's not him, but that damned Patriarch. Ever since those things were found, the man can't seem to let it go of the place. He even has his most trusted *dog* keeping watch. It was his idea, really, to keep the place operational. Using it as a location for stashing away prisoners of war is simply a bonus." He snorted.

Kavriel didn't think that he understood the entire picture. Sure, the location might be ideal for a prison camp, since it seemed to have been some kind of tiny village before even the explorers. It was at a crossroads between Misam to the north and Loellen to the south, and Teltraum to the west. He turned in that direction and noticed a wide road leading back over the hills and valleys toward the capitol. That was when it struck him. He looked at the other road, seeing the signs of use but essentially a narrow track in reasonable condition.

Trade between the larger towns and cities was important. Yet why was there another road *here,* going directly west to Teltraum at the same place as the Oenes Cavern camp? The road was in slightly worse shape than the other, but it was wider and more defined. It was a principal road, leading from Teltraum directly east into the impenetrable Oenes Mountains. It didn't make sense, unless . . .

"What is past this place?" Kavriel asked as his eyes found the stone turret again. Its age compared to the others was obvious.

Ulin thought about it, and his face grew tight. "I'm not sure. When my father was chairman there was a commission formed to explore the region. For some reason it never went through. I never could understand why."

"So there is something more to the Oenes?" Kavriel asked, remembering reading theories about the possibility of settlements beyond the mountains.

Ulin nodded. "Absolutely, although I've never seen it myself." He pointed up to the turret that Kavriel had been looking at. "That place is older than the rest, as you can see. It is now the steward's post, if the book can be trusted, and there are man-made roads that go farther into the range." He looked curiously at Kavriel. "How much do you know about this place?"

Kavriel shook his head. "Not much, actually, besides the scrolls. Is there more to it?" he asked, hoping that Ulin might know something he didn't.

But it was Ulin's turn to shake his head. "That's just it. I think there is, but I don't know about it, and I have been in some pretty high circles. There are too many secrets in politics, I think." Ulin spat on the ground. "I think I might have ended up being a fighter with or without the Rav'agas occupation."

Kavriel looked at the knives adorning Ulin's vest as he nodded. The man had been trained for fighting, that was certain, but there was still quite a bit Kavriel did not know about him. There would be time later for questions, if they got out of this alive. At least the man didn't seem to be angry with him any longer. "Are the Rav'agas planning on exploring?" he asked.

Ulin laughed again. "I don't think so. The steward's quarters are in the farthest outpost, which is a little strange. There are his guards and his prisoners in the camp below him, but behind there are dark and unknown roads. It seems stupid to leave it so open."

Kavriel thought about it. "Unless he already knows what is past there," he suggested.

Ulin let out a grunt of agreement. "Possibly. That bastard Saire has been pulling everyone's strings for long enough that maybe he does know a—"

"Wait!" Kavriel grabbed Ulin's arm. Ulin glared at him but Kavriel wasn't about to let this go. "What name did you say?" he asked.

Ulin looked at him suspiciously. "Saire," he repeated, and immediately Kavriel felt the arrows striking his skull. The world was much too large for it to seem so small. "Heard of him, have you?" Ulin asked sarcastically.

Everybody knew Saire, especially a man whose father had been an overseer, even if it was in some sleepy Highland town. He wondered if Ulin might know anything about what had happened all those years ago, but it seemed more important to wonder why of all the people, General Saire was the man he was heading toward, like a moth to a flame. Kavriel believed in coincidences, not fate, but he must have been cursed, if he had to face that man again. Was there a reason, or was he somehow invisibly roped to the man? He studied the turret again in silence as Ulin studied the rhythmic steps of the Guardsmen below. "Saire is a respected Quetalian general." He spoke in a tone so soft, there was no indication that he believed his own words.

Ulin smiled. "Yes, that's what we were told as well. Funny how things end up, don't they? If I believed that there were bastards out there who lived on pure luck alone, then that man would make the top of my list."

Kavriel thought that a strange thing to say, and when he asked about it Ulin shrugged. "The man is more of a thorn in the chancellor's side than we are," he replied, "yet he must have some kind of wealth behind him in order to be separated yet completely involved in politics at the same time. He has always done what he wants, and seems to be perfect in damn-near everything. My father loved him, and apparently so does the Patriarch."

"He murdered my friends," Kavriel stated, not necessarily speaking honestly but knowing that it was Saire who had been behind all of his problems.

Ulin nodded as if he was stating a simple fact. "Then perhaps you might have a chance for vengeance, little Ghost," he sneered.

Kavriel felt dread that went much deeper than anything his colleague might say. "Why do you think money has anything to do with it?" he asked.

Ulin looked at him as if he thought he was a fool. "Because money *always* has something to do with it. Money or power, and money generally can create power."

Kavriel shrugged. He was still the son of an overseer, and had heard firsthand how certain things were resolved in the government despite the sheer tastelessness of it. "What is he doing here as the steward?" he asked, trying to find his connection in all of this.

"As I said, he is one of the Patriarch's favorite pets, as he was my father's. He was always able to get ahold of resources that even the library scholars did not know about, like he was stashing away information that he would dish out in pieces, like feeding table scraps to hungry dogs. He somehow must have convinced the Patriarch not to have him killed. He does seem to know a lot, and the Patriarch is a curious one."

Kavriel grimaced, thinking of how Xavr seemed to be something of the same thing. "This is about Ciele, isn't it?"

Ulin frowned. "No, this is about finding more scrolls . . . or something that the scrolls mention. I don't know; Saire was the expert and we were just the simple fools who jumped at his requests. The chancellor does not think very highly of him, which I am not certain is either good or bad for us. There are rumors that Saire is only here to watch the chancellor for the Patriarch, but in his own way, by keeping his head in the mountains."

Kavriel tapped the book that was hidden away in his pocket. *The mountains will bury the secrets of my actions until the time comes when I will need to reclaim them, if ever.* He recalled, pressing his lips together. *Sa'rire should not suspect that, but he will most likely search for me or the scrolls in time. I truly hope he never finds them, otherwise he will find the urns of Father's remains.*

Suddenly, like a flash of lightning, Kavriel understood what the book had been talking about, and it scared him like nothing he had ever known before. Saire had been looking for those urns in the mines, and either he had found them or Xavr had put them there to be found.

The urns of the father, Kavriel repeated, remembering more of the verse. Six of them, like the six pieces of the Creator when he had been destroyed by Sa'rire of The Watch. Six urns, two of them emptied during the fight while the four others . . . .Saire had not stopped what he had been doing since the beginning. He was still searching for those remains of the father. He must have known about the sect of The Watch. He either had books similar to Xavr's or he had heard about it from another source.

The man's background was sketchy. Kavriel understood how vast amounts of wealth could buy a background. He knew something that he thought of as extremely important, but he kept himself outside of the politics of the nations, which he only used when he had to. He was like a puppet master, but could easily let the puppets dance on their own while he did other things, or, like a gardener, plant the seeds that he could reap later at his leisure. Regardless, he thought himself outside the rules of man, and it was because of him that Kavriel was where he was today, with no memory, some kind of split personality, and family and friends who were either gone or dead.

He glared at the stone turret high in the mountains as the anger began to burn slowly inside him. He stopped being concerned with the cold, and was only concerned with how to reach that high place, if there was a chance "Steward" Saire might be there, studying his books and his scrolls with bloodstained hands. He had been powerful, and a dangerous fighter, but Kavriel knew now that he could dance the same dance, whether he controlled it or someone else did. Maybe that was his purpose here, and why it now

507

started to feel as if he truly was fated to face Saire once again. They had unfinished business, and he had been prepared to finish it. It was the only explanation.

"How long do we wait?" Kavriel asked, his voice urgent.

"As soon as the sun falls, we move." Ulin cast a glance his way. "Still think that your blade is too dangerous?"

Kavriel smiled with newfound confidence. "We'll just have to find out."

CHAPTER 31

Easy was not the word Kavriel would have chosen for what he and Ulin had done once the valley and the mountain wall darkened toward night. Childs play would be a better term. Either the Rav'agas had assumed that there was absolutely no danger left in the land, that they let themselves be caught so quickly by the black shapes that crept up behind them, or Kavriel and Ulin were walking straight into a trap. The mission invigorated Kavriel, but he wasn't ready to murder unsuspecting Rav'agas just yet. He was still an overseer's son, so any blood on his hands would at least be honest blood. Ulin had either lost or didn't care about such ethics; Kavriel grimaced as the man ran one of his knives across the throat of a Guardsman relieving himself against a tree. The man was still going as he dropped in a heap to the ground, and the only remorse he heard from Ulin was that he wasn't happy to wear piss-stained armor, let alone bloodstained.

Kavriel had used a heavy stone on the guard he had been assigned, and he felt less guilt in listening to the slow breathing from the unconscious man as he removed his armor. "You should kill him," Ulin said while watching Kavriel don the man's ware. "He will either wake with frostbite or the wolves eating at him, or not at all. At least give him a quick death."

Kavriel ignored him, though in the back of his mind he knew what Ulin said was true. Still, he used his tattered clothing to swaddle the unconscious guard like a newborn babe, so he stood some chance. Kavriel also left the man's weapon, for protection against wolves. Ulin just shook his head.

They snuck past the watch towers carved into sections of the mountain and entered a large courtyard encircled by sheds and homes. Firelight burned inside, making their windows glow like the eyes of giants while illuminating across the courtyard. Kavriel and Ulin stood behind a stack of crates while Ulin decided where they should be heading. Kavriel was thinking how quiet it was, despite all the men who were supposed to be imprisoned there.

When Kavriel commented about it, Ulin frowned. "I'm not sure. They could all be inside, or locked up in another area. The logbook did not have as many details about the camp as we'd hoped. I would assume that the company from Misam would keep together." He nodded at a long building that Kavriel had thought was a stable, at the north end of the courtyard. Noises emanated from it. "There, I would imagine."

"Where are the cells?" Kavriel asked, thinking about why they were there in the first place.

Ulin waved his hand. "All around us."

Kavriel looked, finally seeing the dozens of small black cave entrances up the mountainside. He knew he was looking at the famous Oenes Caverns. In another time Kavriel would have been ecstatic, to be part of something so historic, yet now the only thing he could think of was how silly his question had been to Ulin. Of course the prisoners would be kept in the caverns. There was little reason to drag them down to the courtyard, where they might have a chance to escape, even if there was no place to go. He nodded. "How do we get to them?"

Ulin nodded over to a makeshift staircase constructed of flat boards and rope that climbed to the cavern nearest the ground. Two torches on the posts anchoring the base of the staircase illuminated the mountain face, but the hole remained black, like some entrance into the underworld. It reminded Kavriel of the mine back in Mir, and he wondered again about all the similarities in his life leading to this point.

"The caves are connected, more or less," Ulin answered, watching a group of Rav'agas soldiers who were standing near an alley that led away from the mountain. "The bridges above us were built to connect openings so it would be easier to work and study." He nodded over to the side where the soldiers were standing. "Over there is the passage to the steward's quarters. You see those stairs out of the mountainside?"

Kavriel dragged his eyes away from the Rav'agas, who seemed to be exchanging amusing stories. He looked at the impressive staircase that had been carved into the mountainside, climbing hundreds of feet up to the steward's turret. He knew that was where Saire was, and he felt the urge to run up those stairs to confront him once and for all, but that would draw too much unwanted attention. And he didn't want to risk being asked any questions when he passed the Rav'agas soldiers; he was now dressed like them, but he certainly was not one of them.

"Stay here a moment." Ulin moved past Kavriel, watching a second pair of Rav'agas that had suddenly appeared by the cavern entrance.

He sounded curious, and Kavriel wondered what might have caused it. A burst of laughter from the group of soldiers near the alley drew his eye, and he glimpsed something black moving behind them, like a shadow. And something else, like a man dressed in a black cowl. That figure jumped over several crates nearby. Not sure what to make of it, Kavriel walked calmly over to Ulin, who was immersed in a conversation with the two Rav'agas. His mastery of the language surprised Kavriel; Ulin didn't even have a hint of his accent.

The Rav'agas didn't acknowledge Kavriel, who listened in on the conversation, picking up maybe half of it. He had learned Rav'agas from his father and the other elders, but there'd never been a native speaker among them, so the speed and fluidity of the language was always lost on him.

Ulin didn't seem to be affected by that at all; he nodded in genuine concern at what the two men were saying. After a moment, he nodded to them again and they moved away. Ulin spoke something rapid to Kavriel while the soldiers were still in earshot. He didn't get all of it, but he knew that he was supposed to "bring over" or "throw over" whatever it was he was "carrying" or "pulling." He nodded, understanding that it was simply a ruse.

"What is it?" he asked when the Rav'agas were gone and Ulin's expression turned anxious, though he was trying to appear calm.

"We have to move fast. There is about to be a fight here," Ulin stated.

Kavriel instinctively looked around him. "What are you talking about?"

Ulin grabbed him by the arm and guided him toward the caverns. More Rav'agas soldiers appeared, most with weapons drawn. Kavriel became worried. "Ulin, what is happening?"

Before he could say anything more, he saw what looked like three large spiders rappelling down the side of the mountain face toward the courtyard. They were men, of course, dressed totally in black. As unease crept through him, Kavriel wondered if he might be the only one to noticed this. He wasn't.

Ulin cursed loudly and drew both blades from their scabbards just before the rappelling men touched down with incredible agility. They drew weapons of their own and immediately engaged the Rav'agas. As more Rav'agas and more black-dressed attackers appeared out of nowhere, the courtyard became a killing ground. Though he didn't understand what had happened, Kavriel had no choice but to bring up his father's blade. A small group of Rav'agas soldiers pushed him aside, moving in to engage the black attackers.

He felt a hand grab his arm and pull him quickly toward the cavern platform. Ulin raced him up it and only when they were in its temporary shelter did Ulin speak. "Of all the luck!" he shouted as his eyes darted back and forth at the action below. "I didn't think this would happen."

Confused, Kavriel asked, "Ulin, who are these people?" He ducked low and swung inside the cavern opening as a wayward arrow smashed against the rock outside.

"Hielias," Ulin spat as he too pressed his back to the inner wall. "Mountain men, scavengers. They live like nomads out past the wall and attack smaller companies all along the range whenever they get too close." He paused,

513

seeming to count the number of men in the courtyard below, which probably numbered close to fifty. There was a hint of amusement in his tone. "I've never seen this many in one tribe before. They must have seen the ambush and figured for looting. We've had problems with them in the estates around Loellen, but I didn't think that they could get so thick. It might be our lucky day, after all, Ghost."

Kavriel was dumbstruck. He had never heard of such a thing. "So…whose side are they on? Ours?" he asked. Ulin didn't answer, and his expression revealed nothing.

"We have to get to the prisoners." He changed the subject, and he quickly disappeared into the dark cavern behind them. Kavriel had no choice but to follow. His mind was turning in circles, trying to understand any of this. He had never heard of these Hielias people before, not even from his father or from Femaor. He had heard of similar situations in other rural parts of Quetal, but they were generally exaggerated details of the same kind of people Kavriel had been travelling with—smugglers and pirates. Tribal mountain men? Anyone in his right mind might not believe such a thing, and why would such a people want to live in such a desolate place? Still, the Seccacian people of Rav'agas drifted in the desert wastelands, so anything could be possible, and he wasn't about to ignore what he was seeing in front of him now.

It wasn't long before they found the Quetalian prisoners in the caverns. They were a rough-looking bunch, from lack of clean water or decent food, but they were still quite aware of their surroundings. Metal chains connected about a dozen together by the ankle in a larger cave.

Kavriel stopped to guard the entrance as Ulin approached them dressed in his stolen Rav'agas uniform. They didn't put up any kind of defense, though Kavriel could sense their anger. One, an older man who seemed to have been in the confines of the caverns the longest, squinted suspiciously at Ulin as he began pulling the chain loose from the bracket in the wall.

Ulin spoke to him as if they had known each other for years. "There is a bit of a mess outside. I suggest that you find either something to fight with or something to ride away on. You haven't much time."

The old man stared blankly at Ulin for a moment. "The Hielias?" he suddenly asked, and Ulin nodded quickly. "How many?".

Kavriel began to wonder what kind of person the man had been before he'd become a prisoner. His face was dirty and haggard, but still proud. He looked at Kavriel a moment with that same perplexity before Ulin answered with a tinge of respect in his voice.

"All of them." Ulin pulled the chain away. "Now get out."

The group remained where they were. "You are Quetalian?" the old man asked.

Ulin nodded. "I am Ulin Tavrick."

The old man seemed surprised. "Olenson's boy?"

The other prisoners began to wake up to what was happening, gathering whatever meager items they had with them before quickly exiting the cave. Kavriel heard the sounds of fighting growing closer.

Before the old man could ask another question, Ulin quickly removed one of his swords and handed it to the man, who took it with a strong grip. "Please, Lord Aryivan, you must go quickly," he said, his voice urgent, though he made no move to force the man to comply.

The old man took the hint. With a spryness that Kavriel would not have expected from a man of that age, he ran out of the cavern with only a brief glance at Kavriel as he passed.

Now left alone again, Kavriel turned to Ulin, who was already deciding which passage to take, as they seemed to have come to a crossroads in the tunnels. "Who was that man?" he asked, trying to find the name in his memory.

"Jakob Aryivan," Ulin replied without actually looking at him. "He is one of the finest blades in the Eastern Townships." He turned. "One of many that I hope to find still alive here. He was taken at Taivr when the Ay'vol crossed over. He has been here ever since. "

"He knew you," Kavriel stated, curious to know more about the man.

Ulin shook his head. "He knew my family." He nodded toward the left passage. "Come on, before the Rav'agas or the Hielias get here. We have other famous names to free."

They came across and freed about two dozen more prisoners within the next few twists and turns of the passage. Kavriel couldn't help but be impressed. It was obvious that the passages were older than time itself, but the new construction of scaffolds and barrier walls made it seem like a fresh discovery. They seemed to be rising higher in the mountains, and had actually needed to cross two rope bridges that indeed connected several of the caverns together.

When they were out in the open Kavriel could see the battle raging below in the courtyard. He also saw that he was getting closer to the steward's turret high in the stone mountain face, but the second was stairway was separated from them by a fifty foot gap between the jagged rocks of the Oenes.

Ulin was running quickly to the next passages, oblivious to the visual wonder around them, but Kavriel understood his urgency to locate Kell's crew. It was all that he had left.

Turning into a passage that cut across theirs, Kavriel heard a whistle just before Ulin shouted and slammed hard against the cavern wall. A Rav'agas soldier had been lying in wait, ready to defend his shadowed corner with a loaded crossbow. Kavriel and Ulin had moved without caution and paid the price. Reacting solely on instinct, Kavriel rushed the soldier before he was able to reload, and his momentum successfully knocked the weapon from the man's hand before slamming them both against the hard cavern floor.

They wrestled and grappled, Kavriel knowing he was fighting for his life. Before he knew how it happened, he was lying underneath the Rav'agas, his forearm braced against the man's arm as he tried to thrust a wicked-looking blade into Kavriel's right eye. Fire burning in his eyes, muscles straining, the soldier hissed Rav'agas obscenities through his gritted teeth. Kavriel's arm trembled with the exertion.

And then, like a door that suddenly opened when he'd thrown his weight against it, the soldier flew back from Kavriel. He struck the wall and slid down it, his eyes and mouth wide more in shock than pain, for the man was beyond that. A pair of familiar throwing knives stuck out of his throat.

Ulin limped over and held out an arm to pull Kavriel to his feet. "Sneaky bastard," he spat, but his voice lacked strength, which worried Kavriel. His eyes quickly scanned Ulin's body, stopping at the ugly crossbow bolt sticking out just above his breastplate, where his shoulder met his chest.

"Ulin, you're hurt," he said, proclaiming the obvious while reaching toward the bolt, as if he would know what to do.

Ulin shrugged him away like any proud fighter. "Not enough," he replied with a wan smile. With an quick twist of his good hand he pulled the bolt out of his chest. A small amount of flesh and a great deal of blood came with it, and what Kavriel thought was a shrill whistle. He paled, realizing that Ulin's lung had been punctured, and he would need to find medical attention as soon as possible. He tried saying something, but as if already knowing what it would be, Ulin shoved the bloody wooden shaft toward him. "Here. Take it as a reminder not to move around corners without looking first." He laughed madly then clutched a hand over his wound and headed for the passageway.

Dropping the bloody bolt, Kavriel followed him fast, with the dire knowledge that Ulin did not have long to live, if they continued like this. He felt it in the pit of his stomach.

Despite his earlier urgency Ulin did slow down, pausing to peek around corners before moving forward, but Kavriel knew that it wasn't just heightened caution. The man was having problems breathing; Kavriel could hear his rasping breaths echoing in the tunnel. When the clash of steel and the screams of men in anguish drifted to them as if on a breeze from some unseen area farther down the passage, they stopped in their tracks.

Kavriel suddenly felt like turning back. They had gone through about a dozen passages like this in the last few minutes alone, and it didn't seem as if they would find any more prisoners. There were other directions to try, and if they needed to hurry, then they should turn back now, before getting caught up in whatever was happening ahead. He wasn't ready for a full-on attack, and Ulin was certainly in no shape for one.

But Ulin hesitated, curious to know what was going on. He waited until the noise died down before he spoke. "Something is finished up there." Despite his injury, the fool continued forward. Knowing that he wouldn't be able to convince the man that what he was doing was a bad idea, Kavriel reluctantly followed.

Within a few turns they emerged into a large, open chamber with several windows overlooking the mountains in a semicircle ahead of them. Kavriel immediately knew that they had entered one of the several turret-style guard posts that he had seen from the courtyard below, but that wasn't what held his attention. There were Rav'agas in here, several, in fact, but they were all dead, butchered and strewn about the room as if they were in some macabre slaughterhouse. The only one left alive besides them was a figure dressed completely in black linen, standing at one of the open windows as if waiting for others to come.

Ulin cursed. Kavriel felt a strange sensation come

over him, as if he'd just awakened from a daydream to all the details of reality. As if carried on the cool mountain air blowing in the windows, strength suddenly flowed into him.

Before he could say anything Ulin's hands were moving, sending a series of his knives, shimmering like lightning bolts, toward the black figure at the window. Yet before they reached their target, the figure revealed a slim blade that had been concealed behind one leg; moving in a dark blur, it struck away all of the knives. Then the figure moved, so quickly he didn't see it until Ulin was pinned up against the wall by the same weapon that had deflected his knives. He tried moving away from the blade against his chest and gasped in pain.

The figure was directly in front of Kavriel. He instinctively shouted Ulin's name. The figure turned toward him, and the sensation of strength Kavriel had been feeling suddenly became a dull drone of confusion.

Tess.

He knew that it was impossible, beyond all comprehension, but he was looking at her. "Tess," he whispered, and quickly the blade was withdrawn from Ulin's side. He slumped to the floor and keeled over. Kavriel lowered the sword he had been holding in some defiant act of defense as he'd watched Ulin being killed. For the moment there was nothing in his head except memories of his friend, the woman he had been told was executed by the chancellor in Teltraum. This was her . . . but not quite her.

Tess's brightness and warmth had been bleached away by time. Her skin was pale, and a haze filmed her dark eyes; silver streaked the ringlets of her dark brown hair. She had aged fifty years since the last time he'd seen her, but her carriage was still youthful, as if her body refused to believe anything had happened. She was like an animated corpse, refusing the grave to wander the earth like a faded memory of flesh and blood. She *was* a ghost.

The woman who was Tess looked at Kavriel as if seeing him for the first time in her life, and as he whispered her name again, tears gathered in his eyes. She stared at him with an emptiness that made Kavriel think of the glass eyes of a child's doll. She was horrible, so much and yet so different from the person that he knew that he could not think of any words to say. Instead he let his memory loose, and as he stared at his lost friend a connection seemed to form between them, like wisps of smoke swirling around the logs in the hearth before being blown away by the breeze.

His memory became one of many. In the dead reflection of her large dark eyes Kavriel saw things that he had not personally done in his life, yet experienced all the same. He was seeing her memories, and as he lived them he could feel the other part of himself, the dangerous fighter, becoming entranced by her thoughts. Through Tess he saw his family, his homeland, and even the great city of Teltraum. He saw the soldiers and the commanders and the rows upon rows of gallows that had been built in the great courtyard of the capitol city. He saw people that he knew and people that were strangers strung up by the neck and dropped through the trapdoor that ended their lives, and he saw this all through the eyes of the friend whom he thought he had lost.

He started feeling faint, as if his life-force was seeping out of him through his pores. He couldn't keep himself upright. He didn't fall, but he felt his body lean back against the wall. Tess seemed to draw closer to him. His mind blurred, and he understood what was happening. She was sifting through his thoughts as easily as he had hers, yet she seemed to be trying to pull something away from him. Suddenly defensive, he—or the other part of him—ripped free of her as if slicing through the shadowy ribbons that wrapped around the two of them.

Tess stepped back as if he had struck her physically, and immediately turned and ran toward one of the windows. Before Kavriel had recovered the strength drained in the strange reunion with his friend, she jumped through the window. He staggered over in time to see her arcing like a drifting leaf over the space between their chamber and the stone stairway. She landed as gently as if she'd never leapt at all, and looked back at him one last time before vanishing into the darkness.

Kavriel suddenly knew what he must do. He knew beyond all doubt where he must go. Like the moth to the flame, his eyes were drawn to the steward's stone turret, and he felt as if he had just awakened again on the mine floor in the destroyed basin room, where this madness had all begun.

The other part of him connected, and Kavriel could see himself through his own eyes. He had not forgotten the last five years after all. He had been erased from existence during that time, kept in a cocooned state until whatever was preparing him joined with him at the point of his waking, so that he might find whatever pieces remained for him to become complete.

He had been in that place before, that absolute nothingness, walking along the surface of oblivion with the power to decide whether to stay or to go. Yet it had never been his will that decided such things, but someone else's. As if remembering a distant memory from another time and another place, Kavriel saw the face of the young girl Millie . . . or the image of her that had greeted him in the shadowlands that his mind had saved him from reliving. He saw her smile and heard her voice as if she were standing directly before him.

"Yes," the misty voice said, like a master commending a student or rewarding a slave. *"You will do just fine."*

"Ghost…" Ulin whispered weakly from the corner where he had fallen, his voice waking Kavriel from his thoughts as if dousing him with a bucket of cold water.

Kavriel remembered where he was, but had another understanding of *who* he was as the memory of his friend tugged at his heart. He was still fighting the battle inside himself, despite everything.

He rushed over to his fallen crewmate, who clutched at a new hole, one that had pierced his steel breastplate as if it had been made of nothing but air. Blood oozed thickly from it and trickled from the other slightly above, where the crossbow bolt had gone into him, the red of Ulin's blood contrasting alarmingly with the whiteness of his face. Kavriel knelt slowly, unsure what he should say. He had never been with a dying man before. He wished that his concentration could fully be on Ulin, and yet the need to go to the steward's turret tugged at him like a physical thing. It was all he could do not to look away from the bloody man, instead forcing compassion to be his master.

The dispossessed nobleman looked up at him and his arrogant smile slowly drifted from his face. "We have done all that we can, I think," he struggled to say.

Kavriel shook his head defiantly, as if there was something that still could be done for the man that he now considered his friend. "Ulin, we have to find Kell and Seth. They are still here somewhere, and he will be able to help you." Kavriel felt as if he were speaking into a mirror, seeing himself recite the words but feeling nothing in them. The other part of him was too strong now.

Ulin shook his head, oblivious to Kavriel's conflict. "There is nothing they would be able to do. I don't think I'll leave this camp. I never expected to." He smiled smugly. "If you want the truth, I was actually hoping just to cut down a few more Rav'agas before my time came. I am the last of my line, and I should die with some dignity."

"You will," Kavriel summoned to say, his attention drifting to the window Tess had leapt from.

Ulin noticed. "You knew that woman, didn't you."

Kavriel forced himself to nod. "I thought I did, but she has been dead for a very long time now." He wasn't sure why he said such a thing, but deep down he believed it.

Ulin grunted. "We all have been dead for a long time now. We just haven't given ourselves the time to realize that yet." He coughed, spraying bloody spittle. He too looked out the window. "How did she get over there, anyway?" He asked, but his mind was struggling with too much pain for him to truly consider what he had seen. It would have been impossible for any sane man to witness, let alone a dying one.

Kavriel whispered anyway, "She jumped."

"You're going to follow her, aren't you?" Ulin asked, and by his tone Kavriel could tell that there was more to his question than the obvious.

Kavriel nodded. "I can."

Ulin nodded too. "Then the Creator give you speed, Kavriel. I am sorry that we got off to the wrong start. I can see that you are a good man."

Kavriel felt the tears start to come. "So are you, Ulin Tavrick," he choked out. "I'm sorry for what happened to your family, and I promise that I will make it right." His eyes drifted back to the window. "There are many responsible, many who must answer for their crimes." He felt a new kind of heat within him, not out of anger or fear, but something else, like certainty for what he must do. He nodded one last time to Ulin, who was still smiling at him, his breathing shallow, as if to stave off the inevitable for as long as he could.

The caverns were empty now, the battle moved to the courtyard where prisoners, Hielias mountain men, and Rav'agas soldiers were tangled in a bloody web. Kavriel and Ulin were safe high above it. Taking Ulin's hand in a firm grip, Kavriel nodded to the man, who did the same.

Kavriel's story was not about to end here. He knew where he must go. Turning to the window, he ran without care or worry, and launched himself across the impossible gap just as Tess had done. She was what he was, and he was what she was. They were connected by more than just their childhood memories.

Kavriel landed softly on the stone stairway, a good two hundred feet from the bloody battle below and the steward's turret another hundred feet above him, pale and hard as the skull of some perched vulture. A shadowy form stood on the large balcony projecting from it, looking down over the courtyard.

As soon as Kavriel started to climb the stairs, the figure disappeared from view.

CHAPTER 32

Kavriel reached the threshold, and the wind came in hard. He was on a ledge in the Oenes Mountains where only eagles dared, and as moonlight glowed from beyond the jagged peaks Kavriel finally understood their incredible vastness. They did not simply form a wall between Quetal and the unknown, but continued on like a raging ocean far into the distant horizon, perhaps ending in some other world altogether.

A part of Kavriel wanted to stay and admire the terrifying beauty of it all, but he instead turned to the small entrance to the turret. There was no door to open, but Kavriel pushed aside several heavy dark curtains that hung over the entryway like folds of shadows, slipping by them like another gust of wind.

His mind was in a state of semi-drowsiness. He understood where he was but the darkness of the corridor he walked through, faintly lit by torches clasped in wall sconces, seemed to thicken, as if he moved through a smoking chimney. Fear, hate, anger, love—all of Kavriel's emotions swirled together behind his skull as his eyes calmly followed the stone path before him.

He was getting closer to Tess. He could feel her, almost as if she were walking only a few steps ahead of him. He was drawn toward her, like a compulsion, an instinct. It was hypnotizing, and yet there was a part of him that still struggled to escape from her and what she had become. He didn't entirely understand that, but Ulin's words before Kavriel had left him to his lonely death haunted him: *We have been dead for a long time now*. Ulin may have spoken in haughty defiance, but the words stung with truth. He hoped Ulin's death would not be prolonged, and that soon he would be with the family that had been lost to him. Tess, on the other hand, had been truly dead. At least that was what he had been told.

Kavriel entered what would have been considered the grand chamber within the stone turret, if whoever had constructed the shelter so high in the mountain peaks had thought of such a thing. It was an elongated oval with a high, steeply domed ceiling. The balcony overlooking the courtyard opened on one of the oval's long sides, its stone banister heavily carved with images that Kavriel did not recognize. At the other end of the room a fire burned in a great hearth, and before it was a large work table where one man sat in a heavy, throne-like chair, and several others stood alongside. They were not looking at Kavriel, perhaps too deep in conversation to notice his arrival.

Kavriel immediately recognized the seated man, even if his facial features were in shadow. It was almost as if General—or *Steward*—Saire was no longer a man, but a silhouette of some deeper darkness. Kavriel merely glanced at him, and he wasn't even certain the man had seen him. Kavriel's focus was on Tess, who stood at Saire's side like a humble servant. Already he felt himself being pulled toward her as if they were tethered. He was able to keep himself from doing so, but as he continued to walk slowly into the room, he almost felt as if he was separating into mirror images, one part of him continuing toward the center of the room while the other lagged behind, heading toward Tess.

She watched him carefully, and Kavriel felt his

528

stomach turn in circles as he stared back, trying to find some kind of recognition in the girl that he had grown up with and loved like a sister. She was still beautiful, but in a nightmarish, specter-like way, as if he had been visited by the shade of a loved one, long dead. Nothing in his experience could explain what she was now, and other than her physical resemblance to the girl he'd known, Kavriel felt as if she was a complete stranger. It was only that strange, invisible link that kept them looking at one another, analyzing, he both fearful and confused by what he saw. There was no emotion in her gaze, and Kavriel could not be certain if she was as baffled as he was. He didn't think so. Tess was dead, and he was looking at her ghost while she was staring at the nothingness within him.

She turned her head toward Saire at the table, whom, Kavriel noticed, had become aware of his presence, even though he gave no outward sign. On the contrary, he remained as motionless as the chair he sat in, leaning back in it with his fingers steepled under his chin. Kavriel thought he heard faint whispering between Saire and Tess, a subliminal conversation. Saire's translucent blue eyes glowed out of the darkness he was shrouded in like stars at midnight, and he stared at Kavriel, studying him, assessing him.

Kavriel stopped and stood in the center of the great room, his arms at his sides. Strangely, once he did so, it seemed as if the world around him began to move quicker and with more clarity. The crackle of the fireplace grew louder, and the mountain breeze swirled chill eddies around Kavriel's stolen Rav'agas armor. One of the men, large-framed and older, officer's insignia and medals on his uniform, had been leaning over the table with his hands outstretched in some kind of plea when Kavriel entered; now he seemed to reanimate, turning to face Kavriel with a surprised expression.

Blades hissed from scabbards, and a half-dozen Rav'agas soldiers surrounded him, regarding him with mouths grim with anger and eyes wide with terror. Kavriel realized that he had somehow entered the room without anyone's awareness, like another breeze from the mountaintops, and only when he wished it did he become visible. No longer did drawn blades bother him; he had been at the end of them so many times now that it was becoming more annoyance than cause for fear.

Feeling the other part of himself within his skull, like a hawk poised to dive, he smiled. He could rip them apart in the blink of an eye if he willed it. But there was something keeping his violence at bay; he merely watched the men (and Tess), all staring at him as if he were some newly discovered creature. Saire was grinning.

The Ay'vol officer cursed as he too unsheathed an almost ridiculously large blade. Kavriel remembered him from the temple, and as if his life were coming together like the pages of a book into one chapter, Kavriel saw both Kell and Seth standing several paces behind the officer. They had been beaten and looked more dead than alive, but they lived still. Just seeing that they were there made Kavriel forget his other emotions as he looked at them, wide-eyed. They looked at him as if seeing him for the first time, as well.

Two other Rav'agas soldiers behind them, acting as their guards, had crossbows aimed at Kavriel. It didn't take a smart man to realize that he was completely trapped. Still, Kavriel did not feel any anxiety, merely waited patiently to see who would be the first to speak.

"There!" the officer shouted, as if Kavriel had appeared as an example for what he'd been discussing with Saire. "He's the one . . . damn the Fallen, what manner of darkness are you?" he asked Kavriel.

Saire regarded Kavriel calmly. Kavriel didn't reply; he didn't have to. The officer continued his rant. "That's the one, General, the boy that I lost in Misam. How in Creation . . . ? He is some kind of blackness, My Lord, I can assure you. Merely speaking of him has conjured him here, as if summoned. Kill him! Kill him quickly!" he shouted.

Saire quickly raised his hand before the frightened soldiers could make a move. "Calm, Captain," he responded, his voice without emotion. Just the sound of that voice was enough to boil the blood in Kavriel's veins. He would never forgive himself for trusting the man. "There is no need for bloodshed, Bellon." Saire kept his eyes on Kavriel. "The boy is here . . . and I would hate for you to act improperly toward my guest."

The officer Bellon cast Saire an uncertain look, and Kavriel couldn't help but feel uncertain himself. Still, the soldiers had not struck, and their looks had not shifted.

Saire lowered his hand to the table, tipping his head slightly, regarding Kavriel with mild amusement. Tess was a shadow. "So." Saire finally addressed Kavriel directly, and with his words came that strange sensation of tentacles cording around his body. Kavriel stood as quietly, letting the cold sensation bind him. "I was honestly not expecting you. You are stronger than I thought. It's not an easy adjustment for one who has been chosen, but I should have known that there was something about you." He grinned smugly.

Anger surged through Kavriel. He mentally burned away the invisible cords that Saire had been wrapping around him. The general's grin vanished. "Very strong, indeed," he replied, and again Tess looked over to him as if awaiting some kind of order. Kavriel's sadness had no bounds as he stole a glance at her. "What have you done?" he grated.

Again Saire seemed amused. "I've told you. It's not an easy adjustment, but in time the vessel adapts to its contents—in those that are strong enough," he answered lightly, as if everyone in the room understood what he was talking about. The officer's expression and those of the Rav'agas guards revealed it was not.

* * *

"General?" Bellon ventured. "General, what is this about? This is *not* who I sought in that village. You have given me a name but not the man. Explain yourself!" he demanded as he felt his usually solid confidence slowly melting away.

Before Misam, his will had been constantly tested against the weight of the chancellor, but all that had changed when he had led the massive strike against the northeast district, when the metallic smell of blood hung thick in the air. He was the soldier reborn, the man who had been forgotten by his superiors but not by his master. He had been given a blessing from the Patriarch through the message that Saire had sent him, prompting the affair in the

Highlands of that wretched island, when the chancellor would have kept him at a professional distance. He had taken the initiative, and it had been a wise and just choice. Yet what he had not expected to find was this boy in God's temple.

At first, the sheer invigoration he'd felt that night had confused him. His blood was on fire, after the long pause in bloodshed that he had been forced to cope with over the last few years, on that cold island. He had seen the boy fight, but he was not seeing who he truly was, only the memory of the man that had haunted his thoughts. He fought with the strength of vengeance in his attack, but as this new anomaly began to overpower him and his company, Bellon had become uncertain about a great many things.

He had fought with and against many men; he had sampled every skill and talent for death that this world had to offer. He was not easily surprised, but this boy had surprised him. There was something that had been held secret in these Highland communities that he had been quietly ignoring, focused on more pressing concerns in the political duel between the mainlanders and the chancellor. He had never suspected something out of place in those sleepy, mist-laden towns under his power. He had just assumed this man-child who had shamed him was a gem in a field of dull rocks.

Yet there was another . . . and how many more after that? Bellon looked back and forth between the general and the boy. They seemed to be conversing wordlessly with one another, by the way their eyes danced. It made no sense at all. And the woman? The strange woman dressed as one of those mountain vultures currently pestering his Rav'agas soldiers below was yet another oddity in the general's choice of company. She stood there silent as a ghost, and looked the part. He had not seen her before, yet there was something familiar about her, a similarity to the others.

There was more to discover about the part of the world where he had spent the last three years wishing to be away from it. How long had his personal anger blinded him? And how much did this man Saire know about what was going on?

He shouted over to him again, forgetting for a moment the chain of command, thinking only of the boundlessness of conspiracy. "General!"

Finally the shadow man remembered that he was there. His eyes burned with blue fire as they stared at him, disconcerting Bellon.

"I said calm yourself, Captain," Saire replied, pausing for a bit longer than normal as his eyes held Bellon in place. "I gave you a name, yes, and that name still will belong to you. In truth I was honestly expecting the man who bears that name to be present tonight."

* * *

Saire's eyes dimmed as he looked at Kavriel again, as if he were disappointed. Kavriel did not move. "You surprise me, child," he said bluntly. "If I didn't know better I might think that you have been seeking me out, and not the other way around." A smile touched his mouth.

Kavriel responded with one of his own. "What makes you think I wasn't?" he asked, his fingers moving over his father's sword as if of their own volition. He wanted more than anything to kill this man, but he knew that even despite his abilities, he would not make it past all of the Guardsmen around him. As if to prove that, the soldiers tensed at his words, and even Tess seemed to become more focused. Kavriel did not wish to fight her…not her. He heard Seth and Kell shifting in their bonds. Their mouths were shut, but their eyes burned with hatred for their captors.

Saire roared in laughter. "Perhaps you were, child . . . perhaps you were." He finally rose from the throne chair. Kavriel had forgotten how tall the man was and for a moment felt that unease in his gut return as the general towered over them all. He saw the same reaction in his friends, who suddenly grew very still. Saire moved from the table toward the fireplace, turning his attention away from them as Kavriel had first seen him do all those years ago in his own town hall.

He stole another look at Tess, who was still watching him but with distant eyes, her mind focused elsewhere. Kavriel remembered what his father had mentioned about her condition when she and Vaemalin had escaped the mine. She had been afflicted with the red-eye sickness, which might explain her strange behavior, yet it didn't explain what she had done to those Rav'agas soldiers in the other chambers, and most of all, why she was still alive. Kavriel assumed that he had been ill as well, if to a lesser degree, but there was something else there.

His thoughts returned to the basin chamber that they had discovered together, and to the urns that had been found in that basin. The air had changed in the room when one of the containers was destroyed, and it was at that point that things began to turn strange. Was this all a delusional dream? Was he actually here in the Oenes Caverns hundreds of miles from his home, or was he lying in his bed, staring at the ceiling as the healers washed the sweat and filth from him, as they did with others who had fallen to madness. Was this all in his head? Kavriel was beginning to think so, but the more he stared at his lost friend he knew that they were all more real now than they had ever been. They had been poisoned . . . but with what, exactly? Kavriel's hand moved to his side, unintentionally brushing against the book that he had stolen from Xavr's cabin—the memoirs that he had stolen. He began to understand.

"You are Sa'rire," he said to the shadow at the fireplace, and Saire turned to him suddenly with an almost sad expression that Kavriel never would have expected to see on the man. They held each other's eyes in silence for a moment, then the general's lips turned up in a smile.

"I was called that once, a long time ago," he replied softly. "You have discovered much, I see. Again, you surprise me." He inclined his head, acknowledging Kavriel.

The Ay'vol officer seemed to be ready to fall out of his armor with his agitation. "These riddles are becoming tiresome, General," he snarled, radiating anger. "Why have you sent me on this hunt?"

Saire turned to him. "Because you were the best qualified for the job, Captain," he answered. "You are one of the few who have lived to see the greatness that would impress even your Patriarch, and I needed you in order to push the contingent of Quetalian rebels in my direction. I knew that at least one of those I sought would be among them, even if it was not the one I was actually expecting so soon."

The general then turned to Tess, and his eyes lit with humor. "I hope I have not disappointed you, my lady?" he asked, and immediately Kavriel saw the anger flash across his friend's face. It was so foreign on her, it would have been hard not to notice it.

"He was never part of the agreement," she whispered, and if Kavriel thought that his heart might stop simply from seeing his lost friend, then the sound of her voice was another kind of torture. It was hers, but deeper and more resonant, as if she were speaking to him from the entrance to a cave . . . or a mine. What she said went beyond him.

Saire shrugged. "Things never go as they seem, my dear," he replied, but his expression hardened as he lowered his voice. "Yet that changes nothing."

Surprisingly, the Ay'vol officer spoke out. "Have you made a pact with this woman, General?" Bellon growled, keeping his attention on Kavriel while stealing looks at the others.

Saire sighed, but Kavriel understood that the officer was simply trying to understand what was happening. How could he begin to explain? He decided that finally he should speak.

"Xavr was right to keep the remains of the Fallen from you," he said quietly, but with a firmness that caught everyone's attention. Kavriel somehow felt the voice was not his, even though it was him saying the words. It was as if another had stepped into his place for a moment. "You destroyed your brothers and sisters for the sake of becoming what you hated. You forgot what you had been created for. You were only meant to be the inspiration for the children, not the oppressor. You have become too glorified with your own sense of self-worth, your image. Your followers to the south put too much into your head and it has poisoned you." Kavriel felt as if his tongue was on a string being pulled by another, and yet from what he had read in the book, he believed what he was hearing himself say. It all had made sense to him, finally.

Saire—or Sa'rire—looked furious, but his voice remained calm, as if centuries upon centuries had schooled patience. "And what do you know of it, child?" he almost whispered. "You have been given an extraordinary gift from a being that you and your kind have all but forgotten. I had been his servant for longer than your species existed, and yet what did that earn me? What did it earn any of us? Does the night sky look any less extraordinary without the moon, or can the stars, too, illuminate a path for humanity? We were those stars, child, and I will shine brighter than all of them."

Kavriel glanced over to Tess again, whose demeanor had changed. She was blinking more frequently and her expression fluctuated, like a drunk trying to will herself sober. She was struggling with something, and it wasn't in Saire's best interest.

Saire frowned at her before looking to Kavriel. "So you learned a few things." His tone was more agitated. The others in the room tensed, especially Captain Bellon, who seemed to be dancing on his feet. "Yet what you have learned, you can never understand. You are only an experiment."

"And what does that make you?" Kavriel asked, and

for a moment he felt as if he was asking the question with two separate voices, one his own and another much more ancient and forgotten. He and this other were having a mutual debate with Saire. The bits of information he had collected over his journey seemed to glow in his mind, as if being pointed at by the other. "We might have been the Creator's experiment, but you were merely an act of redemption. What do you hope to accomplish by following in your father's footsteps? Another pack of children to follow at you heels?" Kavriel asked. He cast a fleeting glance over to his friend, who still seemed to be struggling with some unnatural symptom. Kavriel could relate.

Saire only smiled. "Oh, what limited vision, little one," he sneered. "You sound so much like my brothers . . . If only they could have understood what Father truly meant to accomplish. Perhaps you shouldn't speak so righteously."

* * *

Captain Bellon finally spoke. "This has gone far enough." His sword seemed to drift in Saire's direction. "Whatever game you are playing, Cielean, I will not let you sully the name of God. The Patriarch will hear of your blasphemous experiments, whatever they may be."

Bellon nearly choked on his words. He had not expected to confront the general. He was the Patriarch's pet, but he was also a man Bellon thought he could trust. He had no idea what was going on between Saire and the Highland boy—or even the other man he'd been sent to "flush out" for him—but he was not a stupid man. He had realized too late that he was here in this place only through the careful maneuvering of Saire and whoever had been his allies. There was some deeper conflict taking place within the normal political arena and if Saire was not working with the chancellor, he was certainly not for the Patriarch, either.

He knew Saire's past—or what past had been created—and he knew that there was always something else at work with him. He had manipulated a great many people before, why would he not continue? He had no clue what these two were speaking about, but he recognized enough in the conversation to know that they were treading on delicate ground with the doctrine. He would not stand for that from anyone. He was a man of god, first and foremost.

General Saire merely smiled at him as if he were a child who thought he understood the workings of the world. Bellon could see cynicism on his face.

Saire spoke. "You are a loyal creature, Captain." Bellon narrowed his eyes, unsure of the meaning Saire's tone conveyed. "Yet you are only a piece in this project of mine, as is your Patriarch. I don't think there will be much use for you any longer. You have not brought me what I wished, but another, and quite a bit more important I see. I thank you, but you have heard too much and like your fellow men at arms in the courtyard, the Hielias will make sure that you are silenced."

* * *

Kavriel wasn't sure what the general meant, but he recognized a direct threat when he heard it. The captain looked as if he had just been stung by a very large bug. He gasped, and his eyes went wide in aggravated surprise. If he too felt as Kavriel had about the general's swordsmanship, then so did the Rav'agas soldiers that were guarding him.

They all turned their attention to Saire, standing calmly beside the fireplace. Even the crossbowmen behind Seth and Kell turned in his direction.

Bellon screamed out his rage. "You traitorous villain! How dare you say such words to me, you foreign bastard!"

He moved around the table separating him and the general as spryly as a man half his age, and the Rav'agas soldiers around Kavriel suddenly moved forward too. They had not forgotten he was there, but there attention was focused on the fireplace where Saire stood.

Saire nodded at Tess and, without any spoken command, she flew from her place, one step onto the tabletop, then another, her foot smashing into Bellon's skull before she landed in front of him. Stunned, the Ay'vol officer staggered back several steps, but anger fueled him now as he came at her.

Out of the corner of his eye, Kavriel saw Kell and Seth both move against the crossbowmen behind them. Their movements were surprisingly fluid, as if they had been saving their strength for a quick attack like this. Seth was able to head-butt one soldier's jaw as his momentum pushed them both against the far wall. Kell used his massive shoulders to ram into the smaller soldier guarding him, disarming him and knocking him off his feet.

Pain suddenly burned through Kavriel's back, and he cried out as he fell forward onto his outstretched hands. The soldiers guarding him had taken the initiative, one of them cutting across his back with his blade as he moved past, toward the other battle.

Kavriel's scream caught the attention of both Saire

and Tess, who looked at the Rav'agas who had attacked then, like a mother protecting a fallen infant, she leapt over him and attacked. Kavriel felt the warm spray of blood over his neck and head as she landed blow after blow on the soldiers. Kavriel looked up just as Bellon lunged at Saire, now that Tess was out of his way.

* * *

Bellon parried the lithe woman's slender blade with his large broadsword with more caution than ease. She was not an experienced fighter, but she was fast, and he almost fell due to underestimation of her ability. Fortunately Bellon had seen how these strange creatures fought, how they somehow altered normal human limitations with their own rules. He knew he wouldn't survive a fight with her in a long duel, but he was hoping at least to wound her enough to get to Saire.

It was by luck alone that one of his men drew her away by striking the young man. One moment she was covering him like a dust cloud, and the next she was gone to slaughter his men. Bellon was not a man to feel despair for fallen Rav'agas soldiers under his command. He had prepared them for both this world and the next and as long as they fought bravely, he would honor them. His target was the general, and if he could not understand the rules of this game, then at least he was going to destroy the central piece.

The general smiled at him, his hands clasped loosely behind his back as calmly as a man about to take a stroll in a garden. Bellon could not help but smile back, feeling that justice was being served as he swung his blade at Saire's unprotected body. He was going to make good on his threat, and if that meant a court marshal from his Patriarch, then so be it. He would explain the reasons for his actions later, when and if the time came. For now he was after vengeance, and God willing, after his men destroyed the mountain savages in the courtyard, he would march them all into Teltraum and cut down the chancellor himself. There was too much garbage in the world to be rid of and he would be rid of it all.

He did not feel his arm snap, though he knew that was inevitable, after the sudden shock as his great sword, forged and crafted by the most skilled swordsmiths, cracked in two as it struck the stone fireplace where Saire had been standing only a heartbeat before. The useless hilt dropped from Bellon's hand as his arm went limp. He looked up into the general's eyes, before him once again, and Bellon felt fear as the general lifted his blade. The blade became a blur of gray as it passed across Bellon's torso, and he felt the steel slicing his abdomen through to his spine. He gasped out with his last breath, and as he fell, his only thought was, *How can he be that fast?*

* * *

Kavriel felt that the battle had moved away from him, or perhaps he had simply been thrust outside its boundaries. Teeth clenched against the pain in his back, he blinked wet eyes and saw Seth still struggling with the Rav'agas soldier he had attacked. They were tumbling across the floor like wrestlers, rolling to and fro, both grappling for the loaded crossbow.

Seth seemed to be fueled by a different kind of anger, wildly directing violence toward a symbol of his broken life, but the soldier was older, more experienced, and bigger than the young man. With a quick turn of his arm he lifted and pinned Seth against the wall, and as the thick wooden shaft of the crossbow smashed against his head, Seth's eyes rolled back.

Kavriel tried to force himself to his feet, but the sword slash flared a painful warning in his back. He was slowly regaining his strength, but he knew it would be too late for Seth. Yet as the Rav'agas aimed his bolt into Seth's chin, another shape suddenly rammed into him with the force of a charging boar. It was Kell, who had easily dispatched his own guard in time to shove the second soldier away.

If the Rav'agas was more than a formidable opponent for Seth, he was no match for the thick-bodied Sai pirate who launched himself into his stomach, nearly picking the Rav'agas up off the floor as he ran him into the wall. He smashed against it with a sickening crunch. Cursing triumphantly, Kell assaulted the other Rav'agas with his bare hands. Kavriel pushed himself to his feet as the man was struggling to protect himself from the savage onslaught. Seth's eyes closed as he slumped into unconsciousness.

Saire stood over the dead body of the Ay'vol captain. He had not looked at Kavriel yet. Feeling the desire for vengeance swelling inside him like a fever, Kavriel drew his father's sword and rushed at the man with fire in his blood, ignoring the pain in his back. His mind might not have been his own, but his will and resolve were sound. He triggered the abilities that he had somehow acquired within himself since the last time he had faced this man, and like a lion unleashed he charged, hungry for blood. Saire's translucent eyes turned his way. As he brought up his own blade to defend himself, Kavriel thought he saw the man smile.

He might not have understood completely how the powers had been gifted to him, as Saire suggested, but Kavriel was at last able to consciously unleash them. He spun and struck as easily as if he were walking down a gentle slope, moving faster than he'd thought possible, his sword feeling feather light as his eyes seemed to target points on Saire's body as if they had been highlighted by a ray of sunlight. He was being guided where to strike, and he used every skill within him, borrowed and gifted and learned. Yet Saire was able to block every attack, his smile never leaving his face.

Kavriel pushed harder, the sweat beading on his brow, the room swirling in a haze of fatigue as he struggled to keep up with the large man, who seemed to be feeding on his energy and turning it against him. Kavriel suddenly remembered that he was not fighting some champion sword master with a hidden past; he was fighting the offspring of a god.

Out of the corner of his eye he thought he saw Kell come in to assist him, but then another black shadow passed, and Kavriel felt his throat lock up as he heard the pirate's scream. Without needing to confirm it with his eyes, he knew that it had been Tess who stopped Kell. Kavriel's sword hesitated in mid-thrust with that knowledge, and Saire seized the opportunity, grabbing Kavriel's naked blade and holding it in place with one hand.

They stared at one another for a moment. Then

Saire's lips curved in a small grin, and Kavriel felt a tremendous *push* emanating from someplace within the man. He let go of the sword as he fell back, only to stop suddenly as, lightning fast, Saire tossed his father's blade aside and grabbed him around his throat with his powerful fingers. Kavriel's body went limp as his feet lifted off the floor, and Saire stared into his eyes, radiating an ancient evil that burned into his very soul. He could not even scream.

"Have you had enough, child?" he sneered, and Kavriel's mouth gaped wide, desperate for air, as Saire squeezed his neck, cutting the breath from his lungs. "You have been holding onto something that doesn't belong to you, and I will now be taking what is rightfully mine." His grip loosened, so Kavriel could respond.

The words wheezed out with painful difficulty. "It . . . was never . . . yours . . . to take." Kavriel knew the tome that he had stolen from Xavr's library was indeed a true memoir, written by someone who had been involved in this sect of super-beings known as The Watch. Whoever they had been, they had succeeded in destroying their father, the Creator and the God of Light in the Rav'agas doctrine. They had been constructed out of the remains of the Fallen, the God of Darkness destroyed by the Creator eons earlier, according to belief, so that he might grant his kindness and gift of life to the mortal realm.

Yet the book revealed another part of the story. This Watch had been created not as an act of kindness, as were the children of the earthly realm, but as a group of "overseers" of humanity. To help or to hinder? That was something the book never mentioned, but the group of six known as The Watch seemed to be just as conflicted within themselves concerning their place in this world as the mortals. The political battlefield on earth also existed in the heavens, and somehow Kavriel, Tess, and Vaemalin had been dragged into it.

Sa'rire had taken the remains of the fallen God of Light and dispersed them in the children. To what end, he could not know, only that it seemed as if Sa'rire was about to collect what he had lent out. It was time to pay their dues, and Kavriel was another victim in this war of gods that had been waged since time forgotten.

He realized all of this as he stared into Sa'rire's eyes as he held him aloft like a child displaying a toy. He felt that gaze pull something out of him like a stitch being removed from an old wound. Whatever power he thought he had over this man, he was terribly wrong. Sa'rire was going to take back what had embedded itself into Kavriel and then destroy him.

A whistle and a flash as metal slammed into the general's outstretched arm. His eyes widened in surprise as Kavriel dropped to the floor. He knelt on the cold stones, clutching his neck and gasping for air, feeling as if he had just been drained of all life-force.

Tess's pained scream drew his head up. The general was growling in a deep and resonating voice, clutching his elbow. His arm was outstretched, and sticking out of his flesh like three sliver shards were metal throwing knives. Kavriel carefully turned his head, his neck tender, and saw Tess on one knee, one trembling hand cupped over something in her chest. Kavriel knew that she must have been hit by the same thing that struck the general, and he turned toward the entrance to the chamber, knowing what he would find, even though there was little possibility it could be real.

Ulin stood swaying on weak legs, his gaze fixed on the general. His vest was open, and his belt of dynamic weaponry glimmered in the firelight. His face was deathly pale, the red stain covering his face to his chin stark against its pallor. In one hand he held three stakes ready while his other hand shakily held out a sword, more to keep balance than anything. Kavriel did not recognize it; the man must have claimed it sometime during his struggle from the prison quarters to the steward's turret. He wondered what kind of strength or resolve had accomplished such a feat. By the sound of Ulin's ragged breathing, Kavriel knew that it was taking everything Ulin had to help him.

Ulin's eyes didn't leave the wounded general, who was grimacing at him as he shouted to Kavriel, "Get up, Ghost."

Kavriel immediately moved away from the general's feet, just as the man dropped his blade and grabbed all three of the knives lodged in his arm with one hand. He yanked them out and flung them to the floor, more angry at the interruption than in pain. He glared at Ulin, who looked past them toward a figure in the corner. By his expression, Kavriel knew that Ulin had spotted Kell.

Kavriel looked over too, remembering the man's attempt to help him against the general. His bulky body lay motionless on the floor near Seth's body. Tess's intervention had been final. As for Tess, Kavriel heard her gasp as she struggled to stand, and as she did, all of his feelings that focused on what she had been vanished. She was dead, just as his father had said she was. Now there was only a ghost, who for some reason had allied herself with Saire. Did she too have the "gift" inside her? Kavriel already knew the answer, and as he crawled slowly over to her he suddenly had a memory of the Wylyn assistant that Saire had brought with him to Rhyol, all those years ago. Had he too been one of the chosen? And if so, what had happened to him? Did Saire simply destroy him to "take back what was rightfully his," as he said he was going to do? And if that was the case, why was Tess fighting for him?

He reached out and put a hand on her shoulder just as she too pulled out the pair of knives that Ulin had thrown at her. She looked up at Kavriel with death in her black eyes. "Tess," he whispered, as if saying a goodbye at a friend's grave. She didn't seem to hear or understand him.

"Kavriel," Ulin called softly.

Kavriel turned and saw that his friend was angling himself between Kavriel and the general, presumably holding him at bay, either so they could get away or he could get over to Kell. Ulin was not a man to take his time when killing someone, and yet he looked hesitant against Saire.

Sensing the breath of a movement from Saire, Kavriel tried to shout a warning to Ulin to get out, but the general moved like a flash of lightning. Ulin screamed in surprise, barely able to get out of the way as the oak table Saire had kicked crashed to the floor where he'd been standing. He gasped from the effort, coughing out a wad of blood and stumbling back on weak legs.

The general was on him by then, and before Kavriel

could do a thing Saire had picked him up by the throat just as he had picked Kavriel up earlier. Ulin's instincts took over. Closing the hand holding the three knives into a fist, he rammed it into Saire's torso. But either his armor was too thick or Saire was impervious to this mortal's attack, because he kept his hold on Ulin's throat, and with a sharp turn of his wrist, snapped Ulin's neck with a sickening crunch.

The last of the House of Tavrick went limp. The general tossed him toward the wall as if flinging a ragdoll. Ulin's arm twitched for a moment before all the suffering and pain he had endured his entire life was finally snuffed out.

Blood exploded in Kavriel's head as he screamed. He didn't remember standing up or when he had retrieved his father's sword, but one moment he was still kneeling by Tess's side and the next he was attacking Saire.

Again the man surprised him with his speed and agility, but unlike the last duel, this time the general parried his furious blows with surreal skill, and finally the sword of Cyr Soelle fell to the floor with a clatter. Kavriel felt his insides burning and looked down at his stomach, where Saire's large sword was buried halfway into him. Kavriel stood motionless, like a puppet, dangling on the sharp string of the master as Saire smiled greedily into his eyes.

"Now." Saire spoke as softly as a healer explaining inevitable death to a patient. "Return back to the dust and the stones you were taken from. I will have what is mine." And with that he shoved the sword to its hilt into Kavriel's gut.

Kavriel felt the leather back of his breastplate split

as the blade exited through his back. He stood paralyzed, gasping for air and choking on blood. Saire narrowed his eyes, seeming to focus on something that was buried deep within Kavriel's head. He could not move, could only hang there in place as the blackness overcame him, as it had so many times before.

Kavriel saw the basin chamber in his mind. He was standing over the open container where the God of Light's blood swirled. He felt as if he *was* the basin, and with every passing moment of his life he saw the liquid slowly evaporating as Saire held onto him tightly. His whispers echoed in the chamber like a thunderclap. Kavriel felt his body dissipating like a cloud of smoke blown away by a breeze. He saw images of his family and his friends, and the memories of his childhood all the way up to this moment, when he was finally reminded that he had died all those years ago, underneath the stones in the mine in Mir.

He had not lost his memory for five years, nor had the red-eye sickness given him a life of delusion. No. He simply had not been there anymore, and by some impossible grace he had been granted, temporarily, this extra time. He had acquired the same bits of God as his friends had aquired, and Saire was here simply to take back what he had lent them. Perhaps Xavr's book was accurate, and Sa'rire was unable to take it directly himself, had needed Kavriel and the others as "hosts" to accomplish his task. Either way, the time had ended, and Kavriel knew there was nothing more holding him to this world. He was being drained of what was never his to begin with, and soon his friends would face the same fate.

He shuddered as death took him, and even the basin

chamber that he had been shoved back to in the weakness of his mind began to vanish. That was when he saw the girl. It was Millie, Seth's lost sister, and the only part of his memory that had no correlation to what he had gone through. She stepped out of the mist, moving toward him with a smile so wide, it seemed almost malicious. She grabbed hold of Kavriel's arms and he felt as if he had just been clamped with blazing hot blacksmith tongs. He screamed a hollow scream in this chamber of death, but the girl's voice launched him out of it and back into the steward's turret, where Saire still held him on his sword.

"It is time, Kav. Wake up!"

Kavriel's hands moved without his accord, and he shoved his open palms hard into Saire. A powerful force, like the gust of a backwind, seemed to follow his movement. It picked Saire off his feet and threw him across the room. He slammed hard into the far wall with the sword that he had killed them with still in his hand. With nothing holding him up any longer, Kavriel fell to the floor, but inside, he knew that he would not die from this. He knew that there was no longer *any* wound that he would die from, and as he saw the general's eyes widen, he knew that he knew it also.

"No!" Saire roared. "How is this possible?" He rose from the floor and pointed his sword at Kavriel. His eyes burned with insanity and rage as he seemed to come to another conclusion. Kavriel struggled to remain conscious. "You will not stop me," Saire shouted. "You think you can stop me, but you will not."

He rushed at Kavriel, screaming, *"You will not awaken! I will not allow it*!"

552

Kavriel might not have been dead, but he certainly was in no shape to try defending himself from the general's attack. However, though the sword thrust through his gut may not be enough to kill him, he wasn't certain that would be the case if Saire took off his head. He pulled himself to his feet and crouched low, bracing for the general's blow, but before that happened Kavriel felt a dark wind pass by him.

Tess had barely touched him as she'd passed by, but in that moment Kavriel had another vision from her past life, as if through contact their memories could be drawn from the same well. He saw himself as a boy, laughing as he played with her. It was her memory, one of times he had shared with her, not entirely vivid, but strong enough to evoke a feeling of happiness, like the scent of a summer breeze reminding him of better days.

The force of their impact as Tess hit Saire was like two stars colliding. The room exploded outward and Kavriel was thrown out of it, crashing through the stone balustrade. As the stone turret shattered, the sound of her voice drifted on the wind after Kavriel as he fell from the mountaintop.

"I am sorry, Kavriel. Please save us . . . please save Vaemalin."

Kavriel landed on the hard ground in the courtyard, below hundreds of feet below where the Rav'agas and the Hielias still fought. His impact shook houses and sent men flying, as if a star had just fallen from the heavens.

CHAPTER 33

The man stood humbly in front of the small recessed window overlooking the remnants of his former village, nervously clutching his cane as he rubbed his leg. It had grown more painful over the last several weeks, possibly due to the unseasonably hot weather that had thrown nature into confusion, flowers blooming in heat normally reserved for the summer months in Rhyol. It was humid, and the humidity could play tricks with your mind as easily as it could with old wounds, Cyr Soelle reminded himself with a sigh. It had been a hot year when he had received the wound that had gimped his leg . . .

They had been foolish to try digging in such a place. The passage was too unstable for any secondary passageways. Yet the symbol was too strange to pass up, and they needed to understand who had been in the mines before them. Had it been another kind of miner, years and years ago, before even the clans had established territories in the Highlands? Or was it something else, something entirely forgotten? They'd been too distracted, and they didn't even have time to understand that they were dying as the walls came down on them.

Cyr closed his eyes, reliving the memory of the mine caving in on his team. The rocks seemed to morph into some giant creature, chewing them up and swallowing them into the recesses of the ground. Cyr's leg twitched, as if he could feel the ore cart he had turned over him to protect himself from the fall of stone. The others had not been so lucky.

When he had crawled out to try to pull a fellow

villager under his dubious shelter, the boulder had crushed his leg, destroying all mobility below the knee. He had been pinned as the earth swallowed them up one rock at a time, and when the cold sea had come in it had buried the bodies of his fellow workmen under its icy cold blackness. Cyr wondered if there was any worse suffering a man could experience. Yet he'd lived, when all others had died. The overturned cart had kept a pocket of air above his head. As the rest of him chilled under the stones and the sea, Cyr had been granted the right to breathe so that his death might be drawn out the longest.

Cyr opened his eyes again, watching the dawn through the window as the sun rose over the trees and hills, fading the purple twilight.

She shouldn't have come.

He had expected the town overseer to send a search party, but he hadn't expected that his pregnant wife would be with the men sloshing through the passages with torches and shovels. She had no business to be there; they all knew about the dangers. Why had they let her come along? She should have stayed away to take care of Vaemalin. The rescuers would have found him alright.

She was so beautiful, light hair with soft skin, pale as milk. As beautiful as she'd been the first day he had seen her, many years before, when he went off to fight the war on the borderlands like all the other young men. She was still beautiful even when the sickness took her mind and body.

Crying, she'd consoled him as the others pried the stone from his leg, telling him everything would be alright even though her hands clutched her rounded belly. Cyr understood later that she had been in pain, and when his second son finally did come four months later, the sickness had taken what strength she might have had left after the birth. She just couldn't recover. Cyr remembered holding his newborn child over the body of his dead wife, their bodies still connected by the mother-cord. She had seen her boy for only a brief moment before she had fallen into the darkness, but in that moment Cyr had seen the joy on his wife's face. At least she had been able to see her son before she died.

Why did it have to take her like that? It shouldn't have been that final? Why did Lyssa have to die?

"Master Soelle?"

Startled, Cyr turned quickly toward the voice, the jerky movement sending pain through his leg that woke him from his memories. Remembering where he was, he watched as the small group of people, cloaked and hooded, entered his room and extinguished the small candles they had carried. Cyr waited for them to settle themselves in the small attic that he had been living in for nearly a month now. Then he asked his question, directing it to the man who had spoken as he entered: "What news?"

The man removed his hood, revealing a head of shaggy black, white-streaked hair. Next to him a short, heavyset woman did the same, revealing a determined though tired face. "They are moving again to the mainland," the man responded.

Cyr frowned, confused. "Again? There won't be many left in Dior if they keep doing this. Are you sure of this, Edan?" Cyr had known the Kessor family a long time and trusted them implicitly. It just seemed strange.

Edan Kessor nodded with a rueful smile. "It's true, and not just in Dior. Glenville, Cold Stream, and Mir Town—all have been moving. There have been orders from the chancellor. The Guard is leaving."

After Edan Kessor gave his report, the other Rhyolian elders who had survived the Rav'agas occupation gave their own. Cyr Soelle nodded patiently as he took in all the information; he knew most of it himself anyway, just from personally watching the odd behavior of the Rav'agas from his secret hideaway.

"What about Captain Bellon and the Dior Guard . . . what of them?" Cyr asked.

Edan shook his head, his expression sorrowful. "Gone. They left the island immediately after they killed my niece, to look for our boys."

He spoke as if still giving a report, but Cyr knew the man better than that. He nodded, feeling the man's pain and hoping he'd get through this. Edan had been through too much.

The heavyset woman, who had been standing next to him, put her hand on Kessor's shoulder. She looked up to Cyr. He nodded. "Amila, have you any news from Teltraum?" he asked, hoping she might have better news about the whereabouts of his and Edan's sons.

She scowled in disappointment. "No, damn it. If Kavriel has made it to Teltraum, he hasn't been able to get to Femaor yet." She paused, glancing at Edan as his face paled. She continued quickly. "Still, the chancellor has been up in arms since what happened in the east. Chairman Richart has simply been trying to stay out of the way of stampeding Rav'agas. Zoren is sending half of his

Rav'agas battalion to the mountains . . . so Aurel says, but you have seen the messages."

Cyr nodded, eyes distant with thought. "Are they going to go after these . . . Hielias?" he asked, returning his focus to her.

Amila Cavyl nodded and smiled. "I guess so. I have no idea who these people are, but they seem to be as unhappy with our new guests as we are. It's a shame they didn't move five years ago." She chuckled.

Cyr shook his head. "No, I don't think that would have been for any good. Still, we don't know anything about these people. They could be dangerous."

Amila shrugged. "A lesser evil, if you ask me. And better that than any Ay'vol Force." She chuckled again, slapping Edan's shoulder. The man actually seemed to become more like his old self again as he nodded and allowed a small smile.

Cyr sighed. "Alright, but this changes nothing for us now. It's begun—all that we have been preparing for." He looked hard at Edan and Amila, who unconsciously stiffened like trained soldiers receiving orders. "Light the flame," Cyr continued metaphorically. His voice grew stronger. "The chancellor is shaken and we must move now, while his attention is elsewhere. We've been waiting for something like this to happen, and whether it's us or mountain men, it makes no difference. The Crypt has been broken, and the chancellor's pillar has been cracked at the base. The Patriarch will not be responding in kind to what has happened. Zoren is choosing speed over judgement to try to clear this mess. We move into Mir tonight."

Edan Kessor and Amila Cavyl nodded as they

quickly turned, with the others in the group, to head down the stairwell. Cyr knew he didn't need to remind them of anything. These were his people, and they had been playing dead, lying in the jaws of their enemy, waiting for the signal. Now it was time, time to rise up from the place of the defeated and break free.

Straight thru the Chancellor's teeth.

EPILOGUE

As the trickle of dirt tickled his nose, Kavriel opened his eyes to find himself cocooned in stone and earth. He panicked, remembering all too well the sensation of being buried alive from the mine, when he had escaped by burrowing through a tunnel toward what he hoped would be the surface.

This time his fingers opened up little blue holes in the roof of his den. He pushed his body up, breaking out of the dirt into sunlight that burned his eyes. Kavriel squinted upward, at the snow and ice high on the peaks of the Oenes Mountains that loomed regally over the courtyard of the Crypt. Opening his mouth, he gulped air like a newborn. The burning and stiffness in his limbs awoke with the air in his lungs and he recognized it as a reminder that he was still alive. He shook uncontrollably for a moment, but as he gradually regained power over his own body, Kavriel began to absorb other sensations, as the world opened up around him.

There were voices, numerous voices, nearby. He turned his stiff neck and saw several groups of Rav'agas soldiers pacing in the courtyard. Occasionally they knelt to collect one of their fallen comrades. They also picked up the bodies of the mountain men who had attacked them.

Kavriel looked at the sky again. Judging by the sun, it was late afternoon. The battle that had erupted the night before had ended with the Rav'agas victorious. He felt an urge to leave this place and placed his hands on the ground to try to force himself out of the earth.

He heard a voice nearby: "Don't move so quickly,

villager. You'll make yourself sick."

Kavriel turned toward the voice and saw a shadow approaching him. A man, dressed in a blue vest embroidered with gold. He nearly blacked out again as the man knelt down, a wicked grin on his face. "Xavr?" Kavriel asked, not sure he believed his own eyes. The man nodded, then began pulling him out of the hole. "How long have you been here?"

They hadn't attracted the attention of the other Rav'agas, but just to be safe, Xavr led Kavriel to a small alcove in the rock, out of sight. Xavr turned to him. "I have always been here, Kavriel," he replied. "And I hope to remain here long after even you are gone." He brushed some of the dirt off of Kavriel's dented and ruined armor, shaking his head in concern.

Kavriel still couldn't wrap his head around everything. The fight in the turret, Saire, Tess, Kell, Seth, Ulin . . . it all seemed to be a distant memory. "What . . . " he stammered, "where are . . . what happened to . . ."

"Easy, easy," Xavr replied, holding up his hand. Kavriel felt too shocked to argue. "Now, you have something that belongs to me, I think." Xavr said, giving Kavriel a determined look.

It took Kavriel a moment to understand what he was talking about, but once he did, his mind seemed to become his again. He reached into his shirt, pulling out the memoir he had stolen from Xavr's cabin, what seemed like ages ago. Xavr smiled as he took it. "You're one of them, aren't you?" Kavriel asked.

Xavr smiled. "Whatever do you mean?" he quipped, but Kavriel wasn't about to play the game.

"The Watch. These are your memoirs . . . you wrote this." He pointed to the book in Xavr's hand.

The man took a long moment before he replied smugly, "Of course they're mine. You took it from my house . . . after I gave you shelter and saved your life, I might add." He narrowed his eyes coyly.

"No. I mean that—" Kavriel began,

Xavr interrupted him quickly. "I know what you mean, and yes, Kavriel, the book is mine. I wrote it a very long time ago."

Kavriel looked into Xavr's eyes. In every respect physically, there was nothing unnatural about him, but he knew that Xavr was no ordinary man. There was something in the eyes . . . the clarity of the color that reminded Kavriel of looking through a foggy window into the morning sky. Saire had those exact eyes, only there was a glint of peril, like the threat of a coming storm still far past the horizon. Anger, cold and unrelenting. But in Xavr's eyes Kavriel sensed only regret. There was something in that look.

"What happened to you?" Kavriel asked softly, forgetting for a moment everything that had recently come to pass.

Xavr smiled humbly. He was obviously able to understand Kavriel's thoughts, just by his change in behavior. "Another time, villager," he replied, and motioned to the towering peaks behind them. "We have to go, or we will be discovered."

"Go?" Kavriel asked as he glanced up at the mountains. He could see the shattered remains of the stone turret that he had been expelled from when Tess went against Saire. The memory of it made his head ring. He felt a hand touch his shoulder and his head immediately cleared. He looked at Xavr questioningly, and again he didn't need to say anything. The man understood him as if there was some unspoken communication between them.

"I mean it, Kavriel. Move now," Xavr ordered.

"Where?" Kavriel asked as he moved with the man, who guided him into the corridors of the mountain, beyond the enemy's line of sight.

"To a place where answers are found," Xavr replied cryptically, but from the little time he had known this man, Kavriel knew that it was probably the only answer he would get.

Strangely, Kavriel sensed a place in the back of his mind that reminded him of a great city hidden away in the mountains. He had no idea where the memory had come from, but he had his guesses. Regardless, he decided to simply accept that whatever connection he had obviously had with Tess when he was reunited with her in the turret was similar to what he had with Xavr.

Xavr and Saire were part of The Watch, and he and Tess were part of something else. What and to what end, he did not know, but despite everything that had come to pass in the turret high above in the mountains, Kavriel knew for certain that his friend still lived. She was no longer here, and for all he could sense she was very far away . . . but she lived. In another way he sensed the same for his brother, but those were more clouded and even more distant. He did not know what that meant, but it was clear that Xavr intended to have him find out. They were all connected to a purpose that went beyond anything that he had ever expected or realized. There was more than just politics and warring nations in his circle of life now. There was something more supreme involved and he could almost taste the answers that awaited him.

"Will I find what I'm looking for?" he asked, already assuming the answer. Xavr nodded without looking back to him. He stopped walking for his next question. "Will it make everything the way it's supposed to be?"

Xavr stopped in mid-stride—perhaps, Kavriel thought, wondering why he had asked such a strange question. He wondered if it was that other part of him playing with his mind again.

Xavr turned his head slightly in his direction. "Probably . . . but let's not hope for that, shall we." He turned fully to face Kavriel. "On second thought, let's not hope at all."

"Why is that?" Kavriel asked, mildly amused by Xavr's strange response, but he could tell from the man's posture as he climbed the rocky mountain path that the comment had more layers than he assumed.

"Because we are going to follow someone else's rules now," Xavr replied.

"Whose?" he asked as Xavr turned back to the Oenes.

"Yours," he replied, and with that the two men disappeared into the Oenes Mountains without another word.

The Rav'agas, cleaning up the courtyard of the Crypt behind them, didn't see them leave.

Back in Teltraum, Chancellor Zoren and Chairman Richart circled one another like aggravated hounds, while the Patriarch continued to send his Ay'vol Force into the north with his blessing upon their heads, and they threatened to claim the nation.

The world was back to the way it was, and Kavriel followed his guide as they calmly stepped out of it.

End of Book 1